Praise for *Black Light*

"Martha Allard creates dark literary magic with her debut novel *Black Light*. She combines the world of '80s glam rock'n'roll with vampiric lore a la *The Hunger*, to create a compelling, haunting love story all her own."
— Dana Fredsti, author of the *Ashley Parker* series

"*Black Light* examines the devastating price of fame and living with love unrequited through a haze of sweat and grit from the '80s. Heartbreaking and bitterly romantic, Trace and Asia will haunt you long after the final page is turned."
— Kacey Vanderkarr, author of *The Stone Series*

"Glittering and grimy as a smear of black eyeshadow, tender and cruel as a midnight kiss, *Black Light* is a heartfelt paean to modern love in all its unlikely and dangerous incarnations."
— Amy McLane, author of "A Is For Apple"

"Martha Allard writes like the love child of Charles De Lint and Poppy Z. Brite."
— Philip Brewer, author of "Watch Bees"

Praise for Martha's short fiction

"Martha J. Allard adorns the pages of *Re-Vamped* with the complex and intriguing story "Getting Fixed." Allard recounts the terrifying tale of a vampire named Casey who has taken up selling her tainted blood to a unique group of junkies with a hunger for the flowing crimson of the damned."
— Jeremy Price, *Up All Night Reviews*

" "Dust" made me want to cry. Martha J. Allard gives us a peek at Peter Pan and Tinkerbell after the death of Wendy. It's a beautiful, if melancholy, ending."
— *Tangent Online*

"Wonderful poetry from Martha J. Allard ("Towered" — "Like any common Prince, he is pale of skin and long/of limb. Like any common Prince, he falls far short/of the advertising.") starts *Turbocharged Fortune Cookie* off with a sizzle."
— *Lady Churchill's Rosebud Wristlet*

Black Light

Cover art by Julia Gollbach at Bioblossom Creative.

Model: Bigstock

Cover design by Mason Jones.

Interior design by Automatism Press.

Copyright © 2016 by Automatism Press.

Paperback ISBN: 978-0-9636794-4-4

ebook ISBN: 978-0-9636794-5-1

To Loren. In 1983 she had all the music.

BLACK LIGHT

MARTHA J. ALLARD

AUTOMATISM PRESS

SAN FRANCISCO

1

1983, Los Angeles

Trace Dellon stands in the wings backstage at the Refugee Club, a narrow shadow. He lights a cigarette, shielding the flame with his hand to protect the dark. In the full house beyond the curtain, he counts dozens of reflections of himself. Boys or girls, hair cut spiky with SpaghettiO-colored dye-jobs, all waiting for him. Every night there's more, but it's not enough, not yet. He exhales a lungful of smoke.

"Trace." Asia Heyes, Black Light's bass player, calls him from the doorway to the basement dressing room the band shares. "Weird's real sick."

"No, he's not." Trace turns.

"Yeah. He is. He's not gonna be able to play tonight. He should—"

"He should be shootin' the hell up, Asia. He's the guitar player and this isn't fuckin' Charity's Place back in Ann Arbor anymore. It's the Refugee Club, where somebody important could be listening." Trace moves farther backstage, past Asia, down the rickety stairs. He smells it, bitter on the air, before he hits the bottom step. Then he hears Weird choking.

Asia is right behind, protesting, "He's almost clean. Don't fuck it up for him."

Trace doesn't answer. Instead of going down the short hallway to the bathroom, he heads into the dressing room. Weird's guitar case is propped against the broken-down leather couch that sags in one corner. Trace flips the case open. Tucked inside, along with the instrument, are Weird's works, just like Trace knew they would be. He grabs the pouch and steps around Asia to cross the hall. Without knocking, Trace opens the bathroom door.

It's a remodeled storage closet, too small for three people. Tommi, their drummer, hovers inside, worry lining his pretty face.

Weird's on the floor, back against the wall, arm draped around the toilet seat, like it's his best friend. In the buzzing fluorescent light, he looks ancient. Every one of his thirty-seven years is etched into his face. His skin is the color of spoiled milk. His long red-blond hair is stringy with sweat. He wipes a hand over his beard, looks up at Trace through slitted eyes and grins. "Hey Dellon, you gonna hold my hair while I puke some more?"

"Are you gonna…? I mean, you are gonna be okay, aren't you?" Tommi's face turns even paler as he squeezes himself against the sink to let Trace all the way in.

"Oh, sure." Weird groans, sucks in some of the sour air. "Yeah, I'm great." Then he looks up at Trace again. "Gimme my damn smack."

"No," Tommi gasps. "No, Weird."

Weird stares hard at Trace. "Gimme m' works, Dellon. Neither one of them will."

Trace nods. He hands the pouch over and turns away.

Asia is leaning against the hand railing of the stairs, shaking his head as Trace exits the bathroom. "So let him go back to killin' himself?"

"You think he can play clean, Asia?" Trace says. "You gonna take that all away from him?"

"That's such bullshit." Asia laughs. "You don't even care, as long as you get what you want. That's all that matters."

Trace looks into Asia's rust-green eyes and takes a breath. All he ever gets from Asia any more is anger and disappointment. Trace won't apologize for telling the truth. He reaches up to brush a stray lock of wavy ginger hair back from his face, but Asia flinches.

"Whatever you need to think," Trace says softly. "It's done. Get ready for the show."

He goes back upstairs without waiting for Asia's answer.

Asia shakes it off. He moves to stand in the doorway. "Wait, Weird. I can play your shit tonight and Trace can play bass."

Weird is up, unsteadily leaning against the sink, already cooking his shit, Tommi looking on, stricken. Weird snickers. "How you think he's gonna do that? Faggot can't even walk and chew gum."

"I don't care." Asia knows he's pleading. He wants to knock the smack out of Weird's hand, shake him. Don't make Trace right, he wants to say. He goes back to begging instead. "We can do it."

"Asia, look, Dellon's a bastard, but he's right," Weird says. His hands don't shake at all when he pulls the plunger back on his syringe to suck the liquefied drug up. "You think that bein' a junkie's ruinin' my life, right? That I'm tryin' to kill myself? See, no, because it's all I am, Asia. No junk, no music. I'm not giving that up."

Weird is tying a piece of tubing around his upper arm. He looks from Asia to Tommi. "You guys got shit to do before we go on, right?"

Not really, Asia thinks, but feels himself give in. He turns away and Tommi follows him.

Trace returns to the shadows behind the curtain. Weird will come through. He always does. No matter what his condition, he lives for the moment the lights hit the stage, almost as much as Trace. Onstage, they always speak the same language.

Trace pauses before he lights another cigarette. Asia and Tommi come up from the dressing room to go out back. Trace stays hidden. He knows Asia needs his space. Once the stage door swings closed, he pulls his lighter out. Disappointment, anger, Trace thinks again. But it's all right if Asia doesn't understand, as long as he doesn't leave.

Trace takes a long drag on his fresh cigarette and pushes off from the wall. He sees the small slim form of Sammy appear from the other side of the curtain. He watches her face brighten as she locates him by the glow of ash. He gives her a wide smile. "Are you my fifteen-minute warning?"

"Just about."

She tilts her head up to kiss him and he feels the sticky exchange of their lip-gloss. Her hands are at the zipper of his jeans. Trace is still thinking of Asia when she slides her hands inside.

Asia and Tommi stand in the alley that runs behind the Refugee Club, leaning against the scarred brick wall, so Asia can breathe a minute before they go on. He feels the tension of stage fright take hold of the muscles in his shoulders and tries to ignore it.

"Trace was right," Tommi says finally, combing his long pale bangs back from his face.

"He's an asshole," Asia corrects.

"Weird's never gonna get clean. He doesn't want to." Tommi laughs bitterly. "'Cause where'd his works come from, huh?"

"Trace got 'em outta his guitar case." Asia frowns. "But, so?"

"And there was what? Like a half a gram of smack? When d'ya think Weird bought it?" Tommi looks at Asia.

"I don't know." Asia shrugs, but gets the sinking realization. He lets out a long sigh. "I wish—"

He doesn't get to finish before the stage door opens and Trace appears, ready for the show. As he steps into the halo cast by a streetlight, his tight tee shirt sparkles. A cigarette trails from his fingers. His eyes are lined in heavy blue, making them electric; the blush against his cheekbones makes them sharper. None of it can make him more beautiful, Asia thinks. It only accents the fact.

"Are you ready?" Trace asks, eyes on Asia.

"Yeah, I guess." Asia looks down at his faded jeans and crackled Harpo's tee shirt. "How's Weird?"

"He's okay. Cleaning up." Trace shrugs.

"Oh, shit, my hair," Tommi says, ducking back inside.

Trace gives Asia a half-smile. "I know you're pissed. If you wanna hit me, now's the time."

"I don't wanna." Asia steps back, as though to get out of range anyway. "I'm not… I just wish things were different, that's all."

Trace takes a drag from his cigarette and drops it on the pavement. He laughs. "Asia, it is gonna happen. Soon. It has to, I can feel it."

Not tonight, Asia thinks, looking away again. Please, not tonight.

The sidewalk outside the Refugee Club is crowded with the tragically hip. They wait in spiked heels and purple eyeshadow. Albrecht Christian stands, unmoving, in this sea of restless youth. It is all familiar to him, but there are differences. Shorter hair, tighter clothes. This new decade has a harder edge. Albrecht catches the eye of a girl packed into a black tube top and red plastic mini. She stares past him and Albrecht smiles like a shark in the neon night, like it means nothing. The truth is he craves youth; he hungers for it. Not his own, the way other men do. Quite the opposite. Albrecht craves youth that will wash away his past.

Now, standing under the Refugee Club's marquee, he feels the ghost of Sean Wilder touch his sleeve. Albrecht's smile softens and he imagines he can catch the faint scent of ginger and cinnamon on the exhaust-laden air.

Sean, Albrecht thinks, savoring the pain of it. And, just like that, he is slipping the snare of time. He closes his eyes, lets the current take him back.

1976.

Albrecht guided the pearl-colored Jaguar away from the well-lit boulevard to a deserted street. The place between Albrecht's shoulder blades itched. Two blocks back, they had been cruising a fashionably seedy area of West Hollywood. Wherever Sean was taking him now was in a feral pocket of the city.

"Turn down here," Sean directed, pointing across Albrecht's arms as he held the wheel.

"Why?"

"Y'scared, baby?" Sean grinned in the shadows, hand wandering to Albrecht's leg.

Albrecht tasted the boy's excitement, felt a warm jolt at the contact. Good, clean, not fueled by cocaine for a change. Albrecht smiled indulgently. "I've got you to protect me, yes?"

"We're almost there, anyway." Sean laughed. "Turn left at the corner. It's halfway up the block, on your side."

Ever patient, Albrecht followed orders. He let the Jag slow to a creep around the corner onto an even more desolate street. There was debris strewn across the pavement now. Albrecht didn't assume that Sean would change the tire if things went badly, nor did he think they'd get very far on foot.

"See it?" Sean gestured again. "This is what I wanted you to see."

Albrecht pulled the car to the curb to regard Sean's find through the windshield. An enormous old theater hulked in the darkness. The surrounding street lights were out, its marquee dead. Above it hung the remnants of the name: A-onis. Not very godlike now, Albrecht thought. Broken glass littered the pavement beneath as though it had just shattered.

Still, in the white of the car's headlights, it had the air of something fine about it.

"*It's perfect.*" *Sean touched his hand and Albrecht felt the spark of the boy's energy jump between them again.*

"*I'll have my office find out who owns the property,*" *Albrecht told him.* "*We'll make an offer.*"

Albrecht knows that standing on queue at the door is unnecessary, but he enjoys the anonymity. The bouncer sizes him up through wraparound sunglasses. Albrecht lifts his chin and sharpens his smile again. A muscle twitches in the big man's neck and he passes Albrecht through.

The Refugee Club folds itself around him as he enters. Now it is the Eighties and Sean is a legend. Inside everything has changed, yet nothing has changed. The concession stand in the lobby is still all brass and glass countertops. The main room still echoes the movie theater it once was. Though the seats are all gone, the dance floor still slopes gently down to the stage. The bar runs along the far wall, carved cherubs and devils above it. Albrecht takes his place there.

He lights a cigarette and waits for one of the bartenders to bring him an ashtray. It is a girl in clumsy drag makeup, the mascara mostly in dark shadows under her eyes, blush streaking up her cheeks in two red bars. Horrifying, thinks Albrecht, amused. The girl's eyes travel from the slim gold lighter Albrecht places on the bar top to the platinum Rolex on his wrist, to the suit he wears. The custom cut of the gray silk is lost on the girl, but Albrecht knows the impression he makes. Wealthy. A little desperate.

It is a lie, Albrecht tells himself. "May I have a gin and tonic?" He knows there is enough Austria left in his voice to set him even further apart.

The girl nods, complying quickly. Albrecht takes a drink and smiles his thanks, but the girl has disappeared.

Albrecht shifts on his stool. There are more people on the dance floor than at tables, all moving savagely to the music that pulses from the sound system.

Sean, Albrecht thinks again, losing the thread of the lyric. He scans over the surface of the dancers, hair sprayed and glittered, lip gloss flashing in the lights. Beautiful, he thinks, but can't feel anything beyond that. They could be mannequins for all they hold his attention.

The music plays out and, in the relative silence, lights on the stage go up. Albrecht spots his little bartender, now turned ringmaster. She steps into the white of the tight spotlight, framed by a heavy red curtain. "You know who I got back here, doncha?" she teases, winking.

The crowd surges forward to pool around the edge of the stage, chanting a name. "Trace. Trace." Albrecht feels himself lean in, muscles tensing.

The bartender grins. "Yeah, that's right." She has to shout over noise, even into the microphone. "Trace Dellon. Ya think you're ready? I can't hear you."

More screams. She has to take a step back from the dozens of hands that reach up to her. The curtain lurches aside and the band is there, waiting. Guitar, bass, drums. So far Albrecht isn't impressed.

The bartender steps away. The lead singer moves into the spotlight and the room explodes. The chant turns to a prayer.

"Everybody comes to the Refugee looking for just one thing, don't they?" The singer grins as the crowd screams. "Well, it's okay. I'm here now."

All lines and angles, his spiky hair is the color of flame. His black tee shirt has the word "Bitch" spelled out against his chest in rhinestones. Albrecht feels the collective intake of breath as the band grinds out the first chords of the song. The energy in the room turns sharp, rakes past Albrecht, hones in on the stage.

Yes, something speaks inside Albrecht. *Yes.*

Trace wraps one thin hand around the microphone, body coiled tight, like a bullwhip. His voice opens a raw, hungry place in Albrecht. Everyone else in the world recedes until it is just him and just Trace.

At the end of the set, Albrecht is breathless. The hunger increases in him as Trace disappears behind the curtain.

"I fucking love him," the bartender sighs, returned to her post.

Albrecht is surprised at how true the sentiment echoes within him. He extracts a card from the holder in his breast pocket. Black with gray Gothic lettering, it reads; "Albrecht Christian, Para Bellum Records." He offers it to the girl along with a fifty-dollar bill. "See that Trace gets the card, please. Tell him I wish to speak with him tonight, without his band."

In the back of the car they take to Albrecht's penthouse, he watches the streetlights play across Trace's skin, shadowing the bone structure of his face, the hollow at the base of his throat. The power that crackles off him from the stage is barely contained now by that translucent skin. Trace catches him looking and gives him a slow smile. Albrecht feels those ice-colored eyes lingering. He is charmed by the honest appraisal.

The Algonquin is not the largest building on the block. Sleeker, taller glass and steel monstrosities have grown up around it in the time Albrecht has kept rooms here. This building is like him. It echoes the past, with its art deco stonework and leaded glass windows. When they arrive, he leads Trace through its hushed lobby to the elevator, where he slides his key into the panel.

"Shit," Trace says as they begin their assent. "You're either really rich, or you're a serial killer."

"Oh, dear." Albrecht laughs softly. "What if I'm both?"

Trace shrugs. "It's a chance I'll have to take."

They come to a stop and the door slides aside. Albrecht steps off. "Here we are."

The main room of the penthouse is entirely black and white, from the tiles on the floor to the walls and furniture. The only color in the place are the Warhols. Blue, red, and green backgrounds, they stand out like graffiti on fresh paint. Trace's jaw drops slightly when his eyes catch on them.

On the canvases, Albrecht is larger than life, blond hair tinted gold and slicked against his skull. His face is lean, sharp, the skin pale and smooth, ageless except for his ancient eyes. His lips are thin, a smile just tilting the corners. "Do you enjoy Warhol?" His smile mirrors the silk-screens.

"Damn," Trace manages.

"Please, make yourself at home."

Trace chooses one of the white couches at the center of the room. Albrecht interprets that as an invitation and sits next to him. He reaches for the onyx box on the table in front of them for a cigarette. "Would you like one?"

"Thanks."

Albrecht extracts two, lights Trace's first. As he offers it, he asks, "How do you like playing the Refugee?"

Trace smiles faintly, pauses to take a drag, then laughs. "It's the biggest stage we've ever been on. It's beautiful. My guitarist is all hot to play the Whisky, but this is better. Everybody comes to the Refugee."

"It's always been that way," Albrecht tells him, lighting his own cigarette. "It's mine, you know—the Refugee. Though I haven't visited it in years, until tonight."

"No shit? But your card said you work for the record label."

"No, I own Para Bellum as well," Albrecht explains. "When I bought the club, it was because... There was a man I loved very much. It was for him." He watches Trace for reaction but can detect none. "When Sean found the place, it was deserted, except by the junkies and homeless. He had this vision, though, of what it could be, and I—" Albrecht smiles, looking away from Trace. "I had the vision of what it had been."

"What do you mean?"

"Oh, I had memories, from pictures I'd seen as a boy in Austria." Albrecht lets regret tinge his expression, the story. "It was the Adonis back then, famous, like your Mann's Chinese now. I remember seeing Errol Flynn going in to some premier. It was very fine and beautiful."

Amused, Albrecht knows that Trace is re-figuring his age in his mind from older to really old. Albrecht continues anyway. "It was how I thought of America, I suppose, before I came here: all glittering and crisp and new. So you see, I had to help Sean save it."

"Wow. I never even heard of it before."

"Of course not," Albrecht says. "In America, forgetting the past is as easy as knocking a building down or putting up new one. You aren't drowning in your history here. Sean wanted to make it into something new and I never told him about my memories."

"Why did you let him change the name?"

"That was my choice. The Adonis had gone, no matter what I wanted."

"Because this is America," Trace guesses.

Albrecht is surprised that Trace understands. He changes the subject. "What do you see as your next move from here?"

Trace's laugh has a hard edge to it now. "Why? Is this where you tell me that I could be rich and famous?"

"Do you need me to tell you that? Because I think you know exactly what will happen and what you'll do to make it so."

"Really? You think I got it all figured out."

"After seeing you perform, I'm sure of it," Albrecht tells him.

Trace takes a drag on his cigarette and taps ashes into the crystal tray in front of them. Albrecht sees a crack in the thick armor of cool he wears. Trace's grin is wide and unguarded.

Albrecht moves closer to trail his fingertips across the sharpness of Trace's cheekbone, along the curve of his jaw. "I didn't know what I was looking for tonight. Not until I saw you." He leans in and as their lips meet, Trace's eyes close. He opens his mouth to Albrecht's. Trace tastes of beer and smoke and something deeper. The promise of power burns against Albrecht's tongue and he swallows it down, lets it bleed into him, feed him. He steals Trace's breath; he could easily use him up, but stops himself. Too beautiful a thing to be squandered in one night.

"I'd like you to stay."

Trace sits back a little and touches his lips with his fingers. "Yeah. Good."

When Trace twists away from Albrecht in sleep, someone else, more compact, softer, takes his place.

Why most especially you? Albrecht wonders, smelling cinnamon and ginger rise from the sheets. Why not some other empty ghost? He does not want this now, not while he has someone warm and alive in reach, but he can't maintain his hold on the present.

Sean curled away from him, small body stark against the dark sheets. "I know you're doing it to me."

"Cocaine is doing this to you," Albrecht reasoned, gathering Sean against him.

"You know that's not true." Sean took in a breath and Albrecht felt the expansion of his ribs, sharp against his skin. "The coke, it's the only way I can hang on. I want you, but when you touch me, I..." This time it was a sob.

"Sh." Albrecht whispered it into the inky silk of Sean's hair. "I don't want to hurt you. Not ever. I love you."

So he did, but even as he spoke, he felt the robber cells of his body stealing Sean's life to feed him. Once it came in torrents off the boy, so strong it dazed Albrecht. Now it was like a trickle of sand, the grains barely brushing his surface. Emptiness grew in Albrecht now, deep and gnawing. He held Sean tighter. "Think about tomorrow. The club."

Albrecht shakes the memory off and gets out of bed. He slips through the French doors to the balcony. He stands naked at the railing, breathing deep lungfuls of heavy, dirty Los Angeles air. This city suits him, more than any other. It is his mirror in many ways. It is something hard and old, covered in a new skin.

Albrecht smiles. He smells fresh cigarette smoke from the doorway and turns. Trace is lounging on the threshold, skin turned blue by the moon.

"I've never seen LA from this high up. It looks just like the movies. Beautiful."

Albrecht laughs softly. "Anything can be beautiful from far enough away."

"The lights go right up to the stars." Trace joins him at the railing.

"It'll be dawn soon," Albrecht warns. "Do you have to leave?"

"I don't want to." Trace leans down to kiss him. This time Albrecht tastes himself.

"Good." Albrecht leads him back inside and shuts the doors behind them. They settle back in bed and Albrecht says, "I want to sign you to my label. We have a studio here in Los Angeles. I want to get a producer in to record with you."

Trace stretches like a cat and turns away from Albrecht. "You heard me sing tonight and then we fucked. Which performance is this offer based on?"

"Do you truly care? Do you think I value your talent less because I'm falling in love with you?" Albrecht fits himself against the sharpness of Trace's back. The press of the full length of his body is like an electric shock, makes Albrecht's heart hammer, his blood pound. Some part of him wants to take this slower, but he can't. He knows that once they leave this room, the world will tangle them up. Other people will intrude. It will never be pure like this again.

Trace turns to move down and Albrecht feels his tongue, quick and wet. He groans and tries to push further in, but Trace moves

11

back. "I love you," Albrecht whispers. "I don't want to let go of you."

When Trace wakes, he's entangled. Christian is coiled around him. Trace moves slowly, works his way out of the puzzle of skin and bone.

He stands at the side of the bed, studying Christian in the unforgiving morning light. His white-blond hair is thick, lank against the pillow. He is so thin and so still, like a corpse. He loves me, Trace thinks, stepping away. He goes to piss in a bathroom as large as his first apartment. He stares at himself in the mirror as he empties his bladder. People have been in love with him before. Asia has been, since they were kids.

Flushing, he thinks, this is different. He steps into a shower tiled in black and dials the water hot enough to bring color to his skin. Standing under it is like a hailstorm, but he takes it.

I love you. Christian had said it. True, they had met less than ten hours ago and true, he'd said it while they were fucking, but there was such a focus to it that Trace finds himself wishing it was sincere. Hoping it was. He thinks of getting back into bed with Christian now, but resists. Trace has always tried to be careful about who he fucked. This happened before he could think. It was still happening too fast.

He leaves the bathroom to collect his clothes from where they'd been scattered last night. He picks up Christian's heavy platinum watch from the nightstand to squint at the time. Not quite ten a.m., still early to Trace, but he is amazed at Christian. Is he so rich he doesn't care if Trace tosses his place?

He turns the watch over in his hands. On the back, he reads the word, "Liebling." He has no clue what a Rolex is worth. More than a recording contract? Whores go through their johns' pockets. Trace's not a whore. Not exactly. "Don't trust me, though," he murmurs, putting the watch back.

He sits on the edge of the bed and touches Christian's shoulder. "Hey, it's getting late."

Christian turns toward him, completely awake, his thin lips curving upward. "Is it? You look well-rested."

Trace catches his glance toward the nightstand and wonders if it is a test. "I had a shower. I hope that's okay."

"I'd like you to feel welcome here."

Trace grins and leans over Christian to kiss him. "I do."

Christian shifts, fingers trailing down Trace's back to the top of his jeans, but stop there. "Perhaps we should have breakfast, yes?" He is pulling away, getting out of bed. "My arrival here was a bit spur-of-the-moment, so I fear the kitchen is not stocked. I could have something ordered in."

Trace hesitates, but shakes his head. "I gotta meet the rest of the band at the Refugee at one for practice."

If Christian is disappointed, he doesn't let it show. "Plenty of time to eat. Shall we have coffee at the club? I'll call my assistant to let them know we're coming. And perhaps we could work out the particulars of the contract as well."

"Herr Christian." Albrecht's little bartender looks apprehensive as they approach. "I'm sorry that I didn't realize last night. Who you were, I mean, I..."

She blushes prettily and Albrecht laughs. "Oh, come now. How were you to know when I didn't wish you to? Still, your service was excellent."

The girl brightens at the compliment, then blushes harder when she sees Trace. Another layer is added to her smile, turns it more intimate. "Hi."

Trace seems amused. "Hi, Sammy." He gives her a toothy grin. "Thanks."

"Uh. Any time." Then Sammy turns back to Albrecht. "Your assistant had breakfast sent over. And I have coffee made, if you like."

She indicates a table nearby set up with fruit and cheese and bread. Albrecht's stomach grumbles and he realizes he's hungry. It's the first time since Sean died that Albrecht has craved more than a cigarette.

They relocate and he watches Sammy nearing with the coffee pot. Her eyes are on Trace as she pours. When she leaves, Albrecht guesses, "There's something between the two of you."

"She blew me last night before I went on stage. We aren't exactly going steady." Trace laughs. "And even if we were... Why?

Jealous?"

Albrecht takes a drink, grateful for the kick of caffeine. "Should I be?"

"It was one blow job." Trace shrugs. "And it was before I met you."

Albrecht doesn't answer, surprised when he realizes he wants more from Trace on the subject. He is jealous. "Of course."

"Where is your lover?" Trace asks. "His name was Sean, right?"

"What?" Albrecht looks up from his coffee cup, afraid that the ghost is somehow visible.

"So you buy this whole place for him," Trace says. "That sounds pretty intense. What happened?"

Albrecht wonders if Trace already knows the story. After all, it is the stuff myth is made of. "You know about the suicide, I'm sure."

Trace frowns slightly. "I heard somebody shot themselves in the john here a long time ago."

"Sean was brilliant and he was beautiful. But toward the end, I remember thinking that he... He used his life up so quickly. When I met him, he was turning tricks on the street and I brought him out of that." Albrecht shakes his head. "The cocaine didn't help, but I could never get him to give that up. I think he saw everything he ever wanted coming true here and was afraid it wouldn't be enough."

"So he killed himself."

Albrecht nods. "He put one of my handguns into his mouth and pulled the trigger."

"Fuck, that's horrible," Trace breathes.

"It was." Albrecht does not tell him that the gun is still in his possession. He intends the story to make him seem tragic and romantic, not frightening. "I miss him."

There is a space in the conversation. Trace brushes his fingers across Albrecht's hand. "I want you to give me the contract."

Albrecht nods. To someone else this may seem like an abrupt subject change, even harsh. But Albrecht is grateful to be done with Sean for the moment. He smiles. "Of course. And I want to give it to you. I shall have my assistant draw it up, but it will be standard, to start with. An album and promotion."

"We'll need up-front money," Trace says. "We're pretty

strapped right now. The guys are living in a hellhole in Encino."

Albrecht nods. "William will have exact numbers, but that shouldn't be a problem. I have a producer in mind. I'd like to get him here to listen to you. You're here for the week, yes?"

Trace nods.

"Good." Albrecht wonders what the other members of the band will think of these arrangements. If that mattered at all. "Good. I'll call William, then, and we'll begin."

Albrecht is in a new position. Instead of the need to consume Trace, Albrecht feels a shift within himself like the clear toll of a bell, from taker to taken.

"Hey." Trace's expression falters. He tries to catch Albrecht's eyes. "Are you okay?"

Albrecht nods. He decides to make it about something Trace can understand. "I was just wishing things were simpler."

Trace takes a piece of toast from Albrecht's plate, tears off a corner. "What do you mean?"

"I admit, having money isn't exactly unpleasant." Albrecht shrugs. "But there are drawbacks."

"You wouldn't say that if you'd ever been short on the rent."

"Perhaps not," Albrecht admits. "But when you're poor, it's easy to guess people's motives."

Trace laughs. "Yeah-right, you think?"

"If you told me you loved me, for example." Albrecht watches Trace's face, but there's no reaction on the surface. "How could I ever be certain you were being genuine?"

Instead of answering, Trace reaches for Albrecht, slides a hand to the back of his neck. Albrecht leans in, aware of how exposed this makes him. There is a steady stream of people milling around them in the club, cleaning, stocking. Trace's lips brush Albrecht's and he is being kissed in public, by a man. This has never happened to him before and he doesn't care. He closes his eyes, opens his mouth, lets Trace take his breath. He feels Trace's hand on his leg, drifting higher. A soft moan escapes Albrecht and Trace stops. He licks his lips and grins again. "If I'm a good actor, does it matter?"

Albrecht takes another breath, lets it out slow. "Let me make the call." He pushes to his feet to use the phone at the bar.

If William is surprised to hear from Albrecht, he doesn't let it show in his voice. He has worked for Albrecht more than a decade and has never so much as raised an eyebrow, no matter what is asked of him.

"I want you to deal with the legalities. This afternoon," Albrecht tells him. "Can you do it?"

"Of course, Herr Christian."

As the call ends, Albrecht feels Trace coming closer again. Albrecht feels closed in, suddenly, and lies, "I'm afraid I have to put in an appearance at the office, but I'll be back later."

As Christian leaves, Trace is surprised at the wave of exhaustion he feels. The intensity of Christian's attention will take getting used to.

Trace ignores the hopeful looks that Sammy flashes. Not now, he thinks, and maybe not ever again, though he liked the flare of jealousy from Christian.

But he decides not to push it. He goes under the stage to the cool, dark little dressing room. He clicks a Ramones tape into the player and collapses onto the saggy old leather couch in the corner.

He doesn't need to look at the clammy wall behind him to know the graffiti signatures of all the bands that came before him in this place. He knows them by heart: Blondie, the Idiots, the Attractions. Trace has yet to make his mark. Soon, he thinks, shifting to peel off his tee shirt. Soon he'll be up there, and past this place. Soon.

Albrecht escapes to the waiting car, tells the driver to drive.

"Where to, sir?"

Albrecht sinks into the leather seat and closes his eyes. "I don't care. Just keep me moving."

He has already lost a part of himself with Trace, feels the connection stretching thin, pulling taut as the distance spins out between them. Albrecht puts a hand to his temples, lack of sleep weighting down on him.

He opens his eyes to Sean, on the floor of the car, his cheek against Albrecht's knee. Albrecht feels the chill. He reaches down to touch Sean's hair.

"Why?" Albrecht asks. "I tried to give you what you wanted."

"It wasn't as much as you took, though."

Albrecht feels the pull of Sean's sable eyes just as if this was really happening. The old grief takes hold of him. Like the rock beneath a wave, he is never broken by it so much as made smooth.

"I knew that if I were dead, you could never leave me."

Albrecht smiles, surprised in spite of everything. Here was a strength he had never touched while Sean was alive. He wonders if it will come to this between Trace and him. He wonders if he even cares.

2

Asia never really sleeps in LA. The best he can manage is a thin sort of doze. This morning is no exception. Somewhere in the building there is a child crying, a pit bull barking, someone arguing in what Asia thinks might be Armenian. Beyond that, traffic noise, car alarms, more yelling out in the street. He gives up the dream of being in his parents' basement, surrounded by cool cement walls, with Trace. Smog-coated heat shimmers through the skin of the apartment.

"Fuck it," he groans, climbing up off his futon to head for the john. He spots Weird in the bedroom off the hallway, stretched out like the dead, full ashtray resting on his chest, burned-down cigarette still balanced in his fingers. Tommi is curled up on the corner of the mattress furthest away from the guitarist.

No Trace, though. Asia isn't surprised. Any time Trace can crash someplace else, he does. And that's most nights since they'd gotten the Refugee gig. Seems like everybody there wants a piece of Trace.

The air in the bathroom is fouler than the smog that settles over the valley in the afternoon. Asia sighs. He knows who will break down and clean it. He squints at his watch. Almost noon. Great. Even if he can get the others moving, it's still forever on the freeway to Hollywood, and the van is just waiting to overheat in traffic. Shit.

He goes back to the living room, where his futon is, to haul out the milk crate that he stores his stuff in. All his stuff, he thinks. Three pairs of jeans and seven tee shirts. When they drove out from Ann Arbor, there wasn't much room in the van after they loaded the instruments and equipment.

It's six months later and all Asia's stuff still fits in one milk crate. He pulls on a pair of jeans and a semi-clean tee shirt. Then he goes to stand in the bedroom doorway. "Tommi."

The boy twitches awake and uncurls himself. "Uh, yeah."

"We gotta start movin'. We got practice. Y'know that new shit

Trace's workin' on."

Tommi yawns and stretches. He combs his fingers through his choppy bleached white hair. "Uh. Okay."

He climbs to his feet and hitches his wrinkled purple parachute pants higher up on his skinny ass. Then he nudges Weird with a toe. "Get up."

"Fuck you," Weird grumbles.

"C'mon," Tommi persists, picking up the ashtray before it spills. "We gotta get outta here."

"Fuck you." This time it's louder. Weird starts to move slowly.

In the kitchen, the phone rings. Asia crosses over to answer. "Hello?"

"Asia," Trace greets. "Just who I wanted to talk to."

"Where are you?" Asia starts to wonder how far away Trace has gotten himself this time. Laurel Canyon? Burbank? Does he need a ride? How will they find him? Will the damn van hold on long enough?

"I'm already at the Refugee, waiting for you guys," Trace tells him. "I'm with Albrecht Christian, from last night. He wants to sign us."

Asia remembers the card, the glimpse he got of a man in a suit. "What? What are you talking about?"

"Last night. He owns the record company and he owns the Refugee. Last night we worked out a deal."

Asia shakes his head.

Trace goes on. "I need you to talk to the others, so they're not caught by surprise."

"We're gonna be late," Asia warns. "But we'll be there."

He hangs up and Tommi and Weird meet him in the living room. "Was that Dellon?" Weird demands, lighting a cigarette with a tiny cowboy boot. "Where'da fuck is he?"

"He's at the Refugee already. He wants us to talk to the guy from last night."

"The fairy in the suit?" Weird snorts. "This'll be good."

Asia sighs. "Yeah, I guess. Trace says he wants to record us."

"Just like that? Because he spent one night with Dellon?" Weird shakes his head. "Or do we all gotta suck his—"

Asia cuts him off. "Remember the card? He doesn't work for that label. He owns it. He listened to us play and wants to make a record. That's what we all want, right? So can y'just act like a human being for while?"

When they get to the Refugee, Tommi and Weird go upstairs, to the stage, and Asia goes beneath it, to the dressing room. He pauses before he descends, letting the air-conditioning envelope him. The whole trip over was stop and start and Weird ran the heater full blast to keep the van from overheating. Asia was sure he would die of it; he felt so sweaty and grimy.

The Ramones, tinny and jangly, echo up from the bottom of the stairs.

"Hey, Trace," Asia calls. "We made it."

No answer. When he steps into the cramped space, he finds Trace out cold, sprawled on the sagging ancient couch in the corner. He sleeps on his back, arms thrown up over his head, wearing only the black jeans from last night. Asia's eye is drawn down to the naked curve of Trace's pale hips above the waistband.

Christ, he thinks, looking away before he can get caught. Stop staring like he's a piece of porn.

Trace wakes to the tape ending. "Hey." He stretches and grins. "What time is it?"

Asia glances at his watch. "Almost two. Traffic sucks."

Trace says, "You talk to Weird?"

"Yeah." Asia slings his backpack off his shoulder and sits up on the cluttered makeup counter. "Yeah, I told him as much as you told me. But..."

"What?" Trace stands up, eyes darkening.

"Just..." Asia props his feet on one of the chairs. "Just, how do you know that this guy is... You know."

"No. I really don't know, Asia."

"You spent the night with him." Asia's face turns hot.

"So? It's not your business if I fucked him." Trace shakes his head, starts past Asia. "Weird and Tommi upstairs?"

"Prob'ly."

"I wanna talk to them before Christian gets back." Trace puts a hand on Asia's shoulder. "Don't be scared of this, Asia. It's what we want."

Asia freezes, like Trace's touch has short-circuited his nervous system. What you want, he thinks, letting his breath out slowly as Trace passes him to head up the stairs. But he knows he's lying to himself. He wants it too. He wants whatever Trace wants. He can't help himself.

Albrecht arrives back at the club at the same time as William. After introductions, William opens his briefcase to begin. Albrecht doesn't expect the band to be a problem. William explains the language of the contract to them quickly. When he writes them the check to cover van repairs, they brighten visibly.

"That went well," Albrecht comments as William packs his case and the band wanders away.

"Yeah." Trace settles in next to him companionably.

Albrecht touches Trace's hand but doesn't go further. He feels something pass between them, more of himself slipping away.

"Are you gonna stick around to watch us rehearse?" Trace asks.

"Do you mind?"

"Not really. But..." Trace shrugs and glances at the stage. "I don't want it to freak you out. This is all new stuff we're workin' on and it's a little rough, y'know."

"I understand."

He watches Trace walk away from him and climb the side steps to the stage. The rest of the band is waiting. Trace takes the microphone from the stand and counts down the first song. They run through it twice, Trace stopping at the same place both times. He and the guitar player argue over the key, but Trace gets what he wants in the end. The third time, the song works, though Albrecht can hear the anger in the guitarist leaking through the notes. The tension is almost visible between them, but Albrecht can hear that Trace makes it work in the music.

Albrecht moves to sit in the back of the club. The rehearsal breaks up as the afternoon wears into evening. Trace and his band are busy preparing for the show and even Sean leaves Albrecht alone in the shadows.

He lights another cigarette. "You should have been happy here."

Only memory answers him.

Sean seemed edgy, but Albrecht put it down to opening night nerves.

21

"There's a mob outside," Albrecht told him. "I don't think you have to worry."

Tonight Sean was luminous. He wore tight silver leather pants with a sheer black shirt that turned the skin beneath bone white by contrast.

Albrecht leaned down to kiss his cheek. "And you look so beautiful."

Sean accepted the brush of Albrecht's lips, but gave nothing in return. "Everything's done now," he murmured, rising.

Albrecht watched Sean walk away but there was a space in his memory where time disappeared. It was after the doors opened. There was a full house and Albrecht assumed he'd only lost Sean in the crowd.

The gunshot cut through the noise at the bar. Even before he'd fully processed what it was, Albrecht was moving toward the sound as everyone else moved away from it.

"Don't—" Someone—perhaps it was William—held him back from the bathroom door, but Albrecht shook free.

The smell of gunpowder, smoke, copper took Albrecht's breath. He remembered being alone as he went through the door.

The first thing he saw was a spill of black silk hair, drowning in a pool of blood. Albrecht choked. Couldn't stop himself from kneeling down, trying to touch Sean, trying to find him in the slick wet smear he'd left of himself.

"Herr Christian?" Sammy approaches him nervously. "Would you like anything?"

Albrecht shakes his head, waves her off, banishing the images Sean has left him.

As the club fills up around them, Albrecht watches Sammy. He imagines the girl is waiting for something. He sees her check her watch more than once. Finally Albrecht does, too. It's 9:30 exactly.

Sammy says something to one of the other bartenders and disappears. Albrecht rises and abandons his cigarette to follow. He stalks backstage to catch her before she gets to the stairs. He pulls her back by the arm, harshly.

Sammy lets out a squeak and Albrecht feels the girl's life quiver under his hand, but the taste is thin, unsatisfying. Albrecht tightens his grip anyway. "Get back to the bar now, or go home."

"But, I—" She looks toward the dressing room, then back into Albrecht's eyes. "That hurts."

Albrecht releases her. He doesn't watch Sammy slink away. The girl is lucky. Albrecht wants to crush her, leave her dry, for meanness sake, and more than that. More than just hurt her, he wants to make her disappear.

He begins his descent to Trace. Albrecht doesn't have a clear plan for what will happen next, until he gets to the bottom of the stairs. He hears laughter from within the dressing room and hesitates before knocking on the door. He feels as though he is losing more of himself, yet can't stop. His knock draws more laughter.

"C'mon in, Sammy," Trace calls.

"I sent her away." Albrecht pushes the door open.

There is a split second of silence and then the band bolts around him.

Trace is sitting at a makeup counter, drawing kohl lines around his eyes. He smiles at Albrecht in the mirror.

Albrecht returns it involuntarily. Trace turns away from his reflection and stands. He is dressed in a black matador jacket, naked chest gleaming beneath, and tight black jeans. Albrecht sees that he is barefoot.

"You don't trust me," Trace says.

"You told me not to, this morning." Albrecht crosses the room. He drops to his knees in front of Trace.

Trace touches his face. "I thought you were asleep."

When they are done, Trace helps Albrecht to his feet, kisses his cheek, then wipes the lipstick away with a thumb. "I just got one more thing to do," he says. "Go on. Don't worry. It's not like they're gonna start without me."

Christian hesitates, but leaves. The sound of Trace's name rumbles the small room around him, like an earthquake.

Trace grabs Asia's backpack to rummage in it until he comes up with a magic marker from its cluttered depths. Uncapping the pen, he climbs onto the sofa and scrawls T R A C E, in fat black letters as big as he can reach, over-writing other signatures as he goes.

When Trace emerges from the basement, Christian and Asia are staring at each other, like they're sizing each other up. Sammy is crying on Tommi's shoulder. The noise from the house is huge. Trace nods to the bartender. "Start us up, Sammy."

She brushes against him as she steps out of the wings. She does her bit like a trooper and the band moves forward.

"Do good tonight," Trace shouts in Asia's ear as they take their places in the dark.

Onstage, Trace knows the band is as good as they have ever been. Asia, keeping his stage fright at bay, is making every note. Weird verges on brilliant, but Trace wants more from them, more from the audience.

He moves to the edge of the stage as he starts the next song. The kids on the dance floor shove from the back, thrusting the ones up front hard against the stage.

Trace casts his shadow over them, leaning in, touching the fingertips of dozens of outstretched hands. He makes his voice sharp and raw as he sings. "Tell me how you want me. You want me."

They scream the words back to him and someone catches hold of his wrist. Instead of slipping away, he grins and pulls back.

A girl emerges from the crowd, all spiky red hair and white, white skin. She is so thin and narrow she could be a boy. She could be him. Wants to be him.

He hauls her the rest of the way up to stumble against him on spike-heeled pumps. He breathes in her scent of sweat and Love's Baby Soft.

"Tell me you want me." He makes the lyric soft, just for her, the screams of everybody else engulfing the music.

The girl's eyes are wide, bright green under her silver eyeshadow. Trace tangles his fingers in her short hair, bending to kiss her. She lets out a cry that he feels more than hears. She goes rigid for a split second, then her mouth opens to Trace. She forgets where she is, gives herself to him.

Trace breaks the contact abruptly, tosses her back into the arms of the crowd, who swallow up her screams.

"Careful on those heels, baby," he says, turning his back on the house as the song crashes to its end.

There is horror on Asia's face. Trace gives him the same cold smile the audience is screaming for right now. Asia shakes his head, but Weird counts down to the next song.

Albrecht lights the last cigarette in his case. He is transfixed by the exchange that goes on between Trace and the audience. Albrecht can feel their need, the desperation in their screams. He sees Trace take it all from them, sees it pulse in him.

Albrecht realizes that he will never possess this. He will never be enough for Trace. Even if he spends the rest of his life deflecting the Sammys of the world, he can't ever offer more than what this audience is giving Trace now.

Albrecht wishes he was the devil, that the contract between them was enough to bind Trace to him forever. In the end, he knows it is nothing more than paper and money.

Onstage, Trace turns his back on all of them, and the children scream harder, as though they will die from the want of him.

When they get offstage, Albrecht Christian is waiting in the wings. Asia forces himself to watch Trace kiss the other man, watch Christian's eyes flutter closed, the breath he draws after they're done.

"Mm." Trace smiles. "How'd y'like the show?"

Asia turns away. This is how it is now. Weird slouches against the back wall and lights a cigarette with a lighter shaped like a dragon.

"Looks like it's you 'n me." He pushes away from the wall and pockets the lighter. "Might as well take off."

"Where's Tommi going?"

"John's back." Weird scowls. "Fucker. Showed up tonight, sayin' he was all sorry."

"Shit." Asia rolls his eyes. The one thing everybody in Black Light agrees on is that Tommi has crappy taste in men. Sometimes even scary taste.

Trace joins them. "I saw that fuckin' John at break."

"Yeah. Tommi saw him, too," Weird says. "He's goin' home with him tonight."

Trace glances toward Christian, who keeps his distance, then back to Weird. "Can't you do something?"

"Yeah, sure." Weird snorts. "Like what? I'm not his dad, Dellon. If he wants to date some dickwad that keeps beatin' the shit outta him, what am I s'posed to do? Ground him?"

Trace narrows his eyes, but only shakes his head. "I gotta go."

Asia looks at Christian, in the shadows, then back to Trace. "I guess we'll see you tomorrow?"

"Yep." Trace grins. He grabs Christian by the hand and kisses him again. "Wanna take me home?"

"C'mon." Weird bumps shoulders with Asia, as the other two

walk off. "Let's get outta here."

Albrecht brings Trace back to the penthouse but tonight the pretenses are gone. There is no small talk. They make love in the shower and again in bed. Trace falls asleep quickly, satisfied.

Albrecht leaves the bed, but he hasn't the stomach for the churning lights of LA tonight. He wanders the cavernous penthouse in the dark, ending up at the black granite bar. Albrecht has been drinking steadily all day, but doesn't feel the effects. Once again, he isn't tired. He isn't hungry.

He has an image of Sean, from long ago, sitting here, smiling through the blue/black curtain of his hair. "Love is never anything good. That's what my Mum used to say."

Albrecht told him she was right, but the boy had only laughed.

Albrecht pours himself some scotch and sits on one of the sofas. He can imagine how pathetic he must look, naked old man alone with his drink in the dark. He wonders at the prospect of unleashing Trace into the world. His audience will only get bigger from this point forward, become more demanding. Trace will take more from them, need Albrecht even less than now.

He sighs, marveling at the brittle sound of it.

When Sean appears, kneeling on the floor in front of him, Albrecht smiles, reaches out to touch his hair. "Your mother was right," he says.

"You're letting yourself fall into your own trap. You believe it when you tell him you love him."

Sean takes the drink from Albrecht and sets it on the side table. His smile warms and he slides his hands up the insides of Albrecht's thighs, pulling a sigh from him. Albrecht leans back, closes his eyes. His body reacts to Sean just as though this were really happening. His blood races. He is hungry on a cellular level. "I do love him."

"As much as me?" Sean asks, drawing back. "Because that's not enough."

The cold truth of it is that Albrecht knows he loves Trace far more, though he suspects Trace isn't capable of returning any of it. Albrecht was fond of Sean, but had no illusions about using him up one day. Albrecht wonders if that is how Trace feels about him.

"Perhaps you're right," he says aloud, but Sean has evaporated.

Albrecht retrieves his glass and empties it. Then he goes back into the bedroom. Sean has made him remember that he doesn't have the luxury of love. For Albrecht, this is survival.

Trace stirs when Albrecht touches him, but doesn't wake completely. Albrecht hushes him, stroking the hollow at his collarbone, his chest, fingers sliding over hipbones. Albrecht wills his body to take the lightning bolt energy that flows through Trace. Albrecht can taste it now, at the back of his throat, like copper. He can take it and leave Trace empty, walk away.

It's what he should do, but Albrecht falters. What would be the point of survival after Trace?

3

Albrecht wastes no time moving Trace into the Algonquin. He also sets William to work out the details of hiring the producer. Black Light's engagement at the Refugee Club is ending over the weekend and Albrecht wants to begin recording as soon as possible after that. He doesn't want to risk boredom for Trace.

Asia is hot and tired and not happy to find that Albrecht Christian is waiting for them in the dressing room. Again. Then he sees that there's somebody else there too. Great. Christian's friend is a lanky black man with long thick dreadlocks, sitting on the couch. He gets up when Trace appears.

"This is Lionel Child," Christian says. "I brought him here to listen to you. He's going to produce your album."

Weird elbows his way around Trace. "I've heard your stuff. You produced for Live Wire, right? The *Shelby Cries* album." He sticks his hand out. "Damn, that stuff is great. And you wanna produce ours?"

The hairs at the back of Asia's neck stand up. Weird loves that album. He bought it new when it came out and Asia knows all the songs by heart, just through the wall of his bedroom in their old place in Ann Arbor.

"That's the idea." The man's voice is deep, accented, Jamaican maybe.

Asia backs out of the room to cross the dark hallway to the john. Trace and Weird can tell him what was decided later. He doesn't have a stake in this like the rest of them.

He strips off his clothes and tosses them on the floor. Then he steps into the narrow booth of the shower before the water warms up. He leans back against the plastic wall and stares up into the darkness of the unfinished ceiling above. Same as every night, he thinks: if this was a horror movie, a guy with an ax would swing down out of there and start hacking. Nights like this, Asia thinks he

28

wouldn't mind that so much. The water cools his skin and washes the sweat from the lights away, and he wonders if he can do this the rest of his life.

After a few minutes he hears the door open. "They're gone, Asia."

He starts and looks through the thin opaque curtain. "Trace?"

"Christian's waiting for me upstairs and Lionel took off. It's safe to come out."

Asia thinks it's strange that he hasn't heard Trace call Albrecht Christian by his first name yet, considering their relationship, but this producer is instantly Lionel. He turns off the water and reaches a hand out to feel around for the towel. "I wasn't hiding. I just figured, y'know, it was crowded in there."

There is no way in hell that Trace is going to leave him alone to get his jeans back on in peace. Asia folds the towel around his waist and steps out, sighing. "And it's not like I know anything about making a record, so I figure—"

Trace frowns at him. "I need you, y'know. I need you to be in the band, with me."

Asia feels his face flush and he can't look at Trace. He swallows hard. "I'm...I'm not going anywhere."

"Weird and me are gonna meet with Lionel at Para Bellum on Monday. I'd like you to come too, but I don't want you to worry about it." Trace touches his shoulder lightly. "Christian's waiting. I'll see you tomorrow, okay?"

Asia just stands there until Trace is gone. He pulls his jeans and tee shirt back on. This is it, he realizes. It's happening, right now, to all of them. He glances at himself in the rippled mirror above the sink, wondering how he could have ever thought it wouldn't.

He lets out his breath and bunches his hair into a rubber band at the back of his neck. Then he heads up the stairs to catch up with Weird and Tommi.

"So what are we waiting for?" Asia asks, joining them in the alley. It's about ten degrees cooler out here than inside. Goosebumps raise on his bare arms and his scalp prickles under his damp hair. Weird snorts and lights a cigarette with a pistol-shaped lighter.

"John's supposed to pick me up, but I guess he's runnin' late," Tommi says apologetically. "You guys can go. He'll be here."

"Yeah-right." Weird talks around the cigarette. "Like I'm gonna leave you standing around in the middle of the night in this neighborhood."

Asia wonders if there's a neighborhood anywhere in LA that is safe in the middle of the night.

Tommi leans against the wall and blows the hair out of his face. "He really will be here."

"So we'll just wait with you." Asia shrugs and smiles, though the prospect of John isn't pleasant. "Not like we got any place to be."

He wants to ask about the producer and about what's going to happen next, but he can feel the tension gathering in Weird and knows that his whole mind is occupied with the promise of John. Asia wonders if they're waiting so Weird can confront the guy.

"What the hell're you doin' back here?" John's voice precedes him as he enters the mouth of the alley. "I told you to be out front."

"No, you didn't," Tommi says. "And it's all locked up now anyway. How come you missed the show?"

"'Cause I got better things to do than be your groupie." John closes the ground between them. He's nearly as tall as Trace, but broader in the shoulders. His fists clench and unclench as he approaches Tommi. "I told you I had stuff to do."

"Well, that clears it up," Weird mutters, dropping his cigarette. He looks at Tommi. "You sure you don't wanna ride with us?"

"He's fine," John answers. When he reaches Tommi, he hooks an arm around his neck.

"Tommi?" Weird prompts as though John hadn't spoken.

"No, really." Tommi smiles first at Weird, then John. He leans up to kiss John on the lips. "I'm sorry," he says. "It's just that I missed you."

"Then let's get home, so you can show me how much."

Tommi giggles as they walk off. Weird just watches until they're gone. "Swear to God, I'm gonna have ta kill that asshole."

Asia doesn't bother to answer. Tommi met John at Black Light's very first LA gig, a dump called the Spyhole. John had been drunk, but charming; at least, Tommi thought he was. Since then, there had been countless bruises on Tommi's arms, even a black eye. They'd been broken up a half-dozen times in as many months, but it never took. "Let's just go," Asia says. "At least there's no traffic this late."

In the van, he stares out the window, not seeing anything. He feels the miles spinning under them and feels empty inside. Maybe John is an asshole, but Tommi isn't alone. That has to count for something. Asia tries not to think about Trace, but it's pointless. Albrecht Christian is different from any of the boys or girls Trace has fucked around with before. There is an air of permanence in the way they touch each other that Asia finds hurts more than even watching Trace with Sammy. Asia feels like something is broken between them now and there isn't any fixing it.

"Dellon told you what we're doin', right?" Weird speaks, as he changes lanes. "I never know with him, so I'm askin'."

"You and him and that guy are gonna be meeting next week." Asia nods. "And then…I don't know what's gonna happen then."

"You're a little freaked out, aren't you?"

"I don't know. I guess I kinda am," Asia admits. "I don't know how to cut a record—do you?"

"A little bit." Weird shrugs. "That's what we got Lionel for, Asia. You don't gotta do anything but play when he tells you and listen to what he tells you to do. It's not like you gotta print the covers or anything."

"You know what I mean." Asia leans against the door and folds his arms across his chest.

The van picks up speed and develops a death rattle somewhere toward the back. Weird turns up the radio and speaks over Tina Turner's wail. "You hear your amp tonight?"

"What?"

"D'ja hear your amp buzzin'?"

Asia frowns, thinking back, a sinking feeling hitting him. Amplifiers are just like cars. They always break down when you need to be someplace and you got no paycheck left. "Shit, really?"

"Yeah. Not that anybody could hear it over Dellon's fuckin' fans, 'cept me, and maybe Lionel."

"Shit," Asia repeats. They had already spent the advance from Para Bellum on back rent and van repairs. Asia doesn't know when they'll start to see any real money.

"So, see, this is a good thing. And besides, Asia, you're a rock star now. You don't ever have to worry about doing another damn thing, except doing what they tell you."

Asia doesn't answer. He wonders if Weird means to be reassuring or not.

Friday is their last show at the Refugee and everybody knows it. It seems to Asia that the number of people in the house has doubled since last night. An impatient rumble vibrates the stage beneath his feet as they wait behind the curtain. He shifts his bass, already sweating under the strap, and glances back at the amp. Weird, from the other side of the stage, catches his look and crosses over. "Don't worry," he mutters into Asia's ear. "Nobody's gonna hear a damn thing we play tonight. Unless the thing catches on fire, nobody's gonna notice."

Great, Asia thinks. Always a fuckin' bright side.

Beyond the curtain, Sammy starts the show. "Now, for the last time at the Refugee Club, Trace Dellon and Black Light."

There is a swell of noise from the crowd, like a massive moan. Then the whole place shakes with Trace's name.

He sweeps past Asia as the curtain opens. Sammy steps back offstage and the lights go up. Trace yanks the mic out of its stand and counts the first song down. Asia can feel himself playing, but he can't really hear it. He watches Trace tease the audience down in front, dancing close enough for them to touch, but always twisting away before it gets dangerous. With each hand that makes contact with Trace, wrapping around his leg, catching at his clothes, his hair, Asia tenses, ready.

"I'll miss you too." Trace laughs at them. "It's okay. Pretty soon we'll be everywhere you look."

They cheer and cry harder for him and he touches as many of them as he can reach. Asia swallows the feeling of dread Trace's words open in him. Asia still wants to go back to the place where he has hope for a normal life. After this gig, Asia's plan had been to get a job at the comic shop on Brand in Glendale, maybe get a regular paycheck for a change.

As Weird slides into the next number, Asia's fingers work on their own and he submits to Trace's music.

Monday morning Asia wakes to Weird's raised voice on the

phone, swearing at John. By the time Asia has crawled off his futon Weird slams the phone back into the cradle. "Fucker."

"What?" Asia knuckles sand from his eyes.

"Fuckin' John wouldn't even let me talk to Tommi." Weird pulls his cigarettes from a shirt pocket and lights one. "We gotta be across town in forty-five minutes."

Asia can see that Weird is torn between driving over to John's to drag Tommi out and making the meeting with Lionel on time. In the end, he fills Asia's backpack with cassette tapes he and Trace have made over the last year and they head over to Hollywood.

Para Bellum is impressive and Asia feels dwarfed by the massive marble and steel lobby.

Weird walks in, already looking like a rock star in his battered blue jeans over cowboy boots. His eyes are hidden behind dark sunglasses. He pauses at reception to light a cigarette with his guitar-shaped lighter. "We're with Black Light," he tells the blond across the desk. "We're here for Lionel Child."

She nods and picks up a phone. Asia tries not to stare at her fingernails, which are the longest he's seen outside of a chopsocky movie. She shakes feathered hair back from her face and tells someone on the other end that they're here and then hangs up. "That elevator, over there. Third floor."

Lionel meets them in the hall. He and Weird shake hands. "Good morning. Trace and Albrecht are already here."

Asia trails them as they pass another blond woman at the desk in the outer office. She nods and smiles.

Inside, one wall is windows that show a postcard view of the city. The opposite displays framed gold records. The other end of the room is taken up with a black grand piano.

Albrecht Christian stands at the window, hands clasped behind his back. Trace is wearing headphones plugged into a reel-to-reel on the wall behind the desk.

"Asia." He grins, pulling the headphones off. "You made it." He glances at Weird. "What about Tommi?"

"He didn't show up this morning," Weird grumbles, crossing the room to tap his ashes into the tray on the desk. "I'll go over to check on him after this."

Asia frowns, uncomfortable with the subject in front of strangers.

Weird chooses one of the leather chairs in front of the desk to slouch in. He peels off his sunglasses to look from Lionel and Trace. "Okay, so what did I miss?"

Asia gives over his backpack and then drifts away as the talk turns technical. He doesn't need to know any of this. He's the one on the outside of the conversation. He can feel distance stretching between him and the rest of them. It's like he's a kid again, sitting in his shrink's office with his mom and dad.

They talked about the sudden changes in his behavior, his grades. The shrink, a guy in a disturbingly powder-blue sweater, made some guesses, but nobody asked Asia what was the matter. It was the first time in his life he realized his parents didn't love him, that there wasn't any way he could make them love him.

Asia spent the session staring out the window at a hawk, circling over a nearby field. He watched it turn in the air and dive on a smaller bird and thought of his brother.

"Are you happy with the arrangements so far?" Albrecht Christian's voice intrudes on the memory, pitched low, as though he is waking a child.

Asia blinks, realizes he's now standing next to Christian at the window. "Uh." This is the first time Christian has spoken to him directly. "Yeah, I mean, it's all great."

He looks up at the other man and is startled at the paleness of his eyes. So gray they're almost white: the color of cigarette smoke. Christian smiles and the space between Asia's shoulder blades itches. "Trace tells me that you are unsure that this is what you want to do with your life."

"It's not that..." Asia stammers, embarrassed that he would be a subject they would discuss. He's momentarily distracted by the sound of Lionel and Weird clattering the tapes in and out of a machine. "I just... It's Trace's decision what the band does."

Christian's smile twitches a fraction wider. "Yes, I suppose that is true. Still, you're an important part of his life. He doesn't want to lose you."

Asia swallows, heat coming up in his face.

"Asia, c'mere." Trace beckons from behind the piano that takes up the other end of the office.

Asia is grateful to escape. He goes to stand against of curve of the grand's body.

Lionel sits next to Trace and Weird stands behind them. Trace has his notebook propped on the music stand.

"We've never had keyboards," Weird says. "None of us really play, so..."

Lionel nods. Asia remembers the out-of-tune upright that lived in the basement of his parents' house. He remembers his brother Eric and Trace beating out their earliest songs on it. Ancient history, he thinks. Before Weird.

Asia wonders how Lionel will interpret Trace's writing. All the songs ever start with are words, scrawled out in Trace's drunken-spider handwriting. Later, Weird adds guitar chords above them, but the melody never gets written down anywhere. Lionel splays his long dark fingers against the keys. "Just sing. I'll find you."

Trace closes his eyes and Asia watches him pull the song from where the music lives in him. The first verse is about a boy who spends his whole life caged in the dark, with only his own voice as company. Trace's voice, naked, is like velvet razor wire. It makes Asia's breath catch, makes him wish they were alone. Then he glances at Herr Christian and sees the same wish on his face.

The piano comes in slow, shadowing Trace.

In the second verse, the boy's voice teaches him to turn himself to smoke, and he escapes. Lionel starts to add layers now, makes the melody darker, playing against the words like a backdrop. By the third verse, the boy is unleashed in the world, and his voice, so beautiful and strange, makes the world mistake him for a god and they kill him for it.

Lionel takes his hands from the keys and smiles. "If you have eight more of these, we have an album."

After the meeting, Trace invites himself along to keep Asia company while Weird heads over to John's. It's been weeks since they've been alone, but Trace can't get Asia to talk. Instead, he stands at the sink, washing plastic bowls and cups, keeping his back to Trace sitting at the table behind him. Finally Asia wipes his hands on his jeans and turns to grab a Diet Coke from the refrigerator.

"I'm gonna go down to the pool. It's too fucking hot in here."

Trace drowns his cigarette in a near-empty beer bottle on the counter. "I'll go with you."

The courtyard below is cooler, with an arid breeze heavy with the scent of curry and deep-fry oil. Trace's stomach clenches at the thought of all that hot food in all those hotter apartments. The smell of chlorine from the pool does little to take the edge off. Fuck, Trace thinks. He doesn't miss this place.

Asia sits on the low wall of a crumbling cement planter that contains a few scraggly yuccas and a crooked palm tree. He pulls his legs up and wraps his arms around his knees. His ginger-brown hair is hopelessly knotted around the rubber band he uses to keep it back from his face. Trace sits next to him but doesn't move to untangle it, though he knows how soft and fine it feels. He lights another cigarette instead. Asia's eyes are on the lone swimmer in the pool, an old man in a black cap.

"What were you and Herr Christian talking about today?" Trace asks.

"What?" Asia takes his eyes off Flipper long enough to frown at Trace. "Oh, nothin'. He asked me... I guess he asked me if I like the studio and contract and stuff."

Trace turns away to exhale. "I know you don't like him, Asia, but could you just pretend a little better? He is our boss."

Asia sighs. "I just—I don't know what to say to him. He's... I don't know. I just never met anybody like him."

Trace smiles, in spite of himself. "Me, neither." He flicks ashes across the pavement. "Look at everything he'd done for us."

Asia chokes out a laugh. "For you. D'ya think if you weren't.... You know. Sleeping with him. He woulda ever signed us?"

Trace feels layers of bitterness under Asia's words, but he can't bring himself to be angry. Instead, he tries to be honest. "He told me that he doesn't value our talent less because he loves me. I believe him."

"You've known him, like three weeks," Asia says. "How do you know he really..."

Trace smiles at the blush that starts at the back of Asia's neck. He remembers the weight of Christian's watch in his hand. "I just do."

"There's something off about him. I feel like I'm talking to a space alien or something." Asia unfolds himself to stand up again. He turns away and lets out a long sigh. "Maybe I'm just jealous.

You're different when you're with him."

Trace watches him walk up the stairs back to the tiny apartment. He's used to the pang of regret he feels as Asia disappears.

Asia pauses before he jiggles his key into the door, hearing voices.

"I was asleep," Tommi says. "He just didn't wanna wake me. He didn't know how important it is."

"Goddamn it." Weird's voice isn't raised, but Asia can hear the frustration in it. "Don't start lyin' for him again. Not to me."

"Weird, I'm not lyin'."

But he is, Asia thinks, sighing as he goes in to break it up. He is lying and it's only going to get worse. When Asia gets inside, he sees by Weird's face that he knows it, too.

"Hey," he greets anyway, like he hasn't overheard anything. "Trace's downstairs. Do you wanna order pizza, or should I make some tuna salad?"

Both of them give him a shudder at the mention of tuna, but Asia doesn't take it personally. "Fine. Order what you want. I'll go see if Trace's stayin'."

Asia pauses on the bottom step, just watching Trace through the bars of the rusty gate. He's right where Asia left him, sitting under the crappy palm. Asia only lets himself linger a few seconds. One day, he knows, he'll be caught looking.

"They're gonna order pizza," he says, pushing the gate open. "You want some?"

Trace smiles, combs his fingers through his hair. He pushes to his feet. "Thanks, but I gotta get back. See you at Para Bellum."

"Yeah." Asia looks away.

The night doesn't get any better. After pizza, Asia resumes washing dishes, though it's a losing battle. At least it gives him something to do while Tommi and Weird argue.

"So, you're not stayin'?" Weird's voice isn't loud, but low and dangerous. "Is he gonna let you show up tomorrow? We need you to be there, Tommi. This is important. This is our first album."

"I get it, okay?" Tommi shoots back. "It's not like he keeps me locked up or something, geez, Weird."

"Yeah-well, you missed today." Weird tilts his chair back, up on its back legs, to lean against the cupboard behind him. "If you go back there tonight, maybe he'll just let you sleep through it again."

"Weird, look, I promise it'll be okay. Okay?" Tommi stands up. "He's gonna be downstairs any minute."

He's gone too fast for Asia to think of something to say to convince him to stay. He sighs at the slam of the cheap door.

4

It's a few rings before Asia identifies the phone. He stumbles up to his feet and lurches into the kitchen, heart hammering. He snatches the receiver off the wall. "What."

"Asia."

The voice is weak, not right. "Tommi?" Asia shakes himself awake. "Tommi, what's wrong?"

"N-nothing. I just need you guys to come and get me." The words sound flattened out.

Asia frowns. "Where's John? Are you at his place?"

"Yeah, I mean, I'm here—he…" The boy's voice drops to a whisper. "Please, Asia."

Asia hears Weird moving in the hallway behind him. The guitarist takes the phone. "Tommi? We're comin' right now. You tell that piece of shit I'm gonna kill him if he hits you one more time, you hear me?"

He hangs up and says, "Let's go."

In the van, Asia asks, "How did you know?"

Weird's laugh is ugly. "C'mon, Asia. Why else is he callin' at four a.m.? To let us know he's havin' really good sex? Besides, what's it been, like a coupla weeks? It was just a matter of time."

Good point, Asia thinks. "Sounded like his nose was broken."

"Fuckin' John."

When they get to the house in Glendale, Asia can see that the front door has been left open. He hesitates to climb the steps of the porch but Weird pushes past him, takes them two at a time. "Tommi?"

Weird crosses the threshold into the dark interior. "Tommi, goddamn it."

He heads straight through the living room for the bedroom while Asia hangs back in the kitchen. The wall phone dangles from where it has been pulled out of the plaster. He sighs, closes the refrigerator, stoops to pick up the pieces of a coffee mug from the floor. Then he goes on, veering off towards the back of the house.

Asia freezes on the threshold of the bathroom. Tommi is propped against the tub. Even in the shadows, Asia sees blood. "Weird—shit."

Again, the guitarist is already there, shoving Asia aside.

"Stupid kid," he mutters, flicking the light on.

Asia holds back a gasp. Under the blood, Tommi is bone white, except for the bruises on his face and torso.

The tiny room is trashed, mirror broken, shards of glass everywhere. It crunches under Weird's boot heel as he crouches next to Tommi. "Hey, hey, kid," he murmurs. "C'mon. Open your eyes."

As he speaks, he takes the washcloth Tommi has in one hand. Weird twists to wet it in the sink so he can start to clean Tommi's face gently. "C'mon, Tommi. You're safe now."

"Weird." He makes a weak grab for the cloth. "I'm sorry. I didn't mean—"

"Don't apologize." There is a shadow of steel in Weird's voice. "Y'didn't do anything wrong, okay?"

He helps Tommi sit forward a little. The boy winces, hand curled to his side.

"Your ribs are prob'ly bruised, at least," Weird tells him. "You need x-rays."

"No," Tommi groans. He tries to raise himself off the floor with his hands, but ends up skittering back down.

"Hey, c'mon." Weird catches him, gently pulls a piece of glass from his palm. "Y'can't even get up, can you?"

"I can't go to the hospital." Fresh tears start at the corners of Tommi's eyes. "They're gonna know what happened, and John—"

"Don't worry about John," Weird says. Asia sees a thin cord of rage whip through him at the name, then evaporate as he speaks again. "We need to worry about you right now. I gotta get you up and outta here, and it's gonna hurt."

He soothes Tommi's pale hair back from his from his forehead. Asia gasps, seeing the main source of the blood, where Tommi's head impacted the mirror.

"Nobody cares," Tommi whispers as Weird gathers him up. "Nobody cares if queers beat the crap out of each other."

"That's just what John tells you," Weird says.

Asia is surprised at how easily Weird manages the weight. "Get a blanket and his shoes," he tells Asia. "And anything else you see that's his."

It's just dawn by the time they take Tommi in to examine him. Asia shifts on his plastic chair in the waiting room and leans his head against the wall.

"Will you be okay on your own awhile?" Weird asks suddenly.

Asia opens his eyes again. "Huh?"

"I got somethin' I gotta do, but I'll prob'ly be back before he's ready to go home."

"What?" Asia frowns. But at the set of Weird's jaw Asia remembers the baseball bat that clunks around under the bench seat in the van. "Yeah. Just..."

"I'll be back for you," Weird says again, but digs into his jeans for a wad of cash. "But if I'm not, take a cab and get Tommi home."

It isn't until Weird's gone that Asia remembers.

They are due back to Para Bellum today to start recording. Never make it, he thinks, panic tightening across his chest. What will Trace do if we don't show?

He pulls Christian's card from his wallet and gets up, stiff from sitting too long, to go to the payphone. He has no idea what the number is actually connected to, or if there will be any answer this time of morning, but he punches it in anyway.

"Para Bellum Records, how my I direct your call?"

For a split second Asia is unsure of what to say. He rubs his eyes with the heel of his hand and blinks. "Uh, I'm supposed to have a meeting there with..." He reaches for the name of the producer, but comes up empty. "Uh, I'm with Trace Dellon's band, Black Light? We're have a studio session this morning?"

The woman on the other end of the phone says, "At eleven with Lionel, I believe. Did you have a message, or are you just confirming?"

"Well..." Asia shifts on his feet. "Uh, see, one of our guys... Tommi, he's had an accident, and we're still at the emergency room. I don't think they'll be done with him before eleven."

The receptionist makes sympathetic noises. "I understand. I'm sure we can work something out. Is there a number where we can

41

reach you?"

"See, I think Trace will be there." Asia again is unsure what to say. He wants to avoid pointing out where Trace spends the night. "I just want him to know where we are, I guess."

"I'll make sure he gets the message," she assures. "Can you tell me where you are?"

Asia tells her the hospital, but keeps the particulars of Tommi's "accident" vague. Trace will know, he thinks. After he hangs up, he returns to his chair, barely noticing when he drifts off.

Asia hears his name and opens his eyes with a start, confused. Then the glare of the waiting room, the noise, the smell, brings him back.

"Was it John? It was, right?" Trace stands in front of him, frowning. Behind him, Asia spots Herr Christian.

"Yeah," Asia answers Trace, pushing to his feet. He doesn't elaborate.

Trace pushes. "How long as he been in?"

"Like, about, a couple of hours?" Asia doesn't really know what time it is now. He's too tired to do the math, anyway.

Christian shifts on his feet and glances at his wristwatch. "Why don't I find some coffee while you fill Trace in? As I've already explained to him, I don't want any of you worried about the meeting today. It's been taken care of."

"Diet Coke for Asia," Trace says as Christian leaves.

In Tommi's room, Asia stands back from the bed, feeling useless. He tries to think of something encouraging to say, but he can barely look at Tommi's face, all bruises and stitches. He's grateful that Weird hasn't made it back yet, to see this.

Trace sits on the bed with Tommi, takes his hand, hushing him when he tries to apologize.

"But I fucked everything up," Tommi insists, voice weak.

"Bullshit." Trace laughs. "We'll just do it in a couple days. You don't worry about this."

He sits there until Tommi falls asleep.

"Should we wake him up?" Asia whispers. "If he has a

concussion, should he be sleeping?"

Herr Christian returns. "They tell me they will wake him up every few hours to check on him. He is allowed to sleep in between." He gives a smile to Trace and touches his shoulder. "The doctor says that he has a hairline skull fracture as well as a broken nose, but the ribs are only bruised. He says that in all, it could have been worse."

Asia shakes his head. Yeah, he thinks, like the bastard coulda killed him.

It starts to look like Weird isn't coming back and with Tommi asleep, Trace and Herr Christian are ready to leave. At first, Asia tries to insist that he needs to stay, but somehow Herr Christian talks him out of it. "You've had an endless night. Let us drive you home to get some sleep. I shall make sure you have a ride back later."

Asia finds he's too tired to put up much of a fight. He sits in the back of the long car on one side of Trace, Christian on the other, and tries not to think about how surreal life has become.

Christian pales at the neighborhood they drop Asia off in.

"I told you," is all Trace says. He slips out of the car to catch Asia's arm. "Get some sleep, okay? I'll call you later."

Asia nods and turns away. As the long car pulls away from the curb, a couple of cop cars roll up, sirens screaming away. Asia's too tired to care what's happening, so he fades into the background fast, heading up the steps before the cops can get out of the car. He walks up to the second floor of the building and jiggles his key into the battered lock. Weird sits at the table in the kitchen, still wearing the tee shirt from last night, smeared with Tommi's blood. Asia stares. At best, it's only Tommi's blood. The guitarist's works are spread out amid the collection of dirty dishes. "They kep' him, din't they?"

"Weird." Asia watches him hold up the hypodermic to tap the air out. "C'mon."

Weird ignores him. He rubs his forearm below the tubing to raise the vein, eases the tip of the needle through his skin. He takes a long, hissing breath, pulls the plunger back a fraction, then down again, over and over. Asia's stomach clenches at the sight of red swirling up, mixing with the heroin solution. Then Weird empties it all into his arm.

"Weird," Asia starts again. "Look, Tommi—"

But Weird draws the needle out and his eyes sag closed. "'m not his dad, Asia. I done everything I can do."

Asia thinks of the bat again. Sitting all crumpled here, Weird doesn't look like he was capable of much violence, but Asia remembers the flash of rage at John's name. "You find John?"

Weird opens his eyes slowly, smiling.

"You did, didn't you?"

Weird tips his chair up to lean against the counter behind him. "You don't really wanna know, Asia."

He can't help imaging what kind of damage that bat could have done. "It's bad, isn't it?"

"I'm not insane." Weird sighs. "I didn't fuck him up as much as he did Tommi. Just scared him, hopefully enough to keep him away."

"Trace and Albrecht Christian came to the hospital," Asia says. "They both said don't worry about it, but we've got a schedule now, and how's Tommi gonna play, all fucked up?"

Weird shrugs and tips his chair back down. "Asia." He smiles wryly. "This isn't that job you had at Kmart that one time. They're not gonna fire us because we get behind or because we call in sick. Besides, Lionel can sit in for Tommi when we lay down the rhythm tracks, if he has to. It's no big deal."

But Lionel isn't a part of this band, Asia wants to say. I don't wanna play with him. He only sighs and shakes his head instead. He watches Weird tidy up his works. What's the point of protesting anyway? Asia thinks, turning away. None of this is up to him.

The next morning Trace wakes up before the alarm, before Christian. He's getting accustomed to this, settling into the routine. He gets up, steals Christian's white silk robe and goes into the kitchen to start the coffee and wait for the guy who brings in breakfast. This is as domestic as he will ever get, he thinks, listening to the elevator door slide open.

Trace greets as the man enters the kitchen. "Hey, Frank."

"Morning, sir." Frank's almost as tall as Trace, with natural red hair. He's dressed, same as always, in a white tee shirt and jeans. He carries a pastry box with him. "Got some fresh stuff for you today. Croissants and fruit for Herr Christian, and," he pauses to set the box down, flashes Trace a shy smile. "A coupla of chocolate custard-filled for you."

"Mm." Trace reaches over to take one out and lick some of the frosting off. "Sugar. The most important meal of the day, I always say."

Frank laughs as he begins to set the table for Christian's breakfast. Trace wonders, not for the first time, what it would have been like to grow up this way, having things done for you by invisible servants. He eats one of his cream sticks while Frank lets himself out. Then he goes in to wake Christian.

"Breakfast," he calls, entering the hushed bedroom again. It's brighter in here than any other room in the penthouse. Trace feels like a black spot on the sun. He takes off the robe to bring it to Christian.

"I'm awake." The other man opens his eyes and reaches for Trace instead. "I felt you leave the bed. I've been waiting for you to come back."

Trace laughs. "Too bad I gotta be at work today, baby. I think it would be a lot more fun to stay here."

Christian arches an eyebrow. "Really? Because when you're there, it doesn't seem that there's anything you'd rather do."

Trace leans in closer to kiss him. "I don't want you to feel like you have to be there every day we are."

"Do I make you uncomfortable, watching you?"

"No, it's not that," Trace says. "It's just, you know, it's gotta be kinda boring. I'm not sayin' you're Yoko Ono or anything...I just..." He looks down, wondering if he's offended Christian. "I just didn't want you to think it was something you had to do."

"Truly, I'm enjoying it," Christian admits. "I know very well that I possess no creative ability, so when I get a chance to watch the process... Watching you create something is quite amazing."

Trace raises an eyebrow, smiles as he gets up again. "Then I'm glad you're there. Are you hungry? Frank brought croissants for you. And there's coffee."

"Frank?" Christian slips into the robe. "Oh, yes, of course."

Trace pulls his jeans on and follows Christian back to the kitchen. Christian looks up from his coffee to ask, "Is Tommi coming home soon?"

"In a day or two," Trace tells him. "It's hard for him, because he wants so much to be at the studio. I wish..." Then he thinks of something else. "I've never said thank you for going with me to the hospital, and everything else you've done."

Christian smiles. "I'm sorry that Tommi was hurt so badly. He seems like a nice young man."

Trace laughs soundlessly at that. "Tommi is nice. He's really sweet and he doesn't deserve shit like John."

Christian drinks the last of his coffee and looks up. "It must be over between them now, yes?"

"Yeah-right, that'd be great, if Tommi can stay away." Trace shrugs. "That's the thing."

"Surely he can see that this...this man is not good for him?"

"It's happened before, just not this bad," Trace tells him. "And when Tommi gets away, John always comes after him, and Tommi loves him."

"Sean used to say, 'Love is never anything good.' I suppose he was certainly right about that," Christian says. "I have been thinking about that neighborhood where the band is living."

"I told you it was terrible."

Christian holds a hand up. "Terrible is not the word. It's simply unacceptable."

"When we start to make money, we can do something about that," Trace points out.

"Para Bellum keeps several places around town that would be suitable. I shall call William and have him begin to prepare one of them. How long do you think it would take Asia to pack?"

Trace laughs. "About a half hour. All we really have is our gear."

"Then I suggest you call him. It should all be done before Tommi is released from the hospital, so he can make a clean start?"

Trace rises and leans across the table to kiss Christian. "That's perfect. Thank you."

"They are your band." Christian's smile is faint. "If they're important to you, they're important to me."

It isn't that Asia likes where they're living. That isn't the point.

He waffles on the phone. "I don't know. I mean, who's gonna pay for it?"

"Asia." Trace's voice shows strain. "I told you. The house is owned by the label. Nobody's gonna charge rent."

He tries again. "But we gotta go back up to the hospital before the studio today."

"Jesus Christ, Asia," Trace growls. "Don't you wanna get out of that hellhole? Wouldn't it be better for Tommi to come home to someplace safe?"

Asia has to admit that it would be. "Let me write down the address."

When he gets off the phone and looks around the kitchen, he realizes that Trace's right. It won't take long to pack their shit. Probably, he and Weird can get it all to the van without anybody noticing, if they leave the futon and the mattress.

Two hours later, Asia's got all his stuff folded back into his milk crates, and Trace's stuff wadded into a couple of garbage bags. The only thing left is the bedroom. He hasn't heard any movement since Weird stumbled in there this morning to sleep it off.

Asia has no wish to disturb him, but Weird has the keys to the van so he has to drive get-away. Finally Asia goes to pound on the bedroom door.

He's not surprised that there's no response. "Crap." It comes out as a tired sigh. He pounds again and is met with silence. "Dammit, Weird, c'mon."

He twists the knob and pushes the door open. "Weird?"

Stale cigarette smoke hits Asia at first, stronger than the rest of the apartment. Then he smells something sharper, more chemical under that. Weird is sprawled on the mattress, waxy and pale, half-wrapped in an American flag blanket.

"Weird." Asia kicks the mattress to wake him, but gets no response. Then he sees the needle on the floor, by Weird's still outstretched hand.

"Shit." Asia kneels down next to the guitarist, leaning close to see the rise and fall of his chest. "No. C'mon, Weird."

Nothing. Asia shakes his shoulder. "You can't do this," he protests. "Not now."

His voice is loud in the tiny room. Asia sucks in a sharp breath. He can't panic. He has to figure this out on his own. He shakes

Weird harder this time. "Wake up."

He sees a flutter of eyelids and Weird groans faintly.

"Wake up," he says, louder, and slaps Weird across the face.

A louder groan answers him and Asia tries again, with a little more force.

The third time, Weird's hand snaps out to catch his wrist. "If you hit me again, I swear to God I'll beat the shit outta you."

Asia sits back on his heels and wrenches free of Weird's grip. "What the hell are you doing?" He gets back to his feet. "D'ya think I need to go back to the emergency room today? D'ya think you wanna be ODin' now, when we're makin' a damn record?"

"Thanks for the concern," Weird grumbles, struggling to sit upright.

Asia sighs and stoops down to help him. "Well, Christ. You scared me. I just don't get why you do shit that's so bad for you."

Weird's laugh is gravelly, broken. "Told you before, you got it backward."

"Bullshit," Asia protests. He doesn't have time to argue. "Get up and get a shower. We're movin' out today."

"What are you talkin' about?" Weird scowls at him, groaning as he climbs to his feet.

Asia explains it all to him, including the need to get all their stuff out in one trip since they're skipping out on the rent agreement.

Weird just smiles. "Don't sweat it, man. Para Bellum will settle up."

He gives Asia the van keys and disappears into the bathroom. Asia listens for the sound of running water, or the smack of Weird's body hitting the tile. When the shower starts, he is relieved. He really doesn't want to go back to the emergency room today. As the water runs, he jams the stuff in the bedroom into a fresh garbage bag, then a second. He scoops the pile of Tommi's clothes that he also uses as a pillow from the corner, then all his Happy Meal toys scattered around the carpet. Finally, Asia spots the black leather pouch that holds Weird's needles and works. Asia's hand closes on it and hesitates. He unzips it and discovers a baggie of brownish power carefully folded within.

"Better let me carry that." Weird's voice startles him from the doorway. He doesn't exactly snatch it away, but tucks it into his jacket pocket. He takes the garbage bag from Asia. "In fact, I'll finish up in here."

Asia backs down. He doesn't want to surrender—it feels exactly the same as Trace handing over the drugs—but he turns away anyway.

In the end, they leave most everything but their clothes and Weird's drugs. The house Trace sends them to is way up in the hills over Encino. It's on the dead-end top of the street, surrounded by tall stone walls. When they pull in, there's already a dark sedan, the contract guy from Para Bellum waiting for them, in an equally dark suit. He takes off his sunglasses as they get out of the van.

"William, right?" Weird begins, hand extended as they approach.

He nods, accepting the shake. "I've brought the keys for you. It's furnished, of course, but I've not had time to stock the kitchen."

Weird gives him a big grin as he takes the key ring. "That's cool. Our last place wasn't exactly stocked either. We can get food at the Ralph down the hill." He switches his grin to Asia. "We get to call the best bedrooms, since we're here first."

"I shall leave you to explore, then," William tells them.

He and Weird re-arrange the vehicles as Asia unlocks the front door. "Jesus."

The floor in the entranceway is black tile and leads through to the back of the house, which is entirely made of enormous windows. Asia walks softly, as though he could scuff the tile with his sneakers, to stand in front of the panoramic view. He puts his palm against the glass.

"I call the one in the corner," Weird announces, coming up behind him. "It's got a cool bathroom."

"Okay," Asia says absently. "Whatever."

"Shit, look at the smog," Weird comments, nodding at the view.

Asia shrugs. "Let's get the stuff in."

Later, Asia sits in the mixing booth, listening to Trace. He's doing the vocal track for "No Outlet" today, the song about a boy with the voice of a god.

Asia wonders what it means. The words to most of Trace's songs are like a code for which Asia has no key. He thinks about how little he knows about Trace's life before they met. Trace's told so many different stories, Asia can't guess at the truth anymore.

Lionel flops into the seat next to Asia and grins. "You sound great on this one. You really get his stuff."

It's been hard for him to work with Lionel. No matter how nice or helpful he is, Asia keeps expecting him to be the one who says, "You don't belong here. You're not good enough." Asia sighs. "Don't get me wrong, but I want Tommi back playing."

"Tomorrow, right? Nobody here doesn't," Lionel says evenly. "I'm sayin' I'm just glad we didn't have to hold things up."

Asia turns back to Trace in the booth. He stands at the mic, eyes closed, face tilted up, living whatever the words really mean as he sings them. Asia stands to get closer.

Weird and Asia go to pick Tommi up the next day. The bruising has faded to shadows on Tommi's face and even the stitches look less angry now. Asia gives up shotgun and lets Tommi sit in front.

Weird heads to the Encino hills without any explanation.

"Where're we goin?" Tommi sits up a little to look out the window.

Nobody's told him about the move because none of them want John to find out. Now Weird smiles. "Wait and see."

"I don't…" Tommi lets out his breath. "I just wanna go home, Weird."

Asia leans over the seat. "That's where we are goin'. The recording company is lettin' us stay in this house they have. It's huge and there's rooms for everybody."

"Yeah. Everybody but that muthafuckin' John, okay?" Weird cuts in, sparing a stern glance in Tommi's direction.

Tommi shifts slightly to look at the traffic. "There's an accident or something up there." He nods ahead to the next exit ramp. "Everybody's stopping."

Weird brakes as everything around them slows. "I'm serious, Tommi. If the bastard doesn't know where you—"

Asia sees Tommi's shoulders slump.

"Weird." Asia stops the coming tirade. "It's gonna be fine. It's a new start for all of us."

Traffic halts and everyone in the van falls silent. Asia thinks about moving Tommi's stuff into his waiting bedroom. And of this morning. The last thing Weird did before they left was to gather the phone off the bedside and yank its cord from the wall. Before Asia could protest, Weird said, "I'm not makin' it easy for him."

When they finally get there, Tommi perks up a little. He is as impressed as Asia had been.

"This bedroom is the size of our whole other apartment," Tommi says, sinking to the edge of the bed.

"Yeah," Asia agrees. "When do you need another pain pill?"

"They make me puke." Tommi's smile is sharp. "I'll be okay."

Asia nods, wishing he could do more. "I guess you're pretty tired. Maybe you should lay down."

"John's not like Weird thinks," Tommi says.

Asia has his back to the boy, focusing on the view of the valley below. "Yeah, he is. Tommi, he put you in the hospital. He cracked your skull."

"I know, but you don't understand."

Asia just shakes his head. He's pretty sure he does, but he doesn't want to make Tommi feel worse, so he changes the subject. "When did the doctor say you could play again?"

"I just have to tape up my ribs so I don't strain anything before it all heals." Tommi shrugs. "So, like, tomorrow, if we're scheduled for tomorrow. Hasn't Lionel been doing some of the rhythm tracks?"

"Yeah, but I like the way you play better," Asia says, turning. "I'm really glad you're okay—we all are."

"I know, Asia." Tommi's tone is layered with exhaustion.

Asia doesn't say anything else. What really is there to say?

Tommi stretches out carefully and Asia slips from the room. He grabs the cordless from the cradle in the kitchen and goes out to the terrace. He sits on the edge of the wall, back to the view, and punches in the number for Herr Christian's penthouse.

Christian's voice greets him and Asia swallows. "Um, it..."

"Hello, Asia," Christian prompts. "Trace is right here. Do you wish to speak with him?"

"Yes, please."

Without preamble, Trace asks, "Is he home? Everything's okay?"

"Yeah," Asia hedges. "I mean, he's…"

"What?"

"Y'know. He still looks like hell. He can't take the painkillers 'cause they make him sick." Asia lets out a sigh. "It just sucks."

"You're right about that," Trace agrees. "Keep an eye on him. I'll see you tomorrow."

You're a big help, Asia thinks, hanging up. The whole situation makes him feel sad and out of control of things.

Weird steps through the sliding door, cigarette hanging in his mouth, beer in his fist. "Don't worry so much, Asia. It doesn't do a damn bit of good."

"Nothing does," Asia agrees, handing over the phone. "You wanna order some dinner?"

Weird decides on Chinese. When it comes, he spreads it out on the low table in the living room. Then he goes to knock on Tommi's door softly. "You ready for some food? I got Almond Chicken for you."

Tommi is moving slower than he was before, as though the weight of being out of the hospital is too much for him. He makes the effort to eat, but barely dents his goldfish box.

Asia pokes at the noodles in his box. If Tommi can barely hold the chopsticks tonight, how can he ever play tomorrow?

The next morning Asia wakes to the shrill chorus of a Thompson Twins song:

I've got a picture
Pinned to my wall

Something is burning, he realizes, rolling over to stumble out of bed. The sticky sweet smell of incinerated Pop-Tart stings his nose. Asia smiles. Both things are proof that Tommi really is home, he's up.

Asia exits his bedroom to find Weird and Tommi standing in front of the mirror in the bathroom. Weird is winding a wide band of gauze over Tommi's bruised torso. He hisses a breath in and Weird murmurs, "Sorry."

"It's okay. It's gotta be tight," Tommi answers.

"If you need more rest," Asia starts, "you can just come tomorrow."

"I need to be there, Asia," Tommi says. "I've missed enough."

At the studio, Lionel goes out of his way to catch Tommi up. He plays what they've put down on tape so far and Tommi grins.

"You guys sound amazing," he says. "Really great."

Trace is standing to the side of the drum kit. "Now it's all perfect."

Asia is watching him for signs of pain, but when Tommi plays it's like nothing happened.

5

Three weeks pass, and the album progresses. Tommi's stitches come out and he doesn't have to wrap himself or dose up with aspirins anymore. Asia is relieved that he is beginning to look normal.

As Asia pulls the van into the driveway, he tries to remember how many songs they have in the can, how many to go yet. He grabs the bag of fish sticks and beer from the passenger's seat and hauls it into the house. The kitchen is empty. He stows the beer in the fridge and the fish in the freezer. The display of afternoon smog that hangs over the valley is fluffy, like amber rain clouds. Like living on another planet, he thinks.

From the living room Asia hears Weird's guitar, muted, just under the TV noise. Asia follows the sound. Tommi is sitting cross-legged on the floor, cereal bowl propped on a throw pillow across his lap.

"No." Weird, sitting behind him on the couch, puts his acoustic aside and pushes to his feet. "I'm not listenin' to this again."

Tommi protests, "Weird, it's not like you think."

"I told you before, if you're gonna be this fuckin' stupid, I can't...." Weird's hands clench into fists. "Just remember, last time you were lucky." He stalks past Asia, radiating anger like heat. He slams out the front door.

Tommi takes a long breath and points a remote at the TV to turn it off. He looks up at Asia, rueful smile on his face. "John wants me to meet him for—"

"Oh, Tommi."

"Just to talk." Tommi holds up a hand to fend off more protests. "He loves me, Asia. And he's stopped drinkin'. I have to give him another chance."

To do what? Asia wonders.

"I know you guys don't want him here, so we're meeting down the hill at the Galleria. It's public and everything, so don't worry."

His smile changes. Now it's so open and hopeful it cuts right through Asia. He wishes that Weird had beaten John to death. He hears the van start up and take off and knows that Weird is wishing the same thing. "Tommi, do you love John back?"

The boy's expression falters a second, like he's caught by surprise. "Of course I do."

It's the first time Asia's heard him say it. "How're you getin' to the mall, then?"

"Taxi." Tommi looks away. "I wouldn't ask Weird to drive me."

Asia sighs again. He remembers how fast Weird had scooped Tommi off the floor at John's. How gentle he'd been. "Tommi, I..."

"You don't have to say anything." Tommi gets up. "I don't expect you guys to understand."

"I wish you wouldn't go," Asia says it in a rush.

"I won't go anywhere else with him, unless I'm sure," Tommi tells him. "Believe me, I don't wanna get hurt."

Asia feels the space between his shoulder blades itch. It's only a matter of time.

Guy Olivier has made Albrecht's suits for twenty years. Like William, he does his job admirably well and asks no questions. Guy still keeps a small space on Rodeo Drive but, being semi-retired, spends most of his time in his native Paris.

It takes more than a little convincing to get Guy on a plane, but now Albrecht sits in a leather chair in Guy's fitting room, sipping a glass of wine, enjoying the unfolding view.

"Please, Mr. Dellon, hold still. Arms at your sides. Shoulders relaxed." Guy prods Trace into the stance he needs and sets upon him with his tape measure like some stooped and ancient creature from a dark fairy tale. Trace catches Albrecht's eyes on him in the mirror and gives him a slow smile. Albrecht smiles back, but sees the boredom on Trace's face as well.

Guy, heedless of the exchange, is making notes, clucking to himself.

"You understand that what I want isn't meant to be worn on the street," Albrecht confirms. "It isn't meant as understatement."

Guy chews the end of his pencil and transfers his attention from

Trace to Albrecht. He answers him in French that is stinging. Of course he understands. Albrecht laughs softly. He is surrounded by artists.

"Let William know when you're ready to have him back for the last fitting," he says as the little man huffs out of the room, leaving them alone.

"But I thought that's what we were doing right now," Trace protests.

"It takes more than choosing a size from a rack to get a good suit, Trace," Albrecht says, rising.

Trace shakes his head, clearly trying to hide his irritation.

"If you don't like it, I shan't force you to wear it," Albrecht promises. He has already given Guy some special instructions. He knows Trace will warm up to the idea when he sees the end result. "Where shall we go to lunch?"

"Weird and Lionel have been working all morning. I told them I'd bring pizza." Trace crosses the room holding his hand out for the earrings Guy had demanded he take off.

Albrecht produces them from his pocket and smiles again as Trace loops them into his ears.

"So," Trace continues, "we can just pick one up on the way there."

Albrecht surrenders the keys to the Jaguar, but draws the line at transporting pizza. Trace has brought him a world of firsts, but he has no wish to discover how long the stench of grease could cling to leather upholstery.

"You can have it delivered."

Trace laughs at his squeamishness.

Trace speeds up as he darts into midday traffic on the 405. Albrecht forces himself to study the other man's profile, not the certain death through the windshield.

"I've been thinking that you need someone to manage the band, day-to-day, arrange a tour to support the album," Albrecht says.

Trace frowns slightly. "I thought Para Bellum was handling that."

"Obviously, yes, but I was thinking of someone with only your interests in mind. I don't think he works for us currently, but that can be remedied." Albrecht smiles at the surprise on Trace's face.

"You know somebody who you think would be good?"

"I shall have William arrange for a meeting, if you would like."

Trace changes lanes around an ancient truck and Albrecht closes his eyes.

When they get to Para Bellum, Albrecht uses Lionel's office. He leans forward to pick up the phone and dial. "William? I need you to set up a meeting for Black Light with Marcus Anthony. Let him know what they need and give him any information he asks for."

William agrees and Albrecht rings off.

Marcus Anthony started his career at Para Bellum, but didn't spend much time there before striking out on his own. His brand of management has proven to be wildly successful in the rock and roll world. Marcus acts as mother, accountant, babysitter, and parole officer in equal parts. He can be anything Black Light needs, Albrecht is sure.

Albrecht checks his watch, wondering how long Trace will be working today. He knows they're getting to the end of the recording process. He also knows that means Trace is closer to leaving him, at least for the tour. Albrecht wonders if he shall be able to cope with the loss.

He pours himself whiskey from Lionel's bar before rejoining Trace in the studio.

Today it's a song from their old set that Albrecht recognizes. Trace is in the booth doing the vocals. Albrecht sits down, closing his eyes.

Trace's voice, raw and demanding, fills the room. "Tell me you want me. Tell me how you want me."

Albrecht doesn't realize he's been holding his breath until he lets it out in time to Trace's last note.

The meeting with Marcus Anthony comes up quick for Trace. By the end of the week, he is driving Christian's Jag to the Denny's down the hill from where the guys are living. Before Trace left, he could tell Christian wanted to come, but knew that it had to be private between Marcus Anthony and the band.

When Trace walks in, the band is in a booth at the very back of the place. Weird, against the wall, catches Trace's eye with a sour look and waves him over. Trace sits down next to Asia, who moves a few inches closer to the middle to escape. Trace peels off his sunglasses and pretends not to notice. "So the guy's late, huh?"

"Not that late," a voice behind him says. "Just a little traffic issue is all."

Trace turns. Sliding in next to him is a dark-skinned man with black curly hair that brushes the collar of his bright blue suit. He flashes a lightning grin and sticks out his hand. "I'm Marcus Anthony and you're Trace Dellon."

Trace grins back, taking the hand. "And this is Black Light."

"Asia,"—Marcus nods— "Tommi, and Weird." He reaches across glasses and salt and pepper to shake each of their hands, too. "Nice to meet you."

"Uh, right," Weird says, smiling wryly. "You, too. You, uh, gonna buy us lunch?"

Marcus laughs. "Good question. Is that the only thing you want me to do for you?"

"Nope. Just the first thing."

"I've talked to Lionel at Para Bellum since Herr Christian contacted me. He's got good instincts. He thinks this album you're workin' on is goin' gold easy and I agree, from what he's let me hear. But you need to get out and sell it, 'cause nobody outside LA knows who you are, am I right?"

Trace nods. "We're gonna do a video."

"Yes. Excellent. And of course, we'll start a tour as soon as it hits, too."

He pulls leather-bound planner out of his briefcase and starts to read dates he's already set up and Trace is amazed. Trace casts a glance in Asia's direction, seeing the color drain from his face, willing him to stay quiet.

Marcus grins again and starts to lay out his plan. "Now, the first part: I've got you opening for another band that I also manage. Live Wire."

Trace nods, waiting.

"You'll meet up with Live Wire for the end of their tour and then I expect to add on dates as we go." Marcus gives them his grin again. "That is, if I'm working for you."

Trace doesn't even look at the others for confirmation. "Yeah, I think you are."

Weird narrows his eyes. "Okay, yeah, but who're you really workin' for?"

"I'm gonna be working for you," Marcus says evenly, before Trace can cut in. "Initially, my expenses will be covered by Para Bellum, but then I'll get a cut of the take from the tour and sales. It's all standard."

Weird shrugs, exchanges a look with Trace. "But your boyfriend—"

"Is still your boss," Trace says, glaring. "What the fuck does it matter if Christian set this up? You think he doesn't wanna make money off us? And for that, we need to be a success. What's so hard for you to figure out about this?"

"Weird," Tommi says.

"I'm just asking," Weird mutters.

Marcus nods. "So you've got an album full of songs to take on tour. That's about a third of what you need."

"It's not a problem." Weird shakes his head. "We've got ninety minutes of stuff already rehearsed and Dellon writes shit so fast that it never goes stale."

"Yeah, but there's keyboards on the album, right? And backing vocals," Marcus points out.

"All we need is the four of us," Trace says. "We can do this striped down. Tommi and Asia can handle the backup. It's always worked before."

"This is bigger than just the inside of a bar, baby," Marcus points out. "It's a whole new deal."

"Yeah, we're ready for it," Trace tells him.

Marcus raises an eyebrow. "Then I'm ready to sign contracts."

They make more plans to meet at Para Bellum before Marcus pays the bill and takes off.

Afterward, Trace catches Asia before he piles into the van with the rest of them. "Hey, let's go hang out for a while."

Asia looks confused, but agrees, climbing into the passenger side of the Jag silently. After they pull out of the parking lot, he says, "You were right."

"What?" Trace glances at him.

"You were right when you said it was gonna happen. It's

happening now."

Though Asia's tone is mournful, Trace can't help his grin. Yes. He was right. But he knows how scared this makes Asia. "It'll be okay, though, you know. You can enjoy it a little. Look at the cool place you're living and stuff."

Asia looks out the window instead of answering. Trace knows he recognizes the route they're taking. He wishes Asia would lose the suspicion and let it be like the old days for just a second or two.

Queen of Angels Cemetery is almost a hundred years old. It was around when Hollywood Boulevard was still lined with orange trees. Trace parks the Jag inside its sagging gates and they walk up the winding road to the top of the hill. They pass crumbling monuments and overgrown graves and Trace thinks about something Christian said the first night they were together. He'd made LA sound like a place that had escaped its past. Maybe not, Trace thinks, looking around at the unruly rows of graves. Maybe we just dump dirt over it.

Back in Ann Arbor, in the summer, Trace and Asia used to go down to the riverbank and talk for hours, but when they moved here, it was this place. Trace knows Asia loves it because so many horror movies had been shot around there. It was the only place Asia had been able to feel at home at first.

Right now, Trace wants all that back, but he knows they can only pretend. Beside him, Asia is different. Trace can see the signs of the record company money, more subtle than his own, but there. Asia's traded his ancient, fraying backpack from his last year in high school for a brand new black one. His jeans are so new they're a uniform dark blue, even in the knees and ass, and he's wearing brand new, bright red high-tops.

Asia stops at the grave at the top of the hill. It's an elaborate tomb in the shape of a sphinx, with a heavy Victorian glass and wrought iron door sealing it. He shoves some dead leaves off the top step with his toe and sits down.

Trace sits next to him and nudges at his backpack. "You got some Diet Coke in there?"

Asia nods and rummages around for a second before he comes up with a can. "It's warm."

Trace smiles. "Yeah."

"Tommi's seeing John again."

"Oh. Shit," Trace groans.

"Yeah," Asia agrees. "It's been like a week. At first it was just to talk, but now he's back over there spending the night. I don't... I just let him go. You shoulda seen his face. He was so happy. I couldn't think of a way out of it."

"Like there's any way to stop him," Trace points out. "Y'know, going on tour might be the best thing for him. John won't be able to fuck with him and maybe he'll be so busy being a rock star, he'll forget about the asshole."

"I guess."

Trace lets the silence stretch between them again. He takes the can from Asia and pulls the tab. He slams a mouthful of the sharp, warm liquid. He smiles faintly, remembering that it tastes better than that Tab shit Asia used to drink.

"I know I'm not doing this right," Asia says. "I feel like I'm way outta my league in the studio and the thought of playin' in front of thousands of people makes me wanna throw up. And now Tommi's bein' stupid.... Shit's just happening all too fast."

Trace leans into Asia slightly, brushing his arm as he hands back the pop. "I keep tellin' you this: it's not Black Light without you. Tommi and Weird, yeah, they're a part of this band, but you and me *are* the band."

Asia draws back from the contact. Asia has rejected him so many times over the years, it barely stings anymore.

Asia says, "I'm not going anywhere."

Trace pulls the chrome case he cadged from Christian out of his back pocket and lights one of the black cigarettes it contains. Asia turns his face away from the smoke and Trace smiles. "Look, I know it seems like we never see each other anymore. Christian just... He's gonna miss me when we're on tour and he just wants to spend time now, while we have it."

Asia shrugs. "I understand."

Trace finally takes Asia back to the house. He heads toward the Algonquin, knowing that Christian is waiting for him, as always. It's as though the other man has tailored his life around Trace's, and Trace has no idea what Christian does when he's not present. It's a little disconcerting, having someone else so dependent on him. Like an audience that never goes away.

6

Trace lies awake, calculating how many miles he's managed to put between himself and the past, wondering if it's enough. Nobody knows where he grew up, not even Asia. Trace smiles, glad that he has this one small square of truth to himself still.

Trace grew up in a trailer park outside of Ypsilanti with his mom. He guesses she might even still live there, not that it matters much to him. Really, he thinks more about Ray than her anyway. Back then, Trace's name was still Mike and by the time Ray had introduced himself, Trace was already looking for a way out.

Ray was that guy that lived at the end of the cul-de-sac like a cliché from an after-school special. Trace was eleven when he caught Ray's eye. It was before Trace's growth spurt and he could have passed for about nine. Ray had been off on disability from the shop for as long as Trace could remember.

"Hey, Mike." He stood on his rickety porch as Trace wheeled his bike past after school one fall day. "Hey, c'mon over here."

Trace stopped and looked up at him. Ray looked just like he always had—old faded jeans and a Led Zeppelin tee shirt. He had about two days' stubble on his chin and a hollow look in his dark eyes. Trace took a step towards him, then frowned. "What do you want?"

Ray's tight face twisted into a smile. "C'mon on up and find out."

Trace stashed his bike behind the trailer and climbed the steps to go in.

"I'll give you ten dollars if you let me see it," Ray said as soon as the door was closed behind Trace. That was how it began.

It was easy and Trace had the money in his pocket when he left. He stopped by Ray's trailer at least a couple of times a week for the rest of the school year. Ray started to offer more money to do more things. "Let me touch it." "I wanna put it in my mouth."

Soon, Trace had enough cash for a new bike, clothes. He bought a guitar. And Ray showed more interest in Trace's life than his mom ever had.

"How was school?" he'd ask, closing the door behind Trace.

"Just like school." Trace would shrug. "Who cares?"

"You should." Ray always frowned. "You wanna end up like me, laid off from the shop? You're too smart for that."

"You sound like my dad," Trace teased.

"Don't say shit like that. You don't even have a dad."

Trace has never been able to lie to himself and pretend he didn't know what would happen. He looks down at Albrecht's sleeping form, wondering if Ray had another boy now. Really, Trace doesn't feel the outrage he knows he should. He had been eager to learn.

Anyway, Ray hadn't been much older than Christian when it came right down to it.

Christian stirs awake and turns toward him. "Do you ever sleep?"

Trace shrugs a thin shoulder, sitting up to reach for the cigarettes. "I don't need that much." He pauses to light one for himself, then another for Christian. "Can we go shopping today?"

Christian arches an eyebrow as he takes his first drag. "I suppose. What do you have in mind?"

Trace grins, sliding out of bed. "I wanna go down to Melrose. I'm a rock star now. I wanna look like a rock star. And I want my rich boyfriend to buy me some shit."

Christian laughs. "More shit?"

There's no sarcasm in his tone. Trace nods. "Please?"

"We can't have you dressing as though you shop at Sears and Roebuck, I suppose." Christian pulls the covers back and rises also. He balances his cigarette in the crystal ashtray on the bedside table. "I'll call for the car. In an hour?"

On the trip across town, Trace loves how ordinary riding in the back of a car driven by a stranger has become for him. He leans forward to tell the driver where he wants to go.

"You know Aardvarks, over on Melrose?"

"Yes, sir."

"Cool."

When they get there, Trace asks to be let off a few blocks away so he can window-shop. Christian gets out with him and Trace smiles. Christian is pale in the afternoon sun, his silk suit the color of the smog in the sky. With his tiny black sunglasses, he looks just like a day-walking vampire.

"You wanna get some coffee, or something?" Trace asks as they pass a small, dark Indian restaurant. "We skipped breakfast."

Christian shakes his head. "I'm fine."

Aardvark's is part overpriced boutique, part Goodwill. When they get inside, the scent of old leather and Armani cologne comes to Trace. A lone boy at the counter looks up from a *Rolling Stone* magazine and nods in their direction. Trace nods back.

He leads Christian on a prowl through the racks that are packed so close that clothing brushes against them as they pass. "There are so many designers that would love to dress you, Trace," Christian says. "This really isn't necessary."

"Oh, come on. This is more fun."

"Indeed." But Christian's expression is one of indulgence and that makes Trace happy. He sifts through the hangers, finding a woman's midnight blue leather motorcycle jacket, a matching pair of pants. Then he heads to the back wall to look at shoes. The boy behind the counter meets him there. "I recognize you. You're Trace Dellon, right?"

Trace looked at him from the corner of his eye. "Maybe."

"I saw you like, five times, at the Refugee Club. I love you."

He looks young, maybe eighteen. His fingernails are painted silver and there are traces of last night's eyeliner under his eyes. When Trace looks him full in the face, the boy takes in a long breath. Trace softens his smile, steps just a fraction closer. "Thanks. We're working on an album right now, y'know."

"Oh my God. That's great." The boy grins. "That's so great."

"Can you take these back to your counter, please." Christian steps in, handing the leathers over sternly. "What else do you need?" He addresses Trace this time.

Christian has effectively frightened the boy away and Trace is amused. "I want new boots, 'cause girl pants are always too short for me."

"Then perhaps…" Christian smiles faintly. "Never mind."

He ends up with four pair: Red Doc Martens, vintage silver platforms, and the others shiny black. He trades his ragged sneakers for the Doc Martens before they leave. Christian tells the boy their driver will be in to pick up the rest as he hands over his credit card.

Back out on the street, Trace catches Christian's hand and squeezes it. "Thank you."

The other man doesn't exactly move away from Trace, but he slips his hand free. "You're right, you know. You are a rock star. You do need to look like one."

Trace wants to point out that the clerk knew who he was, but he doesn't. He lets Christian finish.

"All of you should. And act like it, also."

"Lionel says he has a friend at the *LA Weekly* he can get to talk to us," Trace says. "They're doing a piece on bands in LA, or something."

Christian nods. "It's a start."

"How come you never ask me anything about where I grew up or what my name really is?"

Christian waits until they settle in the car. "I don't know. I suppose I think if you wanted to tell me, you would. Besides, your given name is on your contract, Michael. I just assumed you preferred not to use it."

He has a point, but Trace can't let it go. "You never tell me anything about you."

"I told you about Sean, about the club. What more do you want to know?"

Trace is stumped by that. "I don't know. Like, did you ever like girls? Where are you actually from? When did you know you were gay?" He shrugs. "Stuff that everybody wonders."

"Ah." Christian smiles out the window. "I'm from Austria. I've never felt the need to put a label to who I fall in love with, or why. It has always been that way for me."

Trace shakes his head. He looks out the opposite window, as they get on the freeway, watching the traffic speed by.

"Was that not what you wanted?"

"I don't know. I was just thinking about when I was a kid, this morning," Trace starts. "The first guy I ever... I was like 13 or something." He lies to make it sound less dirty. "He was a lot older. Lived in my neighborhood. Anyway, he showed me stuff that I didn't really understand at the time. I guess he was probably a child molester, but I didn't think about it."

"Because you were a child," Christian says.

It didn't feel like it, Trace thinks. He says, "Honestly, he didn't do anything I didn't want. He always gave me money."

He lets that hang between them for a few seconds. He doesn't look in Christian's direction.

"I do love you, Trace," Christian says. "It's only that I'm not used to giving so much of myself. Sometimes it quite tires me out."

Trace says nothing.

When they return home, Trace models his new outfits for Albrecht, with each pair of the new boots. The silver platforms make him too tall to see the top of his head in the full-length mirror in the bedroom. Albrecht tries to catch his enthusiasm, but feels worn thin. He smiles and rubs at his temples. "You do look beautiful."

Trace tilts his head and looks at Albrecht through narrowed eyes. "Are you all right? You look really tired."

Albrecht laughs softly. "Tired, or old?"

"Oh, come on," Trace says. "You're not old. I just thought you…"

"A little tired," Albrecht concedes. "Yes. I was thinking of a nap."

Trace nods. "That's cool. I told Asia I'd stop over to the house and see how things were going. Do you mind?"

"Not at all. Shall I call for the car again?"

"Well." Trace grins. "I was kinda thinkin' you'd lend me the Jag."

"Of course. You know where the keys are, yes?" To Albrecht's amusement, Trace nods.

Trace leaves and Albrecht pours himself a gin and tonic out of habit. He is not shocked at Trace's childhood story. He has always known that predators seek each other out, as well as prey. He supposes that is what pulled him toward Trace in the first place. Now he is too in love to escape.

At the shop today Albrecht had tried to tap some of the youthful energy that filled the place, but Trace was too all-encompassing. There was nothing left for Albrecht.

He stares at the silkscreens on the wall across the room. They show him hard and sleek and cruel, someone he isn't any longer.

"I love them." Sean's voice pulls him away, into a memory. "Wow. Andy Warhol, right?"

Albrecht raised an eyebrow. "He is the most interesting thing on the East Coast."

"I'd love to meet him," Sean said, brushing his fingers over the lips of the

middle portrait. "If you're friends."

Albrecht laughed. "I don't think Andy has friends. He doesn't seem to need them."

Albrecht had stumbled across the artist early. Warhol existed in his studio like an albino spider, sucking any brilliance that came within reach and regurgitating it out as Soup Cans. What Albrecht found most chilling was the lack of effort to conceal what he was. When Albrecht left, it felt like a narrow escape.

The portraits caught up with him months later, arriving with no explanation. There are nine in all. The first three primaries for LA, the middle three hang in Albrecht's Paris apartment: grays, blacks, and white. The remaining trio is in storage. Albrecht has never displayed them anywhere. They bear Andy's message plainly. Three colorless portraits of Albrecht, featuring a ragged bullet hole in the canvas, in the forehead.

He has stayed out of New York since then. He remembers the bullet holes and thinks he should have learned his lesson about like attracting like.

Trace rolls the window down and hits the 405 like a bat out of hell. He loves the power of the Jaguar's engine and pushes it as fast as he can. He weaves in and out of traffic like he is soaring above it. He ranges his speed from near 100 in the clear stretches to dead stops when he hits the gridlock. He wonders what Christian would do if he got pulled over by the CHP or pasted himself against the back of a semi.

Trace looks forward to hanging out with the rest of the band, almost like old times, except now they never run out of beer.

When he gets there, the front door is unlocked, which makes Trace hesitate. He twists the knob and calls out a greeting. "Asia?" he prompts when he gets no answer. "Weird?"

"They're gone someplace." Tommi's small voice comes from the direction of the kitchen. "They were gone when John dropped me off."

"Tommi?" Trace finds him standing at the sink, holding a bag of frozen vegetables on his eye. "Tommi, Christ. Are you okay?"

The boy's shoulders shake with silent laughter. "I don't know. I guess so. It coulda been worse, huh? I'm not in the hospital."

"Shit." Trace turns him gently to see the damage. Not just a black eye, he realizes as Tommi lowers the pack. The whole side of his face. "That looks like it hurts."

"I told you." Tommi moves away from him and tosses the peas into the sink. "Not as bad as last time. Just don't say anything."

Trace follows him through an archway to a room with a wall of windows that overlooks the valley. Tommi leans his cheek against the glass. He looks so small in contrast to the panoramic view that spins out beyond. "I'm such a fuck-up."

Trace bites back the sharp words that come to mind. "Tommi. Don't."

"He just gets so pissed off." Tommi shakes his head and laughs again. "He loves me, but I make him so mad."

It is a familiar story to Trace. He puts a hand on Tommi's shoulder. "I know he does. But I'm afraid he's gonna kill you."

"It doesn't matter. It's better than being alone."

Trace takes a breath. He knows Tommi is on the edge of something bad. Trace lays a hand against his bruised cheek. "You're worth more than this."

"No," Tommi whispers. "I'm not. Without John, I'm not worth anything."

Trace understands that nobody can talk Tommi down. That he needs more than words now. Trace pulls him away from the window and kisses him slow and gentle until he feels something break down in the boy.

"Stop," Tommi gasps. "Please. John, he…"

"He doesn't deserve you," Trace says, looking into Tommi's eyes. "He doesn't."

When they kiss again, Tommi clings to him. Trace can feel how much he needs, but he stops. "Did he hurt you anywhere else? I don't wanna make it worse."

"You aren't gonna," Tommi breathes.

They go to Tommi's bedroom. Trace undresses him, fingers soft on the ghost of old bruises. While they make love, Trace puts Tommi at the center of the world. They lie next to each other after. Tommi's fingers brush the coin-sized patch of melted skin on the curve of Trace's left hip. He flinches. In the lowering sunlight through the window, he feels exposed. "It's a cigarette burn." His smile has a sharp edge to it.

Tommi frowns, looking up into his face. "How did it happen?"

"Eric."

Tommi shakes his head. "Who?"

"It was before Black Light. Asia's brother. He had a bad temper, but I loved him." Trace shrugs. "I still do, probably. I just couldn't be with him anymore." Trace lets out his breath and brushes Tommi's long white hair back from his face.

Tommi sighs. "Y'know, Weird's gonna so pissed when he sees my face. He told me this would happen if I went back."

"He's not pissed. He just doesn't know what to say. It's hard to watch somebody you care about get hurt," Trace says, circling his arms around Tommi. "I hope you don't walk into that shit again, too, but—"

He is interrupted by the slam of the front door. Tommi reflexively pushes back from him, as though they were about to be discovered by his dad. It's close to the truth. Trace sits up. "Relax, Tommi, I'm not gonna tell anybody anything."

"I just..." Tommi sits up too and looks over his shoulder at Trace. "I really... Thank you. It was..."

"It was nice." Trace softens his smile. The kid is naked and still he blushes. Trace grabs his clothes and dresses fast. He wants this to have been right for Tommi, what he needs. "I'll go out onto the terrace."

He leans across the bed to kiss Tommi one more time and then ducks through the sliding door.

When they get up the hill with the groceries, there's a Jaguar parked in the driveway. Asia sighs and Weird swears, pulling the van in behind it.

It takes them a few trips in to unload the van. Asia begins the task of finding places for all the food in the kitchen when Trace saunters in from the terrace.

"Hey," he greets, leaning against the counter. "Been waiting for you guys."

"We had to park you in," Asia says flatly. He misses Trace living in the same place as him and he doesn't mean to sound defensive right off, but something is wrong. Trace's body language hints at it. "Does that belong to Herr Christian?"

Trace rolls his eyes. "Who else would it belong to?"

Asia shrugs, putting a quart of milk on the bottom shelf of the refrigerator. Then he starts loading bottles of beer into the door.

"John fucked Tommi up again," Trace says.

"What?" Asia straightens. He feels a little sick. "Is he—"

Trace shakes his head. "There's no broken bones this time."

Weird enters from the front, frowning. "Tommi?"

Trace nods.

"Goddamn it," Weird puts his bags on the counter. "Where is he?"

"I don't know where John is, but Tommi's here." Trace glances down the hallway toward the bedrooms. "He pro'bly doesn't need a big lecture right now."

"Yeah, and you know what he does need, right, Dellon?" Weird growls.

Trace smiles faintly. "More than you."

Asia moves just slightly in case Weird takes offense. Then Tommi appears in the doorway and Asia feels sick again. "Oh, man, your face."

"It's not so bad." Tommi shrugs. He looks down at his bare feet. "It looks worse than it is."

Weird's eyes darken, but he only nods. "You were lucky this time too, then, huh?"

Tommi looks up at Trace and blushes. "Yeah, this time I was."

Asia catches what passes between them. Only a split second, but it's like a thunderclap that nobody else hears. Asia feels like he's been smacked hard across the face and blinks through that. He goes back to putting the groceries away as Weird questions Tommi about how bad John hit him and whether or not he'd accidentally gotten any sense beaten into him. Asia doesn't join in. Instead, he goes out back to escape.

Trace follows Asia to the edge of the pool. Asia ignores him, watching the sun set, turning the smog into something beautiful.

"I know what you're thinking," Trace starts.

"You don't."

"C'mon, Asia." Trace laughs at him. "I know you."

"Whatever. It's between you and Tommi," Asia says. He's not surprised that Trace doesn't try to deny it even. "But I'm confused. Are you gonna move out of Herr Christian's now? I thought you were in love with him and shit."

"He doesn't have anything to do with this."

"He doesn't have anything to do with you cheating on him to give Tommi a mercy fuck?" Asia turns, shaking his head. "Wonder if he would think that."

"It wasn't a—" Trace's voice goes cold. "Why? You gonna tell him? When you just got all moved in and comfortable here? What if he gets so pissed off, he fires us and tosses you all out?"

"Nice." Asia is repulsed by Trace's logic. "What about Tommi? Don't you think he's screwed up enough without you havin' to put your dick in there too?"

Trace takes a step back. "Jesus, Asia."

Asia laughs. "What? Tell me that isn't what happened."

Trace holds his hand up to stop Asia. "It's a hell of a lot better than you and Weird makin' him feel more worthless by bitchin' about it all the time."

Asia frowns. "We care about what happens to him, is all. You took advantage of the situation. Just like with Sammy. It doesn't mean anything to you."

"Fuck you, Asia. Tommi needed to be with somebody safe."

"And you think that's what you are?" Asia turns his back again.

"It was what he needed," Trace insists. "It's not his fault he loves the guy. You know you don't just turn shit like that off."

Asia's heart bangs against his chest hard. No kidding, he thinks, but refuses to agree out loud. He just stands there, staring out into the creeping night until Trace finally gives up and leaves. Asia stays frozen while he hears Weird move the van and Trace tear out of the driveway with Albrecht Christian's car. He squeezes his eyes shut and rubs hard at the grit in the corners.

"I'm sorry if I'm causing trouble between the two of you." Tommi's voice precedes him onto the terrace. "He really was just trying to help me."

"Trace is Trace. Don't worry about it." Asia turns and winces at the mass of bruises that cover the right side of Tommi's face. "Can you at least take some aspirin for that?"

"Yeah, it's okay." Tommi shrugs it off. "Please don't worry about me."

How can you let this happen over and over? Asia thinks. He dredges up a half smile. "I'm sorry, it's just my deal, okay? I gotta do the worrying. It's just how it is."

Trace returns to the penthouse to find Christian already in bed, asleep. Not even ten o'clock, he thinks, looking down at the other man's narrow form draped in the sheets. Trace thinks of the first night he spent in this bed. It seems like years, not months, have passed. That night, the sex and the money—and Albrecht Christian's sheer presence—completely knocked Trace off his feet. That night, he was in love. He tries to find some of it now and only comes up with the memory of Tommi. He slides into bed and kisses Christian on the back of the neck. "Hey, I'm home."

The other man stretches and lets out his breath. He turns over to touch Trace's face. "I missed you."

"Good thing I came back," Trace says, wishing he could feel more.

Christian's laugh is soft. "Very true," he agrees. "I am a lucky man."

Later, Christian's lips graze the same scar Tommi found, but don't linger. It's not the same now, doesn't mean anything in this context. Trace curls his fingers into Christian's fine hair to guide him where he wants him.

Wrapped in Christian's arms, the scar of the burn stings and Trace closes his eyes. The memory calls Eric's ghost to him in the dark.

Trace's second year of high school, they took him out of his mother's trailer. He wound up stuck in a foster home down the street from the Heyes family.

Trace had known exactly what Eric was from the beginning. Eric played football; he played guitar. Girls loved him. Trace saw through all that to something else. Eric had a violence that rode just below the skin. From the moment they met, Trace wanted it.

They started writing songs. Eric gave up football so they could put the first band together. That fall Trace practically moved into Eric's basement bedroom. It didn't take long to make the move from Asia's Scooby-Doo sleeping bag to Eric's bed. It was inevitable that Eric's dick end up in Trace's mouth sooner or later.

Trace knew Eric hated the power it gave Trace over him. Eric became like an addict and Trace was his drug. Nobody had ever loved Trace as much as that and he had the bruises to prove it.

Trace slides his hand down to his hip, rubs the scar, knowing it was the only piece of Eric he had left. Except Asia. He'll always have Asia.

7

The next day in the studio, Asia takes note of Herr Christian's absence. Did Trace arrange it? Did he think that Asia would really betray him?

Trace has to know him too well for that. Probably Christian is busy doing... Asia has no idea. Maybe Christian doesn't care who Trace sleeps with. If that's true, he's a fool, Asia thinks.

He watches Weird for some hint that something has changed, but there's nothing. Asia knows what happened shouldn't affect him either. That it shouldn't make him feel like he's dying, but it does. Every time Trace throws a smile in Tommi's direction, it feels just like a cut in Asia's skin. He can't push it down. Not yet.

He sits silently, waiting for his turn in the booth. Today its isolation is welcoming. He angles himself away from the rest of them, puts the headphones on, and plays. He concentrates on Trace's voice. When the track ends, Asia looks up from his strings through the glass to see Weird standing over Lionel. The other man is laughing, Weird nodding. Lionel shifts in his seat to pull a business card out. He offers it to Weird between two fingers. Weird tucks it away and nods again. Then he looks up at Asia and waves him over.

That night Weird drags Asia along to a bar in Century City called Corman's. It's dark and smoky and Asia can tell from the décor that it's named for B-movie director Roger Corman. Shrunken heads dangle over the bar and a fake mummy sits crumbling in one corner booth. Asia relaxes immediately. They sit at the back of the place, Weird drinking beer as Asia nurses a Diet Coke. Asia finally says something. "You know what happened yesterday, right?"

Weird watches the skinny punk kids that tramp up onto the tiny stage at the front. "Tommi told me."

"And?"

"And nothin'." Weird takes a drink of beer and tips his chair up onto the back legs to lean against the wall. "I'm not gonna break Trace's knees, Asia. Don't worry. He's not the one that fucked up Tommi's face."

Asia knows he needs to let go of this, but he can't. "I guess."

He watches the band start their set. The lead singer is a lithe, ageless boy in black vinyl. His ragged hair stands up in choppy spikes. His skin is a stark white against the dark of the bar. He wraps a hand around the mic and leans into it to sing. Asia smiles because he can't help it. It's like he can't get away from Trace anywhere. Without breaking the lyric, the boy locks eyes with Asia and doesn't look away. Asia feels heat on his face.

"I know it has to suck for you," Weird says, setting his beer back within the ring on the table.

That interrupts Asia's concentration and he turns. "What does?"

"Watching Trace do this shit. I know it sucks."

Asia frowns. "No, it doesn't—I don't care about…"

"Forget it. You don't gotta explain it to me." Weird holds up a hand. "Point is, whatever it was between them yesterday, it's over, okay? And Tommi seems fine with that, so what the hell?"

Asia drinks his Diet Coke. "I'm just a little surprised you're takin' it so well."

Weird chuckles. "I'm thirty-seven years old, Asia. Thirty-seven. I've been playin' shitholes like this one for about twenty-five years of that. Y'think I wanna go back to it now? I know damn well without Trace, this is where I end up."

"I thought he was the only one that wanted the whole MTV deal." Asia shakes his head.

Weird shrugs. "Yeah no, actually, I think you're the only one that doesn't."

Asia doesn't answer. He switches his attention back to the band. Their sound is loud and jangly. The singer's vocals are thin and high, like his voice is still changing. It makes Asia smile again. And again, the singer smiles back.

At the end of the set, he comes over and slouches in the chair across from Asia. Up close, Asia realizes that he's made a mistake. It's not a boy.

Weird smiles and offers a hand across the table. "Enjoyed your show," he says. "A friend of mine at Para Bellum Records asked me to give you his card."

He slides it across the table at the girl. She raises an eyebrow as she picks it up. "Lionel Child, the producer. Lionel Child is your friend?"

Weird nods. "Give him a call."

The girl still looks like Trace, wiry and angular, pale eyes, but her grin doesn't have the same edge. "My name's Myrna."

"Uh, hi," Asia fumbles. "You guys are really good. I liked you."

Weird cuts him off with a snort. "I'm Jim Dag and his name's Asia. I'm gettin' a refill." He scrapes his chair back, gets up, and leaves Asia stranded.

"Black Light, right?"

"Huh?" Asia swallows and feels like an idiot. "Yeah, we're Black Light."

She laughs. "I saw you at the Refugee. I wanted to crash backstage, but my date was an asshole, so I had to leave."

"Oh," Asia says, scanning the room for angry boyfriends. "Is he around tonight?"

"Gone now, trust me." She dismisses it with a wave of her hand. "Don't worry."

Okay, Asia thinks. "You wanna drink?"

"Whatever you're havin' is fine."

Asia is mortified. "Diet Coke?"

"Eew. Fuck, no."

By the time Weird gets back with a pitcher and two glasses, Asia is relieved, but it doesn't last long. Weird drinks one more beer, telling Myrna about Para Bellum, about Lionel, and then lets out an exaggerated yawn. "I'm goin' home."

"But..." Asia starts.

"You don't have to come. Take a cab." Weird shrugs into his bomber jacket. "Christ, Asia. That's what the credit card they gave you's for."

In Weird's wake, Asia doesn't know what to say. Myrna pours herself the last of the pitcher and says, "Y'know, I saw you looking at me while I was onstage. That's why I came over here."

Asia contains his puzzlement before it spreads across his face. "I didn't mean to stare." Had he been staring?

"It's okay. It was nice." She arches her eyebrow again. "You hungry? I was thinkin' we could get some Mickie D's."

When they get up to leave, Asia realizes that Myrna is almost a head taller than him. When she slides up against him in the cab, Asia feels small. He catches his breath just as she kisses him.

"Hey." He pulls back. "You don't even know anything about me."

"I know I like you," she says. "What else do you need?"

But she backs off a little. Asia lets out his breath again. What the hell is he doing? Where did he think this would end up?

"So, are you bi or just gay?" she asks.

"What?" He feels heat on his face again.

"You thought I was a boy when I was singing, right? Is it gonna be a problem that I'm not?"

"I thought... I mean." Asia turns redder. "Either way, you're beautiful."

She laughs again. "See, I told you I liked you."

At McDonald's, Myrna orders the biggest fries and two apple pies. "I'm a vegetarian," she explains, just as Asia bites into his Big Mac.

"You're gonna call Lionel, aren't you?" He decides to steer the conversation in a direction he can handle. "He's producing our album. He's good. I like him."

"'Course I'm callin'," Myrna says. "Even if he sucked, it'd be more than what we've got goin' now."

Asia wants to tell her that the next step is all contracts and showing up for work in the morning, that it changes everything in your life, sometimes not in good ways. He shoves some of the tepid fries in his mouth instead.

"Tell me something about yourself," Myrna says.

Asia shrugs. "What do you want to know?"

"Whatever. Where are you from? How long has your band been together?" Myrna smiles. "I wanna know more about you."

"Me and Trace were in a band together before Black Light," he tells her, shoving the specter of his brother into the furthest corner of his mind. "When I was in high school. And I guess we've been out here for about a year. We're from Michigan."

"I was born in Hollywood," Myrna says. "Which kinda sucks, because I mean, where are you supposed to wanna run away to when you grow up, if you're already here?"

Asia laughs. Her logic makes a fractured kind of sense to him. "I don't know. I never really wanted to leave Ann Arbor."

"How come you did, then?"

He sighs. "Because Trace did."

She shifts to look into his eyes, still smiling. "Are you together?"

Asia's slow again and it takes about a half-second for him to get what she's asking. "Uh, well… No, I mean, we're… He's my best friend, but we're not….Y'know."

"Just checkin'." Myrna shakes her head. "'Cause, like I said, I like you and if I'm stepping in the middle of something, I wanna know."

"There's nothing." Asia looks away. Myrna's eyes are as blue as Trace's and their expression is disconcerting.

"If I was your boyfriend…" She slides closer to him again. "I wouldn't be letting you hit on other singers in bars."

"I don't have a boyfriend."

She is so close to him, Asia can feel her breathing. She smells smoky, like the bar, with something sweeter underneath that. She snakes her arm around his shoulders. "I wanna be your boyfriend."

This time he's no less tense when she kisses him, but it's different. He gasps in his breath, closes his eyes, opens his mouth to her. "I want to go somewhere."

"Not my place." She smiles. "It's like one room, and we all sleep there."

"My place's bigger." Asia can't believe he's considering this. Not him. "But we all sleep there, too."

Myrna gives him a squeeze. "But you have a credit card."

Even as they ride the elevator up to the room, Asia can't believe this is happening to him. He feels like he's in movie or something. Then reality hits him as they slow. "Uh, Myrna, I don't have anything to, y'know, like protection."

"I got y'covered. Don't worry." She pats the bulky messenger bag she carries over her shoulder. "I'm like the Boy Scouts, baby. I'm always prepared."

By the time he opens the door, they are both giggling a little. Asia is as terrified of what she expects as he is eager.

"Wow." He pauses on the threshold. It's like they're back in that movie again. How much did all this cost for the night? He hadn't even paid attention.

"Yeah." Myrna pulls him in by the front of his shirt and kicks the door shut behind them. "This beats the hell outta my couch."

Asia thinks of the futon he used to sleep on and the old days don't seem quite so great anymore.

He is painfully awkward at first, but Myrna knows what he needs to know and shows him. Asia loses track of the moment when his fumbling melts away and becomes something else.

Later, he wakes alone in the bed, Myrna across the room. She is sitting in a chair by the window, wrapped in a blanket, holding something up to the moonlight. "Gregory James Heyes."

"What?" He squints in the darkness.

"That's what it says on your license—which is expired, by the way." She rises and returns to the bed.

"You're going through my wallet?" he asks as she hands it to him before sliding back in next to him.

"Yeah, well, you were sleeping." She shrugs, circling her arms around him. "Why did you change your name, Greg?"

"Uh." He swallows, shifting slightly, tossing the wallet to the bedside table. "Nobody ever calls me that."

"Okay, but why Asia?" She props herself up on an elbow. "It doesn't seem like a name you'd pick."

"I didn't," he admits. "Trace picked it. I never asked him why."

"Does he know where you are tonight?" Myrna asks, trailing her fingertips over Asia's bare chest, making him shiver. "I mean, is he missing you?"

"I told you, we're not... We're friends, but even if we were more than that, he's living with another guy, so he doesn't care." Asia tries to keep the bitter edge inside. "I told you."

"I know," Myrna says. "It's just I look a lot like him—and the way you were looking at me while I was onstage." This time her laugh is soft. "It would have been nice to know it was really all for me."

Asia knows he should her tell it was, but he can't lie now. "I'm really fucked up," he begins. "I mean, I never think of myself like... Well, like this. I mean, I don't date. I guess it is Trace. But we're not... We won't ever be together. "

He turns away from her then and closes his eyes. It doesn't

matter, he thinks. He's spent so much time wanting Trace and not being able to have him. He can go back to that.

"It's okay." She stretches out against his back. "You worry too much. Everybody's fucked up somehow."

Asia lets out his breath. The press of her against him is enough to crowd Trace from his brain for a while, anyway. They sleep like that until dawn and then Asia wakes, lies there, staring at the strip of sun that invades the heavy curtains across the room. He has no idea what time it is. He should look, check and see if he is late for the studio, call somebody and tell them where he is. But all he wants to do is memorize this feeling, memorize her weight against his back, the brush of her breath on his neck. He doesn't want it to be tomorrow yet, when he goes back to being alone. Right now he feels whole, like Myrna found the piece of him that was missing and put it back.

But nothing will stop morning, no matter what Asia wants. He moves out of Myrna's embrace to get up. When he looks at her in the gray light, he sees a young Trace, tangled in the sheets.

He turns away, ashamed. Trace is so deep in him, and has been for so long, Asia doesn't know how to stop.

It started at the end of the summer when Asia was sixteen. Trace was staying with the Heyes'. Two things had occurred to Asia during that time. One was that Eric was fucking Trace. The other was that Asia wanted to.

Looking back, Asia thinks it should have been a big deal, figuring out that he was gay, but that didn't occur to him. He didn't want boys; he didn't want girls. All he wanted was Trace. And he knew that Eric would kill him if he ever even hinted how he felt. So when he joined Eric's band, it was like putting his head into the lion's mouth.

It was August, and Trace and Eric were on the verge of blows all the time. Their relationship was unraveling and it spilled over into the band. Asia spent every night they played ready to put himself between them.

Then Eric started picking up girls from the gigs. He wasn't subtle about it, either. He'd make out in the parking lot, after the show, make sure that Trace saw him. Then he stopped coming home.

That night it was too hot to sleep upstairs, so Asia zigzagged around the creaks in the stairs to make it to the living room without waking his parents. He wanted to stare at the TV until his brain would quiet or dawn came. First Asia went into the kitchen looking for a bottle of Tab, but only found beer in the fridge. What the hell, he thought, cracking it open. He was too tired to care if his dad missed it later. Then he saw light coming from under the basement door. Asia stood there, staring at that strip of light, starved for the sound of a human voice, holding his breath. Then he knocked.

"C'mon down, Asia," Trace called softly.

"Hey." Asia pushed the door open to descend. "Eric still gone?"

Trace looked up at him from where he sat cross-legged on the end of the bed, overflowing ashtray on the spread beside him. "He's fuckin' some girl at her dorm room."

Asia didn't know what to say. "Sorry."

"It's better than him bringing 'em home." Trace stabbed his cigarette out and set the tray on the nearby folding table. He rose and took the bottle of beer from Asia. "You're not supposed to be drinkin'. Your mom would kill you."

"My mom doesn't give a shit about me," Asia said. "Eric's her favorite."

"Stupid bitch." Trace shook his head.

Asia shrugged. He took a deep breath. "If I were Eric, I wouldn't be fucking around on you is all I know." He said it quick, staring past Trace to the dusty poster of Mick Jagger that clung to the wall behind the bed.

Trace paused, beer half way to his lips. His smile turned sharp, then softened. "Too bad you're not him, 'cause I'm startin' to think I'm in love with the wrong brother."

All the breath left Asia then. "What?"

"Did I fall in love with the wrong brother?" Trace moved back to Asia, slid a hand to the back of his neck. "Did I?"

Every cell in Asia's body screamed yes, but he couldn't get the air to say it. Trace kissed him and Asia closed his eyes. He didn't even know how to want this.

Then they were on the bed, bodies pressed together. Trace was still kissing him. He worked Asia's tee shirt off and grazed his lips against Asia's chest, hands sliding lower.

"Wait," Asia gasped. "I don't know what to do."

"I'll do it for you." Trace's hand was on Asia's zipper just as the door from the upstairs burst open.

Eric, silhouetted against the darkened kitchen, hesitated for a split second before slamming down the stairs. "What the fuck?" His voice was pitched low, to keep their parents out of it, but Asia heard the threat. "You teachin' my little brother how to be a faggot now?"

Asia scrambled back from Trace, breathing hard, but Trace just smiled up at Eric. *"That bitch you were fuckin' tonight finally teach you to be straight?"*

Asia saw rage burn through his brother. He moved to get between them, but Eric moved faster. He grabbed Trace by the hair and dragged him off the bed. "Did you suck his dick?"

Trace's smile didn't falter. "I was gonna, but then you had to show up."

"Don't—" Asia saw it coming when Eric punched Trace in the face.

Trace stumbled back, laughing. "What'sa matter, baby? You couldn't get it up? You need me to help you with that?"

Eric's next blow landed lower, doubled him over.

"Stop it." Asia finally made himself move. He shoved Trace behind him and glared up at his brother. "Are you stupid? He was just doin' it to make you jealous."

"No I wasn't," Trace protested.

"Shut the fuck up, both of you," Eric ordered, balling up a fist again. "You." He nodded at Trace. "Get your shit and get out of my sight. We're done. And you, little brother, get upstairs and stay the hell outta my way."

That was it. Eric had them both replaced in the band by the end of the week. He went back to ignoring Asia into nonexistence. Trace vanished from both their lives, but Asia spent so much time replaying those few minutes in his mind that they became the only moments in his life.

"Hey, why don't you just come with me today and talk to Lionel?" Asia offers, later, as they're dressing, mostly because he's not really ready to turn loose of Myrna yet.

She smiles and shakes her head. "I wanna meet him on my own terms, not as your boyfriend."

He raises an eyebrow at her joke, but gets her point. "Okay, but I'm gonna call you when I'm done."

"You better." She leans over to kiss him. "Can you come to Corman's tonight?"

"Yeah, and I'll even try to ditch Weird."

"Oh, but I like your dad."

He giggles. "Shut up."

In the end, Asia knows he's going to be late into the studio. He tries calling the house, but there's no answer. Still, he has the cab drop Myrna off first, down in Hollywood. The neighborhood is as dingy and rundown as his old one in Glendale, but instead of the hard-edged concrete and construction dirt, it is filled with older houses, crumbling, but somehow more welcoming.

She kisses him hard and slides out. "Get goin' there, baby. See me tonight."

Asia sighs as the cab takes him toward Para Bellum. God, he feels good. Perfect. She is just perfect and now he can't quite remember why he doesn't just blow off the band and stay with Myrna forever.

Then he thinks of Trace and knows that this feeling can't last.

When he gets there, he's only a little late. Weird's face splits into a wide grin as soon as he enters. "You look, uh, relaxed."

Asia feels his face turn red and smiles back without answering.

Tommi tosses his head to flip bangs out of his face and laughs. "Your mother was up all night worryin' about you, waiting for you to call...." He shrugs at Weird. "Kids."

"Yeah." Weird's expression is only slightly darkened at the sight of the shadowy side of Tommi's face. "Guess that makes you the good one—for once."

Trace looks up from the keyboard, frowning. "What're you guys talkin' about?"

"Asia was out all night," Tommi says gleefully. "With a girl."

Trace says nothing as the teasing goes on from the other two. He catches Asia's eye for a split second and Asia looks away first, smile melted, but the heat on his face amped up. He gets the crazy thought that Trace looks jealous, then almost laughs out loud at himself. Right.

"Hey," he says sharply to stop the others. "I like Myrna and she's prob'ly gonna be hangin' around at the house, so can't y' be decent to her?"

"Yeah, of course," Tommi says. "Doesn't mean we have to be decent to you, though, right?"

8

Albrecht sits on the side of the unmade bed, waiting for Trace to model the second set of clothes this morning. His interview with the writer from the *LA Weekly* is today and he seems nervous. Albrecht can hear him talking while he's still in the walk-in, but can't make out what he's saying.

"He's dating a woman now." Trace re-emerges, sneering.

"I'm sorry?" Albrecht sets his coffee on the bedside table.

"Asia came in late to the studio a few days ago because he was out all night screwing some girl."

The underlying tone of shock would be amusing if Trace wasn't so deadly serious. Albrecht frowns. "But surely you don't begrudge him the time to himself? Perhaps this is a good thing. He seems to me to be a lonely young man."

"Yeah, trust me, a girl ain't what Asia's lookin' for." Trace's laugh is raw. "He's just trying to prove something."

To whom? Albrecht wonders. He's felt the air between Asia and Trace and he has no illusions as to the threat Asia represents. Still, he tries another tack with Trace. "How can you be sure? Do you mean that he could never truly be interested in a woman? You don't believe it's all that cut and dried."

"I just know Asia." Trace's voice drops. "She isn't what he needs. No matter who she is."

Trace's preoccupation with Asia's sex life is more than irritating. Albrecht feels himself begin to armor himself against Trace's touch, as protection.

"What do you think?" Trace asks him, standing between Albrecht and the mirror.

"Hum?" Albrecht blinks as though he's just noticed Trace standing there. Now he looks the other man up and down. He is, of course beautiful, lithe and smooth in his simple jeans and tee shirt. Albrecht at once is hit with a feral hunger, the overwhelming desire to keep Trace here, to himself, forever. He crushes his cigarette out and smiles frostily. "It's a bit plain, isn't it?"

He sees the confidence in Trace falter, just a flicker, but there. Then he shrugs. "It's an interview for the *Weekly*, not a drag show, baby."

"Of course, you know best," Albrecht concedes, lighting another. "This is important for your band. The *Weekly* is local, but its reach is fairly wide."

"I know that." Trace narrows his eyes. "I know what I'm supposed to do."

"Of course," Albrecht repeats. "It's only that you seem upset over Asia and this girl of his. I think you need to be more focused."

"Don't worry about it," Trace protests. "I'm totally focused."

Albrecht smiles thinly. He has no doubt of it, really.

Trace reaches down to pick up Albrecht's wrist, turning it gently to check his watch. "Shit, I gotta go. Will you be here when I get back?"

"Perhaps," Albrecht says, rising.

The location of the interview was Trace's choice. He and Marcus decided on the Refugee Club for several reasons. The most important one is that it's an atmosphere Trace knows well and can control.

He manages to arrive an hour late. He's not really worried. He's operating on Rock Star Time now. He pushes the heavy glass doors open and enters the lobby. He knows that Christian wanted him to wear one of the suits his tailor made, but Trace settled on impossibly tight jeans and sleeveless shirt with the Japanese Rising Sun silkscreened across the chest. Trace spots his quarry rising from his place on one of the padded benches across from the concession stand, in nylon parachute pants and a gray Members Only jacket and knows he was right.

"Mr. Dellon——"

"Trace, please," he insists, taking the offered hand between both of his. "I'm sorry I'm late. Traffic."

"Oh, it's no problem."

Trace leads him into the club, which is quiet and empty, save the distant sound of the bar being stocked. Trace has a flash of the breakfast he and Christian shared here way back when, but shakes it off.

They settle across from each other and the guy introduces himself as Trace lights a cigarette.

"Lewis Ramirez, right. I read your interview with Iggy Pop," Trace tells him. "It was really good. You captured him."

Lewis flushes at the compliment, but covers by glancing down at his notes and turning on his little tape recorder. "You grew up almost in the same place in Michigan, didn't you? Do you know him?"

Trace catches the boy's eyes with his, the lie coming out smooth and plausible. "Our paths have crossed, but you know, he's actually from Ypsilanti and I'm from Ann Arbor."

If Lewis recognizes the bullshit, he doesn't comment. Instead he asks about the album. "What should we expect from Black Light?"

"Music is changing fast now." Trace taps ashes into the tray on the table. "MTV is like talkies were in the Thirties for movies. It's killed a lot of bands out there that can't keep up. So now there's New Wave, with all the hair bands." He waves a hand, dismissing them. "But there's still a void. Something that's missing." He raises an eyebrow and gives Lewis a slow smile. "That's me. I'm here to fill the void."

Lewis smiles in response, blushing again, looking down to write something. "Okay. Let me ask you this: We're still at the start of this new decade. What will make the Eighties different from the Seventies, do you think?"

Trace stabs out his cigarette and shrugs. "It's simple, really. Each second that passes brings us closer to the end of the century. We who are living now are the ones who will be around to see it die. We're starting to see it now: the world breaking down. That, I think, is the difference between 1983 and 1973. One decade closer to death."

"Wow."

Trace laughs. "You wanted me to say something like 'shorter hair'?"

"No, no. It's just a pretty bleak outlook."

Trace flashes him another sharp smile. "Depends on how you feel about the world now, I suppose. Personally, I won't be unhappy to see it all burn. I'd like to be the one holding the match."

"That'd be something," Lewis murmurs.

By the end of interview, Lewis is completely won over. Trace takes his hand again, holding the contact a fraction of a second longer than necessary. "Thank you."

"Thank you," Lewis returns. "Marcus Anthony is having some pictures sent over for the article right? It should be in about two weeks from now."

Trace tears away from the club, happy with the way things went, looking forward to seeing himself in print. When he gets back to the penthouse, he finds it still. That brings him back to the odd exchange with Christian this morning. Trace can feel the distance between them and he's not quite sure how it got there. He wonders where Christian has gone now. He's not the type to slip out for a beer run.

Trace heads to the bedroom and walks into the closet to toe his shoes off. Really, it's like another room, Albrecht's suits hanging on one side like a regiment, a complete contrast to the disarray of Trace's collection. The hangers on his side contain leather jeans, tee shirts, a few sequined items. The boots and shoes scattered beneath are red, black, heeled, jumbled together with his well-worn sneakers. A long feather boa snakes through them.

A note, tucked into the chrome frame of the full-length mirror catches his attention and he has a split second of dread. Is he dumping me?

But it says only, "Lunch at 5345 Wilshire. Please come."

The please makes Trace smile. Of course Christian isn't dumping him. Trace takes his new suit out of the plastic and changes. His smile turns warmer as he imagines the effect it will have on Christian when he walks in wearing it. Worth the trouble.

He stops by the mirror atop Christian's bureau to check the knot in his tie. As he turns, he sees a black-and-white snapshot, yellowed at the edges, on the bureau top. It's the Refugee. Trace recognizes the marquee, but the letters name it the Adonis. Trace frowns, studying the two men standing in front. One of them has to have been Christian's father, judging from the age of the photo. He is identical to Christian, except the wide and unguarded smile on his face. The other has a loose arm draped over his shoulder.

He looks familiar too, but it takes Trace longer to figure out why.

Asia's insomnia. Back in Ann Arbor, Asia was always up watching old black-and-white movies. Trace spent his fair share of time keeping him company. Mostly Asia liked horror, but he liked sword movies, too.

With the smooth, chiseled angle of his jaw and thin mustache, the man with Christian's father is Errol Flynn.

Albrecht waits for Trace at the restaurant. He enjoys the time alone, watching people coming and going. It's been years since he's been here and he recognizes none of the waitstaff. The last time, Sean sat across from him, sampling the Balinese.

He is seated with an eye toward the door. When Trace comes in, he takes Albrecht's breath from him. The dark, crisp lines of his suit both contrast and compliment Trace perfectly. Albrecht looks away as Trace's eyes find him.

"You seem very far away," Trace comments as he settles in across the table.

"Not that far."

"Good." Trace sighs, opening the menu. He laughs and raises an eyebrow. "I can't read this. I don't even know what language it is."

"Sean once said the same thing to me," Albrecht says. "Shall I order for you?"

"Just don't make it gross."

"Agreed."

When the waiter comes back to the table, Albrecht complies, ordering Bebek Betutu for himself and Babi Guling for Trace.

"Snails, right?" Trace teases. "Or roaches?"

"You shall have to wait and see." Albrecht laughs, then relents. "No, yours is grilled suckling pig and mine is duck. They are both excellent."

"Were you thinking about Sean before I got here?" Trace asks. "Is that why you look so sad?"

"Did I?" Albrecht narrows his eyes. "Then I suppose I was, a little."

"You miss him."

Albrecht pauses to sip his wine. "I did. That is why I came back to Los Angeles, because I missed him. I thought I could... I thought I could find something of him here again."

"It's been a long time," Trace says. "Hasn't there been anybody..."

"You're the first man I've been in love with since Sean." Albrecht looks away as he says it. "But still, occasionally, I find him waiting for me. Sometimes I see him when I'm alone."

Trace takes a cigarette from the pack in his breast pocket and lights it. Albrecht wonders what he is thinking.

"Like a ghost?" Trace asks.

"Exactly," Albrecht admits.

Trace drinks his wine, frowning slightly. "Everybody has at least one ghost, I think."

Albrecht is about to comment that he is ready to be rid of his, but Trace sets his glass down carefully and closes his eyes. He seems to be listening to the music that is piped into the dining room softly. Albrecht asks, "Do you know this piece?"

Trace shakes his head. "Not this one. But it's Vivaldi. I recognize his phrasing, all spiky and sharp."

Albrecht nods. "It's part of *The Four Seasons*. Forgive me, but I didn't expect that you'd be much interested in classical music."

"That's because you're a snob." Trace gives him a wide grin. "I get that. But I used to buy stuff like this at Flat Black and Circular back home all the time. There was always something in the dollar bin." He closed his eyes to listen. "It's got so many layers."

Albrecht feels that pleasant jolt of surprise again. It's one of those times that Trace has pulled back the curtain to let Albrecht see what's real about him. Hardly sophisticated tastes, but still. Albrecht takes a drink of wine. "Would you like to go to the symphony? Or the opera?"

"That'd be great. I've never done anything like that before." Trace's hand drifts across the table to touch Albrecht's. "Tell me about the first time you heard Vivaldi. I bet it was like that—live, with a symphony, right?"

Albrecht shrugs one thin shoulder. "I suppose it was. I don't remember, I'm afraid. It's one of those things that seem to have always been with me."

Trace's smile lessens, disappointed. Albrecht is glad for the distraction of the food when it arrives. Trace eyes his plate, suspicious, then cuts into his pork. His eyes widen slightly at the taste. "Not bad."

Albrecht laughs softly. "If I'm a snob, you're no less of one."

"What are you talking about?" Trace tilts his head to the side.

"The night we met. What were you thinking?" Albrecht arches one eyebrow. "Rich old fruit at the rock and roll show? What could he possibly want?"

"You're way off." Trace reaches for Albrecht's hand again, meeting his eyes. "I was thinking: who knew a three-piece suit could ever be so sexy? And then I was thinking, bet it'll look better on the floor."

Albrecht looks away. He hears a sincerity in Trace's tone that touches him. He feels a part of himself falling for Trace again, wishing that first night had never ended. Wishing he had not resisted his instinct to take everything Trace had offered before it was too late.

Trace speaks again, softly. "Hey. I'm sorry. Did I embarrass you?"

"No. I..." Albrecht feels his smile turn sad. "I was thinking about that first night we were together. I wish I could have it back again."

"Take me home right now. You can have it anytime you want it."

After dinner, they do go home. Trace remembers the photo as soon as they get off the elevator. "Can I ask you something?"

Christian arches an eyebrow as he settles on one of the sofas. "I suppose so."

"Hang on." Trace slips into the bedroom for the picture. Then he sits down and hands it to Christian. "Tell me about this."

Christian's fingers brush over the tiny faces and he smiles. "Where did you find it?"

"I wasn't snooping," Trace says, folding his feet up underneath him. "I was looking in the mirror. I just saw it."

"I'm not accusing you of anything," Christian says. "I must have left it out, mustn't I?"

"This is the picture you saw of the Refugee when you were a kid, isn't it?" Trace says. "You never said your dad knew Errol

Flynn."

"I'm surprised you recognized him." Christian's voice is soft. He holds the picture up, gazing as if he could breach the surface and get inside. "You are so young."

Trace isn't sure if Christian is speaking to him or the figures in the photo. "Your dad looks really happy to be with him." Trace shifts to curl against Christian's side, head on his shoulder.

"My father? No, that's not my father." Christian sets the photo aside.

"It has to be. It looks just like you."

"Indeed. Exactly." Christian rises from his seat, hands the photo back to Trace.

"It can't be you." Trace frowns. His fingers worry the edges. "This is like...fifty years ago, right? You prob'ly weren't even born yet."

"As you say." Albrecht smiles. He finds he enjoys this game more than is healthy. He likes dancing along the edge of truth with Trace. Surely he feels what Albrecht is—what he himself is becoming. How can he not? "But it is not my father."

Truly, Albrecht's father had been dead years before and would have heartily disapproved of Flynn. Albrecht sits back down to extract a cigarette from the crystal box on the table and light it. He watches Trace working through the puzzle in his head. Albrecht draws the smoke into his lungs.

"That would make you a vampire or something."

Albrecht laughs softly. "Have you noticed any unusual wounds on your neck?"

Trace sets the photo down. He slides back against Albrecht. "You never see the bite marks until it's too late. Besides, don't you wanna make me one, too?" He kisses Albrecht and murmurs, "Don't you wanna keep me forever?"

"Yes."

In the bedroom, Trace's skin is like an open current. There is no resistance under Albrecht's hands. Trace laughs and yanks his tie off. Albrecht peels the suit coat back from his shoulders as Trace is busy with Albrecht's. He shoves all the clothes off the bed.

"See? Looks better on the floor." Trace laughs. "Told you."

Later, in the wake of Trace's sleep, Albrecht leaves the bed.

"Don't you want to keep me forever?"

Trace's words had sounded sincere, sounded as giving as his body had been while they were making love. But Albrecht knew it couldn't last. Even without Asia between them, they are too alike to last. Simply by nature, they would devour each other.

Albrecht settles in the chair by Trace's side and rakes hair back from his face. Trace gleams in the shadows and Albrecht feels the energy he's stolen shift, yearn towards its true master.

Until now, Albrecht has never thought himself a monster. He knows he is no longer human. War, hunger, fear had burned all that away decades ago.

But Trace held the truth in his eyes tonight. Monster. And so will Trace become one day.

There is a crowd on the steps of the opera house as the car pulls up. Albrecht is slightly annoyed. It appears to be caused by a young actor and his date of the evening, a tall blond woman. They are blocking the entrance with their small army of admirers.

Not quite a mob, but they look persistent to Albrecht. Trace laughs as he climbs out of the car. "It's Tom Cruise," he identifies the actor. "He's even pretty in person."

The young man throws his head back to laugh at something a reporter has asked him. "Not me," Tom denies. "I'm more like an REO Speedwagon guy. Charliee here's the opera fan."

Albrecht is struck with how utterly ordinary the boy looks. All-American to the point of Rockwell, with blinding white teeth and electric green eyes, and completely forgettable features. The contrast between him and Trace is jarring to Albrecht. They can hardly belong to the same species.

Trace steps ahead of Albrecht and calls out a name: "Lewis."

One of the pack turns and greets Trace with a warm smile and a handshake. Albrecht finds himself frowning as the contact lingers and it's a split second before he makes the connection. Lewis Ramirez. From the *Weekly* article. Lewis tilts his head and speaks to Trace.

Albrecht doesn't hear his question, only Trace's answer.

"There's nothing more dramatic than opera. How could I not love it?"

"It doesn't sound anything like your music, though," Lewis says, smile still warm. He doesn't seem to notice that his real quarry has escaped into the building.

Trace fixes him with a dazzling smile, sharp as a bird of prey. Albrecht sees that more of the crowd is caught by him. They linger to hear what he has to say. "Of course, it's the same. What is this opera about? Making a deal with the devil in tight pants? Have you listened to my lyrics?"

Lewis laughs and lets Trace slip away to take Albrecht's hand as they enter the lobby. "I'm sorry. I saw him and thought I should say hi."

"It's who you are, Trace."

"You're Trace Dellon?" someone calls and Albrecht loses his grip on Trace again.

"Yes I am." He turns again.

The speaker has a camera. Albrecht doesn't wait to listen to the rest of the conversation. He continues into the lobby by himself. Ten minutes pass before Trace joins him. He doesn't apologize again. "He works for the *Weekly*, too. He wanted my picture."

Albrecht nods, but says nothing. Trace looks away from him. "It wasn't so bad, was it?"

"It seems a little sacrifice to be with you," Albrecht admits.

"I've someone coming to meet you," Albrecht announces as they stand side by side at the double sinks in the bathroom. "I've hired him for you."

"To do what for me?" Trace finger combs his hair into spikes. "Do I need more people?"

Albrecht steps into the bedroom and lights a fresh cigarette. "I was thinking about last week, outside the opera."

"I told you, I'm sorry about that."

"You needn't apologize," Albrecht says. "It's only that I can see a time when they, your mob, will be less careful."

Trace leaves the bathroom, pausing to kiss Albrecht. "You're sweet."

Albrecht licks his lips as Trace passes by and follows him into the main room.

Albrecht knows that Marcus will have hired security for the tour, that the band, the equipment, will all be looked after sufficiently. He wants more for Trace. For all Trace is driven to become a star, Albrecht finds him innocent of what will be expected of him, how his life is changing. The ring of the telephone interrupts that line of thought.

Trace moves to answer and says, "Send him up."

Albrecht goes to meet Timothy at the lift.

Timothy Snell is the son of one of the Para Bellum board members that Albrecht knows peripherally. Timothy is Robert's problem child, refusing to stay in college, arrested for possession. Bailing him out of LA County lockup at three a.m. was the last straw for Robert. The last rescue, he said.

And so, Timothy needs a job. He'd grown up around the music industry, so Albrecht knew he could cope with anything that might come up on tour.

"Herr Christian." A tall blond boy that Albrecht barely recognizes steps off the lift as the door slides open. "Great to see you again."

He is dressed in blue jeans and a dark tee shirt. He has grown since Albrecht saw him last and now stands almost as tall as Trace. He smiles past Albrecht to Trace.

"Hi." Trace steps forward to offer his hand.

"You're Trace Dellon, huh?" Timothy says. "My dad says you're the next big thing."

Trace laughs. "I'm sure he does."

"My name's Tim."

There's a pause before Albrecht steps back in. "William has told you what I expect, yes?"

"Yeah, I think so." Tim shrugs, sitting in one of the wingback chairs. "You want me to go on tour with the band, watch out for Trace, right?"

"Precisely." Albrecht nods.

"Seems like hard work." Timothy laughs. "All the parties and girls and all. I'll be sure to work my fingers to the bone."

That was the other reason Albrecht called him. Timothy is one of the truly straightest people Albrecht has ever met. Even as a teen, he exuded an air of absolute certainty that he didn't get from his father. He might drink all the free alcohol he can get his hands on, partake of any groupie girl, but Albrecht is reasonably sure he won't sleep with Trace.

Albrecht smiles and excuses himself. "I'll leave you to become acquainted."

Trace watches Christian leave the room. He wonders what prompted this again. Then he shrugs and grins at Tim. "He thinks I need a sitter."

"Y'know, I've been around this business since I was a little kid. I was backstage at a Rolling Stones concert once, with my dad. I was like...twelve."

"Cool." Trace is impressed.

"My dad is a big fan. But we were watching from the back, Jagger was right up there at the edge of the stage, and it was a mob, y'know? And Jagger went down, right in the middle of them."

"Shit." Trace is thinking of one of the little girls at the Refugee, how hard she'd tried to pull him down.

"Yeah, but the band didn't stop the song. Hell, Mick barely stopped singing. The security moved so fast and got him back up before I think anybody could even see what happened."

"So you think your job is to save me from my fans."

Tim raises an eyebrow. "Maybe. If that's what you need." Then he laughs. "I hope not. What I want is to do as little as possible."

It's crowded in the studio today. Asia's finally got Myrna to come with him. Lionel is in the process of explaining what he and Weird are doing at the mixing board when Trace arrives with a strange guy and a copy of his *Weekly* interview under his arm.

"This is Tim Snell," he explains, wry smile on his face. "He's my new bodyguard."

Tim waves and chuckles. "Hey."

Weird and Tommi both shake their heads and go back to work. Asia wonders why Trace would need something like that.

Trace, in the meantime, notices Myrna. "You must be Asia's new bodyguard."

Today they're both dressed in jeans and tee shirts, no makeup, hair unspiked. The resemblance isn't immediately obvious, Asia hopes. Maybe Trace will let it go.

"No," Myrna corrects him. "I'm his boyfriend."

"Lucky boy." Trace murmurs before they trade places and he

sits down at the board. He unfurls the paper and passes it around.

"Great, Dellon." Weird grumbles, shaking the paper back at him. "You practically didn't even mention you were in a damn band."

"That's what the reporter was for." Trace shrugs. "He talks about you guys."

Somehow Asia missed the part where Trace invited himself along to Corman's to hear Myrna play. Trace shows up in a double-breasted suit of brilliant turquoise, the pants tucked into a pair of red Doc Martens, and insists on driving Christian's Jaguar. Asia sighs as they pull up out front. No chance of flying under the radar now. Though it's almost ten o'clock, Trace puts on a pair of tiny black sunglasses.

He is dazzling as he sweeps past the guy at the door. Asia feels like a roadie pulled along in his wake. He tries to steer Trace to his usual table at the back, but fails.

Trace chooses one closer to the stage, where they are visible to everyone. Asia stops for two beers before joining him reluctantly.

Asia tries to concentrate as Myrna and the Leather Boys start their show. Myrna makes eye contact with him as she starts to sing, one eyebrow arched at the sight of Trace next to him. Asia looks away, fidgeting.

It's nothing Trace does, Asia realizes, it's what he is. Trace lights a cigarette and turns toward the stage, keeps his eyes hidden behind the black glasses. The boys in the band start vamping just for him. Then it spreads to the crowd around them. Asia can feel their attention turn away from Myrna to Trace.

People brush by the table close, like they want to touch him. It's like they recognize him, even if they don't know why yet.

The *Weekly* article has been out for about three minutes. What would life be like once the album is released? More of this? What happens when they get the video done? Asia panics a little. He hates the feeling of being observed, but Trace loves it. He makes a show of lighting his next cigarette, exhaling the smoke, lifting his glass to his lips, swaying to the beat of the music. Asia stares at his profile, nearly identical to Myrna's but sharper, and thinks again of what it was like to kiss Trace. Then he shakes himself, turns his attention back to the stage.

"We have a guest tonight," Myrna says. She gives a hard smile as applause breaks out. "Yeah, I thought you noticed. Maybe we should get him up here for a while. What d'ya say?"

She is answered again by claps and whistles. Asia frowns and Trace shakes his head. He shrugs and says, "I don't know? any of your numbers."

Myrna's smile doesn't waver. "Oh, it's okay. We know all of yours, because I'm fucking your bass player."

Trace laughs, glancing at Asia. "Fair enough."

Asia blushes, takes a drink of his beer. Trace rises, leaving the sunglasses with his drink, and joins Myrna. Asia can't read the intention behind her expression.

Standing side by side at the mic, Trace is slightly taller than Myrna. Her hair is black spikes, and Trace's is rusty red, but they are equally thin and angular. "You guys all know Trace Dellon, right?"

The crowd affirms that. Trace leans in to say, "Hello."

Myrna turns back to the boys and says something, then murmurs it to Trace. He nods and grabs the mic to count down.

When they sing, Myrna leans close to Trace. Asia is afraid that Trace will eclipse her, but she doesn't give an inch of the stage to him, matching him verse for verse. They are both looking straight at Asia, so similar that he can't catch his breath. Everybody else in the bar is on their feet, pressing closer to the stage, until Asia's view is swallowed up by moving bodies.

Trace finishes out the set with the Leather Boys. As Myrna is telling everybody that they don't have to go home, but they can't stay here, he laughs and manages to kiss her.

Asia laughs under his breath too, humorlessly. As Trace returns to the table, Asia finishes his warm, flat beer.

Albrecht doesn't look up when Trace walks off the lift. "How was your evening?"

"Okay. Lionel's right about the Leather Boys. They're gonna be good. But what he was ever doin' in a dive like Corman's?" Trace laughs. "Who knows why Lionel does anything, though, I guess."

Albrecht smiles faintly. "I suspect he was meeting a dealer."

Trace shrugs out of his jacket and tosses it over the arm of the sofa. "Really? Lionel, huh?"

Albrecht folds his paper away. He is always surprised when he comes across a patch of innocence in Trace. It's one of the things he still loves. "So, she's talented? Asia's girlfriend?"

"Oh, yeah." Trace flops down next to Albrecht and leans against him. "Yeah, and it's a little creepy. She looks just like me."

"How is that possible?" Albrecht murmurs.

"Looks like me." Trace nudges him. "From the stage. But she's a girl. And she's not me."

"Of course not. You are one of a kind."

Trace doesn't answer. Instead, he kisses Albrecht on the cheek. "Let's go to bed."

Albrecht agrees, submitting to what he knows Trace wants from him, though the comfort he gets from it is thin. When Trace is done, Albrecht rises to take a shower.

When he returns, Trace is smoking a cigarette. Albrecht leans down to take it from him and takes a drag. "I thought you were asleep."

"I was until you got up."

Albrecht slides back between the sheets and Trace takes the cigarette back from him. He finishes it and stabs it out in the ashtray. Then he turns off the light. "How long have you known Lionel?"

Albrecht is caught off guard. "Ten years, perhaps, why?"

Trace shrugs again. "I just didn't know he did drugs."

Albrecht settles in, head on his pillow. "He and Sean were friends. That's how I met him."

"That girl is using Asia," Trace says.

Albrecht opens his eyes and looks up. "What?"

"Asia's never had a girlfriend or anything. He doesn't know what he's getting into."

Albrecht objects, "How can you be such a cynic?"

"She looks just like me."

"As you said, she's not you," Albrecht says gently. "Perhaps her motives are less…"

He breaks off as Trace moves away from him. "Less what?"

Albrecht sits up and sighs. "Nothing. It's late. My English is…"

"Better than mine." Trace's voice is acid. "Tell me what you

98

meant."

Albrecht drags a hand through his hair. "Less complicated."

"What does that mean?" Trace demands.

"Trace, it is nearly three in the morning," Albrecht protests, lying down again, back to Trace. "You obviously want this to be a fight and I am sorry, but I am too old for it. I love you, so please, let me sleep."

He hears Trace let out a frustrated breath. It's a few minutes before he settles again as well, on the other edge of the bed. Something in Albrecht rebels at letting it go without one last dig. "Really, I'd think you'd try harder to be happy for Asia. He is your friend, yes?"

"You wouldn't understand."

Albrecht falls silent again listening to Trace's breathing lengthen into sleep. Then Albrecht moves closer, pressing skin to skin. He tastes the back of Trace's neck, siphoning energy from there slowly, savoring what he can from it before giving in to sleep, too.

"You looked like you were havin' a good time with Trace tonight," Asia finally says, sitting on the bed. He's looking out at the dark garden instead of at Myrna.

"Of course I did." Myrna laughs. "People don't buy drinks if you look miserable when you're up there, y'know."

"I didn't want him to come." Asia shakes his head. "I mean, I just couldn't think of a way to get out of it. I'm sorry."

Myrna flops onto the bed next to him. She puts a hand on his back. "It was okay. He was all right. It was kinda fun."

Asia relaxes a little, lays down. Myrna circles her arms around him and presses against him. Her lips brush his ear when she speaks. "I wanted you to see us together, so you can tell the difference."

Asia catches his breath against the hollow of her throat. "I know the difference. You're my boyfriend."

She rolls him onto his back and straddles him. "Yes, I am."

But when Asia looks up at her part of him sees Trace, so he closes his eyes.

9

"Wear what you want." Myrna says the next morning.

Asia has been dreading this for a week. What he shows up wearing for the album photo shoot will be important. It would come naturally to Trace, but Asia has no clue how to figure it out.

Myrna is perched on the end of the bed, hair sleep snarled, wearing her black leggings from last night and Asia's Whisky tee shirt. Asia sighs. "I don't have anything cool."

Myrna pulls her bag up onto her lap and paws through it. "We shoulda gone shopping. I shoulda thought of it before."

"I never…" Asia breaks off. He assumes it's obvious he doesn't spend a lot of time thinking about clothes.

"Go get a pair of Tommi's parachute pants—black ones," Myrna tells him.

"They won't fit," he objects, but rises to go anyway.

In twenty minutes, Asia is standing in front of the mirrored closet doors, dressed in Tommi's too-tight pants and Myrna's too-tight black tee shirt. She stands behind him to fasten her dog collar around his neck.

"I look stupid. I'm gonna rip the butt outta these."

Myrna smiles. "You look delicious. I'm gonna pierce your ear."

"What?"

"It doesn't hurt. It'll look cool."

Asia reaches up to touch his earlobe. "Myrna, I really don't wanna do it. It just feels…" He shrugs. "I don't want to."

Myrna smiles into the mirror at him, then leans down to bite his other earlobe gently. "Too bad." She laughs and then lets him go. "You're gonna be the prettiest one."

He knows he doesn't have much of a say in it now. She's across the hall in Tommi's room, asking for a sewing needle next.

They drag him into the kitchen and sit him down at the table. Tommi is getting ice out of the door of the refrigerator. "You won't feel it, Asia, honest."

It's not the pain that scares him, not really. Asia thinks of sitting at Corman's with Trace, feeling exposed. This is like that, but he doesn't say it.

Myrna leans against the counter, holding the needle in a flame from a lighter. She smiles at him. Asia smiles back, in spite of himself.

Tommi comes around to hold Asia's earlobe between two pieces of ice. "Just a minute."

Asia closes his eyes, shivering. He surrenders himself, not wanting to see what will happen next. He hears Myrna approach, then the pressure of the ice recedes, replaced by the pressure of her fingers, then the needle. Asia hears the crunch as she forces her way through, but Tommi's right. There's no pain.

"There you go," she whispers close to his ear. "It's in."

She steps away and he touches a thin hoop now looped through his ear. The metal is cold. Then, as he stands up, he feels a rush of blood.

"Oops." Myrna steadies him. "Take a breath, okay?"

Asia nods, dizzy. He focuses on her and breathes. She brushes hair back from his face and smiles. "Prettiest one."

"Asia loves this place," Trace comments as the car pulls up to Monster Court at Universal Studios. "Asia loves old horror movies. He and Tommi wanted to see this place first thing when we moved."

Albrecht nods. He sees that they are the last to arrive. Trace gets out of the car first, resplendent in his dark blue leathers. He walks into the midst of the crew and a hush falls over them. Albrecht reaches into his jacket to hide his eyes behind sunglasses before he submits to inevitable invisibility. He walks across the hollow approximation of old European cobblestones to stand out of the way of the photographers and the band.

Black Light has turned themselves out admirably, Albrecht thinks. Tommi looks very pretty in his ripped tee shirt, skinny tie and white-blond hair, shining in the sun. All hints of abuse have either faded or are covered by makeup. The guitarist wears wraparound sunglasses and a shabby black jacket that Albrecht is sure has graced at least one, perhaps two resale racks. He looks like Johnny Cash on acid. Asia stands with a woman who can only be the new girlfriend and Albrecht sees what Trace reacted to. Tall and sinewy, she is indeed a fractured reflection of Trace. Asia looks as though he is wearing someone else's skin; he is so uncomfortable and stiff. Albrecht wonders if he recognizes the fountain he's standing in front of as the hunchback's. He wonders if Asia would know who Lon Chaney was.

Albrecht goes to stand by Marcus, who is behind the cameras, beaming as though he's watching his babies graduate. Not far from the truth, Albrecht supposes. He lights a cigarette and Marcus gives him a half smile. "You don't really care if that shit kills everyone around you, do you?"

Albrecht exhales his first breath of smoke. "It isn't what everyone around me generally dies of."

He turns his attention to the photo shoot, watching the photographer pose the musicians. Trace needs no help, of course, but Tommi is having a hard time keeping a straight face, which makes Asia laugh. They seem unbelievably young. Albrecht is jealous of the easy history they have with Trace, of the world they live in with him that Albrecht can only watch.

Afterward, Albrecht knows that Trace would rather be with the band for the evening, but he doesn't give in. "You'll be on tour soon enough and then I'll have no time with you," he argues. "Please."

Trace doesn't turn him down. Albrecht knows he won't. He knows Trace feels he can't. Not now, not until his career isn't so dependent. Albrecht isn't above using that to his advantage. They don't talk in the car on the way home.

Asia sits on the side of the hot tub in a pair of cutoff jeans, cooking his legs. Tommi is in up to his chest. He is smoking a joint, laughing.

"C'mon, Asia." Tommi shakes his head, splashing around a little. "You're dating a girl that makes you call her your boyfriend."

"She doesn't make me," Asia qualifies, raking his hair out of his face. "She just…is."

"Yeah." Tommi passes the joint to Asia. "What does that make you?"

Asia stares at the joint in his hand and knows he won't smoke it. He holds it, inhales the smoke a little and knows he won't go any farther than that. Then Tommi takes it back. Asia looks at him sideways, considering. Little Tommi, hopelessly girly and passive. Suddenly Asia sees beneath all that to a kind of strength he could never manage. Under all of it there is a kind of agreement between Tommi and the rest of the world. He knows who he is and exactly how the world sees that.

Unlike Asia, who can't be who he really is even in his own head, let alone anywhere else. "I don't know what that makes me."

Tommi turns and grins at him. "It's okay."

"What's okay?" Weird asks, returning from the kitchen with a fresh beer in each hand.

"That Asia's relationship with his girlfriend—boyfriend is a little fucked up." Tommi giggles.

"Yeah, and you should be the judge of that," Weird mutters, hoisting himself up to sit on the wall of the hot tub.

"Hey, at least I date." Tommi keeps his good nature, even though Weird scowls at him. "And I told you. John's gone from my life."

"Uh-huh." Weird doesn't sound convinced. He twists the caps off the beers and passes one of them to Asia. "Whatever. I'm done with women. Got one ex-wife. Don't need more."

"Really?" Asia asks, partially to deflect the conversation from him and Myrna. "How come I don't know that?"

"You never asked, prob'ly." Weird arches an eyebrow. "And because it was a long time ago. Haven't seen her in ten years. Think about my little girl, though."

"You have a kid?" Asia is amazed.

Tommi's smile is less stoned and more sad now. "You haven't heard from them, have you?"

"No." Weird takes a drink of beer. "No, you know, her mother wouldn't let me see her when we broke up. It was part of the deal. Can't blame her. I was a different person then. Scared her."

"It's bullshit, Weird," Tommi protests. "You'd make a way better dad than the one I got."

Asia drinks his beer and frowns, looking from Tommi to Weird. "What's her name—your little girl?"

Weird rubs a hand over his beard and looks upward. "Sally."

They don't say a lot after that. Weird and Asia drink more beer and Tommi finishes his joint. He finally pulls himself out of the hot tub, saying his fingers are pruney. Asia stares at the trail of wet footprints he leaves and thinks of all the blood and broken glass in John's bathroom. He looks at Weird. "Tommi's right. You'd make a great dad."

Weird laughs softly. "I'm sure whoever Sherry ended up with's doin' a fine job. It was my own fault. When I found out Sherry was fuckin' around, I was pissed off. Stupid. Couldn't really think straight."

Asia doesn't ask for details. He's seen Weird pissed off. While his fuse isn't as short as Eric's, he has the same potential for violence.

Reality is becoming unstitched for Asia more every day. Even though he'd spent the last month working on *No Outlet*, just like everybody else in the band, he let himself believe that they'd never actually be done with it, that he'd never be holding the end product in his hand. But at their next meeting at Para Bellum, there's a box of the album waiting. Marcus gives a copy to each of them in turn, handing them over like checks from the lottery. Asia stares a full second before accepting his. When his fingers close on it, he feels dizzy. Asia barely recognizes the people on the cover. He stares into his own face, standing behind Trace's shoulder, trying not to squint in the sun, and tries to remember what he was thinking the moment the camera caught them. It's not me, he thinks. This is not me.

He feels himself slip; the anchors that keep him in his body give way, bit by bit. Then he feels Trace's hand on his shoulder, gently slamming him back.

He steps away from Trace's hand.

"Now we sell the fuckers." Marcus grins.

Since Black Light stopped playing the Refugee, Albrecht has only heard broken pieces of Trace's music though headphones. It hasn't the intimacy Albrecht had supposed and though he has to share Trace with a few hundred other people tonight, he's looking forward to the performance.

The Whisky is tiny and dark, much more of a bar than the

Refugee Club, but Albrecht understands its significance in the history of a band's career. Timothy, posted outside the dressing room, nods at Albrecht as he approaches. "He's still gettin' ready."

Albrecht is gripped with a sense of déjà vu as he raps his knuckles against the door. There is a breathless pause before Trace answers.

Tonight he gets his own space, but it's the size of a small closet, barely enough room for Trace to sit at the mirror for his makeup. When Albrecht enters, they stand close enough to kiss.

Trace is wearing one of the suits Albrecht had made for him, black and lean, pinched in close at the waist, and tall red pumps. One earring dangles from his right ear, a spill of rhinestones that spell out the word "SEX." His hair is now black, which makes his skin bone white and his eyes even paler.

"You look beautiful," Albrecht tells him, reaching up to touch the spikes. "I like this."

"I stole it from Myrna." Trace's smile turns acid. "Seemed only fair."

Albrecht lets that go. "I have something for you."

Trace laughs softly. "Is it what I think it is?"

He guides Albrecht's hand to the fly of his pants and Albrecht laughs too. "Why don't we save that for later? I have something a little more lasting to commemorate the moment."

He withdraws the box from his jacket pocket and gives it to Trace. "I had them made for you."

"Wow." Trace arches an eyebrow as he opens the box. "I don't know what to say."

Albrecht lifts two bangle bracelets gently out of the velvet. They are platinum, one a plain band, the other two bands twined around each other like vines. "Let me."

He slips them onto Trace's left wrist and kisses him quickly. "I'm going to find my seat. I shall see you after."

Albrecht knows his gift means next to nothing to Trace. Still, Albrecht can't help thinking of the bracelets as his talisman against losing Trace to the world. Enchantment, he thinks, like a fairy tale. He's marked Trace as his with a secret spell. Not the devil, he reminds himself, no matter how much he wants to be. Nothing will bind Trace to him. Albrecht weaves silently through the tight crowd of people that have all gathered here with the same need as his. He can taste the excitement in the air, along with the cigarette smoke. Lets it enter his skin.

During the show, Albrecht stands as close to the stage as he can. He lets the dancers jostle him, brush against him, bring him closer to Trace.

They get away after one encore, though the mob out front still screams for more. Trace is too amped to even sit down. Marcus is the first person he sees backstage. Trace gives him a long hard kiss.

"We were—"

"You are brilliant." Marcus laughs.

"We were *fuckin'* God!" Trace corrects him.

Marcus doesn't deny it. He reaches out to gather up Asia and Tommi as they pass. "D'ya hear that?" he shouts at them over the crowd. "Black Light is God."

Christian begs off the party and Trace wonders if it's a test. He kisses him and tells him he won't be long.

"Are you kidding?" Marcus says as he steers Trace out the back way. "Tonight you're workin'."

Marcus manages to cram Trace, Tim, Asia, and Myrna into his black Trans Am and heads over to Para Bellum. Trace can barely keep still. He turns back to Asia, pale and exhausted in the back seat, his head on Myrna's shoulder. "C'mon, man," Trace groans. "How can you be so mellow?"

"Trace, I just—"

Marcus cuts Asia off. "Now, look, boys. I want to remind you that we're still working tonight. The press that was at the show'll be there, as well as promoters and Para Bellum execs." He glances over at Trace. "Ones you're not currently fucking."

Trace rolls his eyes. "Okay. What's your point?"

"My point for you is: be aware of what you're saying and who you're saying it to." He smiles, teeth white in the shadowy car. "And my point to Asia is: don't hide in some corner, okay?"

The party is lavish, food and champagne flowing freely. Trace spends a lot of time signing album covers and answering the same questions over and over. More people pour into the room. He begins to feel closed in, being led around by Marcus, shadowed by Tim.

Finally, the room is full of too many stupid questions, too much champagne. Trace manages to ditch both his keepers and arranges himself on a sofa near the center.

Tommi stands across the room, with a knot of other musicians. He looks so happy, pretty and drunk. Weird sits at the bar, whiskey in hand, dour, but enjoying himself. Only Asia looks miserable, standing off to the side, while Myrna does his talking for him.

Trace is becoming bored, in spite of himself. He's done with this part of it, he thinks. He's done with LA. He wonders if Christian is asleep yet.

"I read the thing in the *LA Weekly* about you." A boy with a soft English accent stands in front of him, two glasses in hand.

Trace looks up and is captivated by almond-shaped eyes the color of amber. He smiles involuntarily and moves slightly to make room. "Did you?"

The boy offers him one of the glasses and wedges himself between the arm of the sofa and Trace. "And I really enjoyed your show tonight."

"I'm glad."

"My name is Mica," the boy tells him. "After the angel."

Trace laughs, takes a sip. He's never heard of an angel named Mica, but he says, "I can see the resemblance."

The boy blushes slightly. "I wanted to ask you about what you said in the article. About the century dying. Did you mean it? You want to be the one holding the match?"

"I mean everything I say." Trace shrugs. "When I say it."

"Me, too," Mica says. "For example, I really wanted to ask you about that so I could start a conversation with you."

Trace leans forward to set his glass aside, then he turns to face Mica. He really does look like an angel, Trace thinks. All long hair bleached to a soft white, gloss shining on his lips. "Is that what you wanted?" Trace murmurs. "Just a conversation?"

"Not the only thing," Mica admits.

The bracelets are cold on Trace's wrist and he doesn't care anymore why Christian deserted him. He reaches to take Mica by the back of the neck, kiss him, only remotely aware of cameras flashing as their lips meet. "I'm ready to get outta here," Trace breathes against Mica's ear. "You wanna go?"

On the way back to the Algonquin, Trace tries to hang on to his buzz by finishing the one of the bottles of champagne they swiped on the way out.

What if Christian decided to wait up for him? Some part of Trace knows how stupid, even cruel this is. But Mica begins to undress him. Trace lets thoughts of Christian go as the boy unknots his tie.

"How long a ride do we have?" Mica asks.

Trace forgets about what's waiting at the end. "As long as we want."

When the car arrives, Trace sends the driver away and leads Mica through the lobby to the elevator. On the way up, it occurs to Trace to ask Mica about himself.

"My dad was Japanese and Mum's English. That's where I grew up, a place called Brixton," Mica volunteers. "Did you wonder how I got into the party at Para Bellum?"

Trace shrugs. Not really, until just now, he thinks.

"It's my job." Mica gives him a blinding smile. "Marcus called me, you know, for eye candy."

"What?"

"Me, some other boys, a few girls, you know." Mica laughs. "I'm a whore."

"Oh." Trace tries to cover his surprise with a laugh, too. "Am I running a tab, then?"

Mica wraps his arms around Trace. "Not you."

The door slides open as they kiss again to a silent, dark room. The portraits of Christian are in shadow. Trace is torn between relief and disappointment. No confrontation tonight. His plan, decided on sometime between the car and the elevator, is to take Mica to the guest bedroom, but they don't get that far.

In the dream, Albrecht is lost again in the endless landscape of Trace's body. He wanders a velvet road through sharp hills and valleys. He can feel himself starving, wasting, with each step he takes. The beauty of this countryside is cruel. It yields nothing for him. When he wakes, he is not surprised to find himself alone as dawn creeps over the balcony. He shrugs into a white silk kimono robe that Trace has adopted. Albrecht smiles humorlessly, lighting a cigarette to mask the faint scent of him on the fabric.

He leaves the bedroom, thinking of perhaps phoning Marcus, or perhaps Timothy. After all, Trace is his responsibility now.

As Albrecht enters the main room, he realizes that won't be necessary.

Like modern art, the two bodies are so tangled that he has to take a step back to pick Trace out of the field. Albrecht freezes, waiting for some kind of monumental rage to sweep over him. He longs for a deep, murderous anger to rise up and cleanse him of this, but there is nothing.

Trace and a strange boy lay on the sofa in a tight embrace as though they had fallen asleep telling each other secrets. Though an empty bottle lies on its side nearby and their clothes are scattered all over the room, there is something innocent and beautiful about them that makes Albrecht's chest hurt. It hangs in the air, burns through his skin into his blood.

He pulls himself away and goes to the kitchen to find his coffee waiting. When the phone rings, he answers it.

"Trace?"

Albrecht suppresses a bitter laugh. "Good morning, Marcus. Have you lost track of him already?"

"He left with one of the boys from the party—"

"And now they're both here," Albrecht finishes for him.

"Yeah, well, tell Mica for me he's not gettin' a check for this," Marcus sputters. "Trace wasn't who he was s'posed to be entertaining."

Albrecht is almost comforted by Marcus's outrage, though he knows it's not for him. "You'll pay him whatever you promised. Make sure he doesn't feel the need to find compensation elsewhere."

"Don't tell me how to do my job," Marcus protests. "I work for the band, not you."

"Forgive me," Albrecht says, refraining from pointing out that ultimately, it was he who writes the checks. "I'm sure you'll handle it the best way possible."

There is a pause before Marcus growls a goodbye and hangs

up. Then the penthouse goes silent around Albrecht again. He is drawn back to them, unwillingly. He re-enters the room, inhales thin waves of energy. That Trace has left for him, Albrecht thinks. Space in him yawns empty and wide.

They have shifted closer. Mica lays on the outside edge, with his back to Albrecht, head against Trace's chest. Albrecht kneels down, reaches out to touch one pale shoulder and closes his eyes. At the contact, Mica gives a shudder that Albrecht absorbs. He flattens his palm against the boy's skin, covering the pulse. The cells of Albrecht's body suck hungrily at the life there. It's sweet and warm, but Albrecht knows that he could have it all and still never fill the place in him that longs for Trace.

"Shit."

Like a gunshot, Trace's voice cuts through to Albrecht, who opens his eyes and backs away, getting to his feet quickly.

The noise startles Mica awake and Trace has to catch him from falling. Albrecht reaches for his composure. "I see you found a way to amuse yourself without me."

"Don't," Trace warns him, eyes cold. He begins to unwind from Mica carefully. "C'mon," he whispers into the boy's ear. "We gotta get up."

The tenderness needles Albrecht. "I'll leave you to collect yourself." He retreats as far as the kitchen. He sits at the glass and chrome table to open today's newspaper, but can't get past the headlines. Twenty minutes pass before Trace reappears, clothed, smelling damp from the shower. "All right. He's gone."

Albrecht folds aside the paper and looks up. "I gather you enjoyed yourself last night."

Trace gives him a crooked smile and shakes his head. "You're pissed off."

Albrecht meets Trace's eyes and holds them, trying to decide if that is true or not. Then he turns it around. "Trace, what is it that you want from me?"

"What do you mean?"

"Truly." Albrecht laughs softly. "Were you hoping to simply hurt me, or did you want something more theatrical?"

Trace folds his arms across his chest and turns his back. "I was drunk, okay? And I was pissed that you don't give a shit about how important last night was to me. I didn't mean to bring him here. I just didn't think it out."

"If you had, you would have been more discreet, yes?" Albrecht says. "That's comforting."

"Look." Trace whirls. "You're the one who told me to act like a goddamn rock star. I was at a party. The prettiest boy there wants me to fuck him. Was I supposed to turn him down?"

You were supposed to be in love with me, Albrecht thinks. He closes his eyes and sees them again, like interlocking pieces of a puzzle he would never solve, perfect like fine sculpture. "No," he says coldly. "That isn't what I expect at all."

He pushes to his feet. "I'm sorry. I feel quite out of my element with you at times, and I just can't..."

"What?" Trace's voice is softer now.

"I cannot watch you walk away from me when I'm still in the room." He lets out his breath. This is more honest than Albrecht has ever intended to be.

Trace combs his fingers through his ghost-black hair and catches his lower lip in his teeth. "That isn't what I'm doing, Albrecht."

Trace says the name like he's testing it. Somehow, that hurts as much as anything. "It is," Albrecht insists. "You can't help it."

"I'm not in love with him." Trace shrugs.

"That isn't the point." Albrecht presses his fingers to his temples. "You were supposed to save me."

Trace tilts his head slightly, narrows his eyes. "Are you gonna throw me out?"

"I told you when we first met, I never want to let go of you," Albrecht says. "Now I can't."

Trace studies Christian. Underneath all his talk of love, there's something cold and unmovable about him. Trace can feel it buried in Christian, deep and dark. It feels dangerous. Trace longs to wake it.

"I'm sorry," Trace murmurs, closing the ground between them. When they kiss, there's a tremor along Christian's skin, like he's trying to resist. Trace reaches for the robe's sash. "I'm too selfish." He tastes surrender on Christian's lips. "Forgive me."

"I have no choice," Christian tells him.

His tone is unreadable to Trace, but his body is not. Trace lets himself be swept up in Christian's heat, lets himself react to

Christian's silk mouth.

Later, Christian lies next to Trace, studying him.

"What?" Trace finally asks, brushing Christian's fine hair back from his forehead. "What are you thinking about?"

"Mica."

"I told you it didn't mean anything," Trace protests.

"It means something," Christian insists. "You're attracted to him."

"So were you," Trace points out. "I could tell."

Christian smiles and sits up. With his back to Trace, he lights a cigarette. "Is that what you thought?"

Trace stretches and yawns. "Yeah, I mean, when I woke up you looked like you were going to kiss him or something."

"I was caught up in the moment, I suppose." Christian gives a shrug of one shoulder. "You both looked so…"

Trace raises an eyebrow. "Should I be shocked at where this is going?"

Christian sets his cigarette in the ashtray and turns back. "What are you talking about?"

Trace grins. "You never struck me as somebody who liked to watch. Or is this something else?"

Albrecht leans down to kiss Trace and gives him a smile. "If you are thinking of seeing him again…" He gives another shrug and moves to leave the bed.

Trace stretches and yawns, as Albrecht begins to dress. Trace watches him, waiting for him to complete his thought. When he doesn't, Trace asks, "I was supposed to save you from what?"

Asia sits on the side of the bed stiffly. "Fuckin' a." He has to hunch over to clutch his pounding head. "Did I drink a lot last night?"

Myrna laughs through a yawn. "Are you kiddin'? Me an' Weird had to carry you in here."

Asia winces, as glad as he is disconcerted that he can't remember.

"Does your head hurt?" Myrna sits behind him. She lays her cool fingers on the back of his neck. "I didn't even think you really drank anything but beer."

Barely that, Asia thinks, groaning softly. And this is why. This and how bad it got with Eric once he started. Asia only has to think of their dad to know that shit's hereditary.

He arches his back to stretch the aches out and smiles as Myrna's fingers slide over sore muscles. "That feels good. I'm sorry I passed out on you."

"Asia, everybody else I know ends up like that every night." She laughs. "I think you're entitled occasionally. Drink your water and lay back down."

She hands over an enormous plastic glass from the nightstand.

Asia groans again, but knows she's right. He ignores the churning in his stomach and drinks. He forces the water down his throat, eyes closed, head tilted back. He feels everything shift and slosh unpleasantly. "Fuck."

He lays on the edge of the bed, on his side, concentrating on keeping his stomach under control. Myrna stretches out against his back, holds him gently. "I'm sorry. Champagne is bad. We shoulda left sooner. Before Trace and that boy started goin' at it."

Asia groans again. The last image from the evening burned into his brain is of Trace in a long kiss with a stranger, amid a hail of flash. The memory twists in Asia's sour gut. "Myrna, I—"

"That's why you drank yourself stupid, Asia. You know it is." Her voice is soft, but he can hear hardness just under the surface.

He takes a deep breath and lets it out, stares out the window at the creeping smog over the valley. "It doesn't matter what Trace does, because I'm with you."

"You tryin' to lie to me, or yourself?"

He curls tighter in on himself, trying to think of something to say, but trying not to throw up is taking precedence. "Myrna, I can't... I'm sorry if I was stupid, but I am with you. You're my boyfriend."

She shifts closer to him, kisses his neck, making him shiver. "Asia, just close your eyes and start sleepin' it off, like a rock star."

He can't. Will she leave him if he can't give Trace up? Asia doesn't begin to know how to do it. In his mind, he feels Trace's hand on the back of his neck, drawing him in. Asia hears him say, "Am I in love with the wrong brother?"

No, he thinks, stopping the memory. Trace is done with this. I have to be done, too. Asia tries to push it all down deeper, bury it in some dark part of himself, and let it die there. He sucks in a lungful of air and lets it out quick. He turns to Myrna, circles his arms around her to press tight against her. "Don't dump me," he murmurs before kissing her.

"I didn't say that," she protests. "I just want you to be honest with—"

He kisses her again, hoping he doesn't taste as bad as he feels. "I don't care about what Trace does. You're my boyfriend."

"I am." She shifts them both so she's on top of him now.

Later, they lay face to face and Asia asks, "Do you really wish you were a boy?"

The corners of her mouth twitch upward. "What?"

"Because, you know, if you wanted..." He feels himself start to blush. "I'm gonna get paid a lot for the record, and if you wanted, we could find..."

"Asia." She laughs. "Are you offering to get me a sex change? Do you want me to be a real boy?"

"No. I mean, I don't care. I mean, I really like you, and I don't want you to have to be something you don't wanna be." He starts to inch away from her. "I kinda know what that feels like."

She pulls him back. "Asia, I would be crazy to ever dump you, wouldn't I? I would never find anybody like you again."

He blushes harder. He knows he's no one special.

"Have you ever had sex with another guy?"

That makes him frown. "What?"

"Trace, or anybody else?" she asks.

"I—" This time he does move away from her. He sits up on the edge of the bed, closes his eyes. There's a wide spot in Asia's brain where there's no memory at all. I'm not sure, he thinks, though he knows it makes no sense. He shakes himself and stands up. "Why?"

Myrna props herself on an elbow. "No reason, I guess. I just wondered."

"I'm not... I mean, I wasn't a virgin, before." Asia keeps his back to her, trying not to sound defensive.

"Okay."

"I mean, I—"

He's cut off by a pounding on the door. "Rise and shine, Sunshine." Weird's calling. "We gotta be down the hill in like an hour for some shit Marcus wants."

Asia forces himself out of bed and to the door. He opens it a crack. "Okay, already. Give me like ten minutes."

He's in the shower, face turned up to the water before he realizes that neither he nor Myrna answered the questions.

Asia rides in the back seat of the van, arm still curled around his middle, resisting the urge to lie down. Tommi turns to grin back at him sympathetically. "Asia, you look awful."

"That's good," he says. "Wouldn't want to be accused of false advertising."

Weird chuckles, wrenching the van around the corner at the bottom of the hill and lurching it into traffic. "Eggs. You need some protein. You drink that water?"

"Yeah." Asia narrows his eyes. He should have known the water was Weird's idea.

They meet Marcus at the Encino Denny's. Asia stomach clenches at the smell of grease and hash browns in the air. He reaches for his waiting water. Weird's cure of drowning has to kick in soon, Asia figures.

Marcus waits for everybody to slide into the booth, eyebrow raised, giving each of them a look that reminds Asia of his mother. He does not look pleased.

Marcus speaks finally. "Well, that could have gone better."

Weird shrugs. "Went better for some of us than others."

"What I mean is, now is the time for you to start to change your attitude. All of you." Marcus pauses as the waitress brings him a plate of eggs and chicken-fried steak. He cuts into the meat, then continues. "The performance was great. You're always great onstage. Offstage, you're like four guys waiting to see who fucks up first. We can't have that now."

"Okay, wait. I only see three of us here this morning." Weird scowls. "And none of us were the one who picked up a little hooker-boy in front of everybody and took him home. So, what the hell?"

Marcus holds up a hand and nods. "Okay, yeah. Trace's the one who makes things happen. That's his job. But you guys are the ones who need to keep this going. You guys are the wheels. His behavior has always been outrageous, right?"

Asia took another long drink of water, aware that Marcus was looking only at him. He nods slowly.

"Right. And you have to be the balance to that. Touring is hard work and this one will be fast and dirty. The sad fact is that you're not gonna be livin' like rock stars. You're only gonna be pretending to live like rock stars."

Weird pulls the ashtray across the table and gets his cigarettes out of his jacket. Today his lighter is shaped like a coffin. "We're cool, Marcus. But nobody can control Dellon. All you can do is hope to contain him."

10

The lobby of the Pantages Theater in Hollywood is the location for the video. It's been closed up for years and the crew has played up the dust and litter. Trace stands at the top of what had been the grand staircase, staring around at all the tarnished gilt wood, thinking of the Refugee Club and Christian's father.

Trace is dressed in the leathers he wore for the album cover with heeled red boots that go up to the knee.

There are candles on every available flat surface, from tiny nubs to a few huge pillars and candelabras, leaving the stale air oily with the scent of burning wax. The rest of the band is positioned on the way down, Weird and Asia with their guitars, Tommi leaning on a shred of hand railing. The director is one of Lionel's assistants, a dark-skinned woman with a fall of inky hair. As she tells them what she wants, Trace is fascinated with her long rainbow-colored nails.

Trace lip-syncs along with "No Outlet" as he descends, carefully stepping around the holes in the ruined carpet and the candles. Weird and Asia pretend to play as he passes them on the way down.

Trace misses Christian's presence during filming. In the process of recording the album, Trace fed off the hunger he read in Christian's eyes, used him as the audience, singing to him through the glass. He has come to rely on Christian as a substitute for the real thing.

They film quickly and are packed up some time after midnight. Trace knows that the rest of the band will stop for a beer on the way home. He'd like to go with them, talk about the tour, or just hang out, but he doesn't. He knows Christian will be waiting for him.

Trace finds him out on the balcony, leaning against the railing, gazing out at the city.

"Hey." Trace joins him, standing close.

Christian smiles, but doesn't look at him. "Did you enjoy the filming?"

Trace smiles back. "It was fun, but I missed you."

"Really." Christian sighs. "I thought perhaps I'd be in the way."

"Never." Trace frowns. "You never could be."

Christian answers him with silence, smile turning brittle. Trace feels the chill and is gripped with the unfamiliar feeling of uncertainty.

This distance has been between them since before Mica. Neither of them has spoken the boy's name after that morning, but Trace knows it changed things. Each time they've fucked since, Trace has wondered if Christian has found something lacking between them. That couldn't be, could it? Trace has no frame of reference for leaving a lover unsatisfied. "I was thinking about Mica this morning."

"Were you?" Christian's tone is cool. His smile doesn't falter. "What were you thinking?"

Trace stares out at the night sky, perfect as a movie set. No matter what, Albrecht Christian still owns the best view in the city. "That I wouldn't really mind sharing him."

"Ah." Christian finishes his cigarette and crushes it in the crystal tray on the railing. "With me?"

"Of course." Trace laughs. "Who else? Isn't that what you've been thinking? I saw how you looked at him when he was here before."

"Are you truly so bored?" Christian asks softly. "If you loved me, you wouldn't feel the need for this, I think."

"I don't know. Maybe I am in love with you." He reaches for Christian's lighter and pulls his own cigarettes from the pocket of his leather jacket. He lights up, using the pause to think. "I don't know what it feels like."

"Like losing parts of yourself all the time. Like dying, yet you don't want it to stop." Christian laughs. "You're wondering now why anyone would submit to this, yes?"

"No, I…" Trace has to look away. Is that what Christian meant when he said 'I love you?' "I don't mean it to be like that."

Christian walks away, pausing at the threshold to the bedroom. "Invite him to dinner."

"Are you sure?" Trace raises an eyebrow.

"You will see him whether I want it or not, yes?"

Trace shakes his head. Lying seems like the kindest thing. "No. Not if you don't want me to."

"Invite him to dinner, but call him tomorrow. Come to bed tonight."

Trace does, but stays only until Christian falls asleep. He's restless. He knows there's a piece missing from him. Christian has brought it to his attention. Trace wonders if wanting to love him counts for anything.

He sits in the moonlight that streams in through the French doors and watches Christian sleep. He tries to find some of the wonder he felt the first night, that morning, staring down at Christian. When he closes his eyes, he gets flashes of Mica, warm and soft against his skin, and it opens a treacherous longing in him.

He gets up to rummage around in the guest room, where most of his things are now. He opens the case that holds Eric's old twelve-string and his notebook. He brushes his fingers over the strings of the guitar, pulling a whisper from them, but leaves it, taking just the notebook.

He drifts into the living area of the penthouse and curls up in a chair by the window, opening to a blank page. He leans his head back and closes his eyes, this time holding the vision of Christian, cold and hard and perfect. I'll stay with you as long as I can, Trace thinks, touching the pen to the paper. Not for love, but for the want of it.

When it comes, it sweeps both Christian and Mica away. The melody rains down on Trace like a hailstorm, catching him inside of it. Words spill onto the page. He loses track of the moment he stops writing and sleep takes him, but he wakes again as dawn pales the window. He closes the notebook without reading it and goes back to Christian. He slides into bed and fits himself to Christian's body, kissing his neck and lips.

"Trace." Christian lets his name out on a sigh.

"Mm." Trace murmurs as Christian's arms circle him. "I wrote a song for you."

"Really?" Christian opens his eyes and smiles. "For me or about me?"

Trace laughs softly. "Is there a difference?"

"Will you think of me every time you sing it?"

Trace kisses him, opens his mouth against Christian's and

thinks, yes, every time. When they're done he says, "Always."

Christian's hands slide downward on Trace's body. "Good."

Trace picks Mica up in Christian's Jaguar. He's happy to see Mica again, but a little nervous about how the evening will play out. In some ways, Trace knows he's still a boy from the Midwest. Three-ways are the stuff of fantasy, but he's never considered it literally. On the way back to the penthouse, he looks over at Mica and grins. "I guess you made a pretty good impression on Herr Christian."

Mica smiles back. He is digging around in his overnight bag. Trace frowns involuntarily when Mica comes up with something familiar. Trace asks anyway, in case he's wrong. "What's that?"

Mica shrugs, unzipping his works. "Just a little bump. It's coke. I'm gonna need to shoot up before we go in, okay?"

Need to? Trace wonders. He hasn't considered that this life might not come naturally to Mica. He shrugs. "Okay. I thought people snorted coke."

"Sure, if you wanna lose your nasal membranes." Mica laughs. "This is much neater."

Ten minutes later, parked in the Algonquin's garage, watching the needle slide into Mica's ivory skin, Trace wonders if that's true.

Albrecht has spent all of dinner watching Trace with Mica, keeping himself from them. They are easy with each other, sharing the same language that Trace has with the band. Trace's smile is softer for Mica, his laugh lighter, quicker. As the evening progresses, Albrecht stays back, stays the observer. At first in the bedroom, Trace is shy under Albrecht's scrutiny, then, true to what he is, he starts to enjoy the audience. He settles his gaze on Albrecht over Mica's shoulder, drawing Albrecht in.

When he joins them, he reaches for Mica, brushing his fingers against the softness of the boy's fine skin. He presses Mica between them and stretches to kiss Trace. He pulls back and licks his lips, then kisses Mica.

The boy shimmers with Trace's energy and Albrecht takes it from his lips, then his skin. Albrecht hears himself moan and

Trace's eyes catch him again. Albrecht feels like an addict, with just the taste of what he needs. Enough to keep him alive, but not enough to make him want to live.

Still, he can't stop. He searches Mica's body for more whispers of Trace, taking the energy beneath it too.

It heals him, almost against his will. Everything goes away but the heat of Mica until it's over.

Trace and Mica sleep and Albrecht feels the flow of energy pulse in him. He feels as though he can transmute himself into something more than earthbound, soar off the balcony and over the city, a pale, hard bird of prey. That makes him smile. This power is so fleeting that by the time the sun has burned through the smog, it will be gone.

It's been months since he felt this way. No, years. Since long before the first night Trace spent here, he realizes.

The next morning Albrecht sees changes in Mica, though neither he nor Trace notice. Not yet.

Albrecht separates himself from them once again as they eat. He takes his coffee at the breakfast bar, secretly relishes the feeling of being filled before it fades. He turns his back on the tender scene the two of them make at the table. He doesn't want to see Trace's fingers slide through the length of Mica's hair or the smiles they share. Albrecht hears the soft clink of the bracelets, links of a chain that Trace doesn't feel.

"Did you hear me?" Trace breaks into Albrecht's thoughts.

"What?" He looks up. "I'm sorry, no. What were you saying?"

"I think Mica should come on tour with me."

Albrecht frowns.

"I need somebody to help with hair and makeup and clothes back stage. And to make sure it all gets to the next gig, right?"

"I suppose, not that you don't already have one assistant." Albrecht looks at the boy now, still shadowy from last night. "Do you have any experience with this sort of thing?"

When Mica meets his eyes, Albrecht feels a connection, an understanding, on some level of what has been taken from him. Albrecht looks away first.

"No," Mica says evenly. "But it doesn't really sound like rocket science."

"And you would prefer it to what you're doing now?"

The boy laughs. "You mean tricking? What do you think?"

"I'm gonna tell Marcus today," Trace decides.

"I'm sure he'll be thrilled," Albrecht says, gathering up his coffee cup to return it to the kitchen.

"What do you mean?" Trace follows him.

Albrecht shakes his head, feeling cornered. "The world is bigger than just the inside of the club now. There was a picture of you kissing him in the paper—on MTV. More people are talking about that than your album."

"Who gives a shit? Fuck, it's not as though I'm in the closet. I never have been." Trace frowns.

Albrecht sighs. That innocence again. "No. And your audience understands you. They always have. Part of the allure is that unspoken dare you offer them. But this is different."

"Really." Trace's voice loses the anger. "I don't get it."

Mica joins them. "What he means is, you can be gay or bi, or whatever you want. You can hint that you are, too. But people don't want to see it in action. Pisses 'em off."

"But that's bullshit." Trace shakes his head.

"It's the way it is." Mica gets up and comes to Albrecht, lays a light hand on his shoulder and smiles. "I hope you were entertained last night."

Albrecht smiles back, feeling an echo of Mica's energy ghost through him. He reaches up to take the boy's hand, meets his amber eyes. Sean, Albrecht thinks, pressing his lips to the palm. "I…. You know I was. In fact, I'm not at all sure I want you going anywhere."

A shiver passes through Mica as Albrecht slides his hand away. His eyes are on Trace next. "I think I'd prefer Mica here, with me, while you're out conquering America. I'm bound to be lonelier than you are, yes?"

Trace frowns slightly. Albrecht knows he's put him in a box now. To protest would prove to Albrecht that he's jealous. So Trace shrugs one shoulder and says, "Whatever Mica wants."

Mica takes a soft breath, still standing next to Albrecht. The connection has been made; Albrecht feels it, the pull within him, for the boy. The part of him that still cares for survival wakes, hungry again.

In the end, it will win. Albrecht knows it. He will win. He sees in

Trace's eyes that he knows it, too.

The first time Asia sees the pictures of Trace in the *LA Weekly*, it's a shock. It's surreal enough, seeing him pose for the camera, but Asia can't shake the feeling that the end result looks nothing like Trace. Of course, the picture that Asia is looking at now in the nightlife section of the *Weekly* isn't posed, at least Asia doesn't think it was. It's Trace, with the boy from the party, frozen in a kiss that leaves nothing to the imagination. It's everywhere Asia looks. Almost every day, Marcus has a new article that contains it. He says he's pissed off, but it's obvious the publicity pleases him. Asia thinks back to what Weird said about containing Trace. It wasn't possible.

Asia wonders what Herr Christian thinks about it. Was he as jealous as Asia? Why did he let Trace go to the party alone anyway?

Asia shakes his head. It's not his business how they run their affair. He doesn't really want to know, does he?

There's a knock at the door and he sighs, tosses the paper down and climbs to his feet. That would be Trace, the only one on time for the meeting. He wonders how long before the others show. It's not that Asia doesn't miss Trace; it's just that it's getting more and more awkward between them. There seems to be so much less to talk about now.

"Trace—uh, hi," Asia says as he opens the door, and then freezes. The fact that Trace is standing on the step with Herr Christian and the boy from the picture does nothing to put Asia more at ease. "Hello, Herr Christian and…"

Trace smiles and walks in, the other two trailing in his wake. He leads all of them back into the living room. "You didn't meet Mica at the party, did you?"

"Uh, no." Asia looks away as the boy says hello. He folds the picture inside the paper as he sits back down.

They all settle on the couch, Albrecht Christian between Trace and Mica. "I've heard your album," Mica begins, smiling shyly. "It's really good. It's gonna be a big hit."

He looks Asian, but has an English accent. His hand discreetly slips into Herr Christian's.

"Thanks," Asia says. "I hope so."

The rest of the band shows up finally and Asia is grateful not to have to make small talk with the strange trio. It's hard enough to think of something to say to Herr Christian, but now it's all Asia can do not to stare.

Marcus opens his Day Runner and begins to give them dates. The place between Asia's shoulder blades itches. The video is set to play on MTV next week. The first gig on the tour is at the beginning of next month, in San Francisco. Asia feels a protective numbness set in and he can't absorb the particulars. Somebody will tell him later, he knows.

Trace lies across Mica's rumpled bed, staring at the water stain that spreads from the light at the center of the ceiling down the wall to the window. The room is barely big enough for the bed. The only other furnishings consist of a collection of battered milk crates, stacked like shelves, stolen McDonald's trays laid out on the top to hold a little TV with rabbit ears, a boom box, and makeup and cassettes scattered between the two. Somehow the cramped bareness of it all makes Trace homesick. He misses Asia, as though they don't see each other every day at the studio.

"I don't know what to pack," Mica says finally, after pawing everything over. He dumps his partially filled bag on the bed. "I can always come back later, I guess."

Trace doesn't respond. When he sits up, his bracelets jangle softly. "I didn't think things would end up quite like this."

Mica pauses, sitting next to him. "Don't be like that. Albrecht said you were the one who suggested calling me again in the first place."

Trace raises an eyebrow at the familiarity. After one night, Mica's moving in and using Christian's first name. Trace feels a bitter smile sharpen his lips. "I didn't think he'd take you away. I just wanted to see you again and I didn't want him to be jealous." He looks into Mica's eyes and wonders if the angel thing is really true. Then he laughs. "I guess he's not jealous."

Mica touches Trace's face, pulls him into a kiss. "He loves you, Trace. When he was watching us, it was all you. I could tell. His eyes never left you."

Trace remembers. He'd been performing for Christian, but then he'd lost him somehow. He tries something else. "You'd rather be with him than me?"

Mica's smile is unreadable. He eases Trace down onto his back. "What do you want me to say?" His hands slide up under Trace's tee shirt, nails scoring his chest.

Trace closes his eyes. Mica is a whore, no matter how much Trace likes him. He turns his face away to look out the window as Mica's hands go to his jeans, unbuttoning and unzipping. Trace feels himself respond appropriately, but it's from very far away.

"It's business with Albrecht," Mica tells him, as Trace catches his fingers in Mica's white/gold hair. Trace pulls his mouth where he wants it, savoring the warm softness of it before the boy can tell him which he is, business or pleasure. Trace pushes himself deeper in, not wanting to know.

While they're fucking, Trace finds himself listening, trying to translate the sounds Mica makes, wondering if they're true, or for Trace's benefit. He thinks of watching Christian with the boy. Of Mica's face when he came. Was it all show? Is it now?

He thinks of Christian saying, "How would I ever know if you were being genuine?"

What does it matter? Trace thinks again, thrusting one last time into Mica. I'm a good enough actor and it matters not at all.

He rolls to the edge of the bed and stares at a toppled plastic *Empire Strikes Back* cup on the milk crate shelving unit. Bad printing of sweet-faced Luke Skywalker stares back at him. This doesn't matter. Trace takes a breath. The tour, the album, the band: that's what matters.

"Albrecht will wonder what you've done with me," Mica says.

"No. He won't."

That night Albrecht and Mica go to bed and Trace is alone with his notebook again. The words that come out of him this time are cold and strong, the chorus like a razor.

Your smile shatters mirrors
That lie together
Make me pay and pay
Cracks spider through your face

And you make me pay and pay
'cause I'm your best trick of all, baby,
The one you don't forget

He feels the music rise in him, bitter and sharp, and it makes him smile.

The bedroom door is ajar and he hears movement, Mica's soft moans beyond. Trace pauses, but decides to move farther down the hall. He goes into the spare room and takes Eric's guitar out this time. He sits in the middle of the bed, curled around the instrument, head over the strings. He feels like Asia, way back in Ann Arbor, alone in the middle of the night.

Trace sat next to Asia on the couch and took the glass bottle of Tab out of Asia's hand for a swallow. He shuddered as he sucked it down. "Fuck me, I don't know how you drink that shit. It's gonna rot your colon out."

Asia took his eyes off the television screen to look at Trace. "I know."

He seemed so sad, resigned. Trace smiled faintly. "Maybe you could just lean your head back and close your eyes. I'll stay with you until you're asleep."

Trace lets out his breath, blinking the memory away. Asia had once told him that he felt like the last survivor in a zombie movie at 4 a.m., like he was the only person living in the world. Trace chords the guitar and strums softly, thinking that might have been the moment he realized he loved Asia.

Trace lets the night crash around him. He lets his breathing become deafening inside his own skull. He tries to think of Asia, sitting in front of the television tonight, staring at the images, resolutely drinking his Diet Coke, waiting for dawn to save him, too.

Albrecht wakes warm and satisfied, Mica curled in his arms, but it doesn't last. He lets out a sigh and puts the boy aside. Mica barely stirs before burrowing against the pillow Albrecht's just left.

Albrecht goes to find Trace. He is asleep in his clothes on top of the coverlet on the guest bed. He lies on his stomach, stretched out next to his battered old guitar. One bare foot trails over the edge of the bed. Albrecht brushes a finger up the length of its sole.

Trace twitches awake at the contact and twists toward him, dislodging the spiral bound notebook that ended up under his folded arms.

"You must have fallen asleep while you were working," Albrecht says. He bends to pick it up, carefully folding it closed before handing it back.

Trace combs his fingers through his hair. "It was late. I didn't want to disturb you."

Albrecht arches an eyebrow. It's not hard to hear the edge in Trace's tone and the irony's not lost on Albrecht. If Mica was going away with Trace, Albrecht doubts he'd have left them alone all night to sulk. Albrecht refrains from pointing this out. He loves Trace and doesn't want to waste the time they have left with this. He sits down. "You said you wrote a song for me."

"Yeah, I did."

Albrecht says, "May I hear it now?"

Trace laughs, looking away, and Albrecht is certain he sees a hint of embarrassment in his eyes. "I guess. I haven't been over it since, so I don't know how it'll sound."

Of course that is a lie, Albrecht thinks. Trace knows exactly. "Please."

Trace sighs and combs his hair back again. Then he shifts a bit to pick up the guitar. His voice is soft over the chords. He keeps his eyes down on the strings as he plays.

The song reaches into Albrecht and pulls everything to the surface. He feels exposed. He closes his eyes, lets out his breath. Trace's voice is unrelenting, Albrecht feels struck by the words. There's no love there for him, nothing but truth. When Trace stops singing, Albrecht opens his eyes again. "I don't expect to live through losing you."

Trace's mouth twitches up at the corners for a split second, then he sets the guitar aside. "You're not losing me."

Not yet, Albrecht hears the rest of the sentence as though Trace had added it. Not while you still need me, he thinks, but knows it's more complicated than that. "It's a beautiful song, Trace. I don't know what to say."

Trace shrugs. "I… I wish you would just come with me."

Albrecht is not so naive. Certainly, that is what Trace wishes at this moment, but that won't last. Albrecht is sure he doesn't want to be there when Trace realizes that. "I am sorry I brought Mica here," he says. "I'm sorry you feel that he…interferes with you and I."

Trace shrugs again. "I'm the one who called him, right? I shouldn't be surprised how it turned out."

"I love you, Trace," Albrecht says softly. "More than anyone I can remember. More than…" More than his own life, Albrecht realizes, but keeps himself from saying that. Instead, he reaches for Trace, traces the angles of his face softly. When they kiss, Albrecht keeps his eyes open, watches Trace's close, the brush of lashes on his glass-smooth skin. He feels Trace pulling him closer, his hands on Albrecht's body, then, in the silence of the penthouse, a shower starts. Trace opens his eyes too, pulls back, and bites his lower lip.

"I know that you love me." He looks down at his bare feet. "I have to get going today. Marcus has stuff planned."

Trace knows he's being bitchy for no reason. He understands the practicality of Mica for Christian. He understands that Christian now needs a substitute for him, that he can't bear going back to being alone. It takes nothing away from how Christian feels about Trace. Still, Trace thinks as he hits the freeway in the direction of Para Bellum, he feels like he needs to punish Christian somehow.

It's not that he expects to be faithful while the band is on the road. Trace's never been able to stay monogamous. He doesn't understand the concept. But he begins to understand how other lovers might have felt betrayed now. And he doesn't like the feeling.

At Para Bellum, he rides the elevator up to Marcus's office and gives a big grin to the girl answering phones. "Hi, Allie."

"Mr. Dellon, hello." She smiles back, blushing when he comes around to sit on her desk. She is about Tommi's age, with short choppy hair dyed blood red and purple eye makeup and nail polish. "He's on the phone, but you can go in."

"I'll wait." Trace brushes a finger against one of her nails. "That's pretty," he says. "Is it Wet N Wild?"

"Yeah." She pulls her fingers up into a fist against the desk. "It takes a million coats though, 'cause it's so cheap."

"Tell me," Trace laughs, wiggling his own ragged sky blue ones back at her. "Look at this."

"I love the album." She tells him, more at ease now. "I went out to buy it last night."

"Thanks," Trace says. "It's been sellin' great and the video's gonna be on MTV this week."

"Ooo," she gasps. "That's amazing. You guys are going to be so big."

Damn right, Trace thinks.

Allie glances at her phone and one of the lights goes off, then flashes. She snatches the receiver up and says, "Marcus, Mr. Dellon is here."

When she puts it down again, Trace says, "Call me Trace."

"Go on in, Trace."

Marcus is driving him over to one of the TV studios to film a MTV spot for the video. They ride in Marcus's Trans Am with the top down. Trace leans back and closes his eyes. He smiles as the hot wind off the highway whips at his hair.

He's glad Marcus doesn't attempt conversation. Instead Trace replays his morning with Albrecht Christian. Maybe, he thinks, this is love. Not since Eric has Trace missed anyone's presence like he'd missed Christian last night.

The motion of the car and the sun on his face send Trace to sleep, deeper than he'd gotten last night. In his dreams, Christian and Eric smear into each other, the textures of their skin, the taste of them.

When they stop, Marcus flips down the visor on Trace's side and says, "Do something with your hair."

They enter the studio and Trace gets it in one take. He stands in front of a giant MTV logo and blows a kiss. "I'm Trace Dellon. Don't miss me and my band, Black Light, in our new video, out at midnight, Eastern Standard time on J.J. Jackson's Garage."

11

The record shop on Brand Street in Glendale is small, so it looks much more crowded than it really is. At least that's what Asia tells himself as he sits at the end of the table, like a spectator. Tommi and Weird sit between him and Trace. Around them, people jostle each other for a chance to ask Trace to sign their album cover and, more occasionally, the rest of the band too. Asia nods and smiles at all the wishes of good luck on tour and assurances of how great they are and longs for it just to be over. He can't go back, he thinks again, for the hundredth time. He watches Trace take a few seconds with each person. He shakes hands or smiles, winks or kisses, depending. Asia knows that for the time Trace focuses on them, touches them, they feel like they're the only person in the world to him. Asia looks away, remembering his few minutes of that attention.

After it's over, Asia drives Myrna to her gig. He blinks in surprise as the DJ on the radio says the name of the band. At first, there's nothing familiar about the song that follows. Asia can't connect himself to the music, until Trace's voice, tight and sharp like fine diamond sand, twists the words, so that they cut straight through Asia. Even over the shitty car speakers, Trace's voice reaches for him. Asia leans forward, turns it up.

"How does it feel?" Myrna asks, turning the volume up even farther. "Is it the first time you've heard it on the radio?"

There's a lump in Asia's throat. He nods and swallows past it. "It feels...like it's somebody else."

Myrna slides closer to him on the seat. "It's not, Asia. That's you."

No, he thinks. It's not me. Trace's voice, without Trace present, chills him. The permanence of what they have done settles on him. Asia stares at the slowing traffic ahead of them. Now, no matter what else happens, this would always be them, this song, frozen in this moment.

At Corman's, he sits at his regular table, hating that there is only a finite number of shows left that he'll be allowed to watch. He knows what Myrna will say, "You'll be back. It's not for that long," but Asia feels like this is the end of everything between them.

As the band starts on the last song of the last set, Asia pushes to his feet to go to Myrna's dressing room.

Asia stands up as Myrna enters. She slides an arm around his waist and pulls him against her so she can kiss him. Asia closes his eyes and lets out his breath as their lips meet. Her fingers tangle the hair at the back of his neck.

"Mm," she says. "You seem happy."

"You were great tonight." He avoids the subject, trying to memorize the lines of her body against his. He tries to kiss her again.

"Wait." She laughs, kicking the shut the door to the tiny room. She reaches a hand between his legs. "You're in a really good mood."

Yeah-right, he thinks, welcoming the electric current her touch sends through him. He unbuttons the leather vest she's wearing and lets her guide his head down to her breasts. He can taste sweat on her skin, feel the hitch of her breath under his mouth. Maybe, he thinks disjointedly, he won't go. He'll quit Black Light and be Myrna's roadie. She's pushing his head lower and Asia kneels, hands skimming up her thighs, under her skirt.

After he's caught his breath, he looks up at her face and says, "We're leaving in eight days."

"That's great. It'll be great, Asia." She smooths her skirt back down and sits on the van bench that serves as a couch. She pulls Asia down with her. "Do you know where you're playin' first?"

He shrugs. "They were talking about it, but I..."

"Asia." She sighs out his name, throws her arm around his shoulder. "This is how you do it. They're playin' the video. The single's on the radio. Now people wanna see you."

He corrects her. "They wanna see Trace." He puts his head on her shoulder and closes his eyes. Right now, it's just the two of them. The sounds of the bar throwing the drunks out is muffled through the door and Asia wishes it could always be just like this. No Trace, no album, just Myrna and him. "I don't wanna go away. I'll miss you too much."

She laughs low in her throat. "You won't, 'cause I'm comin' with you."

"But," he lifts his head again, "you gotta play here. And I don't know if I even get my own room, or anything. I don't——"

"Asia." She laughs again. "I'm your boyfriend. I'm not lettin' you go without me. Trust me, Marcus won't mind. You'll be one less guy that needs looking after."

"Can we just go home now?" He's too tired, suddenly, for anything else.

"Poor baby." She laughs, getting up and dislodging him. "Success is so hard for you."

When they get to the house in Encino, it's dark and the van isn't in the driveway. Asia smells pot smoke as he crosses the threshold of the front door. Myrna smiles and says, "Well, Tommi's here."

There's a burst of laughter and splashing from the terrace and a voice, along with Tommi's. Asia tenses, thinking of John, and goes out to see.

"Hey, guys!" Tommi is in the hot tub with another boy, sloshing water over the side. "This is Justin. He was at the record store today, y'know, for my autograph."

"Really." Myrna walks over to take the joint from Tommi.

"Yeah, he saw me on MTV and thought I was cute."

"Yeah." Justin splashes over to Tommi and kisses him, sloppy. "I'm his groupie."

Myrna passes the joint back to them and turns to kiss Asia, puffing smoking into his mouth as their lips meet. "Well, try to keep it down out here, will ya? Me and Asia are gonna go fuck."

Later Asia sits on the side of his bed, listening to the giggling and towel snapping, wishing he could be as happy as Tommi. He is depressed by the jumbled mess of clothes strewn around his room. They are a combination of both his and Myrna's. He wonders how he'll decide what to take. He remembers a packing list from summer camp and wonders if Marcus will give him one of those. Toothbrush, towel, deodorant, underwear for each day, plus extra in case.

The plane to San Francisco is the first one Asia's ever been on. He clutches his can of Diet Coke and closes his eyes, stomach tightening at the sensation of being hurtled through the air. After takeoff, Myrna reaches over and unbuckles him. "It's not gonna do you much good if we suddenly slam back into the ground, baby," she teases, kissing him.

"Thanks." He's more frightened of actually getting to their destination than the ride there. They've never been to San Francisco. He knows it's not going to be like a show in LA. Hell, in LA the audience was half full of people who'd fucked Trace. They were set up to love him. Nobody up north knows them. "I'm okay. I'm not gonna puke or anything."

"Good, because you'd definitely be less cute, hurling in my lap."

He laughs despite the fear curling around in him. "Then I guess the honeymoon is over."

It is too short a flight for him to get any sleep, but he manages to close his eyes, burrowing against Myrna's shoulder. Under the engine noise, he can sense the rest of the band, scattered among the other passengers. He breathes in lungfuls of Trace's cigarette smoke from the back of the cabin, wonders how his stomach is doing. A few rows ahead of Asia and Myrna, he hears Tommi pestering Weird with his expectations of the new city and Weird's low rumble in response. Asia knows at this moment he is still a part of them, would always be part of them, no matter what. The thought smooths out the knots in his stomach. He sighs a deep breath, the scent of Myrna making his life perfect.

It doesn't last. The puking comes later, before the show. Asia is crouched at the toilet in the bathroom backstage, Trace—not Myrna—hovering over him. "I'm sorry," Asia chokes out. "I can't—"

More acid from the Diet Coke burns its way out of him and all he can do is shudder. Trace's fingers are cool in Asia's hair as he gathers it back. He lays a damp cloth at the back of Asia's neck. Somehow, that makes him shudder again. "It's okay." Trace bends, speaks close to Asia's ear. "We have plenty of time before we go on. You're gonna be okay."

Why, Asia thinks dissolutely, did he ever think he could do this? "Trace, I can't."

He hates the broken, weepy sound in his voice.

"You can." Trace pulls him to his feet, turning him so they face each other. He uses the washcloth on Asia's face now, gently. "It'll be just the same as the Refugee. You don't even fucking look at them. You just look at me."

Asia tries to breathe through his mouth. The tiny room around them is soured now, but Trace doesn't give any indication he smells it. He is so beautiful tonight; he doesn't even look human. He looks like he is made of light and glass, his skin shimmering against the suit he wears, cut tight in at the waist, accenting his hips. Asia looks down, to stop himself from blushing, and focuses on Trace's bare feet, nails polished a sky blue.

Asia steps away, catching the contrasts between them in the mirror. "I'd better get another shower, huh?"

Trace gives him the cloth and smiles. "You gonna be okay alone then?"

Asia feels heat on his face and nods, but thinks: no, don't leave me.

Trace steps out of the bathroom, closing the door behind him gently. He wonders if this will happen to Asia every night they play. Trace lifts his hand to comb his fingers through his hair and is distracted by the clink of Christian's bracelets, chilling his wrist, under the cuff of his shirt. Trace slides them off to look at them. He runs his fingers around the inside of each, one smooth and plain, the other like two vines twined around each other. He felt how much the gift meant to Christian the night he gave them, the first night of Mica. Instead of replacing them, Trace puts them into his suit pocket. They mean nothing to him, not with the memory of Christian and Mica together so fresh.

Tommi walks in and glances toward the bathroom door. "He sounded bad."

Trace smiles faintly, thinking how odd to be having this conversation about Asia. "He just needs a shower. Once we get on stage, he'll be okay."

They both know that isn't entirely true, but Asia will at least get through it.

Of course, Trace is right. The Fillmore is a little bigger than the Refugee, but Trace isn't intimidated by size. Asia stays back, close to the drums. When Trace glances back between songs, Asia seems sweaty, like he has a fever.

Even though they are here to see Live Wire, it doesn't take long for the audience to make their decision about him. Trace feels it when they surge forward and he meets them at the very edge of the stage. He leans out, reaching for them, as Weird begins the intro to "No Outlet," and hands grasp for him. Trace grins as he starts singing, stretching further out, feeling dozens of hands brushing his body and face. From the corner of his eye, he sees Tim, in the wings, tensed, waiting. Trace has the urge to fling himself into to the mob to see if they would catch him.

He doesn't get the chance to find out. As their hands close in on him, he feels himself snatched back from behind. Tim, he thinks, letting himself be reeled back. But he's wrong.

"Be careful." It's Asia, shouting in his ear above the music and crowd noise. He lets go of Trace and retreats back to his spot.

"They always said it never rained here." Mica shakes his head. "That's why I came here. It's always raining in England."

Albrecht smiles faintly. Of course. Hollywood never let it rain in the films. He rises to push the doors open and step out onto the balcony. This is one of the beautiful things about this place. If you believed all the lies, it could take you by surprise. Albrecht lets the rain cool his skin. The sensation brings him a scrap of memory, sweet and painful.

"Whatever are you doing out here?" Albrecht asked, from the stage door of the club.

Sean stood in the alley behind the theater amid castoff lumber and trash from construction. His face was turned upward, toward the raindrops. He stretched his arms out, eyes closed, as though he could catch the storm in his hands. Albrecht stepped into the downpour to pull Sean into his arms and bent to kiss him.

"I thought it never rained here," he murmured into Sean's wet hair.

Sean shivered. "Not often."

Albrecht kissed him again, tasting the faint chemical taint of the liquid smog clash with the spice of Sean's lips. Albrecht's eyes closed too, feeling Sean feed him. He parted Sean's lips to feel the catch of the boy's breath inside his mouth.

"Hey."

Mica's voice intrudes and Albrecht loses the ginger of Sean's lips on his. He is only cold and wet. He opens his eyes and turns to the boy. "Yes?"

"It's cold. C'mon back to bed. We can watch the rain from in here."

Albrecht lets Mica lead him inside. The rain pelts the windows, streaking the room in marbled gray. Mica undresses him and Albrecht surrenders himself. He lets his body take what it needs from Mica.

"Is it Trace?" Mica asks him finally. "Why did you insist on staying here, when all you really want is to be with him?"

Albrecht lets out his breath, smiling in the darkness. "I was thinking of someone else, actually, just now, but I suppose it is always Trace, at the heart of it, isn't it?"

Mica doesn't answer, but Albrecht gets the sense that he is waiting for more explanation. Albrecht continues, "I would only be in the way on a rock and roll tour, don't you think? I have no wish to illustrate to him how far removed I am from his life, really."

"He knows how much you love him," Mica tells Albrecht, sliding up against him again. "I think it scares him." He pauses to kiss Albrecht. "I can't imagine running away from something like you, but I think that's what he's doing now. If you loved me, I would never leave you."

Albrecht sighs again, feeling Mica's hands glide over his skin. You'll never leave me regardless, he thinks.

He doesn't sleep the rest of the night and only has the sound of the rain for company. Sean won't even appear in his mind again and Trace is lost to him. Albrecht can feel the boy sleeping in his arms becoming more fragile, brittle from the contact, and knows that this won't last forever either.

12

The fact that all the guys in Live Wire turn out to be assholes doesn't stop Asia from feeling a little sorry for them. Their first album was a huge hit. Every song seemed to chart, become an instant classic. The second album: not so much. Until Black Light joined the tour, ticket sales had been slow and they are not exactly grateful to Black Light. Every time Trace steps onto the stage, he steals their audience right out from under them.

Tonight is no different. Black Light tears through their set. Asia can barely hear himself play over the cries of the crowd. He has to keep his head down, eyes on his strings. Trace's name, screamed by a thousand different people, rips at Asia's concentration.

When they're done, the crowd begs Trace to stay, then to come back. Hunt Bail, Live Wire's lead singer, passes Trace sullenly in the wings. Trace gives him a sharp smile. "Have a good show."

"Faggot," Hunt growls.

As they file into the green room, Trace laughs. "I guess they won't ask us to open for them again."

"Fuckers." Weird narrows his eyes, lighting up a cigarette. "Gonna get my money back for their record."

Back at the hotel, Marcus has insisted that everybody show up for the party. Asia wonders what he's hoping for. Fistfight?

The suite is packed with people. Not just the band, but roadies and press, too. And of course Live Wire's usual attendance of groupies. Asia immediately seeks out a place in the corner and waits for Myrna to get them drinks.

Hunt Bail is in the thick of it, still in his spandex, his silk shirt open to the waist. He has a bottle of whiskey in his hand and is surrounded by four bleach blondes. Asia wonders, as he watches one of the girls go for his crotch, how old he is. He looks exhausted, crow's feet at the corners of his eyes. He seems way more interested in the bottle than the attentions of the girls.

Marcus cruises by and takes it away, saying something to Hunt. The singer shakes his head and laughs. "Fuck you, Marcus. Keep that little faggot away from me."

Asia sighs, can't hear Marcus's response. Myrna sits down next to Asia and passes him a cold Diet Coke. "Won't be sorry to see the last of them, huh?"

"I guess," Asia says, halfheartedly. He sees Trace begin to cross the room. He has that same razor-tipped smile on his face when he gets to Hunt. Side by side, the comparison is cruel. Trace is graceful, lean in his clingy jumpsuit, while Hunt isn't even making the effort to conceal his beer gut.

Asia climbs to his feet, just in case Hunt takes it bad. Marcus tries to deflect Trace, but Trace shakes him off. He makes a show of offering his hand. "Enjoyed working with you."

Before Hunt responds, one of his girls stands up and kisses Trace hard on the lips. "I think I love you."

"It won't be like this forever," Hunt tells him as Asia approaches. "You won't always be what they want."

Albrecht stabs out his cigarette and shifts to watch Mica fold himself up to slide a hypodermic needle between his toes. When he's done, he discards it to the bedside table on his side.

Albrecht thinks of Sean. "Do you need that to do this?"

The drug hits Mica and his muscles twitch. He grins. "This is easy. I need the coke for other things."

The sex is satisfying. Albrecht takes what he needs through the contact as though Mica is giving it willingly. Afterward, though, the boy is exhausted, the drug not enough to replenish him. Albrecht is restless. He gets up finally to call William.

"I don't know where he is," he explains, lighting another cigarette. "Can you find him?"

"Tonight, Herr Christian?" William asks, sounding as crisp as if it were noon and not one a.m.

"Yes, tonight. They're bound to be done with the show, and I need..." He breaks off, afraid of what he wants to admit. "Please, if you can track him down."

Albrecht rings off after a promise from William. He sits in one of the dove-colored wingback chairs, phone resting in his lap. He closes his eyes, feels himself begin to drift, when it rings sharply. He snatches it up. "Yes."

"Hey, baby." Trace's voice invades him, over the sound of many other voices. "I sang your song tonight."

"I wish I had heard it," Albrecht says, taking a sharp breath.

"Me, too. I miss you."

Albrecht stops himself from analyzing the tone. "I'm glad."

"Tomorrow we start headlining and we're sold out."

Albrecht shifts in the chair. Marcus had arranged the tour to overlap with Live Wire's in order to give the album time to gain speed. Albrecht has always had faith in Trace's talent to fill seats, but he understands Marcus's need to hedge his bets. "I'm glad things are going well for you. I know you must be busy. I shall see you in Ohio."

"I can't wait."

Albrecht doesn't say I love you as he hangs up. He goes back to bed, rousing Mica by taking him in his arms. Albrecht kisses him hard, hungrily sucking down more of the boy's life.

Mica edges back this time. "How is he? Is the tour going good?" His voice is sluggish now, eyes sagging.

Albrecht sits up again. "I want you to stop using drugs," he says softly. "I watched Sean destroy himself. I won't, I cannot watch it again."

"It's not that easy." Mica's smile is slow and painful.

"Indeed." Albrecht pushes to his feet and goes the bedside table. "I do understand that, yet I won't have it here."

He opens the drawer and takes out the cocaine, the pouch with Mica's needles. "But I'll help you."

"Albrecht, don't—"

He steps into the bathroom to flush the drugs.

"Hey." Mica is standing in the doorway behind him. "That's mine."

"Sean died," Albrecht insists, stepping around the boy. He returns to the main room to sit on the sofa. He waits for Mica to follow.

"That was mine," Mica tells him, frowning.

"I am sorry." Albrecht sighs. "But while you are with me, I shan't permit it."

Mica folds his arms across his chest as though he were waiting for Albrecht to relent.

"Do you want to stay here?" Albrecht asks softly.

"Yes. I would do anything for you," Mica says, rubbing his arms.

Albrecht nods. He feels the bittersweet connection between them strengthen. "Do this."

It saddens him, knowing that as he grows stronger, Mica will grow weaker and emptier until Albrecht has used him completely. Yet Mica will never leave him, will cling to him until the end.

That is Albrecht's talent: ensnaring beautiful things to destroy them.

All but Trace, who Albrecht wants in the long, cold night more than anything. Trace, whose body fed from him as greedily as Albrecht ever had. Albrecht longs for Trace's vampire touch.

When he shakes himself away from these thoughts, Mica has gone back to bed. Albrecht stays where he is, waiting for the sunrise.

Trace puts the phone down and pushes to his feet, picking up a bottle of whiskey. The party is winding down now and most of the members of Live Wire are passed out with their groupies. There's no sign of Weird and Tommi is making out with a boy Trace doesn't recognize. Asia is with Myrna.

"Can I borrow your boyfriend?" Trace asks her as he approaches.

She snorts. "He's not my property."

"Good point." Trace grins, then looks at Asia. "C'mon and talk?"

"Uh." Asia narrows his eyes and tilts his head slightly. "What do you want?"

"Asia." Trace softens his smile. "Just talk."

Asia frowns but gets up. "Okay."

Trace leads him out of the suite and down the hall. They get into the elevator and Asia is struck with how surreal the scene is. Trace is still in full costume with bare feet, clutching a bottle of Black Velvet by the neck. Asia trails after him in ragged cut-off shorts and a Pretenders tee shirt that Myrna lent him.

Trace leans against the paneling and takes a slug from the bottle. "Fuck, I'm tired."

Asia takes it away from him. "This isn't gonna help that."

Trace opens his eyes and grins at Asia. "I'm supposed to get stinkin' drunk after a show, maybe trash a hotel room. That's how we do it. Ask Hunt."

"Yeah-right." Asia lets out a sigh. He takes a drink of the shit himself, as though it will help him avoid the pull of Trace's mood. "'Ash' sounded really great tonight," Asia offers.

Trace laughs. "Thanks."

Asia is quiet. He remembers the first time Trace played the song, backstage in Denver, a week ago. It seems like a whole other lifetime—with other people—now.

Trace picked up Eric's twelve-string and settled it across his lap. Asia looked down at his sneakers. The guitar brought the ghost too close for him. Trace chorded a few times before he started, head tilted back, eyes closed.

Though it burns you
I'll stay
Though you're ashes
Though you can't ask it of me
Stay
Because I burn
Because I'll burn through this razor-sharp affair
Stay

The lyrics cut into Asia. They swept Trace farther from him and he wondered what effect they had on Albrecht Christian. Asia sucked in a breath as it ended and looked up into Trace's frozen eyes. "It's good."

"Yeah, damn, Dellon," Weird agreed. "You want me to work on it some? We could add it to the set."

Asia shook his head. "He should do it without us. Just like that." He wanted no part of the song. It was too much like losing Trace for him.

Now Asia asks, "Does Herr Christian like it?"

"What?"

"I mean, you wrote it for him, right? Does he like it? I don't know how it would feel if somebody did that for me."

Trace takes the bottle back. "I don't know. I didn't ask him."

Asia frowns. He wants to ask what is wrong, but is almost afraid. He's grateful when they reach the rooftop, if only to be released from the close space.

The doors slide open to a garden. It's raining.

"You're gonna freeze out here, Trace," Asia protests.

Trace shrugs. "I won't."

Asia feels guilty in his shoes and tee shirt as he follows. "What are we doing?"

"I can't sleep." Trace walks along the main path, bare feet on concrete. He sets the whiskey down on a bench and wraps his arms around himself tight. "That's all. I just can't."

Asia frowns. "Because of the tour and record and shit?"

"Y'think?" Trace smiles bitterly. "I don't know. Albrecht called tonight, but then didn't wanna talk to me."

"Uh." Asia doesn't know what to say. He has to take a split second to match the name. He's never heard Trace use Herr Christian's first name. "Maybe he just misses you. Maybe he wanted to hear your voice."

Trace leans one hip against the oversized railing and looks out over the side. "He's got Mica. He doesn't need me."

Asia shivers, rain soaking through his shirt. "Come on." He takes a breath and touches Trace's shoulder. "That can't mean anything. It's just that you're not there."

Asia draws his hand back, reaches for the bottle of whiskey. He takes a slug and thinks, if I were him, I wouldn't be in bed with somebody else, ever. I'd be right wherever you are.

Instead of saying that, he drinks some more, wondering why it doesn't warm him up like his dad always said. "Look," he tries again, "I'll stay up and talk to you, but let's go back to the suite—"

"Too crowded." Trace shakes his head. "There's some girl waitin' for me in my room. I don't wanna go back there."

"Let's go to my room."

"Myrna."

"She won't care," Asia says.

"She thinks she stole you from me." Trace turns to face him, touches his cheek with an icy hand. "She hates me."

"She does not. And anyway, it's my room, Trace," Asia argues. "If you catch pneumonia, we'll be fucked. Marcus'll be pissed."

Trace laughs. "Yeah-right. Let's not let the meal ticket damage himself."

"That's not what I meant." Asia frowns. "I just—"

Trace's expression softens. "I know. That was bitchy. I'm sorry."

They wake up Myrna, but she's pretty cool about it. Asia talks Trace into laying down on the other bed and he's asleep as soon as he does.

Myrna flops back onto their bed and yawns. "Stop worrying so much about him, Asia."

"Yeah." He stares at Trace across from him, face streaked with makeup. He looks ravaged somehow. "I know. I'm sorry."

Myrna lays her fingers against the back of his neck. She kisses him. "Just lay down and close your eyes."

"Myrna," Asia protests, but she pulls him down.

"He's out cold, Asia. He won't hear anything." She's smiling when she unzips his shorts and straddles him. "C'mon. I missed you."

In Asia's brain, he's mortified, but his body doesn't care. He gasps as Myrna grinds into him. He closes his eyes and turns his head to the side. As Myrna fucks him, Asia watches Trace sleep through slitted eyes.

The next day, they pack the Tower Records in town. Tim stands at Trace's elbow. The minders that Marcus hired organize the mob and hold them back from the band about five feet or so. For Asia, it's smaller, but more threatening than the concerts. Everybody's at eye level and there's no barrier of sound between them. They shout things at Trace mostly and he responds appropriately, blowing kisses and grinning. The minders let the kids closer about ten at a time. Asia finds himself moving between them and Trace, out of reflex.

The local radio DJ leans close to Asia. "This is just the beginning for you guys, y'know?"

Asia fumbles a nervous smile and nods. He does know. Trace steps past him, into the knot of kids. There's no hint of the exhaustion from last night. He is luminous. They all try to touch him and he endures it with a sharp grin.

"You wrote that song for me," one of them tells him, thrusting an album cover at him. "'Ash.' It's my song."

That makes Asia sad, somehow, for both Trace and the girl, but Trace only laughs and reaches for her hand. He turns it palm up to kiss and says, "Yes, it is."

In the car later, on the way to the airport, the DJ interviews them into a tape recorder. Asia fidgets mostly, letting Trace tell embellished stories of their checkered past. Asia has learned by now that the truth is only important if it is useful, or entertaining. He leans back into the leather and closes his eyes.

He wakes again as they pull to a stop. "Sorry."

"It's okay, Asia," Trace says softly. "I know you're tired."

The shimmering beautiful Trace is gone and he looks pale and defeated again. Asia frowns. "Really, Trace, are you okay?"

He nods as the door is opened for them. "How can I not be? This is everything I ever wanted."

They are done with the West Coast and traveling east, working their way back into the country. Traveling backward, Asia realizes, as the plane takes off. It seems strange to him that after all that effort to reach the edge of the world in LA, that success should turn them around this way. He turns to Myrna, but she's already asleep.

"How long until we play Detroit?" He kicks the back of Tommi's seat. He is listening to his new Walkman so loud that Asia can almost place the bass line of the song.

"What?" The boy turns and lifts a headphone off, letting Gary Numan jangle out.

"How many weeks until Detroit?" Asia repeats. "I can't remember how many more shows we got."

"Twelve, unless Marcus adds some on the way," Weird says, over his seat. "Which he will. We got two and a half weeks before we get to Michigan, if that's what you're askin'. Why? Gonna invite your parents?"

"Yeah-right." Asia shakes his head. "Like they'd come. I haven't spoken to them since my brother…"

"Yeah, sorry. 'Course not." Weird shifts so he can hang over the seat further. "You're just ready for this to be done, I bet, huh?"

Asia nods. No matter how many records they sell or how many gigs Marcus gets them, Asia knows that they all know he'd rather be living in Ann Arbor. "Aren't you kinda tired?"

Weird snorts. "Kinda? I'm old, man. A'course I'm tired, but I got a gold record, too. So who gives a fuck?"

Tommi nods. "Asia, be happy. We're havin' a good time, remember?"

Asia nods too, but he leans out into the aisle to spot Trace, farther up in the plane, sitting next to Marcus. He doesn't look like he's sleeping. As Asia watches, a girl walks unsteadily past him to stop beside Trace. Asia can't hear the conversation, but he knows what she's saying. She crouches in the aisle beside Trace's seat. He turns, kisses her, and signs something for her. She squeals a little and kisses him back, then scampers away. She smiles at Asia, a little puzzled as she passes this time, like she almost knows who he is, too. Asia looks away and Tommi and Weird both chuckle.

"Yeah," he admits softly. "I'm ready to be done with this."

He gets up and walks up the aisle. Trace is writing something on the legal pad he has balanced on one knee. Asia smiles at Marcus and says, "Can we trade seats for a while?"

Marcus shrugs and collects his drink to sit with Myrna. Asia settles in between Trace and the window. "How're you doin'?"

"Tryin' to work on this song. Marcus wants us back in the studio when we're done with the tour. I need new stuff to record."

Asia frowns. "You got lotsa songs, Trace. I know you've got enough for another album. At least one more."

Trace shakes his head. "They're not good enough. Bar band crap. This is for the next album."

Asia doesn't argue with him. Trace's never had a problem writing before. If anything, it was the rest of them having to keep up with the constant flow of new stuff. "Can I see it?"

Trace rips the page off and crumples it. He tosses it to the floor and lights another cigarette. "It's nothing."

"Trace." Asia bends to retrieve it. "Don't."

He smooths out the sheet and realizes that Trace is right. There's nothing written on it but scribbles. "Let it go for now. Get some sleep while you can."

Albrecht has spent the day in meetings. Since Trace left, Albrecht has developed more of an interest in Para Bellum. He's never sure whether it annoys William to have him underfoot again or not; William's too good an actor. Mica, however, has no such distractions. When Albrecht returns to the Algonquin in the afternoon, Mica is fairly vibrating with boredom.

"Shall we go for dinner—perhaps take your mind off other things?" Albrecht suggests.

Mica smiles. "Dinner, like a dress-up dinner, or can I wear, y'know…"

"Normal clothes?" Albrecht arches an eyebrow. "What would you prefer?"

In a half-hour, Albrecht is wearing a charcoal suit and Mica has indeed chosen jeans, tight black ones with thick stripes in rainbow colors. His shirt has been artfully customized with a plunging neckline. He is not exactly in drag, but the eyeliner and lip gloss make him something more than either gender.

"Very pretty," Albrecht pronounces as they step onto the lift. Boy or girl, Albrecht is certain they make a striking if not inappropriate couple. "Do you enjoy curry?"

Mica laughs. "As spicy as I can get it."

"Mm." Albrecht smiles. "In that case, I have a place in mind."

There is a new band at the Refugee Club, but neither of them have the heart for it.

"Take me up to Mulholland," Mica asks. "Don't you wanna see how this car drives up there on the curves?"

Albrecht smiles. "I know already."

"Don't you wanna show me?"

Albrecht sighs. Tonight he does. Tonight he wants to make Mica happy. "Yes. I do."

He guides the Jaguar up the narrow, winding street faster than is wise. Mica leans forward a bit and smiles in the darkness. "I haven't been up here since I first came to LA."

Albrecht raises an eyebrow. Mica's accent, though flattened out by living in the valley, was proof that he was from somewhere else, yet Albrecht has always thought of him as a creature of this place. "Were you young?"

Mica shrugs. "I've been here six years. I was fifteen."

Albrecht shakes his head at the staggering distance of years between them. "This was Errol Flynn's house once," he says, instead of commenting. He slows them to a stop in front of a broken set of gates that lead them to nothing but weeds and the shell of the building beyond. "There's nothing left now, but once it was quite beautiful." As he speaks, the echo of light and laughter fills his mind.

"That's so sad," Mica says.

Albrecht shakes away the memory of Flynn's warm hand on his shoulder. "Times change. People move on. They forget. Everything is so fleeting. But, yes. It was very beautiful."

He takes his foot off the brake and moves them on. Mica catches his mood and sighs. "I'm sorry. This isn't very fun for you, is it?"

That makes Albrecht laugh softly. "I am afraid I'm a bit old for fun, my dear. Did you know that Houdini's house was up here also?"

"Yeah," Mica says. "All that's left of it is the stairs, right? And he's supposed to come back on Halloween."

Albrecht nods. "He promised, but no one has ever seen him."

"Too bad," Mica says.

Albrecht begins back down the hill, the familiar curves making him daring. Mica rolls his window down and lets the wind stream his hair back. "You miss Trace."

Albrecht spills them back out into the traffic and admits it. "I do. Don't you?"

Mica shrugs. "You'll see him soon."

13

After the show, Asia goes straight back to the hotel. It hasn't taken long for the party schedule to get old for him. He meets Myrna in the hotel bar for nachos and a Diet Coke. All he really wants is a shower and to get as much sleep as he can get, but he shovels the microwaved chips and near-cheese into his mouth. It's almost closing time, so they have the place to themselves. Jim Morrison's voice echoes low and dark in the stuffy, smoky room.

"People seem ugly when you're unwanted."

As though even the Lizard King was frightened in the dark.

"Streets are uneven." Myrna picks up the lyric with her whiskey-honey voice, as she steals a chip from his plate and dips it into the barbecue sauce that came with her chicken wings. "That boy was fucked up."

"Yeah," Asia agrees, thinking of Trace. "It's too bad. You think if you're a genius, you'd be able to deal with shit a little better."

"They found crap, I guess, at the end. Stuff he wrote, y'know, and they thought it would all be songs, like, brilliant stuff he'd kept back, but it was grocery lists jumbled up with letters and poetry." She shook her head. "Like he didn't know the difference."

"No one remembers your name."

Myrna leans across the table to kiss Asia, but he can't stop thinking about the aborted lyrics on Trace's legal pad. Was that what killed Jim Morrison? Is that what is happening to Trace?

Myrna senses his thoughts and frowns. "Asia." She pulls back from him. "Trace's not Jim Morrison."

Asia blinks. "I wasn't thinking about him."

"I can see it in your eyes," Myrna counters. "You're always thinking about Trace."

Asia sighs. He'd like to protest, but it's pretty much true. He doesn't want to fight about it tonight. He is too tired and it isn't going to solve anything. "I think I'm gonna go for a walk before I go to bed."

He pushes to his feet and avoids her eyes. He blinks hard against the brightness of the hotel hallway. A steady breeze of recycled air chills his skin as he digs into his pocket for change for a Diet Coke.

He comes up empty and heaves a sigh. Figures. He heads to the lobby, hoping to get at least a nap there.

It's still bright, but it's silent. He sits on one of the leather sofas across from the desk and lets out another sigh.

He wants Myrna to stop. More than that, he never wants to hear Trace's name from her lips again. She knows, he thinks desolately. And she's always forgiven me for it before. What's changed?

But then he thinks of Trace, the pale line of his neck as he lay on the bed opposite them. Asia remembers feeling Myrna take him, hold him inside her, and it not being enough when Trace was so close within reach.

He flinches, wishing he could just shove it all away. He leans his head against the high arm of the sofa and makes himself close his eyes.

"Sir?"

He wakes to a light touch on his shoulder. "What?"

"Sir." It's a very young girl in a blue polyester blazer. She's bent over him, speaking in a soft voice. "Are you a guest here? I can't let you—"

Asia blinks, sits up, and regrets the pain in his neck. "I didn't mean to fall asleep. I'm Asia Heyes and my room's..." He can't remember the number.

"Oh." The girl straightens and blushes. "Oh, with Black Light. I'm sorry, I didn't recognize you."

Asia rakes his hair back from his face, fingers catching in the snarls. No, he thinks. All sprawled out here in his sweaty tee shirt and jeans from the show. He probably looked like a bum. "It's okay." He smiles and stretches out the kinks in his back. The girl looks about seventeen, despite the uniform. She has long, smooth fox-colored hair, gathered at the back of her neck in a braid. Is this your first job? Asia wonders, envious. He never had a real first job. Trace got him fired too quick. "Can you tell me my room number? My girlfriend has the key and I can't remember it."

On his way there, though, he notices Weird's door open, just a bit, and stops. "Hey," he calls softly, pushing open further.

When there's no answer, Asia hesitates, but knows he has to

continue. He's always known he would be the one to find Weird. It's always been in the back of Asia's mind, since the first time he saw a needle in Weird's arm.

"Weird?"

"Yeah, Asia, 'm not dead." Weird's voice is gravelly. "C'mon in."

Suddenly, everybody seems to know what Asia's thinking. As soon as he crosses the threshold, he smells the sharp scent of heroin cooking. He closes the door. "Aren't you at least afraid of getting busted?"

Weird is sitting cross-legged on one of the beds. He chuckles. "That'd be a picture, wouldn't it? But no, not really. You ever know anybody that's been busted?"

"No..." Asia pauses. He is about to say he doesn't know anybody that did drugs, but that's stupid, as he watches Weird holding his spoon over his lighter. "It's five a.m.," he points out instead. "What the fuck are you doing up?"

"This." Weird shrugs. He puts the lighter down and picks up the needle. "What the fuck are you doing up?"

Asia looks away at the rest of the ritual. "Me and Myrna. She's mad at me, so I..."

"You look like shit." Weird chuckles again. "I tried to warn you. Women."

Asia looks back in time to see the needle slide home in Weird's vein. "Things are going really good, aren't they? With the tour and the album. Why do you still need to shoot that?"

Weird is absorbed with the drug though and doesn't answer. He barely bothers to loosen the tubing around his arm before slumping back against the headboard and closing his eyes.

Asia stretches out on the other bed, pulling the pillow from the spread to bunch against his body, closing his eyes, too.

He jerks awake to the phone and Weird's cursing. For one split second, Asia thinks he's back in Encino again, waking up on his futon.

"Yeah, okay," Weird growls into the phone and slams it down. "Git up. Your girlfriend's lookin' for you, and we got a half-hour before the car comes for us."

Asia sits up and rubs his eyes. "'Kay."

Weird chuckles as Asia stretches and yawns. "You really do look like hell.”

“Thanks.” Asia manages a smile. Then he sobers. “Do you think Trace's doin' okay?”

Weird shrugs a shoulder. “With Dellon, who the hell knows? Anyway, aren't his boyfriends meeting him when we get to Ohio? That oughta cheer him up.”

Maybe, Asia thinks, but doesn't answer.

At the Akron airport, Albrecht gets into the limousine and finds Trace waiting. Without preamble, Trace pulls Albrecht against him by the lapels of his jacket, crushes his lips with a hard kiss. Albrecht gasps at the taste of Trace, so strong it threatens to daze him. Albrecht reaches for him, fingers scraping under the tight tour tee shirt he wears, dancing along the waistband of his jeans. *Now.* Albrecht gasps again, not caring how exposed he is. He needs Trace now. He wonders how he could have ever survived this separation.

Then Mica climbs in and the door is shut behind him. Trace lets Albrecht go and slips to the other corner of the seat. Mica settles across from them, behind the driver, and smiles. “Hi, Trace.”

“Hi.” Trace smooths his clothes back down and takes a breath. “How was the flight?”

“Mica slept, so he would have no idea,” Albrecht says, if only to draw Trace's attention back to him. “He was asleep from the second we took off to the moment we touched down. For me, it was uneventful.”

“*No Outlet* went gold, didn't it?” Mica says, grinning. “Congratulations. That's cool as hell.”

“Last week,” Trace agrees. “I thought Marcus was going to have an orgasm when we heard.”

Albrecht smiles slightly. He gives up contributing to the conversation for the time being. He's trying to remember why he brought Mica. He doesn't want him here; he wants Trace to himself, above anything else. Albrecht leans his head back against the leather seat and closes his eyes.

“I have to get to the hall to do my makeup and shit,” Trace says. “So if you want to see the show, we can have your stuff sent to your hotel."

Albrecht rubs at his temples. "I think… Forgive me, but I think it would be best if I went straight on to the hotel. The jet lag is quite getting the better of me."

He opens his eyes to read Trace's expression, looking for some indication that he is disappointed. Albrecht is rewarded with a flicker, then nothing. Trace moves closer to him again and takes his hands away from his face. He kisses Albrecht's forehead gently. "It's okay, baby. You go ahead and nap. There's always tomorrow's show."

The brush of Trace's lips flares up a starvation in Albrecht that he thought was gone.

As soon as the car takes Christian away, Trace misses him. Tonight, he thinks, they can be together. It shouldn't matter that Mica is here too, Trace reminds himself, but he thinks of the nights before he left, alone in the spare bedroom, listening to them down the hall. His choice, but it didn't seem like he really had one at the time.

"I know you miss each other," Mica says, as Trace sits down in front of the long, lighted mirror backstage to begin his routine. "I'll let you alone with him while we're here."

Trace scrubs his fingers through his hair and sees a quarter-inch of light brown root. He grins tight. "That's sweet. What makes you think it's what he wants?"

"He misses you," Mica says it flatly, with no trace of jealousy in his voice. "He doesn't sleep, or when he does, he dreams of you."

"Hm." Trace applies one thick stripe of silver shadow to each lid. He wants to believe Mica. He does believe him, yet something keeps him from admitting the same. "What about you?"

Mica sits up on the counter, back against the mirror, and perches one foot on Trace's chair, up between his legs. "You're my favorite rock star. Of course I dream about you."

Trace trails his fingers up the inside of Mica's leg, knowing exactly what is expected of him. Mica leans down, eyes sliding closed, to kiss him. Trace studies his face, up close, still beautiful, paler and drawn since the last time they'd fucked. He pulls back. "I gotta finish. You're gonna get me all smeared up."

Eventually, Mica leaves the dressing room and Trace uses the time alone to stare at himself in the mirror. He can't tell if he looks any different than he did. When he emerges, everybody else is out in the green room. Weird is eating an apple and drinking a beer from the bottle. Asia is sitting on a folding chair in the corner, clutching a can of Diet Coke like he wants to strangle it. Tommi is on the couch, legs stretched out, getting a foot massage from Mica.

"Hey, Dellon, I was wonderin' if you were gonna join us mere mortals, or what tonight," Weird greets.

Tim sticks his head in. "You've got eight minutes."

Asia swallows. He stands up and Trace smiles at him. At least he's not still puking his guts out every night.

"Get your shoes on, Sunshine," Weird prods Tommi. "We gotta go."

Albrecht watches the city pass from the car window, feeling something more than exhaustion settle on him. Akron is like every Midwestern city he's ever been to. Industrial air washes all the color from things in a way that LA smog never seemed to. It was not unlike the Berlin of his youth. There was a time he could have flourished in a place like this, but that is all past for him.

The bitter gnawing need for Trace is there, deep in Albrecht, but rising. He replays the taste of Trace, the press of his body, but it helps him not at all.

He closes his eyes. He should have kept Mica. To replenish him.

When had his tastes become so rarified, Albrecht wonders, lips curling into a hard smile. In his youth, the will to survive won out over appetite and he was never so particular. Perhaps Sean had cured him of that. Sean, who made him feel something more than sated. Before Sean, Albrecht was a hunter. It took Trace, though, to make him into prey.

Trace and Mica join Albrecht at the hotel around eleven o'clock. Albrecht has had time to order room service and have the meal waiting for them.

"Mm." Trace sits at the table. "This is way classier than the Buffalo wings at the Knights Inn 'cross town."

"Indeed." Albrecht falls into his role of rich, indulgent boyfriend easily. He's too close to Trace now. He'll say anything to keep the air pleasant between them. "Your next tour shall be grander, I expect."

Trace laughs. "Than this one? It'd have to be."

Albrecht sips his wine and watches Trace cut into his steak. Mica recounts the concert enthusiastically and Albrecht is jealous. He isn't part of this world and he'll never separate Trace from it now.

It seems to Albrecht that Trace doesn't address him directly, if he can avoid it. When he is finished with his meal, he stands up and kisses Albrecht before saying, "It's Asia's birthday, so I gotta get back, but I'll see you tomorrow."

Albrecht manages to catch Trace's left hand, hold it to his cheek. He closes his eyes and opens them again. Trace's wrist is naked, he realizes, all at once. The bracelets are gone. Albrecht looks up into Trace's frozen eyes and sees the lie. "I've missed you more than…"

Trace's smile is hollow. "Tomorrow."

14

"Asia, wake up."

It seems to Asia that he'd just laid down and closed his eyes. It's the middle of the night, he thinks, but he opens his eyes anyway. Myrna stands over him, hands on her hips. "I'm goin' back to LA."

"What?" He sits up and rakes his hair out of his face.

"Yeah, I've been talkin' to Lionel about getting' the Leather Boys' studio time moved up on the schedule. It looks like it's gonna happen."

She is grinning and Asia wants to be supportive, so he wraps his arms around her waist and leans his head against her middle. "That's so great. When d'ya start?"

"In three weeks." She slides her fingers through his hair.

"Then you don't have to go back right now." Asia looks up at her and sees her smile lessen.

"No," she admits, stepping away from him. "But I am."

"But…" He gets up, takes a breath. "Why?"

"Asia." Her tone reminds him of a parent. "Because this hasn't been workin' for a while now, and you know it."

He catches her arm, like he can stop her. "What are you talking about? Please. Wait a minute and talk to me. I don't want you to have to sit and wait for me all the time——"

"This is your tour, your band, your turn." She slips free of him. "No, that's not the problem. If it was just you and me, there wouldn't be a problem. But it's you and me and Trace."

"Myrna, don't." Asia shakes his head. "You said that it didn't matter and you believed me that there was nothing."

"Yeah, but you're in love with him, no matter what, Asia."

"I'm not," Asia insists, but just saying it twists in his stomach. "It doesn't matter, Myrna. You're my boyfriend. I need you."

"I wish that was true, but it's not." She smiles and laughs. "C'mon, all I've done this whole time is stand in for him. And watch you wish you were with him."

She kisses him and turns away. "I'm not mad. I know you can't help it. But I can't, either."

Asia wants to argue with her, but he's lied to her so much already. He swallows. "You're going home?"

"Yeah. I gotta get back to the boys. If we're gonna cut a record, I gotta get them focused."

Asia nods. "Will you call me when you get there?"

She laughs again and then looks into his eyes. Her gaze is ice blue and painful. "No, Asia, I won't call you."

He thinks he should know what to say, but nothing comes. His chest feels tight as she walks out the door. When she's gone, he closes his eyes, feels the silence settle in the strange room around him. Something in him is envious of Myrna. All Asia wants to do is go home. But he can't. Trace is here and so Asia has no home.

Myrna is right about everything.

Then he remembers, "It's my birthday." He says it to the empty room. He sits on the edge of the disheveled bed and rubs at his chest. Myrna doesn't know. Now she never will.

He is twenty-four tonight, stranded in this hotel room. When he lies down, he smells her on the pillow and inhales deep. Trace, he thinks, helplessly. Even if Asia wants to blame Trace for this, it would be another lie. Trace didn't take Myrna away. Asia let her go.

Just as he closes his eyes, there's a knock on the door, and Trace's voice on the other side, calling him.

"Hang on." When he opens up, Trace is standing in the hallway, wearing jeans and a tight scooped-necked tee shirt that says, "I'm with the band." He steps inside, grinning. "Happy birthday, man."

Asia smiles back against his will. "Thanks."

Trace passes him to flop down on the extra bed. "I know you hate the party thing, but I just wanted you to know I didn't forget, y'know?"

"Thanks," Asia says again, sitting next to him. "Really."

"Where's Myrna?"

Asia takes a breath. He knows he will have to answer this question over and over. "She went home. She broke up with me."

"Oh, man, that sucks." Trace groans sympathetically. That was all. Not: why? Or: did you have a fight? Maybe Trace knows the reason already.

Asia shrugs. Now that the initial shock has worn off, he doesn't feel like he's been hit in the chest anymore. He doesn't really feel anything. "I'm okay. Aren't you staying at Herr Christian's hotel for the night? I thought he came to see you."

Now Trace shrugs. "He's jet-lagged. Besides, it's your birthday. I wanted to see you. He understands."

Asia looks at Trace, whose face betrays nothing. "He brought Mica with him?"

Trace nods. "It was a little fuckin' crowded over there for me, y'know?"

Asia doesn't answer. Why anybody would need more than Trace is beyond him.

"But, whatever." Trace grins again. "I got you somethin'."

Asia tilts his head and narrows his eyes. Trace's never done this before. Never had money to buy his own cigarettes, let alone things like birthday presents. "You didn't have to."

"I know that, but I did. It's in Weird's room." He stands up again. "C'mon."

Asia follows Trace down the hallway. When Weird opens his door, a cloud of smoke rolls out with him. He grins. "Happy birthday, man. You're almost not a kid anymore."

Asia nods. Sometimes he feels like the oldest person he knows. He is afraid the room will be stuffed full of strangers, but it turns out to be just them. Tommi is perched on the low dresser across from the bed, his back up against the mirror.

"Myrna went back to LA," Trace announces. "So don't ask."

"What a bitch," Tommi says. "Did Trace tell you what your present was?"

"Not yet," Trace says. "It's on the bed."

A slim black case lays on the spread. Asia's breath catches when he opens it. The bass guitar inside waits for him, the body a rust/green color that reminds Asia of fall.

"Oh." Asia sucks in his breath. "Trace..."

"Weird's always bitchin' about your old one and I wanted you to..." Trace touches Asia's shoulder. "I saw it and thought of you."

There is something embarrassing about having them all watch him pick it up, put his fingers on the strings, but he does it anyway. When he looks up, it's to Trace's eyes. "Thank you."

"We have like, ten hours off or something, right?" Trace says. "Let's do something. I don't wanna sleep."

Asia thinks of Herr Christian, but doesn't bring him up again. They are in Ohio tonight, only about four hours away from Ann Arbor. It's September, with the cold just creeping into the air. Asia has only lived in California a year, but already his body has forgotten the feeling of seasons. "Okay. What?"

Weird shrugs. "I used to play in this jazz band, when I was a kid around here. I bet I can find some music someplace."

Trace laughs. "Jazz?"

"Yeah." Weird crushes his cigarette out in an overflowing ashtray. "Froggie and the Gremlins."

Now Tommi laughs. "Gremlins? That's stupid."

"Oh, yeah-right, and grown men should be callin' themselves Black Light." Weird points out. "You want the guided tour, or not?"

Asia can't let go of the bass, not yet, so he takes it with him.

Albrecht looks out on the city chilling below him, feeling the pull of Trace, though he is across town by now. Albrecht regrets this. Perhaps he could have made a clean break if he'd only kept enough distance between them, but not now. Albrecht feels as though he is dying again.

He hears the water start in the bathroom. He extinguishes his cigarette and rises, dropping his robe as he enters, unannounced. He crosses the granite tile to join Mica in the shower, large enough to be a room by itself.

Mica is standing under one of the nozzles, face turned up to the spray, eyes closed. His pale skin is darkened by the heat.

Albrecht calls his name and the boy turns. Albrecht takes the hand he offers and steps under the scalding water to kiss Mica through the torrent. "I'm sorry," Albrecht murmurs. "This is not how you envisioned this evening ending, I know."

Mica reaches for him. "I'm not disappointed."

The boy is pliant, yielding under Albrecht's touch. He takes Mica against the wall of the shower, pressing into him to seek that heat he knows is there. He feels it coming from deep down, but he can't reach it. It's gone for Albrecht now. He finally stops.

He walks out of the water and lies across the bed, one hand draped over his eyes. He feels Mica sit beside him.

"Please." Albrecht breathes before he has to endure Mica's touch again so soon. "Please sleep in the other room."

"But I—"

"Please," Albrecht says again.

Mica leaves without another word. Albrecht knows he has devastated the boy with the rejection. He stares at the wall and lets the silence win out for as long as he can stand. Then he gets up again. He crosses the main room of the suite to knock on Mica's door.

"May I come in?" he asks, easing it open, spilling a sliver of light into the room.

"I'm your whore. You can do what you want."

Albrecht sighs. "I don't want you to feel that way."

Mica is sitting on one of wide windowsills, legs folded against his chest, arms wrapped around his knees. He looks like a ghost already. "It is that way, so why not?"

"If you're unhappy, I won't stop you from leaving."

Mica chokes out a laugh, turns his face away from Albrecht. "Don't pretend it's that easy."

Albrecht crosses the room, brushes his fingers against Mica's cheek. Mica catches his hand before he can take it away, holds it there. Albrecht shivers at the touch of Mica's delicate breath in his palm.

"You," Mica whispers. "It was never Trace, not after the first time you touched me."

Albrecht closes his eyes. He feels the tragedy of it all so clearly. He can't love Mica, just as Trace can't love him. "I—"

"Don't say anything. I'm your whore. You can't understand. Hell, I don't understand it." Mica unfolds from the windowsill and goes to the closet to shrug into another of the hotel's robes. "I've never been one of those boys that dream about some daddy coming along to give 'em a better life. But then you came along and gave me one." He meets Albrecht's eyes. "How'm I s'posed to not love you for that?"

"Mica." Albrecht thinks of all the times since he met Trace that he wished he was the devil. The tears on Mica's face are proof to Albrecht that he has achieved that. "It's late. I'm cold. Come to bed."

Mica gives in. They lay skin to skin, Albrecht's body warming at the contact. He takes what he couldn't before. After, as Mica clings to him, Albrecht feels him waning, just as Sean did. Soon he'll fade, if he stays with Albrecht. "Please," Mica whispers. "Just tell me why."

And as Sean did, Mica has figured it out, Albrecht thinks, sadly. As much as he can on his own.

Albrecht begins his story softly. "I am really much older than I look. I was born in the final minutes of the last century. I believe my mother died, but my father never talked about her, and I never asked. We lived in a fine house, with beautiful things, until the war."

Mica looks up. "Which one?"

"The Great War. Austria-Hungry declared war on Serbia in retaliation for the assassination of Archduke Franz Ferdinand. All of Europe was dragged into it before the end." Albrecht smiles faintly at the history lesson. "But I was young and what I remember about it was that we lost our home, Father and I. We were hungry, cold, wasting away. My father died."

"How old were you?" Mica asks.

"I was...perhaps seventeen?" Albrecht says. "My life before faded quickly. It became like a fairy tale I told myself in the dark."

"What happened to you then?" Mica asked him. "How did you survive?"

"Just as you do now. I sold myself for what I could. At first it wasn't much. Food, warmth. But I learned quickly that I could take more than money from these encounters."

Mica shifts and rakes his pale hair back.

Albrecht finds himself wanting to say it all out loud. What could it matter if Mica knew? He was like all of them: so fleeting. "Europe smelled of smoke and ash and rot. The energy of decay hung in the air, clung to my skin and my hair. I fed from the darkness that the war left, took from others with my touch. Perhaps if I had lived in a different time or place, I might have been different, but as it was, it left me with a talent for destruction. It is how I still survive. From the energy of others."

"That's why when you touch me I feel..." Mica pauses, but doesn't move away from Albrecht. "You take my life."

Albrecht closes his eyes in the face of the naked truth. "I suppose this is a fairy tale still." He slides his fingers through Mica's hair, so like Sean's in the dark. "But I'm not the prince. I'm the monster."

Mica gives another soft, jagged laugh. "I'm not the prince, either. Trace is."

Albrecht sighs. "No, he's another monster. I shouldn't have brought us here. He...drains me so."

Mica settles against Albrecht's shoulder. Albrecht listens to his breath lengthen into sleep and tries to match it, to follow him.

Albrecht is not surprised to find himself at the Refugee Club in his dreams. He's surrounded by busy workers and sounds of construction. The scent of ginger and cinnamon comes to him over the smell of fresh sawdust. He turns to find Sean, smiling at him, silver pistol in his hand.

Albrecht smiles back, though he knows it's a dream. "Are you trying to frighten me?"

"Would that be possible?" Sean arches one thin eyebrow. "I felt nothing, you know. I felt nothing when I walked away from you, and nothing when I put the gun in my mouth."

"You ruined your face," Albrecht protests.

"I wanted to erase my beauty from your life," Sean agrees.

"You couldn't, not even then." Albrecht closes his eyes and accepts the memory of Sean's silken hair drowning in so much blood.

Sean moves to Albrecht. He gently traces the line of Albrecht's jaw with the chill barrel of the gun, then tilts up on his toes to kiss Albrecht. There is a faint tang of copper to his mouth. Albrecht gives himself to it. When it's done, Sean says, "You'll never really leave Trace now. You know that."

The dream dissolves around Albrecht to the unflinching Midwestern sunrise. He jerks awake to find that Mica has escaped him and retreated to the edge of the bed. Albrecht is holding something hard and cold and impossible. He doesn't have to look down. He recognizes the weight. His hand curls around the grip like a lover. He sits up and puts the barrel into his mouth, tongue seeking traces of Sean in the taste of oil and metal. I feel nothing, he thinks, and his finger tightens.

Black Light have spent the night drinking, first at bars Weird remembers, then, after closing time, down at some riverbank, sharing a forty-ouncer and a couple of joints Tommi has in his pocket. It's freezing, but none of them complain, pretending that being stoned enough will keep them warm. Right before dawn, reality sets in and they realize that they have to get back to the hotel before they're missed or late for something. They stumble into a stop-and-rob nearby and give the clerk fifty bucks to call them a cab.

Since then, the sun's come up and the cabbie is driving them right into it. Tommi groans, hides his face in Asia's shoulder, as the rest of them cover their eyes.

"Fuckin' daylight," Weird mutters around a cigarette from the front seat.

"Uh-oh." Asia sits up and leans forward, shifting his bass between the front seat and his knees awkwardly as they approach the hotel. Marcus is standing outside, mid-pace.

Trace snickers. "Looks like we're gonna get grounded."

Something about the way Marcus's eyes settle on them as they stumble out of the cab sets Asia on edge.

"We shoulda let you know we—"

Marcus cuts him off with a shake of his head. "Trace, I need you to come in and sit down with me."

"Told ya." Trace laughs again.

"Please." Marcus takes him by the arm and steers him inside to the deserted bar beyond the desk. "Sit down."

Trace's smile fades. The others trail them in, moods deflating along with his. "What happened?"

"When you left Herr Christian at his hotel last night," Marcus begins, "did you have a fight?"

"No." Trace narrows his eyes, heart banging against his rib cage. "Why?"

"Because he shot himself in the head this morning, around sunrise."

Trace concentrates on trying to breathe. Breathe in, breathe out. He calls up the last moment of Albrecht, his smile, hiding layers of hurt, maybe anger, and Trace's own selfish, childish pleasure in that.

The world tilts, shoves him off.

"Trace? Did you hear what I—"

Marcus's voice is eaten by the static that fills Trace's ears. Then

162

everything blinks to darkness.

"Fuck!" Asia lurches forward as Trace goes over. He drops the bass to catch Trace, but only manages to ease his fall a little. "Shit," he mutters, crouching to hold Trace awkwardly.

Trace reaches up to touch Asia's arm. "Is he dead?"

"I—" Asia looks at Marcus, who nods, then back at Trace. Asia speaks past the lump in his throat. "Yeah. I'm sorry."

Trace presses his face against Asia's chest. Asia feels him shudder. "Can you get him some water?" he asks Weird, skin burning under the touch of Trace's skin.

Weird nods and leaves.

"Oh my God." Tommi speaks softly. "What—I mean, he shot himself?"

"Mica was there—or I guess he woke up when it happened. The cops are talking to him," Marcus says. "Now, I need you to focus."

He is looking directly at Asia, who swallows.

"Nobody knows who Albrecht Christian is in relation to any of you. We're gonna keep it that way. I know this is going to be hard, but we need to blow town this morning and get to Detroit, just like we planned."

"Fuck you, Marcus." Trace looks up. "I'm not singin' tonight. And I'm not leavin' Mica with the cops."

"You can't cancel a show now," Marcus protests. "This is not an option."

Asia helps Trace to his feet and Trace wipes at his eyes. "Your bass, Asia. I'm sorry."

Asia had forgotten all about it. He picks it back up, unharmed, but somehow it doesn't feel as good in his hands now. He slings it around to his back. "C'mon. We'll deal with this later. Right now, let's get upstairs and change clothes and crap."

"Mica was right there when he did it," Trace protests. "He shouldn't have to…"

Asia shakes his head.

Marcus speaks again, voice not as hard. "Listen to me. I'll fix it for Mica with the cops. You're right, he's been through something terrible. I won't just strand him here."

Weird returns with a glass and passes it to Trace. "Man," he says, but stops there.

Asia braces himself to steady Trace as they get out of the elevator, but Trace walks out ahead of him to the room and slides his key into the lock. Once inside, he collapses on the bed and lets out a long, shuddering breath. "I was so mean to him. I just walked out."

"Trace, it probably didn't have anything to do with you."

Now Trace laughs. "Of course it does. It has everything to do with me."

Asia lets that alone. It seems painfully true and denying it won't help Trace. "If you don't wanna go on, I'll stay with you. I don't care about Marcus."

I just care about you, he thinks. He takes the bass off and leans it against the bed. Trace turns over to look at him. His mascara is smeared into black streaks under his eyes, like bruises, and it makes Asia think of Eric. He sits down and brushes his fingers against Trace's. He wants to offer comfort, but even this much contact is too much for him. He shrinks back and swallows. "I'm so sorry."

"I gotta wash my face." Trace smiles faintly and sits up. "You'd better get packed and shit, too."

"Uh." Asia is surprised at Trace's fast recovery. "Okay."

Trace gets to his feet and puts a bag up on the desk. He rummages around for a second before coming up with two bracelets. "He gave these to me, right before we left. They're platinum."

"They're beautiful," Asia says. He remembers the first time Trace wore them, at the Whisky, but doesn't remember when he stopped seeing them.

Trace jangles them together. "I took them off as soon as we left LA. I know he noticed they were gone last night."

"Trace, you were pissed off," Asia argues. "It's still no justification for what he did. You can't make it so much your fault."

"Go pack," Trace tells him, instead of going over it again. "Come and get me when you're done."

15

By the time they get on the bus, everybody's feeling the lack of sleep. Weird and Tommi sack out immediately, but Asia can't. He's sitting next to Trace, also not sleeping. The bass, in its case is on the floor, leaned against the seat between them. Asia hasn't known what to say since this morning, so he says nothing. Trace stares out the window as they cross the border into Michigan.

The sky gets darker and darker, until they're in a full-fledged thunderstorm. Asia leans his head back against his seat, closing his eyes to listen to the storm. The rain pelts the bus roof. Every so often, lightning invades his lids, flashing pink. This is what he misses from his childhood: the feeling of heaviness in the air before the storm, the electric release of it. In LA, the air is always the same: arid, damaging.

They get to Joe Louis late for the soundcheck, so the pizza backstage is cold. It's a big, concrete arena and Asia knows if any of this was still important, he'd be terrified to go on. He tries to find some enthusiasm for finally playing his new bass, but he can't even care about that now. He gnaws on a stale piece of crust, watching Trace put on his makeup.

"Don't worry so much, Asia." Trace stares into his own eyes, frozen open as he applies mascara. "I'll be all right."

"Trace." Asia hates the resignation he hears. "I'm…." He wants there to be a way out for both of them, but he can hear the audience, already in the arena, restless, calling for Trace. It's too late. "I'm sorry."

"Don't be." Trace doesn't take his eyes off his reflection. "I'm not."

The smile Asia sees is chilling, empty. He doesn't answer, just shakes his head. He takes a deep breath and asks, "Do you want to cut 'Ash'? It's not like it's even on the album. They won't expect to hear it."

"They pay to hear it, Asia. I'm not cutting it."

"Trace, nobody wants you to have to—"

He's interrupted by Tim, slipping into the room. Trace looks up at the other man's reflection.

"You need anything to get you through tonight, Trace?" he asks, resting a hand on Trace's shoulder.

Trace takes a breath and grins his plastic grin at him. "Not right now, okay?"

"Okay." Tim shrugs. "You ready to go, then?"

Trace nods and Tim shadows them as they make their way to the stage. They pick up Weird and Tommi as they go. Asia can feel the rumble of the crowd, louder, rougher, through the soles his feet, shaking his bones as they get closer.

The band takes their places and Trace sees Asia steel himself for what comes next. He's clutching his new bass like it will protect him. Nothing's gonna do that, Trace thinks, as the lights hit them. The massive sea of people surge forward to stretch their hands out to him. Trace takes the mic out of the stand and drops to his knees as Weird begins the intro for "No Outlet."

Trace takes a breath to start the song and the crowd hushes back a notch, as though holding theirs. He closes his eyes and starts singing, offering the lyrics up to be swallowed by their frenzy. By the chorus, Trace pushes back to his feet. He leans out, letting them touch him, hold him, yank him closer. He sees Asia move closer, too, from the corner of his eye. Tim, just offstage, does the same. Trace tries to see just one face separated out of the screaming dark, but he can't focus. He knows if he lets himself slip below that mass of hands and upturned faces, there will be no getting him back.

Trace pushes back to his feet and puts distance between himself and the edge of the stage, turns back to the band, meets Asia's eyes. It's all right, he mouths, knowing he isn't fooling anybody. He sings the end of the song, lets the world kill the boy with the silver voice, and drags a grin up from down deep to begin the next song. And the next song.

Until it's time. Trace feels their want, their excitement at the prospect of having him to themselves. Weird and Tommi head offstage, but Asia lingers. When Trace turns to reach for the twelve-string, Asia hands it to him. He nods, then looks away, follows the others to leave Trace onstage alone. The crowd calls his name. Some call the name of the song. He settles the strap of the guitar across his shoulder and thinks about silencing them by telling them that the instrument belonged to a lover who was now dead—and he is going to use it to play a song he wrote for another lover, who was also now dead. It would make them love him more, but he needs to keep it for himself. He steps close to the mic as the spotlight tightens around him. They give a gasp as he gives them the first chord. In the breath he takes before singing, Trace closes his eyes, lets Albrecht go, separates himself from the song, and lets it belong to everybody else.

At the end, Asia is right there again, taking the guitar back while the audience screams. "Thank you," Trace breathes into the mic, before darkness washes the stage.

"Are you doin' okay?" Asia asks in his ear as they step into the wings.

"Listen to that." Marcus meets them and sweeps Trace away from Asia and into one of his wide hugs. "The more tragic you are, the more they love you. Trust me, concentrate on that."

Trace doesn't want to. He wants to be left alone to cry, not expose the wound to a couple of thousand people like this. Tonight he doesn't want to get caught in that sharp tangle of adrenalin and lust. But the rumble of them, screaming, needing, sweeps him up. He nods and wipes at the corners of his eyes with the heel of his hand. "Yeah, okay." He looks from Asia to the rest of the band. "Ready to go again?"

As lead singer, Trace now rates a suite, presumably larger and nicer than what they've all grown used to, but Asia's room is as tiny and crappy as ever. He lies on his back on the lumpy bed, staring at the ceiling. He wonders if Myrna would talk to him if he called. Then he remembers that she didn't give him a number. He gets up to check on Trace. During the show, even Asia had to watch him closely to see that something was wrong. Now Asia's scared, because maybe he was just putting the breakdown off. He knocks softly. "Trace, are you awake?"

He hears hushing noises and low-pitched laughter. He starts to back away, but realizes it's too late when the door opens.

"Hey." Trace stands, blocking Asia's view to the shadowy room beyond. He's bare-chested with bare feet. "Are you checking up on me?"

Asia feels heat on his neck, hearing that laughter again, behind Trace. "I wanted to see if you were... I guess you're okay, though, huh?"

Trace gives him a sharp half-smile. "Yeah. I'm great. You better get some sleep. You didn't get any last night."

"Yeah." Asia glances down at his bare feet, then turns away. "See you in the morning."

Trace watches Asia go, before closing the door. He turns back to the room, letting the smile soften. "Did you keep my place for me?"

The boy had been waiting for him, drinking from the bar in the main room when he got here after the show. Trace just assumed it was Marcus's doing. He almost asks if he is running a tab, but then realizes it doesn't matter. He doesn't even ask for a name.

When they fuck, Trace takes himself out of it, separates himself from the performance. When it's done, he falls asleep at the edge of the bed, hoping for emptiness.

It doesn't last long. He's wakened by sunlight and the ring of the phone. He's momentarily disoriented when he hears another voice answer. Mica? He wonders, but knows that's not right.

"I'll tell him." It's the boy with no name, leaning over Trace to hang the phone up again. On the way back, he kisses Trace's bare shoulder. "That was Marcus. He says he's got Mica all settled. He's gonna stop over to see you this afternoon."

Mica or Marcus? Trace wonders, but doesn't ask. He can't imagine Mica will ever want to see him again. "Good." He rakes his hair back and rolls over to face no-name-boy. "I was afraid he was callin' to get me outta bed for some bullshit publicity thing."

The boy nods. "You must be tired, after the concert and everything."

Trace presses against him, giving him a grin. "Yeah, not really. I wasn't exactly thinking of sleeping in."

Asia wakes freakishly early and lies there until the sun creeps into his eyes. Then he gives up and pulls on his jeans to go down the hall to get a Diet Coke from the machine. He runs into a threadbare-looking Weird on the way. "What're you doing up?"

"Hungry," Weird grunts. "Gonna get outta this hotel for a while. Wanna come?"

Asia curls his toes into the carpet and looks down. "Well... I need to get a shirt and some shoes, but... yeah."

"'Kay." Weird nods. "We should get Tommi. He could use some protein."

Asia dumps his quarters into the Coke machine and gets a can of Diet to take the edge off the morning, then goes back to his room to find a shirt and shoes. He meets up with Weird again in front of Tommi's door.

"Hey," Weird calls as he bangs. "Git up. We're goin' to breakfast." He waits maybe ten seconds before he bangs again.

"Okay. Shit." Tommi laughs as he yanks the door open. "Geez. Gimme a minute to find some pants and junk."

He's wearing a pair of purple underwear and nothing else. He opens the door farther and turns back to the room. Over Weird's shoulder, Asia sees the flash of another pale boy, peeking out of the sheets. "We're gettin' breakfast," Tommi tells him.

"We'll meet you in the lobby?" Asia says, smiling a little in spite of himself.

As they wait, Asia cracks open his can of Diet Coke. He swallows about half on his first drink, closing his eyes as the carbonation hits him, savoring the tang of aluminum. Weird chuckles. "I swear, you love that shit like I love smack."

Asia takes another, smaller drink and shakes his head. "Maybe. But at least it's legal."

He's ready for another by the time the boys join them. Tommi's friend is wearing a pair of Tommi's army surplus pants and a Black Light tour shirt. With his bleached hair and jangling earrings, he could be Tommi's twin.

Weird groans as the sunlight hits them and slides his black sunglasses on. He pauses to light a cigarette and says, "There's s'posed to be a pretty good place around the corner."

"Billy's," Tommi's friend confirms. "It's good and cheap."

Asia tilts his head, looking at the pair of them. "I'm sorry, but I don't think I know your name."

The boy laughs. "It's Cale."

"I'm Asia."

Cale laughs again as they round the corner. "I know."

"He was at the signing yesterday afternoon," Tommi tells them. "And then he came to the show last night. He was waiting around here so I, uh, could sign his album, you know, privately."

Both boys laugh at that and Weird snorts. "Whatever."

Trace sits in the chair by the bed, listening to the shower run. He's ready for the boy to leave. He lights a fresh cigarette off the butt of the last, before crumpling it into the ashtray.

"I'm sorry about your friend," the boy begins as he emerges, dressed, from the bathroom, towel-drying his hair. "Marcus said he…"

"He killed himself," Trace finishes, steadily. "Night before last."

"I'm sorry."

"Me, too," Trace says, but keeps his voice cold. "Do you need cab fare or anything?"

"No, that's all been taken care of." It's as if the boy senses his dismissal, but accepts it easily. He brushes past Trace, kissing him before he goes to the door. "Bye."

Trace says nothing. He lets himself adjust to being alone, for the first time since it happened. He calls room service and asks for a bottle of Black Velvet, lies down on the bed to wait for it. He squeezes his eyes shut and lets out his breath. He imagines himself in Mica's place, in that bed, covered in Albrecht's warm blood. Did you scream, he wondered, wondering if he would have.

When he wakes up again, the whiskey is waiting for him on a prim little tray, single shot glass accompanying it. Trace cracks the seal and drinks it straight out of the bottle. At first, his empty stomach protests, clenching around the alcohol, but Trace ignores that, taking another belt. This is the way, he thinks, feeling as though he is falling farther and farther away from himself. This is the way to get through the rest of it. He can do anything if he can just stay out of his body. He thinks of Mica and the feral flash in his eyes when he slides a needleful of cocaine under his skin. "Sometimes I just need something," he'd explained, "to stop my brain from thinking."

Exactly, Trace thinks, retrieving his cigarettes from the bedside table to light one up. Keep me away; keep me numb. Tim could get him coke, Trace knows, or anything else he wanted, but the whiskey feels better, a cleaner brick to smash his brains out.

Asia can't stand the thought of eggs, so he orders a grilled cheese sandwich and another Diet Coke. Weird orders something called the Hungry Boy special, and Tommi and Cale share an order of bacon and cornflakes. They sit at the corner of the booth, leaning against each other and giggling. Weird slouches next to them, eyes still hidden behind black sunglasses. He leans around them to talk to Asia. "What do you think is goin' on with Trace?"

That sobers Tommi. "Trace's lover shot himself," he explains to Cale, who makes sympathetic noises.

Asia shakes his head. "I don't know. He seems fine, doesn't he? Said he was okay. Show was good last night."

"He was better than he's been in a while," Weird admits. "But if he's gonna go off, it'd be nice to have a little warning."

In his head, Asia agrees, but the irony isn't lost on him. This was a business discussion. Weird wasn't really worried about Trace's well-being. Asia thinks back to last night, wonders again who was in that room with him. The look on Trace's face had been dead, cold. "He won't. He always shows up to play, if that's what you're worried about. Doesn't matter how bad he feels or how fucked up he is. You should know that."

Weird lets it drop as the food arrives. The waitress sits down next to Asia in the booth, smiling at him. "I was there last night. I saw you. You were amazing."

Asia feels heat on the back of his neck. She means Trace was amazing, of course. "Thank you," he tells her anyway. "I'm glad you liked it."

"I have your album, too. I play it every night before I go to sleep."

"Uh, thanks," he says again, wondering what he should say.

Fortunately, Weird leans over and saves him. "As soon as we get back to LA, we're makin' another one."

Asia wonders if that will be true, ultimately, but it makes the waitress even happier. She leans over to kiss Asia on the cheek shyly. "I can't wait."

She gets back up to take other orders and Asia stares at his Diet Coke. He sighs. It is almost over. Last week, that's all Asia was living for: the prospect of the tour ending. Before they left, he knew he would hate it and he wasn't wrong. It has been endless bus rides and car rides and plane rides, shitty hotel rooms and worse food. Even if they had been free of the drama, it still has been awful. In each place they stop, the audience gets bigger and more demanding. Now that they're in Detroit, he finds he's even too tired for stage fright. Besides, now he has the added fun of worry about Trace. Before, Trace had been looking worn around the edges, when he thought nobody could see, but now he looks so glass-boned and brittle that the audience might shatter him with their applause.

Asia is glad that it's all ending, but he has this awful feeling that it'll never be the same, even when they get back to LA. Trace will never be the same. He's almost happy that Marcus added the extra shows at Joe Louis. It's not because he's missed Michigan, or feels any connection to this place, but at least it's putting off the inevitable, at least for a week or two.

16

Detroit.

Home. Or near enough for Marcus's publicity guy. They've added enough shows that Trace feels like he's frozen, like he'll never escape here again.

He sits in the rain on the narrow ledge outside his open window. It's gentle, cool on his face. It counteracts the effects of the whiskey he is drinking, keeps the hard edges on all the facts in his life.

Fact one: Albrecht is dead.

Fact two: Trace might as well have pulled the trigger himself.

Fact three: that does nothing to stop the fucking show from going on.

Trace finishes off the bottle of Black Velvet and lets it slip from his hand. He watches its long fall to the rooftop below, savoring the hollow shatter as it explodes on contact. Easy to let it slip. Easy to let himself slip.

He pulls the curtain back and rises to get another bottle from the bar, still too steady as he opens it and returns to his perch. He tries slamming it fast this time, but the only effect is that the bottle doesn't last as long. Please, he thinks. Let me be numb.

He ignores the knock at the door, at first tentative, then insistent. Whoever it is will get in, whether he opens it or not. Everybody has a key.

In Trace's mind, Christian—whole and golden—demands his attention, his smile like razor wire. *"For example," he says. "If you were to tell me you loved me, how could I ever be certain you were genuine?"*

How, Trace agrees, when I never knew myself? He traces the vines entwined on one of the bracelets he wears. The platinum is cold. It rejects the little body heat he has.

A key rattles and the door opens. "Trace, I'm letting Mica in." It's Asia's voice. "Are you okay in here? It's colder'n hell."

"I'll find him." Mica steps through the door.

Trace watches him approach through the soft shroud of curtain. Mica looks completely different than the beautiful boy Trace met at the Para Bellum party. Still beautiful, but now he's dressed in a black pinstriped Armani that could have come out of Albrecht's closets. His white-gold hair is gathered sleekly at the back of his neck. They could have been father and son, Trace thinks, looking away.

"Get down from there." Mica comes close enough to pick up Trace's empty. "Before you get hurt. You're giving poor Asia heart attacks, y'know."

Trace doesn't move. Mica pulls the curtain away. "Even you wouldn't make me watch you kill yourself, too."

Trace lets out his breath, swings his legs back in and stands up. "I'm sorry. I haven't known what to say to you, since…"

"Since Albrecht shot himself while I was in bed with him?" Mica raises an eyebrow. "I'm sure not."

"I'm sorry." Trace says it again, but he knows it means nothing.

"I knew you would be. From the second you walked out that night." Mica's smile is sharp, but then it fades. "He wanted to leave you then. I just thought… I didn't think it would be like this."

Trace reaches for his shoulder. "Mica."

"Don't touch me." The boy steps back. "I came to tell you that he's getting buried tomorrow. There's no funeral. I'm flying back tonight."

Trace doesn't say he's sorry again. He walks back over to the bar for a fresh bottle of whiskey, because he's not drunk enough yet to deal with this.

"That's brilliant." Mica laughs. "Get so hammered you can't play tonight. That will prove you feel bad."

"Fuck you. You don't know anything," Trace snarls before he can stop himself.

"You didn't love him. All you wanted was what you could get from him."

"I tried to give him what I could, but then he wanted you."

Mica moves around Trace to slide the window closed. "Asia's worried you'll give yourself pneumonia or something."

"Look, I get why he killed himself. I know it's my fault," Trace says. "I don't know why he did it with you right there. That I don't understand." But Trace can't stop his brain from imagining how it must have been for Mica, waking to the shot, all the blood.

"He wanted—needed you." Mica turns away as he speaks. "If you're jealous of me, you're stupid. I was just…easier for him."

"Wait." Trace reaches for Mica again and this time he doesn't pull back. "Wait. I want to go with you, back to LA. Can we get a flight out tomorrow morning?"

He feels Mica's muscles relax a fraction under his hand. Mica draws a breath. "I can call William. He'll arrange it. Do you have to play tomorrow night?"

"I don't..." Since Albrecht shot himself, Trace has only been thinking about an hour into the future. He tries to pull himself out of that and focus. "No. Not tomorrow. The next day is the last show." He thinks to ask Mica to get them to put off the burial, but decides not to.

Mica tilts his head up to meet Trace's eyes. "He did it while I was with him because he knew I'd still love him."

That hits Trace hard. The last second he had with Christian replays in his brain again, and he squeezes his eyes shut against more tears. He can't breathe. He feels the same as when Eric died, like he'd broken something in himself and there was no healing it.

"Trace." Mica touches him, holds him tight. "Trace, stop."

"I didn't mean it," Trace whispers, burying his face into the warm curve of Mica's neck. "I don't know what to do now."

"Come with me tomorrow," Mica says. He takes the whiskey from Trace's hand and leads him over to sit on the sofa in the main room. "I want you to come."

Trace tries to kiss Mica then, suddenly hungry for the taste of him, but Mica stops him with a hand to his chest.

"Don't. Please."

Trace pulls back, stung. "I—"

"I can't." Mica withdraws his hand.

Trace swallows and nods. "I have to get ready for the show. Marcus'll have somebody up here in a minute, making sure I'm dressed and shit."

"I'd like to stay for the show tonight," Mica says. "Can I call William from here?"

Trace nods, getting to his feet again. He looks back at Mica, eyes narrowed.

"What?"

"You're different."

Mica's smile is painful this time. "How can I not be, Trace?"

Mica comes with him to the show and Trace is glad for the company. They ride to Joe Louis in silence, until Trace asks, "Albrecht had a picture of his dad and Errol Flynn standing outside the Refugee, back when it was a movie theater. Do you think William would let me have it?"

"You can ask. But it wasn't his father, y'know, Albrecht's, I mean."

"That's what he said, too, but it had to be," Trace insists. "It was too old to have been him, but it looked just like him."

"Albrecht's father died during World War I. He told me," Mica says. "He told me that he was a lot older than he looked."

"He told me that too, but…"

"If you didn't believe it's him, why do you want the picture?"

Trace doesn't answer. Because it's impossible, he thinks.

Tonight Trace lets the audience take him into their panicked frenzy. As Black Light tears through the playlist, Trace lets himself enjoy it all again. As "Ash" approaches, he welcomes the chance to sing it, give it away. This time the words come out different.

You've burned, burned me with your fire.
Burned me, but you don't stay

By the time it ends, Trace has no more breath. "Thank you."

They don't hear it. The roar of the crowd swallows everything. As Asia leads Trace offstage, he stumbles against him.

When they're done, Trace finds he only has a few hours, really, before he has to make the plane to take him to LA. Mica has booked himself a room elsewhere in the hotel and Trace decides to leave him alone.

He is far more tired at the end of this show than he used to be, at the beginning of the tour. He feels as though he's aging by the minute when he collapses across the bed and closes his eyes. He thinks of Asia, briefly, as sleep takes him. Poor Asia, wanting nothing more than to be normal. Never happen in Trace's company.

When Trace dreams of Albrecht this time, he's different. He's smiling, laughing, and there's no hint of the bitterness that tinged everything when Trace knew him.

He dreams Albrecht dancing with Errol Flynn, happy in the other man's arms. He is sleek and beautiful, golden hair slicked tight against his skull, his skin pale like porcelain in contrast to the black he wears. Trace sees him sigh and rest his head on the other man's shoulder, eyes closed.

"He was born at the turn of the century in Austria." Mica's voice drifts above the Vivaldi that pours spikily over the scene. "He knew Errol Flynn. I think they were in love, that's what it looks like. When the cops came and got me, they wouldn't let me wash. There were strands of his hair in the blood dried on me."

Trace's eyes open again and he sits up fast. His stomach seizes and he rolls over to puke on the floor. "Fuck, fuck this."

There is no one there to catch him. No one to brave the night with him. He collapses back down and reaches for the phone to dial in the dark.

"What—Trace?"

He closes his eyes and takes a deep breath. "Asia." There's a pause. Trace says, "Are you asleep? I mean, did I wake you?"

There's a short, weary laugh on Asia's end of the phone. "No. I'll be right there."

Asia puts the phone down and looks at the other two. "He sounds bad."

Weird rolls his eyes. "Thought he'd have his hooker with him, keepin' his mind off it."

"Weird," Tommi protests. He stubs his joint out and rises. "Don't be an asshole."

"Yeah," Weird grunts. "Whatever."

As they leave, Weird pauses, meets Asia's eyes. "Call if you need help."

Asia nods, but doesn't say anything. He grabs his key and pulls on his shoes.

He walks down the corridor to Trace's room, trying not to jump to conclusions. There's part of Asia that can't stop thinking that now it should all be different. Now that Albrecht Christian is dead, Asia should be all that Trace has left.

When he knocks, Trace opens the door but just stands on the threshold.

"Hey." Asia steps around him to get inside. "Trace, what's goin'

177

on?"

"I just can't sleep." Trace shrugs. "I gotta fly back with Mica in like four hours to deal with Albrecht's funeral and I guess I'm not really looking forward to it."

Asia takes a breath of the sourness in the room and says, "Were you sick?"

Trace laughs. "I had a dream and when I woke up, I got sick, yeah."

"I can clean—"

"You don't have to, Asia. It's a hotel."

Asia doesn't point out that somebody still has to clean it up. Instead he says, "Why don't you come to my room to crash. Or talk, or whatever."

Trace blinks hard at the wash of light when they step into the hallway. Asia looks at him for the first time tonight. He's thinner now than he's ever been, purple shadows under his eyes. Asia's room is around the corner. When they get to it, he unlocks the door and Trace turns off the lights when he crosses the threshold.

"Trace," Asia starts, then pauses, trying to think of what to say. "You can't let this…."

Trace goes to Asia's rumbled bed, collapses into it, head on Asia's pillow. "It's okay. There's nothing you can say."

Nothing he can do, either, Asia realizes, watching Trace curl into the bedding and close his eyes. From where Asia stands, at the door, to where he wants to be is too far a distance. "You can't let what he did ruin your life. That's all I mean."

"Thanks," Trace murmurs, but says nothing else.

After a couple of minutes of watching him sleep in the shadows, Asia goes to the other side of the bed. He kicks his shoes off and lies down on top of the covers. He closes his eyes, but knows he'll never sleep as long as he can hear Trace's breath coming so close.

The next day, it seems to Trace that they arrive in LA almost before they left. They're at Queen of Angels Cemetery by two. As the car takes them to the gravesite, Trace begins to wonder if they will be the only ones there. Did Albrecht have any family? Any friends? As the car slows, Mica's hand finds his.

It's arid and bright and the grave smells of dried dirt. Nothing is said as the casket is lowered in. There's only William and the two of them to watch. Trace can't connect the closed box to Albrecht Christian, beautiful, golden-haired, tragic. He watches Mica's face as the casket comes to rest, but the boy betrays nothing. The questions Trace has for Mica aren't ones that can ever be asked, so he stays silent, thinks about the first night he and Christian had together, how much he had wanted Christian back then. The memory is almost painful. He shivers, despite the unrelenting heat of the LA sun.

As they are driven away, he says, "He was the man in the picture, somehow, wasn't he? That's what he told you."

"He told me it was like a fairy tale," Mica begins, sliding his hand into Trace's again. "He said he was the monster. I think he thought it would make me want him less and I would save myself, but nothing could have made me want him less."

Trace closes his eyes and lets his head fall back against the leather of the seat. He is so tired of being sorry. He tries to focus on Mica's story, all about impossible things that Trace can't imagine and doesn't care about right now. The boy's hand feels so good, so warm in his that suddenly all he wants is more contact. He reaches for Mica, strokes his face and feels that warmth again, traveling up from his fingertips. "Please, Mica."

Mica draws back and touches his lips. He frowns and sucks in a long breath. "You're just like him, aren't you?"

"What?"

"You both take," Mica says. "He needed you to give him energy, but all you could do was take it from him. And it was too much for him. He tried to get away from you, but it was too late."

"You make me sound like a vampire," Trace protests, but he begins to see the horrible sense it makes. In his memory, Albrecht says, *You were supposed to save me from all of this.* But that hadn't been what Trace had done. "You can feel... Am I doing it now? Because I didn't know..."

Mica smiles. He relaxes back against Trace. "With him, I developed a taste for it, I think. So, yeah, I can feel it."

Trace's mind is racing, serving up memory after memory of touches, kisses, sex that suddenly all turns predatory, as he relives them. Is that what he is?

"It's your power, Trace. That's why people love you," Mica

murmurs. As the car takes them back to the airport, he kisses Trace, this time with no resistance. Trace savors the touch of Mica's hands, his mouth. He wants to stop the boy, but he doesn't know any other way to lose himself. In the end, he knows that Mica's right. This is all he is. He takes what Mica gives him.

Before they get to the airport, he asks, "Does it hurt...taking your energy?"

Mica nods, as he straightens his clothes. "But I needed him."

Trace thinks about Albrecht's sad story of his other lover, Sean. Did Sean take that way out because he felt himself weakening? Did he fade, like Mica seemed to, under Albrecht's touch? Then Trace remembers Eric, how much Trace needed from him, the power he'd felt over him, how much he hated Trace for making him need it. Then he thinks of Asia and feels something change within him.

He takes the flight back alone and it's much longer than the one they took to get there. For the first time ever, Trace doesn't want the audience. He doesn't want the music.

Asia is waiting in the suite when Trace gets back, dozing on the sofa. He startles when Trace comes in and rubs his eyes with the heel of his hand. "Hey, Trace." He smiles uncertainly. "Glad you're back."

Trace takes a breath and knows, right then, what he wants. "Asia."

Under everything else in their lives, there has always been a pull for Asia. Since the first kiss, it's been there. Now it's so strong, Trace wants to feel Asia's breath in his mouth, Asia's life, seeping into his skin. He wants to be inside Asia until there's nothing left of him. Vampire, he thinks, taking a breath. He tosses his key onto the table in front of the couch, but doesn't move any closer.

"How was it?" Asia asks, sitting up a little straighter.

Trace shrugs. "I don't know. It was...quiet. We were the only ones there."

"It must have been hard," Asia says. "God, I wish things..."

He didn't finish the sentence and Trace smiles to let him off the hook. "I do, too. I wish things were different, but they're not. You were right. I can't let what he did ruin everything. I'm not gonna, anyway."

Asia looks surprised, but relieved. "Okay. Well, um, are you hungry? 'Cause Weird and Tommi found this great place that's down the block, and it's open twenty-four hours, and they serve breakfast all the time…."

He looks so hopeful that Trace breaks down and gives in. From the moment he met Albrecht Christian, he's been separated from the band, and he knows that at least Asia feels it. He nods. "Yeah, I could have pancakes. What time is it? D'ya think the guys'll wanna come?"

It turns to be more early than late, right around four a.m., but nobody seems really put out when Asia wakes them. It's chilly on the walk, but the inside of the place is warm and smoky. Trace slides into the booth with the rest of them and lights up a cigarette as they put in their drink orders.

It's just like old times for the rest of them. Weird orders the heart attack special: meat, meat, with a side of meat. Tommi gets onion rings and a side of coleslaw with an orange pop. Asia decides on macaroni and cheese and Trace has the waiter-boy bring him a stack of blueberry pancakes and sausage. Tommi flirts shamelessly with the poor guy. For a while, Trace is amused just to watch.

"So, after tonight, we're back to LA, right?" Weird says, between bites of bacon. "Got your shit together for the studio?"

Trace taps ash into the tray in the middle of the table. "'Course." He shrugs. "We can start back as soon as we get there. Unless you need a break."

Weird laughs. "What do you think, Dellon? I need another gold record."

"Okay." Trace grins. "Then we start as soon as we get there."

As Asia pays the bill, Trace hangs back. He catches the eye of the waiter again, to pull him back over.

He's young, with close-cropped jet hair and skin the color of coffee and cream. The shirt he wears has the name of the diner stitched over his heart. It's baggy over tight black jeans. "Did you want something else?" His lips quirk up into a shy smile. "Trace?"

Trace returned the smile with one that overpowers the boy. "No. I just wanted to tip you." He digs a wad of cash out of his pocket, peels off a twenty and offers it between two fingers. "You done here soon?"

The light is changing outside, spilling harsh white dawn into the place around them.

"'Bout an hour." The boy shrugs. "Got a class at ten."

He takes the money and Trace dangles his room key in front of the boy. "Can you skip it? I'm staying down the street."

The boy stares at him. Then he smiles wide, reaching for the key. "It's stupid, anyway."

Trace smiles and turns to join the rest of the band. On the way back, he feels Asia's eyes, but there are no questions for him. Trace keeps his distance. He knows the boy will show up. He wants to think it will distract him from Asia.

When they get back, it's almost eight and Trace feels like he's been awake forever. He gets the guy at the desk to let him into the suite and tells Asia that he's going to crash while he can before the show.

Trace stands in the shower and wishes he could wash the last two weeks off his skin. Now everything in his life is suspect, needs to be re-evaluated. With his death, Albrecht has pushed him further and further into the dark, but Trace knows Asia is still there. Asia will always save him.

He's pulled out of the water by a knock at the door, then a voice calling him. "Um, Trace?"

He smiles. The diner boy, right on time. "I'm in the shower. Hang on."

He climbs out and wraps a towel around his hips, finger-combs his hair back from his face, noting, in the foggy mirror, the band of light brown at the roots. It's been weeks since he's felt like re-dying it. Maybe this afternoon.

When Trace emerges to the main room of the suite, the boy is standing in front of the door, still holding the key, staring around like he doesn't know what will happen next. He has changed out of his work clothes into a tight black tee shirt and jeans with enormous holes ripped into the knees. "I'm glad you could make it," Trace tells him. "Have you seen us play yet?"

The boy is having trouble holding eye contact. "I couldn't get tickets."

"Would you like to see us? Tonight's your last chance." Trace crosses the room. "I can get you comped."

"That'd be..." The boy's Adam's apple works as he swallows. His neck is long and smooth. Trace brushes his fingers against the pulse there, beating madly. "Great."

"What's your name?" Trace asks him. "How old are you?"

"It's Derrick. I'm, un, seventeen." He smiles shyly, eyes darting down to Trace's towel, then off behind him. "I'm almost 18."

Trace wonders if Derrick is telling the truth, but knows it wouldn't matter. Seventeen is still older than he'd been. When Trace touches Derrick again, he feels it, like a live current under the skin. This is what Albrecht needed, he thinks. I want it. He knows, from the touch, that he'll be the first for Derrick and that makes it even better. "Do you want to sit down?" he asks softly, fingernails scoring over the thin tee shirt. "Want me to order you some breakfast or something to drink?"

"No." Derrick shivers. "No, it's okay."

Trace leads him to the couch and gives him some space when they sit. "So, do you have our album?" he teases.

"I've seen you on MTV," Derrick says, moving closer to Trace. "You... You didn't look real."

Trace laughs. "Oh, I'm real." He takes Derrick's hand and holds it to his bare chest. "See, completely solid."

The boy's touch is so soft that Trace closes his eyes. He wonders what will happen to Derrick. Trace has no illusions, now. He takes Derrick's hand again and kisses the palm. "I'm glad you decided to come," he says. "I've been really lonely. It feels like we've been on the road forever."

"I..." Derrick swallows again.

Trace leans in to kiss his lips this time. He feels Derrick's breath as the boy opens his mouth to him.

"I've never fucked a guy before," he tells Trace quickly. "I don't know what to do."

But his hands are on Trace's towel, working it open. Trace smiles as they slip lower. "It's okay," he says, pulling at Derrick's shirt. "I'll show you."

They end up in the bedroom, falling onto the bed in a tangle. Derrick kisses Trace like he's been waiting for Trace to save him from drowning his whole life. Trace drinks it in, pulls the glow from Derrick's dark skin, the warmth from his body. Trace feels like he's starving suddenly and remembers Albrecht's touch the first night they were together.

When they finish, Derrick falls asleep, but Trace leaves the bed.

His mind is racing and he feels better than he has in months, really. He can't imagine this fading. He rummages around in the bag where his notebook has been since Albrecht died and yanks it out. He feels like he can write the whole album right now, today, in the aging afternoon.

Songs that have hung on the edge of his brain become solid things and he sits down at the bar to pour them out on the paper. Asia is there, in the dark, among the words and Trace thinks, "Wrong Brother."

The verses come out of him fast and he can hear it as he writes. Then the warmth Derrick gave him begins to falter and the rest of the music slips through his fingers. Trace puts his head down and lets out his breath, empty. He's too cold, suddenly, and pushes to his feet to return to the bedroom.

Trace crawls back in next to Derrick. He pulls the boy against him and kisses him. "It's almost time to get dressed."

"Almost?" Derrick grins.

"We have a little time. What did you wanna do?" Trace takes a deep breath of Derrick's warmth again, letting it transfer to him. He reaches up to touch Derrick's face and Albrecht's bracelets clink softly.

"Well..." Derrick kisses his fingers, slips his tongue across the pads. "Whatever you wanna do."

Trace studies Derrick's face carefully, looking for loss there, some sign that he's taken something, but he can't. "You were wonderful," he tells the boy softly.

"It was so..." Derrick's breath catches. "You're so beautiful, I can't believe it."

Trace laughs, but doesn't deny it. He presses against Derrick, savoring the shiver that runs through him.

17

At the curb outside the hotel, Derrick catches Trace's sleeve. Trace is done with him now, but doesn't want to be unkind. He gives Derrick one last kiss, tasting the lingering desperation of the boy's mouth. "Enjoy the show tonight," Trace says before handing him off to Tim. "Make sure he gets a good seat."

Tim nods and Trace climbs into the limo without a backward glance. The others are already there and he sits next to Asia, whose eyes are on Derrick as they pull away.

At Joe Louis, the limo pulls past a line gathering at the front and Trace stares at dozens of red-haired copies of himself, all bad makeup and glitter. It reminds him of the Refugee Club and he has a brief yawning sense of homesickness for the place. The limo ghosts past quickly and takes them back to the stage entrance before the crowd can realize who is inside. How will it be, waking up tomorrow without anyone screaming for him?

In Trace's little dressing room, things have already been packed. There's only his makeup left and the suit he's meant to wear tonight. Black pinstriped. Trace has to stop himself from thinking of Albrecht. He decides not to change at all. He's tired of having to go on stage so heavy with Albrecht's ghost. Let it be for now, he thinks. He sits in front of the mirror to begin his makeup, staring into his own eyes.

It's Asia, knocking softly. "Hey, Trace."

Trace smiles. "Hey. How's your stomach?"

"Fine." Asia comes in to sit next to him. "Did you get any sleep at all?"

"A little," Trace says. "Tomorrow I can sleep in, so it doesn't matter."

Asia doesn't say anything else. He watches Trace go back to his eyeliner. They're silent until Tim's knock. "Five minutes, guys."

"You're not dressed." Asia comments finally.

"I didn't feel like it tonight," Trace tells him. He pulls his bracelets out of his black jeans and slides them onto his left wrist. "Tonight I want it to be old times."

He can see by Asia's face that it's all Asia wants: for it to be like before all this. Trace pushes to his feet and touches Asia's shoulder. "C'mon."

Asia wonders if they oversold the show. It seems more packed than ever, the crush of people more threatening. From his place, he sees Trace's silhouette, tiny against the wall of sound and bodies up front. Trace yanks the mic from the stand and counts down the first song.

The noise is so bad that Asia has to feel his way through the set, following the beat that rumbles underfoot. Trace has no problem. He stays right up front, just out of reach of a hundred hands that yearn for him.

Finally he says to them, "This our last show of the tour."

They scream their disappointment back at him and he placates them. "It's okay. We'll be back. You've been great. You know I love you."

There is a pause, then they sigh all in unison, and Trace turns back to give Asia a smile. Weird begins the last number. It's really the end, Asia thinks, wondering why he doesn't feel more relieved.

After the plane lands, they learn that Marcus has arranged for new apartments for each of them, since Para Bellum has installed the Leather Boys in the house in the hills. Asia wonders, bleakly, if Myrna is staying in his old bedroom. He thinks about calling over there, but knows he won't. They've been on the red-eye and it takes a while to get everybody deposited in their new places. Trace goes in a separate car and Marcus takes the rest of them. He drops Weird, then Tommi, off, and Asia is almost asleep by the time they get to his new building.

The apartment is just off Sunset Boulevard on the eleventh floor. Asia hesitates on the threshold, but Marcus shoves him over.

"It's too big for one person." Asia lets his backpack slide down to the floor, staring around.

"Asia, c'mon," Marcus urges. "You've earned it. Enjoy it."

Asia sighs and Marcus laughs at him.

"Okay, or at least try not to be so miserable."

Asia sits tentatively on the couch at the middle of the room and smiles. "You think I don't appreciate everything that's happened to us and everything you've done for us."

Marcus laughs again. He tosses Asia's new set of keys on the low bookcase by the door and comes in. "No, I think you're a good boy, Asia. Just stuck in a life you didn't ask for." He sits down on the other end of the couch. "It's been tough. The last couple of weeks, especially. I know that."

"Trace's just so...I mean, shit. He's freaked out." Asia shakes his head. "He thinks it's all his fault. Honestly, Marcus, I don't know."

Marcus shrugs. "Who the hell could tell, with Albrecht Christian? I knew him for ten years on and off, and I can't tell you anything about him. I never could get any read on him."

Asia isn't surprised. Really, Herr Christian scared the hell out of Asia. Even if his relationship with Trace had been different, he still would have made Asia uncomfortable. He was like the adult you ran from as a child. You never quite knew why you were running, you just knew you had to.

"You're about ten minutes away from Trace," Marcus tells him. "I almost stuck you in the same building, but this is close enough, I think. You can still pick him up on the way to the studio when we start up again."

Asia laughs softly. Marcus still wants to believe that Asia can contain Trace. "Yeah-right."

And then Marcus is gone. Asia takes a lap around the living room. The only indication that it is decorated with him in mind is the *No Outlet* sleeve art on the wall over the couch. Asia stares at it, wondering if he can stand to be faced with the blank look on his own face, just behind Trace, every single morning he stumbles in here. It creeps him out, more than a little, that someone he doesn't know packed up all his stuff and then unpacked it again. He crosses the living room to test out the door on the other side. He finds the bedroom waiting for him. It's all browns and beige, the bed big enough to sleep crosswise on. Asia dumps his backpack out on it. The dirty socks and underwear mar the magazine look of the spread and carefully arranged pillows. It makes Asia feel a little better. He goes into the bathroom to put his toothbrush and razor away and catches his reflection. He is pale against the stark background of tile, with dark circles under his eyes. He runs some water to splash over his face. He wonders if he will be able to sleep here.

The driver carries Trace's bag up and takes it to the bedroom. Trace looks around the place. It's not as big as Albrecht's penthouse, but it comes close. It sure as hell beats anything Trace has had before. Instead of the somber black-and-white deco of Albrecht's place, Trace's new apartment is splashed with color. The living room is reds and blacks with an oriental feel, the furniture low to the ground. The bedroom carries the theme. The bed is low and wide, the accents red and gold in here. The driver hands the keys over and leaves Trace alone.

Trace flops onto the red silk and buries his face into a cool, soft pillow. He wonders how Asia is coping with floundering in his own new rock star pad.

Trace lets himself relax, puts off thinking about the album for a while. They have more than a week. He thinks about Derrick, about the transfer of his energy into the music in Trace's head. It hadn't been enough. Trace doesn't think an endless supply of victims would be enough. It's as though his body is more selective at choosing. Not like the vampires in Asia's movies. The life it wants is Asia's. Now that Trace is beginning to understand that, everything that Albrecht did makes so much more sense.

Trace rolls over and reaches to the lacquered bedside table for the waiting remote to channel surf until he has no more thought in his head at all. Settling on MTV, he waits to see himself.

It's not long before he's staring into his own eyes, lit by candlelight, at the foot of the staircase at the Pantages Theater. The camera pulls back and Asia and Tommi and Weird are all behind him, in the shadows. Trace closes his eyes, wondering if he even looks like that now. He doesn't feel like it.

He knows that Para Bellum has plans for reshooting that video right away, this time as a little movie, with him in the role of the boy-god. Trace laughs softly. Before the tour he would have loved that. He can imagine standing in front of the camera, Albrecht watching him from behind the lights. Now it doesn't seem to have any point, just repackaging what he's already sold. The song isn't even his anymore.

The VJ talks about the tour ending, about the anticipation building for the next album. "Can't wait to see more from this band," she says.

Me either, Trace thinks. He clicks her off and gets up again. He takes Eric's twelve-string from its stand in the corner. There's a cassette player on the dresser nearby and he picks that up too. He re-situates himself on the bed, cross-legged, and chords the guitar randomly. He hesitates with the words, knowing the truth of them will be another thing that Asia misunderstands. "I don't know if I wanna use this yet," he admits. "Asia will hate me."

Saying it out loud makes it easier, though, and the lyric comes out of him, shifting with the soft chords his fingers find.

He zones out for a while until he hears the front door open. He puts the guitar aside and clicks off the recorder.

"Trace?" It's Tim.

"Yeah, I'm in here."

Tim pushes the door open and walks in. "So, you like?"

Trace smiles faintly, wondering if Tim had a hand in the furnishings. "Yeah, it's great. Looks like a rock star lives here."

Tim leans a hip against the tall narrow chest of drawers by the window. "I need to go over your schedule with you, okay?"

Trace raises an eyebrow. That sounds pretty official. Tim's version of this on the tour was to bang on Trace's door a half hour before he was needed and tell him where they were going on the way. "Okay, hit me."

Tim smiles again. "Thursday, you're having a guy from *Rolling Stone* over to talk about your rise to fame and crap like that. I'll be here for that. He's gonna drop by about ten for drinks. That's two days from now, in case you're jet-lagged."

Trace nods, listens to three or four other things planned for him, then interrupts. "Do you got Asia's phone number?"

"Sure," Tim says. "I left it on the fridge in the kitchen, by the phone."

"Where is he, from here?"

Tim moves over to the window and points toward Sunset Boulevard. "Right over there." His finger rests on another tall building. "He's right there."

"Does he like it?" Trace asks, starting across the rooftops between them.

"I don't know. Why wouldn't he?" Tim shrugs.

Trace almost laughs again. Spoken like someone who really didn't know Asia. "I'm gonna call him."

"Okay." Tim runs a hand over his scraggly beard. "Well, y'got food in the kitchen, but I could also call for something else, if you want."

Trace shakes his head. "No it's okay. I'm okay. You don't have to babysit me."

Tim frowns. "You should get some sleep. You look like hell. You need something?"

"Do you got something?" Trace knows he does. Tim can always be depended on for chemical help.

"Yeah, I do. But take one at a time, okay? I don't wanna have to explain to Alb—" He aborts the name. "Sorry. I just mean, I don't wanna have to tell Marcus if you gotta get your stomach pumped, y'know."

"I know. I'll abuse your prescriptions responsibly. I promise." Trace holds out his hand.

Tim digs in his pocket to come up with two pill bottles. "These ones," he hands the smaller of the two over, "are to help you sleep. And these ones," he adds the second, "are to get you up. Don't mix 'em up, either."

Before he leaves, he reminds Trace where Asia's number is, but it doesn't matter. Trace has already decided to keep his distance. He feels the distraction Tim has provided recede even before the other man gets out the door.

Tim pauses. "Look, I been talkin' to my dad and he says he wants me to try school again. I think I'm gonna."

"That's great," Trace tells him, without even looking up at him again. He tosses the pill bottles on the bed, eyes drawn to the window.

"Yeah, and I'm gonna need to register and everything pretty soon."

"So you're quitting to go back to your dad's," Trace guesses flatly.

Tim shakes his head. "Not today. In a couple of weeks. It's not that I don't like the job, I just—"

He wants to go back to his real life, Trace thinks. He smiles thinly. "No, it's okay. I understand."

Or he would understand, if he cared at all. Now he's just indifferent. More, he finds he wants Tim gone. What is he now, but one more connection to Albrecht?

After Tim leaves, Trace lays back down, rattling the pill bottles. He wonders if they would work. The whiskey had almost made him numb, but then Mica showed up. Then everything changed. Suddenly Trace didn't have to wonder about why it happened; now he just has to figure out a way to forget it all.

"You're just like him."

It would have been easy to ignore. Mica could be just a coked-out whore, but Trace knew he wasn't making it up. As Mica explained it all to him, there was a rightness about the story that Trace couldn't turn away from. His subconscious keeps replaying scenes from his time with Albrecht that just reinforce the facts like a tape loop from hell. After it first happened, all Trace wanted to do was stay unconscious. Now the last thing he wants to do is close his eyes.

But he doesn't even feel it when he slips under.

It's not Albrecht, but Asia that comes now. Asia, beautiful and worried, waiting for Trace to take anything he needs. Trace inhales the damp chill of the muddy riverbank they sit on. He tosses his cigarette into the water, smiling at its tiny death hiss as it drowns. Asia doesn't move away. Trace puts his arms around Asia tight, kisses him hard. He thrusts his tongue into Asia's mouth, deep. Trace feels Asia shudder, open under his touch. Everything Asia has rises to the surface for Trace to take, and he does. Asia's energy enters Trace's body through his skin, melts into him at all the contact points as if they were becoming one body. Trace feels his greed pull harder on Asia until his soft, warm mouth turns paper-brittle. Asia's eyes open, all the green-gold fading out of them, until they're almost as colorless as Albrecht's—and still Trace can't let go of him. He's starved himself for so long, he can't stop it. Asia moans, but clings to Trace and it goes on, until Asia's grip falls away, his head falls back, and Trace is holding the hollow husk of a thing he doesn't recognize.

But then he doesn't care. He has everything he needs now. He feels Asia inside him.

Trace wakes cold, empty, and sour.

He shakes himself and gets off the bed. He grabs one of the bottles of pills and shakes a couple into his hand. Without trying to retrace the directions Tim gave him he tosses them down and swallows hard.

Fuck Albrecht for putting this in him, he decides, but can't get a grip on his anger. Asia, he thinks, and feels his body react immediately. He's so hungry for Asia now that it frightens him. He finds himself drifting back to the window, finger finding the building that Asia is in.

Trace knows he can't stay away forever.

Asia pauses as the elevator doors slide shut behind him. He hears the unmistakable blare of Adam Ant from the end of the hallway. He sighs and then laughs and follows the racket to what has to be Tommi's place. When he gets there, the music does a breakneck flip-flop to Gary Numan. Asia gets ready to pound, but see that the door is already open a crack.

"Hey!" he yells, stepping through to find himself in a crowd of people. "Hey, Tommi!"

"Asia!" Tommi shrieks, breaking away from a boy that he's dancing with in the middle of the living room. "Sorry, but I thought if I told you it was a party you wouldn't come."

Asia almost admits that's true, but Tommi looks so happy it's infectious. Asia inhales the thick stench of pot and cigarette smoke that fills the place and closes the door behind him. "Don't you worry if your neighbors call the cops on you?"

"They're mostly here." Tommi laughs, waving his hand around the place. "Everybody, this is Asia! He's in the band with me and Weird."

There's a lull in the activity when everybody looks at Asia and he starts to blush. Somebody calls his name on the other side of the room and Asia follows it. "Sammy?"

Trace's fluffer from the Refugee waves and grins at Asia. She pushes through, brandishing an album and pen. "Will you sign this for me? I've got everybody else but Trace."

Asia blushes harder. "Sure, I guess. How y'been doin'?"

When he writes his name over his face it reminds him eerily of high school yearbooks.

"I'm okay. Still at the Refugee, but it's not the same since you guys left."

Asia doesn't know what to say to her after that, but it doesn't matter. Sammy is swept away by the tide of partiers and Asia finds a place out of the way, on the end of the couch.

He spots Weird, in his own corner, nursing a whiskey. Tommi weaves in and out of his crowd, which is a combination of people they knew at the club or Para Bellum and with Tommi's new neighbors. It's not until much later that Trace shows up and the party turns predatory.

"Trace," one of the girls calls out as he enters and everyone's attention shifts to the door.

He looks better than the morning they landed, Asia thinks, knowing how easily that could be a lie. Tonight Trace is definitely dressed for an audience. His jeans are black, along with the tee shirt he wears. On anybody but Trace this would be understatement, but the tight clothes make him look like he's carved from night sky and moonlight to Asia. His hair shows signs of having been just cut and dyed again. He smiles across the room in Asia's direction, but can't wade through the people between them to make it over. Sammy is right there, kissing Trace hard, album cover in hand. Several other girls in a multicolored collection of halter tops and leather pants are next. As Asia watches, he sees a crack in the mask Trace wears, sees the restless, tired Trace show through. This isn't where he wants to be either, Asia thinks, rising. Someone pushes a joint into his hand as he braves the crush to rescue Trace.

"Trace," he interrupts a tiny boy whose hair matches Trace's. "Are you okay? You look like you could use some air."

He grabs Trace's shoulder before he can deny it and pulls him away, passing the joint to the boy.

"Asia," Trace mouths as they make their way to the sliding doors and out onto the balcony. "I've been going to call you."

For five days? Asia thinks. He slides the door shut behind them and wonders how long they get before Trace's fans push out here, too. "I figured you were busy." He shrugs. "I just wanted to give you some space."

Trace shakes his head. "It was quiet. My place is so quiet."

"Sorry," Asia mumbles. He leans out as far as the railing will let him, gulping lungfuls of air that is marginally less smoky than inside. "Yeah, my place is quiet, too."

Trace joins him, leaning with his back against the railing so he can look at Asia. He pulls a pack of cigarettes from his pocket and lights one. "I know I've been... a mess."

"Nobody blames you," Asia protests. "I don't. I'm just glad you look better."

"I'm not drinking myself to sleep anymore, if that's what you mean," Trace tells him flatly. "I'm working on stuff, but it's not... Not ready."

Asia draws a breath in. He knows Trace has been struggling. It hurts that Asia can't seem to figure out how to help. "I keep telling you: we don't gotta do new stuff. All your stuff is great. Don't worry about work right now. "

Trace takes a long drag on his cigarette and exhales over Asia's head. When Asia meets Trace's eyes, he realizes that they're almost all pupil. He shakes his head. "So then, what are you taking now that you're not drinking?"

"Tim gets it for me," is the only explanation Trace offers.

Asia frowns. He swallows and pushes away from the railing, but Trace catches his arm, pulling him back hard. "Don't."

"Trace." Asia blinks at the cold pressure of Trace's hand. "I didn't say anything."

"Don't leave me."

Trace pulls Asia closer and Asia has to steady himself.

"I'm not... Nobody's leaving you, Trace. C'mon." Asia tries to gently disentangle himself, but Trace won't let go.

"Asia."

I'm the only one left, Asia thinks again, unable to break away from Trace's eyes. He lets Trace draw him in. Asia takes a breath and closes his eyes as they kiss. Trace tastes the same; just the same as he did the first time. Asia opens his mouth, gasps again. He wants to collapse against Trace, fall and never stop.

Then he remembers where they are, who he is, and pulls back. "Trace, I—"

Trace lets him go, licking his lips. "I know, Asia. I'm sorry."

"No, it's not that." Asia shudders at the loss of Trace's skin against his. "Please."

Trace's smile turns sharp, becomes the plastic rock star smile that Asia has come to hate. "I need a fuckin' drink." Trace stalks past him, back through the sliding doors again.

Asia feels like he's been punched. He follows Trace, but hangs back, watching him work the crowd, finding Sammy and bestowing a long, open-mouthed kiss on the girl. Tommi breaks it up by whispering something in Trace's ear.

"Yeah, cool." Trace grins and follows Tommi into the bedroom, Sammy in tow.

Asia feels heat on his face as the three of them disappear. He hates himself for hesitating and hates Trace for giving him another chance, then taking it away.

Trace watches Tommi and Sammy, at the foot of the bed, chop up coke with their razorblades. Since when did Tommi do coke, he wonders, because as the boy regiments his pile into neat rows on a mirror, he looks like he knows what he's doing.

"This is good stuff," Sammy assures, and again, Trace wonders when she started.

But he doesn't ask either of them. He instead sprawls across the midnight satin of Tommi's bed and heaves a sigh. "You both look beautiful tonight," he tells them.

Tommi looks up from his mirror and blushes. Sammy meets Trace's eyes, smiling. "You ever done this before?"

Trace shrugs and shakes his head. He shifts to crawl to the end of the bed and says, "No, you'll have to show me."

When it's his turn, Trace does his first line and wonders when it will hit him. The other two have already begun to vibrate. He doesn't feel anything instantaneously. Then Sammy kisses him and Trace feels the drug light up everything inside him. He grabs Sammy and kisses her back hard, mashing her lips, sucking at her tongue, as though he could pull her share out of her.

Sammy shudders, hands trying to undress him. "I miss you," she breathes, working on his jeans. "Come on."

Trace feels himself respond, laughing. "Don't you want the rest of the coke?"

"No, I want you," Sammy insists. "I want you."

Tommi laughs too and Trace wonders if this was planned. Tommi and Sammy were always friends. Maybe they both still wanted him. Of course they did. Maybe this was an ambush. Then he thinks of Asia and lets Sammy get on with it. He reaches out to Tommi, but the boy shakes his head. "I got guests."

So this is all for little Sammy, Trace thinks, as she unbuttons his jeans.

When they're done, she looks away from Trace. "I really, really missed you," she tells him softly. "I keep seeing you on MTV and hearing you on the radio all the time. It's hard not to feel..."

Trace knows he's the devil. Sammy has been in love with him from the moment she touched him, way back before their first gig at the Refugee, before Albrecht Christian even existed for him. Trace imagines her lying on her bed at night, hungry for him, staring into his cold eyes on the album cover.

If he cared about her in the slightest, he'd know the thing to say to release her. But he doesn't. All he cares about is what he can get from her. He grabs her hand and kisses her. "You wanna come back to my place? The rest of the people out there are boring the shit outta me."

He leads her out of the bedroom and through the crowd that closes in as soon as he emerges. Trace smiles, feeling Asia watch him take Sammy away. He glances back, making eye contact for a split second, wondering if it's anger he sees in Asia's gold-green eyes. Hoping it is.

When they get back to the apartment, Trace is confused to find Tim waiting for him. He looks up from his place on the couch and smiles. "Interview over drinks? At your place?"

"Shit." Trace laughs. The remnants of Sammy's coke make him feel as though he's moving slightly outside his body. "Why didn't you come and get me? I was just at Tommi's."

"Yeah, because it doesn't mention that you'd be there on my schedule. And none of the rest of them answer their phones." There is a strain in Tim's voice, but the smile is still pasted on.

"It was kinda last minute, I guess. Tommi just had a buncha people over." Trace smiles, reaching for Sammy's hand. "Luckily, Sammy rescued me before I got mauled or something. She knew me from before I got famous."

Tim glances at her before pushing to his feet. "It was *Rolling Stone*, Trace. Marcus is gonna be pissed. Shit, I'm pissed. This was a friend of mine and I set it up."

"Call him," Trace demands, tired of the lecture.

"What? It's like, one a.m."

"So? Call him. Let me talk to him. I'll get him back here."

Tim lets out his breath, then obeys, picking up the phone and punching in the number.

He speaks after a minute. "Norm? Did I wake you? Well, Trace just turned up and he wants to know if you'd still be up for speaking with him."

Asia has to admit that, even though he is the only one that isn't stoned, it's still better at Tommi's than his own apartment alone with a late-night horror movie. He holds a can of Diet Coke and sits on one end of the sofa, watching the activity. Tommi's living room has turned into a cross between a disco and an orgy. Asia inhales all the stray pot smoke he can, wondering if it will slow the speed of his thoughts.

"Hey!" Tommi bounces down next to him, sloshing warm beer onto Asia's jeans. "Hey, how're y'doin'?"

Asia shakes his head. "It's kinda loud in here."

"Yeah, that means people are havin' a good time." Tommi laughs. "Are you havin' a good time?"

Asia laughs. Tommi is so happy, he's glowing. Asia envies his ability to enjoy everything. Asia wishes he could catch it. He shrugs. "Yeah, I guess."

"Trace looked okay, didn't he?"

Now Asia wonders what Tommi wants from him. The truth? Or reassurance. "A little. Maybe."

"I saw you outside, the two of you, I mean," Tommi tells him, shifting to catch Asia's eyes. "I mean, I wasn't trying to spy on you, but I just happened—"

Asia feels heat on his face, in spite of everything. "It's okay. It's not exactly private."

"Why did you..." Tommi shakes his head. "Asia, if anybody ever kissed me like that, I don't think I coulda walked away."

Asia sucks in a long breath of smoky air. Walking away? Is that what Tommi thought he saw? "I gotta go, Tommi."

He tries to get up, but Tommi catches his hand, and Asia has to stop himself from snatching it away. "Wait. I'm sorry. I shouldn't have said anything."

"It's not you," Asia tells him, but slips out of his grip to escape. No, it's all me, Asia thinks, stumbling through the dancers to the hallway. He hits the button and leans against the wall, eyes closed, as he waits for the elevator.

By the time Trace's done with Norm from *Rolling Stone*, both Tim and Sammy are crashing in the guest bedroom. Trace doesn't begrudge Tim anything. Maybe Sammy could be his goodbye present, Trace thinks.

He leaves them alone until dawn when he shoves the bedroom door open and sits down next to Tim, shaking his shoulder.

"Jesus Christ," Tim groans, disentangling himself from Sammy's limp form. "Don't you ever fuckin' sleep?"

Trace grins, knowing that when he does crash, it's going to be from very far up. "Only if I feel like it."

"Did the interview go okay?" Tim pushes himself up from the mattress, bunching the sheet around his hips.

Trace nods. "Of course it did." He circles the bed to lean down and kiss Sammy's cheek. "Good morning."

She stirs, eyes fluttering open. "Mm, hi."

"Hi." Trace reaches out to smooth back the cloud of dark hair from her face. He feels brittle hairspray on his fingers when he pulls back. "You look hungry."

She catches him for a kiss before he straightens. Her warm drowsy energy collects in his chest.

"I am," she tells him.

"Sorry I had to work last night."

Tim clears his throat. "Uh, Trace? Maybe we could get a little privacy to get dressed and shit?"

Trace laughs again. Tim sounds annoyed. "Sure, I guess. Do you want coffee?"

"Hell, yeah," Tim grumbles.

After coffee, Tim offers to drive Sammy home. Trace knows he should call Asia, try to talk to him, apologize or something. But he doesn't. Asia must have some kind of built-in defense against Trace. Last night was proof of that. Trace sits at the bar that divides the kitchen from the living room and stares into his notebook. He knows it all comes back to this, this collection of broken phrases and scribbles. He forces himself to think of Albrecht, hums the melody of "Ash" under his breath. He knows he's not done with this, that if there's even one more song in him,

Albrecht will color it, no matter what Trace wants. He rests his pen on a clean page and closes his eyes. No more coke, no more Sammy, just him and the page. He feels unsteady, his hand shakes. He puts the pen down and reaches to the end of the counter for an unopened bottle of Black Velvet. He cracks the seal and takes a drink. It hits the bitter coffee in his stomach hard and he welcomes the pain. Takes another drink.

The bottle takes it all away and he lets it.

After a while, Trace becomes aware of a pounding on the door. He stumbles a bit on his way to open up.

Marcus stands on the threshold, looking displeased.

"'llo," Trace says, returning to his place.

"Trace." Marcus follows him, taking the bottle away and replacing the cap. He sets it with the others on the bar. "What are you doing? It's not noon yet."

Trace shrugs. "I haven't been to sleep yet from yesterday, so it's not morning either."

Marcus's concern creases his brow. "Are you trying to burn yourself out?

"Yeah, Marcus, that's what I'm trying to do." Trace laughs at him. He flips the cover of his notebook shut and stalks into the living room to collapse onto the couch.

"Look, all I meant is, I know you've had a setback, but you can't let it—"

Trace laughs again. "You don't have any idea what is happening to me, Marcus. What if I wanna quit?"

"Well, baby, then you're in trouble," Marcus tells him. "'Cause you're not workin' for your boyfriend anymore. You're actually working for Para Bellum and you're under contract to deliver an album. This is not the time for you to flip out. This is the time that you get in there and make something out of all this."

Marcus sits opposite him and opens his briefcase onto the coffee table. He pulls out a slightly rumpled piece of legal paper. "Look, it doesn't have to be that hard. Here's a list of possible numbers for you guys to start working on in the studio. Weird put it together from your old set."

"I don't want them," Trace tells him, not even looking at it when Marcus shoves it at him.

When he's gone, Trace retrieves his bottle and notebook. He

throws himself on the sofa and thinks of Asia, of the taste of him, the feel of his hair in Trace's fingers. Trace closes his eyes and doesn't fight reliving it. How long had the contact been? Ten seconds? Twenty? Too long, Trace knows. He touches his lips with his fingers, opens his eyes again. Music comes back, soft, reproachful. Asia. This time Trace doesn't push it out of his mind. This time he puts it down.

18

Dawn creeps over the city. Trace watches the sun igniting the wall of windows in his bedroom. He lights a fresh cigarette off the butt of the last, which he stubs out in the crystal tray that lies next to him on the red silk coverlet. What if he falls asleep and lets the whole thing burn? There doesn't seem to be much hope of that.

He thinks about taking some pills, but doesn't. Now that Tim's gone, it might be harder to replenish the supply. Of course, he thinks, taking a long drag on his cigarette, it shouldn't be more than a few weeks before Tim runs out of money and grows tired of school. Trace still has his number.

Things have changed for Trace. Since Tommi's party, things have changed. He exhales smoke on a sigh.

Now every word that has come out of Trace is colored with the taste of Asia. Just like Albrecht had ruled Trace's music, now it's Asia. The difference is Trace doesn't want to let this go.

He knows what he should do is take the tapes in and give them to Lionel and Weird. Maybe just being with the band might break him out of this.

But he knows he won't. He can't imagine being so close to Asia now. He can't imagine trying to function when all he really wants to do is take Asia.

Trace knows he could try to do what Albrecht did—find a substitute. Mica would surely volunteer, but Trace finds that longing for Asia has paralyzed him. He stubs out his cigarette and sighs again, changing his mind. He reaches for the pills on the side table. He shakes a couple out and dry swallows them. They make sleep heavy, mostly dreamless. He likes the insulation they provide him with, something to stuff the emptiness.

When Trace doesn't show at the rehearsal, nobody's surprised.

"We don't need him," Weird points out. "Not yet, anyway. We got stuff to work on."

Asia wants to protest. Trace should be the one making decisions about what this next album will be. It's as though Weird is launching some kind of takeover, trying to shift the power away from Trace. We're still his band, Asia thinks, but says nothing. He doesn't know if he's ready yet. He hasn't seen or spoken to Trace since Tommi's, but he's thought and dreamed about almost nothing but that moment. Asia has no idea how he can go back to pretending it never happened.

Black Light play through a few old numbers, but Asia can't concentrate. Without Trace's voice, the music comes out wrong. His fingers feel swollen, awkward on the strings of his bass. He has to keep stopping, making them start over.

"Sorry," he says again.

"It's okay." Weird lights up a cigarette and hangs it in the corner of his mouth. "We haven't done this stuff in six months at least. You're rusty."

Asia appreciates Weird's words. It doesn't get any better, though. Asia's brain keeps going back to the feel of Trace against him, the taste of Trace's lips, his tongue, then the sudden lack of all of it. Asia's fingers falter again.

Afterward, Marcus stops him on the way out. "I want you to check on him before you head home, okay? Call me."

Asia sighs, but agrees.

Asia rolls down the window of his new used Chevette and heads past the exit to his own apartment building and on to Trace's. He wonders if Trace is even home, if he's alone. He wonders if Sammy has moved in yet. Jim Morrison's voice on the radio makes Asia laugh bitterly.

"C'mon, c'mon, c'mom and touch me, babe."

Appropriate. He thinks of the story of Morrison trading a blow job for vocals. Maybe Marcus could work something out with Sammy to tempt Trace into getting the album done.

Asia changes the station, trying not to think about it anymore.

Trace answers the door on the first knock, looking surprised. "Asia. How did rehearsal go?"

Asia shrugs. "Okay, except that you weren't there."

"I was sleeping," Trace tells him, stepping aside to let him in.

"Trace," Asia protests. He begins to reach for the other man's shoulder to give it a shake. Then he remembers. Stops himself, avoiding Trace's eyes. "I know we need to talk. I should have—"

Trace laughs and it has a bitter, hollow ring to it. He collapses to the couch, picks up his notebook and offers it to Asia. "Is this what you want?"

Asia sits next to him, taking it hesitantly. He's unnerved by the intimacy. Trace's kissed him twice in his life, held his hair while he puked countless times. He has seen Trace do all sorts of things with groupies backstage and at parties that Asia's traitorous brain has then turned into X-rated dreams at the least opportune times.

But Asia's never read anything out of Trace's notebook.

"Go ahead." Trace sits up a little to reach for his cigarettes.

At least the first half of the pages are covered with aborted lyrics. This is what Asia has been dreading. Sometimes the whole space is taken up with a single word over and over; sometimes one line fights its way through the vicious knots of ink. Asia swallows a sinking feeling and goes on. As he gets farther in, there are occasional bursts of coherence, angry, broken. Asia sucks in his breath.

Then he turns another page and the words at the top freeze him.

It's the Wrong Brother
that torture wants,
and it wants what it wants
world lit all in bruise-colored light
won't heal, just a scab of love

Make me a desert
to lie in this cage
until someone I love
is no one I know

Asia brushes at the words, as though he can draw the pain off with his fingers, but it makes no difference. I'm sorry, he thinks, throat dry. The thought of having these words committed to tape, having to play whatever Trace hears along with them is terrifying. There are other songs there, but he closes the notebook and sets it between them. He swallows. "Weird and Lionel are gonna start with stuff from the old set."

Trace doesn't respond. Asia begins to think he's asleep already and wonders how hard it would be to carry him into the bedroom to bed. He's so thin now; he can't weigh more than a child. Asia stares down at him a long time, even entertaining the thought of staying, but knows he doesn't have the nerve. I'm the wrong brother, he thinks. Instead, he gets a blanket from the bedroom and spreads it over those sharp white shoulders.

Asia thinks of checking the kitchen for food, but knows it's a waste of time. Trace has never eaten anything that requires more work than pouring it into a bowl. Asia knows nobody's shopped since Tim quit. Maybe, Asia thinks, he should call for a pizza, stay to eat with Trace.

That's exactly what he should do, but he can't. Not with the ghost of that song between them. I love you, Asia thinks, as he sneaks out of the apartment. Why isn't that enough to make everything perfect?

It's almost ten by the time he gets back to his place and Marcus has left four messages on the machine. They're all pretty nice. He sounds calm on the outside, but Asia hears what he's really saying: "Call me back and tell me if we're fucked or not."

Asia sits at the chrome kitchen table and folds his arms to rest his head for a few minutes. He knows it's not that late, but right now it feels like that place in the night where everything he wants is so far away. He should call Marcus, just to chase the feeling away with another human voice, but there's only one voice he wants right now, and he's just walked away from it. Ran, he corrects himself.

The metal of the tabletop and the chair chill him through his clothes, but Asia doesn't care. He closes his eyes and waits for Marcus to find him.

When the phone finally rings, Asia jumps. He reaches to the wall jack to snatch it up. "Yeah."

"He's okay?" Marcus asks.

"He's not okay." Asia laughs. "He's not... I don't know what to do, Marcus. He's not okay."

"We can deal with it," Marcus says. "We can get him some help. But we gotta get him into the studio right now. We gotta get the album done. Once it's all down, Lionel and Weird can mix it, and Trace can take a break."

How will that help? Asia wants to ask. How will it bring Albrecht Christian back to him? Or fix what I've broken between us now? Asia draws a deep breath, knowing Marcus doesn't have the answers to those questions. "Okay. But I don't know if he'll be in tomorrow."

There's a pause. It's not what Marcus wants to hear and Asia knows it. The other man finally says, "Well, we'll see. You get some sleep now and we'll deal with it tomorrow."

Asia clicks the phone off and hangs it back up on the wall. "Right," he says to no one. He wanders into the living room and throws himself onto the sofa, catching up the remote to turn the TV on. He clicks through the channels absently, desperately searching for something familiar. He stops on the image of Jack Palance and his plastic fangs, clutching at a young girl. Finally, Asia thinks, closing his eyes to her screams, knowing it's a poor substitute for Trace.

The next afternoon, when Asia gets to Para Bellum, he's nearly an hour late. Weird and Tommi and Lionel and Marcus are already crowded into one of the rehearsal rooms, waiting. He pauses on the threshold, holds back a sigh.

Weird looks up from lighting his cigarette with an Oscar-shaped lighter and gives Asia a grin. "You workin' on Rock Star Time too?"

"Sorry." Asia shrugs. "I fell asleep in front of the TV. Didn't hear the alarm."

"'S'okay," Weird says. "We're just gettin' started."

With what? Asia wonders. He breaks down and asks, "What about Trace?"

Marcus is chewing on the end of a pencil. He shakes his head. "I sent a car, but he sent it back. He won't pick up the phone, either."

Asia thinks of Trace, sitting alone, with that notebook staring back at him. "I told you," he starts. What? He's too sad to work? Too fucked up to work, Asia corrects himself silently. "I can't make him."

Marcus claps him on the shoulder and smiles tightly. "I'm not askin' you to. Not yet, at least."

Asia can't stay in the room with the rest of them, so he slips out into the hallway. Would Trace pick up the phone if he knew it was Asia? Would he talk?

Once the idea is in his head, Asia knows he has to find a phone. He goes up a floor to Lionel's office. The receptionist lets Asia in and leaves him alone behind the big desk. Asia remembers how imposing it had been the first time they'd been here. He remembers standing next to Herr Christian at the window, feeling utterly at a loss as to how to interact with the older man.

Asia picks up the phone and dials Trace's new number, and waits. He hears Tim's voice on the recording. "Trace's way too fuckin' busy to talk to you, but leave a message and his people will get back to you."

A month ago, that might have been funny, but not now. "Trace, c'mon. Trace, I know you're there. Just pick up the phone. I don't care if you come in, I just wanna talk to you."

He's rewarded with nothing but a beep and then a dial tone. Asia puts the receiver down and lets out his breath. He hadn't expected an answer on the first try, right? He dials again and repeats himself. Still nothing. This time he puts the phone down a little harder than necessary. He's trying to be patient. Please, he thinks, let me have another chance.

But he won't commit that to tape.

Asia knows that everybody else, the guys, Marcus, they all expect him to know how to fix Trace, as though he has the secret key to unlock him. Never did, he thinks, staring at the phone.

After three more tries, Asia's interrupted by a knock on the door. "Yeah?"

It's Marcus. "Hey, Weird wants you for a second, okay?"

Asia looks up. "Yeah, okay."

"You get him?" Marcus asks as they head back.

Asia just shakes his head. Marcus smiles faintly. "I know this is hard on you, Asia. He's puttin' you through the shit."

"He can't help it," Asia protests, but can't put any real feeling behind it.

"He's lucky he has you," Marcus tells him.

Asia almost laughs. That is becoming more and more of a lie all the time, he thinks.

It goes on for more than a week like that. Marcus calls Trace and Trace ignores him. Asia knows that eventually he's going to be forced to drag Trace in. Soon he'll have to come or they'll have to reschedule and postpone the album's release.

Today they've moved into the studio to put something down on tape. It's one of the songs from way back in Ann Arbor. Trace wrote this one with Eric. At first, Asia has trouble reconciling himself to this version. It triggers too much of the past for him, that Tommi and Weird have no idea of.

Asia's fingers are stiff; he's tense, like he's waiting for the impact of his brother's fist to snap his head back. He'd learned early on, to lean into the punch, not to flinch. Eric would just hit again if Asia tried to dodge. Without the lyrics to carry him through, he has to imagine Trace, conjure him up from memory to push Eric out. He closes his eyes and sees Trace, glowing and sweaty in that tiny bar in Ann Arbor, clutching the mic stand in front of him, mesmerizing the crowd on the dance floor just like he did at the Refugee, just like he had in every town Black Light played on tour. Back then, it was more intimate. Back then, Asia only had to share Trace with about fifty other people. He hadn't known how lucky he'd been.

"That was great," Lionel said after they'd gotten to the end. "We can use that." He paused and exchanged a look with Weird that made the place between Asia's shoulder blades itch. "But what we need now is to get vocals down." Lionel looked at Asia next. "Just something temporary, so I can hear what I'm really working with."

"What?" Asia starts to shake his head.

"You know it as well as Trace," Weird says. "C'mon, Asia. Just a tape."

"What makes you think I know the words?"

"They're Trace's words. You know 'em," Weird insists. "I don't got the voice and neither does Tommi. Just sing it."

Asia lets out his breath. He doesn't have any more protests, not ones he's prepared to share. He steps up to the mic and glares back at Weird. "Fine."

Weird counts it down and Asia takes a breath. Weird's right, they are Trace's words. And Asia knows every one of them. He opens his mouth for the first line and he sees Trace's mouth opening, taking the breath he takes now, releasing the first note.

Asia sings, but he doesn't hear himself. He hears Trace, not singing for a faceless audience; he sees him, sitting cross-legged on Asia's bed, back home, Eric's twelve-string guitar across his lap, slim fingers on the strings, singing for Asia alone.

The last verse comes and it's over before he knows it. There's a split second before anybody in the room breathes again. Marcus walks over from his position by the door. He gives Asia a smile. "That was great."

Asia feels heat on his face. He feels like he's betraying Trace and wants to make Lionel erase the tape. He knows he can't. They won't listen to him now any more than they ever have.

The session runs on for what seems like hours. They make Asia sing a few more numbers. He keeps thinking about Trace. Asia starts to feel anxious. In the end, it's not Marcus who prompts Asia this time, it's Trace himself. As Asia drives away from Para Bellum, he knows he has to see Trace. Maybe this time, Asia can think of the right thing to say.

19

Asia feels his resolve falter as he drives. In the dark, he takes the long way to Trace's place.

What, exactly, does he think he can say? You're wrong. I love you. I always have. No, Asia can't imagine those words ever coming out.

There's no answer when Asia knocks, but he's not surprised. He fishes the key that Marcus gave him out of his pocket and slides it into the lock. It's dark and silent inside. He is drawn further in, but something stops him from calling Trace's name.

The bedroom door is ajar and Asia pushes it farther open gently. Still silent in here, the scent of whiskey and Aqua Net and stale cigarette smoke. Asia's chest tightens.

Trace is sitting, folded in a tight knot in the middle of the bed, sheets strewn around him. He's naked, gleaming milk blue in the moonlight.

He lifts his head. "Asia."

"What's wrong?" Asia's throat dries. Anything he thought he was going to say drains away.

Trace's laugh is like a paper cut. He uncoils himself and closes his fingers on the whiskey bottle tangled in the bedding. He belts some back. "What makes you think there's something wrong?"

Asia makes a grab for the bottle, anger flaring unexpected. "Just fuckin' stop this, would you?"

Trace just laughs again. "Somebody will just bring me more. I got people, and that's their whole job, to bring me shit to fuck me up."

"You don't gotta drink it." Asia rounds the bed to snatch the four or five pill bottles from the nightstand. He takes them into the adjoining bathroom.

"Like you really care." Trace's voice drops and he folds in on himself again. "None of you."

Asia lets out his breath, the words not coming, just like he knew they wouldn't. He stares at his fists full of amber bottles. When did he become June Carter Cash, following Trace around, flushing his stash, for Chrissake? It's pathetic. He does it anyway. He dumps all the pills into the toilet bowl and flushes, empties the whiskey down the sink.

When he comes back, Trace says, "I'm sorry."

"What?"

"I'm sorry. I didn't mean it," Trace tells him, in that same dead tone. He's back to his original, almost fetal position, knees drawn up tight against his chest, face turned away. "It's just I feel so... Nothing works anymore. That's all. I don't know why."

"Trace." Asia's breath catches in his throat. He freezes, tries to stop the speed of his thoughts. Then he makes himself move again. Now, he thinks, drawing Trace into his arms, feeling the frail outline of bones through chilled skin. Trace presses his face against Asia's neck. Asia shudders, cold too, like there's a window broken somewhere. Trace's lips are against his pulse, then on his mouth. When they kiss, Asia feels like Trace is drawing something out of him.

Take it all, Asia thinks, falling, falling.

Until Trace pushes him away gently. "Go home."

"What?" Asia's voice breaks.

"Go home." There's a sharp edge to it this time. "I don't want you."

That hurts, but it's a lie. Asia reaches for Trace again, to prove it to him, but Trace is too fast. He stands, wrapping a dingy white kimono robe around himself.

"You love me," Asia protests.

Trace's laugh comes out jagged. "You know me, Asia. Do you even think I'm capable of that? Do you think I wanna be?"

Asia remembers all the times Trace's eyes have found him across a room, every time Trace's hands have touched him and thinks, yes. I do know you. He says, "I just..."

"You just what? Wanna fuck?" Trace snatches his cigarettes from beside the bed and pauses to light one. "Come back when I'm in the mood."

Anger ambushes Asia like a crowbar to the back of the neck. Heat licks up through him, the urge to rip Trace apart screams in every muscle. He takes a step forward. Trace seems to read it and moves to keep the bed between them. "Go home, Asia."

Asia can barely hear over the blood rushing in his ears. You love me, he thinks, as much as I love you. But he can't find any of it in the steel of Trace's eyes. For the first time, maybe ever, Asia begins to understand his brother. A hundred things crowd his mind to be said, begged, cried, screamed, but he can't speak. He turns away.

Trace lets out a long, shuddering breath as the front door slams. He sits on the side of the bed, rests his cigarette on the lip of the tray and shivers. "I'm sorry." And he is.

Trace is certain that if he closes his eyes right now, Christian will be there, in the dark, waiting for him. "Is this how it happened for you?"

"Yes." Christian's accented voice makes him sound cruel. "I loved you too much to hurt you, and so you could be of no use to me. The alternative is this."

In Trace's mind, Christian's voice comes from a bloody half-face. That face turns its smooth and beautiful side toward him, still protecting him. Christian yearns toward him. Trace accepts it, full on, ruined lips against his, ribboned tongue searching his mouth. Trace doesn't fight it. Asia is gone and Trace is in hell now. When Christian has taken everything, Trace accepts that, too.

Asia sits in his car, so angry he's shaking too hard to put the key in the ignition. No, he keeps thinking, over and over. No, you can't do this to me. I'm all you have left.

But he did, Asia thinks. He forces himself to drive away. After Asia's whole life of waiting, Trace is done with him.

He can't go home; he can't bear to get that phone call from Marcus: "He's okay?"

No, Asia thinks. Trace and I are done. Nothing is okay.

He thinks about the freeway and wonders if he can make it back to Michigan without falling asleep. How long would it take him? Would they look for him? How can he ever look at any of them again, now that Trace is done with him?

But he doesn't head out of town, because he knows he can't leave. It doesn't matter what Trace wants of him, Asia's stuck here. He knows he has to swallow this rejection and pretend like nothing happened. He doesn't know what else to do.

A horn blares behind him, and he jumps, wondering how long

he'd been sitting here, how many red lights has he spent, idling? Asia puts his foot on the gas and moves through the intersection. He feels like he needs to keep driving, as though stopping, going home and going to sleep would bring morning faster. He doesn't care where he goes; he doesn't want to face the sun when Trace is done with him.

So, finally, in the deep night, he finds himself back at Trace's place, sliding his key into the lock again. Now that he's let that piece of him that longs for Trace out of his own brain, he knows there's no going back.

He walks in and pauses. It all seems the same. Silent. Dark. "Trace?" Asia has to force himself to take the breath to get the words out. "I can't leave it like this. I don't know if I can say anything to make you understand what I..."

He stops at the bedroom door. It's wide open, just like he left it when he slammed out of here before, but he gets no sense of anyone inside. "Trace?" His voice falters as he enters. Then he chokes altogether. "Trace."

Trace is in bed, twisted in the sheets, unmoving. No, Asia thinks, rushing over. No.

And then he's falling again, but this time he can't stop himself, there's no bottom. He sinks to the mattress, fits himself against Trace. Asia gathers him close, seeking some scrap of heat, some proof that he's wrong.

But he's not wrong. Trace is gone. There's nothing left in Asia's arms but meat and bone. He presses his face into the pale curve of Trace's neck and sobs.

Time disappears with everything else.

20

"Asia."

He hears it, but it's so far away he doesn't bother to open his eyes. If he doesn't move, time stays frozen. If he doesn't move, he still has Trace.

"Asia." It drops into a gentle tone. There are warm hands on his shoulder, touching his hair. Fingers against his cheek. "Please open your fucking eyes."

Asia manages to gulp in a breath of sour air. The bed dips behind him. "Asia, baby. Let him go."

He can't. He won't give in. Part of him knows that Trace has left him, but he refuses to let the message get to his muscles. "Leave me..." His voice is raw from tears. "Leave us alone."

"He's gone, Asia." It's Marcus's voice, close to Asia's ear now. "You can't be here. Let me take care of him."

Against his will, Asia feels the world reanimate around him. He feels air on his skin with Marcus's movement. Asia opens his eyes to slits, seeing the back of Trace's neck, barely an inch away. Asia stares at the stubble of natural brown at the hairline. He smells the sticky scent of nicotine and Aqua Net and death. He takes one more breath of it and uncoils himself from the body. He is stiff, has to let Marcus take his weight when he tries to stand.

"Listen to me," Marcus says, holding Asia by his arms. "Look at me. Did you take something, too?"

Asia would laugh if he could remember how. He just shakes his head.

"Okay. Good boy. Now, you need to tell me what happened."

Asia looks over his shoulder, down at the mess of sheets and barely recognizes Trace anymore. Death has changed him, taken the sharp lines of his body and made them translucent, wax. A hole's been ripped in Asia's chest. He rubs at it, fighting for a normal breath. He feels Marcus's eyes on him and knows that he can't explain.

Trace is gone. The rational part of Asia's brain is tearing more things out of him, secret things that now no one will ever know.

Marcus wipes at the tears on Asia's face. "I'm so sorry."

He steers Asia into the living room where Mica is waiting. Asia wonders, fleeting, where the boy came from. He thought Mica was done with Trace. Then Asia's brain stumbles over that.

"Where's Trace?" Mica asks, taking Asia by the arm.

Asia closes his eyes again.

Marcus speaks. "Dead. Prob'ly OD'd, it looks like."

"Oh." Mica's voice sounds hollow on the word. He swallows, then tries to catch Asia's eyes. "Let me take you out of here. Can you make it? Do you want me to get you some water first?"

Asia doesn't speak. There's no point. He digs his keys out of his pocket to hand them over and lets Mica lead him away.

Mica drives them out of the garage, into the harsh morning sun. Asia cries silently.

Mica speaks softly. "He loved you more than anybody else."

Asia chokes, like he's been hit in the throat. Last night when Trace kissed him and Asia held him in his arms, felt the burn of his body: right then it had been true. Asia can't deny it. Can't defend himself against it. He hears himself choke again. "I tried to stop him, but he...I should have stayed, no matter what he said. I should have found all the fuckin' pills."

Mica drives awhile before he speaks again. "He loved you, but he couldn't be with you. He knew what it would do to you."

A ghost of the taste of Trace, the glass-smooth texture of his skin, invades Asia so hard and fast that he bangs his head against the window to stop it. Then, to regain a shred of normality, he says, "I have to call Weird and Tommi. And Lionel, pro'bly too, I guess."

"I'll do that. When we get you home. I'll stick around, 'cause I don't think you should be alone."

Asia almost laughs again. Now he'll always be alone, no matter what else happens to him. He is so tired, like he's been treading water for a year. When they get to his sterile new apartment, Mica unlocks the door and guides him in. Asia looks away from the print of *No Outlet* that hangs in the living room.

All those people died last night, he thinks.

The day of the funeral, Mica gets him out of bed and dressed. Asia retreats so far into his head that the past meets present now. He stares at himself in the mirror as Mica knots his tie. The last time Asia'd worn a suit was for Eric.

They'd both been pallbearers: Trace in front, Asia in the middle because he was so much shorter. Because of their positions, Trace took most of the weight that time. Eric hadn't seemed to weigh anything at all to Asia, but he knows that Trace will be heavier.

The service is at a sprawling Gothic church someplace in Hollywood. It's jam-packed with people and more lining the steps outside. A gospel choir sings and Asia sits through it all motionless. Trace lays twenty feet away from him, dressed in the black suit he'd worn when they played the launch party, surrounded by blinding white satin. Asia stares at his translucent hands, folded across his body, the platinum bracelets visible above the cuff of his silk shirt. Asia tries to keep himself from looking at Trace's face. He can't see Trace dead anymore.

Marcus talks about the tragedy of talent lost. Tommi, in tears, tells about Trace saving his life. Asia barely hears them. He spends the time reliving snatches of Trace in his brain. Then it's over and they're taking Trace to the grave.

Asia takes the front position this time, Weird on the other side, Tommi behind him. The casket is so heavy Asia feels his feet sink into the soil with each step they take.

They all stand around the grave as Trace is lowered. Asia can't feel his body anymore. He doesn't know what keeps him standing up. Someone puts a rose in his hand. He is vaguely aware of the sound of cameras as he lets it drop, but he can't hear it land. Weird and Tommi toss theirs and a handful of dirt. Asia does same. That he can hear, like a hard rain, landing on the casket.

Afterward, Mica drives him to the Refugee for the memorial. Asia doesn't move to get out of the car when they park. He leans his head back and closes his eyes.

"You're doing good." Mica touches his hand. "Only a little while longer, I promise."

The gathering is eerily reminiscent of the tour launch party. A lot of the same people are here, few of whom Asia knows by name.

When he enters the lobby, he's assaulted by the larger-than-life painting of Trace, from the new album. He's leaning against a bar, backlit in neon, cigarette balanced in one hand. Asia swallows on a dry throat, remembering the exact moment of that pose, Trace's eyes reaching into the shadows for Asia. *No Outlet* is playing over the speakers, Trace's voice echoing softly under all the conversation in the room. Asia squeezes his eyes shut and wavers on his feet.

"I'm gonna be sick," he says to Mica as they move across the room. "I gotta go..."

He doesn't finish the sentence, shouldering through the loose knots of people toward the doors to the main room. He slams into the bathroom and collapses over the toilet in the first stall. He gasps in air, but can't seem to let it out again. He tries to puke, but nothing comes except choking. He feels tears burn their way from the corners of his eyes, hears himself moan, and can't do anything to stop it, so he finally gives in. Trace is gone but even if his brain believes it, his body rejects the knowledge.

Suddenly someone is touching him. He feels himself being pulled up to his feet, folded hard against another body, wiry arms tight around him.

"Asia." Weird's voice is raspy in his ear. "You're gonna be okay."

Asia pulls away from the guitarist, out of the stall. What is he to Asia now, but a broken down old junky looking for a fix? Asia swallows hard. Anger, like nothing he's felt since Trace died, sweeps him and he clenches his hands into fists. Asia fights to keep his voice low. "Don't fucking touch me again, Weird. You always hated Trace. What are you even still doing here? Your meal ticket's gone. Time for you to go back to Michigan and be a mechanic now."

Weird freezes, and Asia sees his anger flare up too, like the crack of a whip, then die back. "I get that you're hurtin', Asia," he says quietly. "I get that he's something you can never have now."

Asia sucks in his breath hard and squeezes his eyes shut for a split second. "Fuck you, Weird."

But when he opens them again, Weird's gone.

Asia rinses his mouth out under the faucet and goes back out to the lobby. Weird's standing with Marcus and Tommi. None of them look in Asia's direction. He feels other eyes on him, though, as he stalks across the room. Trace would be in his element here, Asia thinks, and even searches the crowd for his narrow form before he can stop himself. All these people think they love him, but it's the idea of Trace that they love. Asia still feels the brush of Trace's lips on his skin, still smells cigarette smoke and Aqua Net. He leans against a wall for support. He needs to cry 'til he's empty, until there's nothing left of him either, but he can't let go here. Not with all these other people. He can't take comfort from any of them, because none of them can ever understand what he's lost.

Still, he's drawn to the sound of someone else crying from across the room. He follows to where Tommi has settled, sitting with Mica. The boy is crying into Mica's shoulder and Asia stares at their long pale strands of hair mingling together, different shades of bleached gold. He hates them both for being what Trace wanted.

He can't watch them now. It's too much. He tries to turn away to slip out.

"Asia, wait." Tommi lifts his head. He separates himself from Mica. "What did you say to Weird?"

He wipes at his eyes with the heel of his hand and Asia suddenly feels powerful. For the first time ever, he has the power to make someone feel as shitty as he does. "Same thing I'm telling you: we're done. Trace's dead, so you're gonna have to find some other way to support yourself."

"Asia." Tommi's voice breaks on his name. "I know you loved Trace, but so did I."

Asia chokes out a laugh. "Loved him?" His voice raises enough to halt all the conversation around them. "Just 'cause he fucked you once? Do you think he ever even thought about you at all?" He looks from Tommi to Mica. "Neither of you meant anything to him."

He turns his back on them, shielding himself from the shock that must be on their faces. People get out of his way as he slams the glass doors back hard to get out of there.

At first he walks aimlessly, half expecting someone to come after him, but nobody does. Asia yanks at the knot in his tie, unbuttons the top button of his dress shirt so he can breathe. He wads the tie and stuffs it into the pocket of his jacket. Nobody will come, he decides, and gets a cab.

Asia ends up at Trace's, because he can't stay away. Or maybe because he's been away too long. He doesn't know what else to do. He unlocks the door and enters. All the blinds in the living room have been raised, and the sun is scattered around the carpet in patches. It hurts Asia's eyes, so he retreats to the kitchen, sits at the breakfast bar. He tries to imagine Trace, sitting here, alone. Did he hate himself as much then as Asia does right now?

The place is nearly the same as Asia left it, maybe tidier. The futility of the cleaning service coming in for Trace and picking his clothes up from the floor and washing dishes now seems ridiculous to Asia. How long will it take Marcus to empty this place out and erase Trace from it?

There is still a half a bottle of Black Velvet on the end of the bar and Asia reaches for it. He longs to be like Trace, incapable of love. When he takes a drink, it burns, but that doesn't stop him from forcing more down. He can't feel that it has any effect on him until he stands. Then walking to the bedroom feels like he's walking down the aisle of a bus taking a fast corner.

He hesitates on the threshold, has no idea why his body is moving him back in here. It's just a room now, he thinks, nothing left. How could there be?

But Trace's whiskey forces the desire to hurt himself up to the surface and he pushes himself through the door.

The smell of bleach hangs in the air and Asia's throat constricts. This is where they would have started destroying the evidence, Asia thinks, and he hears himself laugh. Of course they did.

The bed. Their bed. The mattress and box springs have vanished, leaving only the brass headboard to lean against the wall. Asia laughs again. The only evidence of them is gone, shoved in a dumpster somewhere. He feels anger, but it's too far away, he can't get hold of it. There's nothing to protect himself. Asia lays on the floor, on his stomach, rests his head on his folded arms. He curls in on himself, inhales the total absence of Trace, tries to let it take away what still lives in his brain, tries to make it his world now.

But all he gets is dark.

21

Asia wakes stiff. The floor is hard, but somebody has thrown a blanket over him. He groans as the whiskey rebels in his stomach. Then it hits his head. He begins to get why Eric was such a son of a bitch. Asia is sure he'd feel better if he could just punch somebody.

"I wondered how long you'd stay passed out." It's Mica, sitting in the chair by the window, his feet pulled up under him. "I did try to wake you.

"How'd you know I'd be here?" Asia asks.

Mica just laughs at him, getting up and coming over. "Please. What do you think? I'm not stupid. And I still work for Para Bellum. I'm supposed to watch you."

"I told you I didn't want to see you." As though anybody ever cared what he wanted. "Didn't want to see you again."

"Yeah." Mica sits on the floor next to him. "Big deal. I'm a whore. Do you think you can hurt my feelings so I'll go away, like Tommi?"

Asia flashes on Tommi's face, tear streaked, and sighs, ashamed. He uncoils himself a fraction at a time. "I shouldn't have said any of that."

When Asia moves, his muscles protest, but he doesn't feel sick. "How long have I been here?"

"It's tomorrow, Asia. You've been here all night. It's the most you've slept since it happened."

Mica helps him to his feet and Asia tries to smooth out some of the wrinkles in his suit. When he catches sight of himself in the mirror, he realizes it's a waste of time.

As they leave, he pauses in the living room. Trace's notebook is still on the middle cushion of the couch. It draws him in and he pretends, for maybe a full second, that if he opens it, feels the texture of Trace's pen marks on the paper, it will skip him back to the moment Trace surrendered it to him. Maybe he could read the code better.

He shakes himself, gathering it up, as well as Eric's guitar, which was leaned against the coffee table. Trace's guitar. He corrects himself. Mine now.

Mica doesn't speak to him on the way home. Asia knows he should apologize again, but he can't. He can't forgive Mica for the pieces of Trace he has. He tries to stop himself from re-playing the scene of their kiss, the briefest flash of Trace's tongue into Mica's mouth. Asia tries not to hold it against Mica, but can't stop now.

Later, Asia stares at the TV until it's reduced to colors and noise. Mica hands him a couple of pills and a glass of Diet Coke. "Take these. You'll be able to sleep, I mean, really sleep."

Asia frowns up at him, but doesn't argue. They have a bitter tang against his tongue, but the Diet Coke covers it with its own. He wonders if these are the same pills that Trace choked himself with.

If they save Asia from this shadow-life, Mica should get a truckload.

All they do is make his dreams sharper.

He's in Trace's bed again. The scent of cigarette smoke and Aqua Net clings to the pillows and he turns to find Trace, looking back at him. Asia has to catch his breath. Beautiful. Trace smiles. His hands are on Asia's skin, lips on Asia's lips. He's warm, so alive that it chokes Asia.

"Stop," he gasps, as Trace pulls him closer. "Stop it. You don't love me. Stop it."

"Asia." Trace changes their positions, so he's pressing into Asia. "You're the only one I ever loved."

Trace is inside him. Please, Asia hears himself breathe Trace's name, begging. He needs more. Asia closes his eyes. He needs this, just this, forever.

"Asia."

The voice comes from outside Asia and he cries out as the dream explodes to smoke around him.

"Asia, wake up."

It's Mica, crouching down by the side of the bed. Trace's dead, Asia reminds himself. He's dead, and that was a dream, and it never happened like that.

"Asia." Mica touches his shoulder. "Marcus is coming over this afternoon."

Asia wonders if Mica had heard him begging in his sleep. Would Mica find it predictable? Asia rolls to face the boy. "Did you love him?"

"Trace? No. Not like you do, at least. I liked him. A lot. I wanted to be his friend, but there was always Albrecht between us."

Something dark in Mica's tone makes Asia understand. No. It wasn't Trace that Mica loved. Asia swallows. "I'm sorry. What happened to Herr Christian. It must have been terrible for you."

"It was. It's over now." Mica's smile is brittle.

Mica doesn't bother to try to force food on him and Asia is grateful for that. After he's up and dressed, Mica lets him retreat back inside his own head again.

"I'm going to run some errands, okay?" Mica tells him. "But remember Marcus should be here pretty soon."

Asia just nods. He's barely aware of Mica leaving. He stares at the morning news shows, fascinated with the brief rehash of Trace's death, a flash of himself, going into the Refugee for the memorial. Asia is surprised at how impassive he looks on the screen. It looks so painless.

Marcus lets himself in. When Asia doesn't acknowledge him, Marcus leans over to take the remote and turn off the TV. Then he sits down across from Asia. He says nothing about Asia's outburst. He just gets right to the point.

"The fact is, you could walk away from it all right now and live fairly comfortably."

Asia smiles sharply. "What about the money from the studio? And the rent on this place? What about the new album?"

"I didn't say you'd be living like a rock star," Marcus admits, looking startled at Asia's response. "But the fact is I know this isn't the life you want."

Asia drinks his Diet Coke and waits. Marcus is working up to pitching something and it's not hard to imagine what.

"This is the life Trace wanted, isn't it?"

"Yes." Asia makes the one word as hard as he can.

"So you could just go back to Michigan now and pretend none of this happened."

The thought makes Asia laugh out loud. "Yeah, I don't think so, Marcus."

"Well, okay, maybe not. I'm just saying, if you *could* have anything."

"I'd have Trace back," Asia tells him. "Just get to the point. Fact is I'm not going back to Para Bellum now. I'm sorry if that fucks you over, but what am I gonna do? Trace was the band. He was the music and he's dead."

"Asia, we can finish the album. You can finish it for him."

Asia's stomach coils into a hard knot. No, he protests in his head. "We can't... I can't make up for not having Trace there."

He feels himself cracking open again and tries to get a grip on it.

"Look, we have those four tracks that Trace put down for *No Outlet* that he dropped, remember? The vocals are done, mostly. And then we have your old set, with you singing." Marcus stares at Asia for a few seconds, like he's trying to decide something. "I think you love Trace too much to let any part of him be lost."

No, Asia thinks again, but knows it's not true. It doesn't matter what Asia wants, not even now that Trace's dead. He wants whatever Trace wants. He still can't help himself.

"Nobody thinks it'll be easy," Marcus says.

"Weird wants to do this?" Asia says softly. "He wants me back? He doesn't hate me?"

"Asia." Marcus gives him a sad smile. "Of course he doesn't. He knows you didn't mean what you said."

Lies, Asia thinks. Weird knows he meant every word. If what Marcus says is true, it just means that Weird isn't holding a grudge. The promise of another gold album is probably enough to let bygones be.

"I need time to go through Trace's stuff." It sounds cold to Asia's ears and that's a relief. If only he can stay numb enough to get through this.

Marcus nods his agreement. Asia finishes his Diet Coke and speaks again. "You call Weird and Tommi and tell them. I'm not ready to talk yet."

That makes Marcus frown a little. Asia knows he's acting out of character—he's supposed to be the communicator, the peacemaker. But that was before, when he had a reason to make peace.

"I'll go with whatever you decide Asia," Marcus says finally. "But you need to do this."

Asia doesn't laugh in his face, only waits for him to become uncomfortable enough with the silence to leave. When he does, Asia pushes to his feet from the couch and goes to the bar in search of something stronger than Diet Coke. There's a bottle of vodka waiting for him and he cracks it open and takes a drink. It's supposed to be tasteless, but when he swallows it—just like Trace's whiskey—it burns his throat. He almost chokes, but takes another drink. Burning is good. If he could burn all of it out of him, then the problem would be solved, wouldn't it?

If he gets drunk enough, maybe he'll pass out and choke on his own vomit. Then who would finish the fucking album?

But he doesn't get the chance to pass out. The alcohol hits his empty stomach and seizes it almost immediately. Asia bolts for the bathroom, but doesn't quite make it.

Mica returns to find Asia lying on the tile panting, next to his puddle of puke. He doesn't say anything, but Asia can't meet his eyes. First Mica helps Asia up, sits him on the toilet lid, then gets down on his hands and knees to clean up the mess. They don't speak as Mica helps him into the shower. Asia can't meet his eyes. Mica holds him up as the water rinses the stink from him.

Post-Trace, Asia thinks as Mica puts him back into bed. This is how I live in the post-Trace world.

"Pretty soon you're gonna have to eat something," Mica warns him.

Asia groans at the thought. Mica combs his fingers through Asia's wet hair, trying to untangle the worst snarls, gently settling him on his side. Mica rubs at the knots in Asia's shoulders. Asia shudders and rolls onto his stomach, lets Mica soothe him.

Just don't let his name come into your mind, Asia thinks, concentrating on Mica's touch, the warmth of his hands. Asia closes his eyes, feeling Mica's hands lower on his back. Asia's breathing becomes slow, measured. When Mica leans over him to kiss his neck, something breaks in Asia. Take me, he thinks, muscles jumping under the brush of lips.

Afterward, Mica lays next to him. Asia says, "They all still wanna finish the album. They think I can work on it now."

"Marcus said he was going to talk to you. He said he thought it would help you."

"Help him, more like," Asia protests bleakly. "Trace will be twice as popular dead. There's no way he can deny that'll make money."

"Asia." Mica leans up onto an elbow. "Of course it's gonna make money. And of course Marcus wants that. He'd suck as a manager if he didn't. But he also really believes in you. Not just in Trace, but you, too. He believes you have this in you and it should come out."

That does sound like Marcus, Asia thinks wryly. "I can't believe Weird and Tommi want me back after the shit I said."

"They're your band, Asia. C'mon."

Asia curls around his pillow. "Not mine."

"When Albrecht shot himself, I thought he'd shot me, too," Mica says softly. "There was so much blood and I couldn't hear anything. I couldn't understand what happened to him. And it was like I was outside my body for a while, y'know? Then after I figured it out, I wished he had shot me, too."

Asia's throat tightens. He squeezes his eyes shut. He doesn't want to care about anybody else's pain.

"And I wanted Trace to suffer, because I knew it was all his fault." Mica gets up from the bed. "But I realized that it didn't matter. Albrecht was still dead. What difference could it make?"

"You're saying it doesn't matter what I do to myself now, because Trace doesn't care?" Asia laughs into his pillow at the thought. "No shit. Trace never cared when he was alive."

"I'm sayin' you'll do the album because you love him, regardless. You should stop fighting both those things. You can't live like this forever."

In a post-Trace world, it's the only way for Asia. But he only laughs again and says, "You think I wanna live now, without him?"

"I can think of faster ways to kill yourself."

At least two, I bet, Asia thinks, ashamed at putting Mica through any more shit. Asia shifts and opens his eyes again. Mica stands at the foot of the bed, in his jeans and one of Asia's old Hard Rock tee shirts. He sighs. "You just don't want to want to live. But that will come back."

Asia feels himself go cold inside. "It that why you fucked me? To give me the will to live?" He tries to laugh again, but the coldness turns sharp in his chest and it hurts to breathe. "It's gonna take a lot more than that."

But he can't stop himself from replaying it in his head. Mica felt so different than Myrna. The moment of Asia's orgasm had been so perfectly pain-free. Trace had lifted away from him.

Asia can't let it happen again.

"That isn't why," Mica protests softly, coming around to the other side of the bed. "We need each other. Don't make it more or less than that."

Asia doesn't answer. He can't let Mica in again. He has to hang onto Trace tight, or else he'll be gone.

He remembers staring at Trace's feet, in the casket. Bare and pale and so beautiful that the air hurt Asia's lungs. When they closed the lid, Asia felt like he'd lost a layer of skin.

"Asia." Mica's voice drags him back. "C'mon. You're done hidin' in bed all day. Get up and call Tommi. He's left a message every day."

Since when? Asia doesn't remember the phone ringing. How many days have passed since the funeral? "I don't wanna talk to him."

But Mica's gone. Asia knows he's being an asshole. Before Trace left him, he never would have said such horrible things to any of them. He never would have let himself slip and need Mica so much. He doesn't want to live, but he doesn't want to die either.

Trace never understood what Asia saw in horror movies, but if this were one now, instead of real life, the devil would appear, and Asia would only have to promise him a hand, or maybe a virgin, or his soul, and he'd get his wish. Trace would reappear in a puff of white smoke. But this isn't a horror movie. This is the post-Trace world and Asia's alone.

Mica returns, but Asia has closed his eyes again.

"You could use another shower." Mica thunks a pile of folded clothes down next to Asia. "And get dressed."

After a few minutes, Asia relents. He decides it'll be easier to obey and gets up, shuffles into the bathroom.

Later, he finds Mica in the kitchen, pouring orange juice. Asia gathers his hair back into a rubber band and sits at the table. "Can I ask you something?"

Mica turns away to replace the pitcher in the refrigerator and sets the glass in front of Asia. "I guess."

"Trace was..." Asia takes a breath. "I never—we never slept together."

"Asia." Mica stops him gently. "What do you want to know?"

Nothing, Asia thinks, feeling his skin flush. Except that Mica had a piece of Trace that Asia never would. His lips twitch up into a painful smile. "We never... Tell me."

"The first night, when we met, he was so..." Mica gasps in a tiny breath. "He was tender and perfect. I fell in love with him then."

Asia's breath catches, too. The ice in his chest starts to crack.

"After the first time, Albrecht was there and Trace changed." Mica slides up onto the black granite counter and kicks his socked heels into the cupboard. He looks away from Asia. "Then it was all a performance. It felt like he was onstage."

Asia pushes back from the table as the ice breaks. He feels himself collapse back into the hole, falling again. "I just... I just..."

He rubs his eyes hard and feels tears.

"It's okay, Asia." Mica moves to touch his hair. "It's okay."

"No!" Asia pushes him away. "No, it's not. He hated me when he died. He didn't want me. He made me leave when we almost..."

Asia chokes on the rest. He stumbles back and has to catch himself on the doorframe. "It was all a lie."

"If you believed that, this would be a lot easier," Mica says softly.

Asia turns his back on Mica. Easy. No, there was no way any of this could be easy. "What choice do I have?"

His voice is a whisper. He can barely force the words from his throat. He just stands there, wondering how to hide from Mica now. Asia is trapped and he knows it.

"Trace loved you. Anybody who knew both of you could see that," Mica says, unrelenting. "I think that he was afraid it would hurt you, like it did Albrecht. That's why he did what he did."

"Why he killed himself?" Asia demands. "For me?"

"Sit down." Mica is behind him, steadying him, guiding him to the couch in the living room. "Just sit down and breathe, okay? I'll get you a Diet Coke."

"No." Asia grabs Mica's hand before he can escape. "Tell me. What did Trace tell you?"

Mica looks down at Asia's hand tightening, before he speaks again. "We talked about Albrecht, you know, when we flew out here together for the funeral. I told Trace some of what Albrecht said the night he died, what Trace meant to him, how he made him feel."

The boy sits next to Asia and shakes his head. "Albrecht said that both he and Trace had the ability to pull energy from the people around them. You must have felt it, right? Albrecht said that was what attracted him to Trace in the first place, but Trace was stronger than he was. He took too much, but didn't understand that he was doing it."

Asia stares at Mica, trying to guess his motives in this. "I don't believe you."

Mica touches Asia's hand softly. "Neither did Trace, at first. But I guess he didn't really have much choice."

"Did you know he would do this, then?"

"Look, I didn't ask Albrecht to tell me his life story and then blow his brains out. I thought if Trace knew, if he could understand, then maybe he could learn how to control it." Mica shakes his head again. "He said I made him sound like a vampire. But I think about them more like a drug—Trace and Albrecht. I know I was addicted to Albrecht. I needed to feel him taking it from me. It was better than coke." Mica's smile turns bitter. "And nothing will ever be the same. Because I'll never find anybody else like him."

Asia narrows his eyes and thinks, unaccountably, of Jack Palance, sinking his plastic teeth into the flesh of virgins. Asia had wanted nothing more that night than to go back, give himself to Trace.

Asia leans back and closes his eyes. He feels far too calm. He doesn't have any strength to deny what Mica has told him. Hasn't he always known that Trace was magic? Somehow he can't stand that Mica knows, too. "You have to go." He says it quietly.

"Asia, I know how hard this is to process, believe me, but you have to."

Asia yanks his hand away. "I don't have to do anything. You just told me that that Trace swallowed all those pills because of me. No, because of what you told him he was. You made him afraid of me, when it wouldn't have mattered what he took.... You have to go."

22

Asia doesn't let himself miss Mica, or wonder what would have happened if he'd stayed. Asia has to keep himself focused on Trace. He spends his time trying to hear the music in Trace's notebook, but the songs are out of Asia's reach. All he can do is let memories come.

He sat on his rumpled bed, cross-legged, next to Trace, who held the guitar. Asia reached awkwardly to adjust Trace's fingers on the strings. "No, see, that's D. Now D7th."

Asia tried not to let the contact linger. When he leaned close, he felt Trace's breath against his hair. Asia pulled away, too quickly. There was a pause where Trace looked up from the strings at him, then back again.

"I get it," Trace said softly, moving his fingers.

Asia lets the image fade. He sets the guitar aside. Had he felt it then: the taking, in Trace's fingers, in the touch of his breath? Asia pushes to his feet to get a drink, knowing it won't wash the question away.

He brings the bottle back to his place on the sofa, wondering when it was that he had become such a cliché. Halfway there, he hears a knock and goes to answer the door.

There's a girl standing in the hallway dressed in a long pink tee shirt, tied at the hip over black leggings and ankle boots with Cuban heels. "These are from Marcus." She hands over a shoebox.

It rattles when Asia takes it and he knows, with sickening certainty, what's inside. He thanks her and shuts the door as fast as he can.

He collapses back onto the sofa and flips the top off and finds that he's right. The box is filled with cassettes. Asia twists the top off the vodka and takes a drink before he even touches one of them.

What if he never played any of them? What if he ripped the tape out of each and shredded it? He won't and he knows it. This is something real and concrete of Trace, something he can hold.

The first one he lays his hand on is dated two weeks before it happened. Not from the last album, then. Asia's stomach tightens. Marcus was holding out on him.

It's Trace's voice. It's all there is.

Asia gets up to click it into the stereo and hit play. He leans on the wall beside the entertainment center and waits.

Trace speaks. "I don't know if I want to use this yet. Asia's gonna hate me."

He hears sadness there, even in the chords that Trace starts with. Minor and so soft they're like the ghost of a song.

It's the wrong brother
that torture wants.
and it wants what it wants.

Asia stumbles back, falling into the chair behind him. The lyrics unfold to encompass every time Trace had touched him and every time he'd drawn back from it. He hears the dream-Trace saying, "I love you more than anyone else." He feels the lie he's been clinging to crumble around him. There's no hate for him in this song: only longing, only regret.

There are three other songs that follow. Trace's comments all deal with how Weird's guitar should sound, or the tempo, or some production points. Trace is still talking about the future.

Asia begins to arrange the rest of them by date, gets out Trace's notebook. He goes into the bedroom closet to find the little tape player that he knows is floating around in there and brings it, the box, and a legal pad to spread out on the kitchen table. He gets a glass bottle of Diet Coke from the fridge and pops off the cap with a drawer pull. He turns one of the chairs around to straddle it and listens to the tapes again, trying to find the corresponding page in Trace's notebook. He stops making notes and closes his eyes. If he concentrates, he's sitting next to Trace again, on his bed at his parents', Eric's guitar between them.

Gradually, that feeling slips away from him, as Trace's voice gets softer, more desperate. Asia can hear the regret he holds for other things coming.

"I can't ever seem to get away from this, no matter what. I only played it for him once, before we left. I thought if he heard it, he'd know that I tried to love him," Trace says softly, over the opening chords of "Ash." "I know it's gotta go on the album, but now it's so hard..."

The gentle, choked version of the song that follows is painful. This was Trace, stripped of his audience, feeling the loss. Asia rubs at his eyes, takes a long drink of the Diet Coke. He puts his hand on the last tape. Trace has written "Savior" on it, instead of a date.

There's the chunk of Trace clicking off the tape, then starting it again. Asia can hear a phone ring in the background, then the murmur of his own voice. He hears himself pleading for Trace to just pick up. It could have been any of the dozens of calls he'd made, but to Asia it sounds like the last of them.

"Shut the fuck up, Asia," Trace mutters. "Let me think. I need to get this outta my head."

Asia's heart bangs hard against his ribs. Then Trace starts singing.

> *I know what I do to you*
> *I know the*
> *taste of your breath*
> *I used to dream of your love but I wake*
> *to its phantom*
> *What you give me is pain*
> *Like your breath*
> *what you give takes me to the dark.*

Asia freezes, the Diet Coke burning in his stomach. There's more. Asia can hear everything between them in Trace's voice. The song stretches out to encompass what they both lost. Then it stops and Asia hears Trace take a long breath, hears him put the guitar aside and the tiny hiss of ignition when he lights a cigarette. Asia listens to his first drag before Trace says, "I can't do any of this anymore."

It's the suicide note. Asia pushes from back from the table and goes to collapse on the couch again, feeling every one of Trace's words carve itself into his body. The feeling that bleeds from them Asia has no word for. Grief, love, hate: it is all those things, but worse, more.

Asia closes his eyes. In their history together, Asia always believed he escaped being the target of Trace's writing eye. Asia recognized that Trace wrote about himself, he wrote about his audience, Eric, Herr Christian, but not Asia.

All of what Mica told him comes crashing back. Asia knows what he's always been too terrified to accept. He was the one. He was the one that Trace needed.

Trace's voice, like velvet sandpaper, replays in Asia's mind now. How could he have been the object of such desire? The apartment closes in on Asia. Trace's voice filled the hollow in him only to widen it with its absence now. The silence is too much. He gets up with no clear plan but to put some space between himself and the ghost of Trace's voice. He catches sight of himself in the mirror in the bedroom and realizes that he hasn't shaved since Mica left him. Asia scowls at his reflection and goes to the bathroom to take care of that. He drags a comb through the tangle of his hair as well, and gathers it into a ponytail holder. Then he collects a change of clothes from the dresser too. He trades his frayed sweat pants for a pair of black jeans and a black sweater he's pretty sure he didn't buy and knows he's never worn. Then he drags his red high-tops out and laces them up. He rides the elevator down the lobby of the building and goes out to walk toward Sunset Boulevard.

He realizes that he doesn't know what day it is. He barely remembers the month. How long has it been since he's seen Mica? How long since the funeral? LA spreads out for miles around Asia, hazy. The light is so low and bright he shades his eyes and squints; he can feel the chill collecting in the breeze. He wanders past a used record store, a magic shop, and finally ends up at a little restaurant about five blocks down.

He stops at the payphone by the door and digs through his wallet for the card that has Mica's number on it. He leans against the wall as it rings, then a machine kicks in.

"Leave a number and anything else you know that's interesting, and I'll call back," Mica's voice tells him.

"It's me—it's Asia and I don't know the number here. I'm at, uh…" He tries to remember the name on the sign outside. "Andy's, on Sunset, down the street from that one used bookstore. I know I'm not…" He laughs. "I'm not that much fun. But I really need to talk. If you can. I'll be here for a while."

He hangs up and lets the lone waitress, a girl with a bleached and teased beehive, seat him in a booth. She gives Asia a menu and he stares a full minute, without reading it. Finally he says, "I might need a little time to decide what I want. Can I have a Diet Coke?"

She agrees and Asia tries to concentrate on the menu in front of him. He has put himself into the position of having to eat, or at least plan to eat something, but the decision is hard. It's like he's forgotten how to do it.

"I have your album," the waitress opens with as she returns. "I really like it. I'm sorry about your friend."

Asia feels himself try to hide behind the wall in his head, but manages to answer her. "Thank you."

"I saw you, on TV, coming out of the church. You look a little better today."

He smiles faintly. "Thanks."

"My girlfriend killed herself in high school, when we were seventeen. I never knew why, so I just..." She shrugs. "I was going to say I understand, but I hated that whenever somebody tried to tell me that back then. Sorry."

"No," Asia insists. "I appreciate it."

He is almost surprised to find that it is true. He orders a hamburger and wonders if he can actually eat it, but is nearly finished when Mica shows up.

"Hi." The boy grins and sits down next to Asia in the booth. "I was just thinking about you."

Asia feels a smile spark across his face. He reaches out to touch one soft lock of Mica's hair that's spilled over his shoulder. He looks so beautiful, perfect in his tight jeans and lip-gloss, just like he's walked out of a video or something.

"I'm glad to see you out of the house," Mica continues. "You look better."

"You're the second person in the last twenty minutes to tell me that."

"Then it must be true." Mica laughs. "Are you buying me lunch?"

"Yes." Asia waves his waitress back over to take Mica's order.

As she leaves again, he says, "I've been thinking about what you told me about Trace."

"Asia," Mica begins.

"No, I mean, I believe you. It would be stupid not to. And I'm not mad. I just..." He lets out his breath. "Marcus sent some tapes over that Trace made before he died. And they're..."

"Oh," Mica says softly. "Asia."

Asia blocks out the memory of Trace's accusing apology and

reaches for a half-smile again. "It's okay. I mean, it was hard to listen to, but I'm grateful. It's Trace's voice."

Mica nods.

"I'm gonna take them back tomorrow and I guess I'll talk to Marcus about getting in to finish the album."

"I'm glad, Asia, but..." Mica tilts his head and narrows his eyes.

"Yeah, I know." Asia shrugs. "I guess I just don't feel like being alone tonight. I know I've been an asshole, but can you..."

He doesn't finish. He doesn't know how make himself sound like something other than a john to Mica.

Mica takes his hand, pulls it under the table to squeeze it. "When we get home, I have to make a call, but yeah, I'd like to stay with you."

"I don't wanna make you rearrange anything." Asia feels himself blushing now.

"I said I'd like to stay with you, Asia," Mica leans over to bump his shoulder. "I mean it. I'm glad you called."

Back at the apartment, Asia waits for Mica to ask him about the songs. Finally, when he doesn't, Asia offers.

"I'll play them for you."

Mica is seated on the couch next to Asia. "If you want."

He moves away so Asia can get up and Asia wonders if he really does want anyone else to hear what Trace wrote. "I didn't know I was going to go in to talk to Marcus until I told you," Asia says as brings the box of them in from the kitchen, along with the player. "I guess maybe I can think better when you're around."

Mica leans against Asia again as he clicks in the first tape. "Other Brother" spills out, along with Trace's comments. Asia doesn't fill in the history for Mica. He watches the boy for reaction to the words, but Mica's face is careful. He says nothing.

Asia goes on to the next: "Ash." When Trace speaks, Mica answers him. "He did know. Albrecht did know how much he tried."

Asia only chokes when he put his hand on the tape containing "Savior." He can't put it in the tape player. In fact, he knows he has to keep it just for himself, no matter what else happens. Though he's sure Mica recognizes the writing on the label he says,

"This one's mine. It got in there by mistake."

He shoves it into the pocket of his jeans.

"Thank you," Mica says softly. "Thank you, Asia, for playing them for me. I think they'll make a beautiful album."

"Yeah, Trace's a—" Asia catches himself. "Trace was a genius."

Mica stands up, pulls Asia to his feet too. "C'mon. Bed. You gotta get up to be at Para Bellum tomorrow, right? Let's get some sleep."

Asia is about to laugh at the thought of it, but Mica kisses him softly, and that takes the rough edges off the prospect. Asia follows Mica into the bedroom without protest.

Mica smooths the covers back and fixes the pillows.

"I don't expect you to..." Asia feels himself teeter on the edge of saying the wrong thing and does it anyway. "You don't have to fuck me, if you don't want to."

Mica looks up and laughs. "I really am glad you called me, Asia."

He starts to undress and Asia reaches to turn off the light before he sheds his own clothes. He slides under the quilt and closes his eyes. This is all he wants, right now, just the sense that he's not the only one left in the world at three a.m.

Mica shifts closer, moves so his head is on Asia's pillow. He circles his arms around Asia.

Asia catches his breath against Mica's skin and thinks of the tape, still in the pocket of his jeans, crumpled on the floor. No one will ever know, he thinks. No one will ever hear.

Mica moves on top of Asia, his long hair falling around them like a curtain. Asia sighs out Mica's name and closes his eyes again. Trace is there, in the dark, but it's Mica's hands on him, it's Mica's weight pressing into him. Asia lets it happen, lets Trace dissolve in a lightning flash of orgasm.

Mica loosens his hold on Asia when it's over. Asia touches Mica's face in the dark. He leans up to kiss Mica, feeling the guilt return. "I'm sorry."

"Asia." Mica pulls back reproachfully. "Don't."

"I can't be anything to you, Mica. You know that. Even if I want to be, I can't—"

"I don't want anything." Mica cuts him off.

"When I asked you to come over here, it was because I...I

missed you."

"Don't say anything else, Asia." Mica pulls him close again. "I know you feel like you're cheating on him. It won't feel like that forever."

Asia shows up at Para Bellum the next day, with all the tapes he can surrender under his arm. He walks into Marcus's office and puts the box on his desk. "Thanks."

"Sorry I didn't tell you about them straight off. I thought you should have them but I was afraid you..." Marcus shrugs. "I needed time to have them copied, but I shouldn't have sprung them on you with no warning. I found them at his place before I called the cops."

"So you've heard them." Asia's heart bangs out of time at the thought of another copy of "Savior" somewhere.

Marcus nods. "Most of them, not everything."

"He showed me his notebook, a coupla days before he..." Asia shakes his head. "But it wasn't anything coherent. I didn't know he had anything else."

"I think he wasn't ready for you to hear them, Asia. I don't know if he would have ever been." Marcus rolls his chair up close to the desk, peers into the box.

"I didn't bring them all back. These are the ones I want to use. I mean, I don't mind using old stuff if we have to, but I want..." Asia breaks off, distracted by how coherent he sounds.

"Okay." Marcus laces his fingers together and cracks his knuckles.

"I want Lionel to go over them and see what he can use. I don't know how it would work, exactly, but I want to use Trace's voice as much as possible. Can't he take it off the tapes, and use it for the vocal track? Weird can figure out the chords and stuff." Asia almost smiles. He sounds like an idiot, but he's done his level best not to learn anything about the process of recording.

"If this is what you wanna do, Asia, we'll figure out how to make it work," Marcus assures. "Though you'll still have to stand in for him on a few."

Asia feels himself close up and fights it. He knew this was coming. He nods.

"I saw your face that day, when you did it before. Nobody thinks it'll be easy for you, but...I know you can."

It doesn't hurt as much as Asia imagined it would. He swallows hard. "Let me know when you've got something scheduled with the others."

He gets up, turns to leave.

"He was making them for you," Marcus says. "The tapes."

It's pointless to deny it. "I know."

"Asia." This time Marcus rises too, moves around the desk to grab Asia's arm. "Look, man, I know you think this is never gonna get better, but it will. Each day. You just need time."

Asia swallows and pulls away. He thinks of Mica, sleeping warm and welcoming beside him last night. He shouldn't want that. He doesn't want it. Each day that's easier to live makes Trace farther away, harder to feel. "It's not that I don't appreciate what you're trying to say."

Marcus arches an eyebrow. "I don't want to lose you too, Asia."

On the way home, Asia turns the radio up to drown Trace's lyrics out of his brain. He feels the press of the cassette against his thigh in his jeans pocket. Hidden, he thinks. It's still hidden. Even if Marcus heard it, he might not remember it. And if he did, maybe he wouldn't mention it.

No, Asia thinks, hand resting on the outline of it. No, nobody can hear it. It's the only way he can do this, finish the album, turn himself inside out. He has to keep this one song. This one piece of Trace has to stay with him. The prospect of work feels better than Asia wants to admit, sort of like coming back to life. He'd felt it with Mica as they'd shared fries last night, and later.

When he gets back to the apartment, he dials Mica's number again, expecting the machine. He's startled when Mica says, "Hello."

"Hi." Asia leans against the wall in the kitchen, shrugging the phone between his ear and shoulder.

"Asia. How did it go?"

Just Mica's voice stirs something in Asia. He closes his eyes. "It's all fine. We're gonna start pretty soon."

"That's great, Asia. Good for you."

"Yeah." Asia wonders what he will say next. He is sick of talking about the album, with anyone. He wants to put Trace aside, for just a few minutes. He takes a breath. "I guess. What're you doing, right now? Are you busy?"

"Do you want me to come over?"

Asia's heart speeds up a fraction. "Yeah, that'd be great. In fact, can you stay with me a while?"

If Asia had ever once asked anyone out on a date, he imagines it would feel just like this, awkward and nerve-wracking.

Mica laughs. "I'd love to, Asia. Are you sending a car, or picking me up?"

Asia finds himself smiling, blushing, alone in his kitchen. "I'll come get you, okay?"

The first day of recording, Asia is the last to arrive. He walks into the studio and the shift of power his way is obvious. Both Weird and Tommi look up and conversation ceases.

"Glad you could make it," Weird greets, around his cigarette.

His tone is completely free of sarcasm and somehow that makes Asia even more ill at ease. He takes a breath, glances toward Mica, who is sitting over with Lionel. "Look, you guys, about what I said before... I'm so... I didn't mean any of it."

Weird stabs out his cigarette and pushes to his feet. "Asia, it's done. We know that. We know all we're doing here is picking up the pieces, okay? We just want to finish this one last thing."

Asia nods. He tries to catch Tommi's eye, but the boy won't look at him. Asia gives up. Did he think an apology would fix everything? He's ruined whatever they had left. Weird is right. They can only pick up the pieces. Asia freezes up and Mica steps in. He gets up and crosses to Tommi, pulling a lock of his long hair out from behind his ear. Asia sees for the first time that it's dyed a brilliant blue.

"I like this." Mica laughs. "Except that now I don't get to be your twin anymore, huh?"

Tommi smiles up at him and shrugs. "Unless you want my girl to do yours, too."

"Won't match my eyes like it does yours," Mica says. "But I'll think about it. I'm glad you look so good."

Weird snorts. "Are we gonna play or trade fashion tips, girls?"

"Yeah-right." Tommi gets up from his seat. "Like I can't do both. C'mon, Asia."

"I like your hair, too," Asia tells him as they get set up.

Lionel shifts in his chair on the other side of the glass and catches Asia's eye. He flips a switch and leans into the mic. "Asia, you want me to play the tape?"

"Marcus found these on cassettes in Trace's apartment," Asia explains to the others.

Lionel put all the usable songs onto one tape, except for one. At Asia's nod, Lionel fills the room with Trace's voice.

"Oh." Tommi's soft smile melts off his face.

Weird picks up his guitar and closes his eyes. He begins to add to Trace's phantom chords on the tape, making the song solid. He hums the melody under his breath, then opens his eyes to look from the empty mic to Asia.

Asia pulls in a shaky breath. The second cut belongs to him. He braces himself. Trace speaks. "I don't even know if I wanna use this yet. Asia will hate me."

There's silence, then Trace starts singing. Asia feels both Weird and Tommi react to the lyrics, feels their eyes on him, but can't look at them. The other tape is safe, in his pocket where no one will ever know about it. He closes his eyes.

Asia tries to reduce it all to the series of math problems Lionel will hear, to the progression of chords for Weird. But Asia can't do it. He's not a musician, not really, and all he can hear is Trace, lean and pale, glaring at him, the bed between them. The melody is gentle against the anger in the lyric. Unlike "Savior," it's an apology for things that almost happened, that will never happen now. It doesn't get any easier to hear it. Asia can't imagine how it ever will.

"Can you... Lionel, can you turn it off a second?"

"It's beautiful," Tommi says. "I'm sorry, Asia."

Asia feels himself redden. He doesn't have the energy to be pissed off at Tommi for making the correct interpretation. "I don't think I want... I don't think I'm the one to sing it. But I wanna use the song. I wanna use Trace's vocals." He looks up at Lionel, who nods. "I wanna use his vocals as much as we can and just play along, sort of? There are at least six complete songs here. And then we can just fill in with stuff from the old set, right?"

Asia has a memory of one of the girls catching Trace after a concert. "'Ash' is my song. You wrote that for me."

Trace hadn't corrected her, like he already knew the song wasn't his anymore. Asia wonders how it will feel when this song is taken from him. Less painful? He knows that isn't what he wants. He says, "Can we use him talking on the track too? I think people will want to know what he was thinking."

Asia knows he can give almost everything else away. He knows it's what Trace would want, so he has no choice.

23

"Let's go to Han's, over on Hollywood," Asia suggests as he drives out of Para Bellum's parking ramp. "I want dim sum."

"Umm," Mica says. "Dim sum."

Han's isn't fancy. They get takeout there about three times a week, but Asia knows that will make Mica happy. He loves Chinese. When they walk in, Asia sees that the hostess recognizes him and gives them a table up front, by the big picture window. Asia feels other eyes on them, trying to place him, trying to figure them out. He feels like he's sitting in a fishbowl. He takes a breath and ignores it to focus on Mica. "I want to thank you for all of this."

"You're welcome." Mica laughs. "For whatever you're talking about. You're always very welcome."

His tone makes Asia blush, but he stays on the subject. "I couldn't have done any of it without you. If you hadn't been there to drag me out of Trace's apartment after the funeral, I don't know what would have happened. There wouldn't be another album, that's for sure."

"There would have," Mica protests. "Somebody else would have been there for you."

"No." Despite the whole world of Hollywood Boulevard passing by beyond the glass, Asia reaches for Mica's hand. Out of the corner of his eye, he sees the hostess who recognized him take note, but now he doesn't care. Mica's hand is warm in his. "Not like you. I needed it to be you."

Mica surprises him. "I needed it to be me too, Asia."

Suddenly Trace doesn't exist. Mica is the only man in the world. Asia knows the reprieve won't last, but he savors it while he can. "I thought when I started this that I would get the album done and leave. I always wanted to just be the guy I was supposed to be, y'know? Maybe go back to school; maybe get a job."

"Now you don't?"

"I don't want to leave you." He takes a breath and lets it all out. "I want you in my life, from now on."

Mica hesitates long enough for the waiter to intrude. Asia keeps Mica's hand as he orders wine and appetizers for both of them. Asia is determined not to back down. "Neither of us can have what we thought we wanted, but now…" Asia breaks eye contact. His heart is beating so loud it almost drowns out his words. "Now I want you."

"Asia. I feel…" Mica lets the sentence die as their waiter interrupts, bringing glasses and the bottle.

Asia waves him away, trying not to look annoyed. "I'll pour."

Asia fills Mica's glass, surprised his hands don't shake. He's having his first date with a man he is trying to learn to care about. It makes him dizzy. "What…were you gonna say?"

"That I want you too, Asia." Mica says it so easily, just like it doesn't cost him anything.

Asia wants it to be easy for him, too. Suddenly he's numb. He has trouble catching his breath. Trace is stirring in him somewhere, reminding him that this is all temporary. As happy as Asia wants to be, the echo of the song he's kept back won't let him go. He thinks again of telling Mica about it, but he can't. Mica wants the shell Asia has built around the secret. If the secret escapes, the shell will crumble.

"Asia? I want to tell you that all the time, but I'm never sure you want to hear it." Mica's fingertips touch Asia's again, but don't linger.

Asia forces a smile, tries to put Trace away again, let Mica be the only man in the world for a while longer. "It's exactly what I want to hear."

The rest of the album goes fast. Asia barely realizes they're finished when Tommi says, "I think we should call it *Ash*. I mean, I think it seems…" The boy shakes his head, canary blue locks falling into his eyes. "I keep hoping they're happy, y'know, where ever they are."

Asia can't fault the sentiment. He swallows. "Yeah, that's a great idea, Tommi."

Weird lights a cigarette and nods, but says nothing.

Trace's vocals take up the first side and Asia's are on the second. Lionel's production has made it impossible to tell that

Trace wasn't in the studio. It's beautiful and Asia can barely stand to listen to it. Every note, every word makes it impossible for him to keep Trace in the past.

Weird and Tommi do the press. They talk about how tragic it is, how they miss Trace. They both shake their heads and say they had no idea it was so bad, how much they regret not being able to do something to stop him.

Asia says nothing. The cassette is a constant reminder that he could have done something, if Trace had only let him.

On the day the album goes platinum, Black Light officially dissolve. Marcus pushes Asia for a solo album. Asia doesn't turn him down flat, just puts him off.

Everyone is happy with the success. Asia tries to be. But Trace's voice keeps ambushing him: when he's clicking through the channels and he catches a flash of Trace on MTV; when he and Mica are driving to Ralph's for groceries, Trace's voice splits through the plastic pop songs on the radio. It's harder, out of the studio. Always makes him remember the song he's kept trapped. Reminds him that this is all a lie.

Ash stays on the charts for months. Asia knows it should be getting easier. He knows that time is passing and he should move forward. He should call Marcus and get back to work while Para Bellum is interested in a follow-up.

But he doesn't. Asia has no voice of his own. Whenever he tries to write, he gets nothing from the twelve-string but disjointed chords. He ends up passing out on the sofa with a bottle, trying to summon Trace in the empty dark.

Sometimes, when he's sure Mica's asleep in the bedroom, Asia plays "Savior" softly, lets it wash over him, remind him again.

Mica fights it at first, doing his best to pull Asia out of the depression he's slipping into. Asia can see how patient Mica is trying to be, how gentle. It's almost like the weeks after the funeral and he hates to put Mica through it again. He doesn't want to lose the biggest piece of his post-Trace world.

"Do you know what today is?" Mica's voice wakes Asia from a murky sleep as he opens the drapes remorselessly. He rounds the sofa to gather up the near-empty fifth that Asia slept with.

Asia stifles a groan. "Um, Tuesday?"

"Pretty good for an alcoholic agoraphobic, I guess," Mica admits. He disappears into the kitchen and Asia hears him clink the bottle into the trash before he returns.

Asia appreciates the effort and tries to show it by sitting up. The light from the window feels like it's stabbing directly into his brain and he hears Trace saying, *"I have people that it's their whole job to bring me more."* But Asia won't do that to Mica. He smiles. "What is it besides Tuesday, then?"

Mica leans down to kiss him. "It's our six-month anniversary."

Asia pulls back to study the other man. He's always struck at how different from Trace Mica is. Skin milky, not silver-cast, his hair long and pale. He's curves and softness where Trace had been lines and angles. Asia wonders if Albrecht Christian found himself in the position of comparing the two men, wanting one, wanting to want the other. The bullet in his brain makes more sense now. "Mica, I…"

A smile flickers over Mica's face and disappears. "So I thought we should go to Han's for dim sum. To celebrate."

Asia agrees instantly, eager to make up for letting time slip away. He gets up, showers, shaves, and gets dressed. When he reappears, Mica's smile lingers longer.

"There you are," he says, catching Asia's hand to pull him close. He brushes Asia's cheek with the backs of his fingers. "Feels like I haven't seen you in weeks."

"I've been right…" Asia takes a breath at the press of Mica's body. "I'm just right here."

"Good." Mica lets him go. "Right where I want you."

Asia blushes hard. He thinks again of Albrecht Christian.

At Han's, the table up front is waiting for them. Asia sits just where he sat a half a year ago. Would they do this again in six months? In three years? Would they get the chance?

This time it's Mica that prods the waiter on his way. Then he lifts the top off the bamboo basket and plucks out a steamed dumpling. He offers it across the table to Asia between chopsticks. "Careful." He laughs. "It's pretty hot."

Asia leans forward to accept the food, holding it between his teeth before biting down. He laughs. "No kidding." He reaches for his water. "Not this hot at home."

"It's a shorter trip from the kitchen," Mica points out.

Asia nods but Mica doesn't let the silence linger. "I love you, Asia. That's why I'm still with you. I thought I wouldn't be able to love anybody after Albrecht. But you…"

"I wouldn't try to take his place."

"No, you've made your own with me." Mica's smile becomes brittle. "But…I can't seem to do the same."

"Mica," Asia protests. "I don't…"

"Trace takes up too much of you." Mica holds Asia's eyes with his. "I need you, Asia. I need you to trust me."

"I do," Asia tells him.

"I know you're sad," Mica says. "I don't expect that to just go away, but I need to know what's going on with you."

"I'm just…" Now Asia pauses. He doesn't want to lie to Mica, but he thinks if he could explain, it would ruin things between them. "I'm supposed to be writing stuff. Marcus wants a record, and I can't. I don't know what I was thinking. Trace was the one who wrote the songs."

Mica shakes his head and smiles. "He couldn't have ever done it without you, Asia."

Asia almost argues, but the lyrics of "Savior" rattle around in his head and he can't. Instead, he grabs Mica's hand. "I'll work it out. I'll try to be better."

They don't linger over dinner, but as Mica drives them back to the apartment, Asia asks if he'd like to go someplace else. "Do you wanna get a drink or go dancing?"

"I would never put you through that." Mica laughs. "Besides, the only place I want to take you is home."

The kiss Mica gives Asia in the elevator on the way to the apartment is long and complicated. It promises to lead to something else. He pushes Asia against the wall and hooks a hand to the back of his neck to pull him close. Asia opens his mouth to Mica's. They part as the door slides open to their floor. Mica leads Asia past the twelve-string in the living room to the bedroom.

Afterward, Asia is on the edge of sleep. Mica shares his pillow, face inches from Asia's, so close Asia feels Mica's breath.

"What's the song you play in the middle of the night, Asia?"

Asia closes his eyes in the same split second Mica opens his. Trace's voice wraps around Asia, echoing against his skull, soaking out and turning him cold.

"I hear it when you can't sleep, but I don't know it from the album. It sounds like Trace, but is it yours?"

Mine, Asia thinks, shuddering. I own every word. "No."

"Is it something you could use as a starting point for your own writing?"

"No." It comes out stronger this time. He feels this last secret is ripped away.

"*I know what I do to you.*" Trace sings it right behind Asia's eyes now. He pushes to his feet before Mica can touch him.

"I didn't realize you were still spying for Marcus."

"Asia."

He doesn't need to see the hurt. It's all there in his name. Asia leaves the bedroom, lets himself out onto the balcony.

At ten stories up, the railing is chest high and made of cement blocks. Marcus is so fucking careful. Jumping isn't impossible from here. It would just take a little extra effort.

Asia only leans against it, staring out at the river of light below. He thinks of the old days, on the muddy riverbank in Ann Arbor with Trace.

Asia doesn't want to slip, fall into the past again. He wants to love Mica right now, tonight, write songs for him to prove it. But Mica broke the shell and now Asia is nobody.

The night is turning to ice and Asia is freezing along with it. But then Mica is there, draping a robe around his shoulders.

"I'm not Marcus's spy," he says sharply. "And fuck you for thinking that, after everything I said just said to you."

The thread of anger makes Asia turn to look at Mica. "You shoulda left it alone. That song is between me and Trace."

Mica's eyes darken. "Trace is dead." He spits it back at Asia. "He can't love you now. He can't give a shit about you. But I'm right here, Asia, and I do. I love you."

Asia narrows his eyes, shrugs the robe off. "And you want me to give up the last piece of him—of me, because, why?" Asia's whole body tenses, like he's about to take a punch. "Because you *love* me? Bullshit. I'm your fucking job."

Under everything, Asia hears the ghost off Myrna's goodbye.

"There's three of us." He pushes that away. "If you meant any of that, you'd understand."

"Just..." Mica's voice drops to barely a whisper, like he can't get the air. "Just stop it, Asia. Stop. I don't know if you think you're punishing yourself, or you have to hurt me because I get it. But I know I love you."

Asia hears him break on the last word. Trace still sang behind his eyes, voice velvet sandpaper. Asia goes back inside, settles on the couch in the dark.

He hears Mica come in after, hears him in the bedroom. None of it registers until Mica reappears with his duffle bag.

He picks up the cordless from the end table next to Asia and punches a number in. Asia clicks on the light. He can see no anger left in Mica. But the tears are still there. Asia realizes he's ordering a car.

"Mica." Asia pushes to his feet. "It's the middle of the night."

Mica's laugh is strangled. He flinches back when Asia tries to touch his face. Asia knows this is how it has to be, but he wants to be able to fight it.

"I'm gonna wait in the lobby," Mica says, wiping at his eyes with the heel of his hand.

"I'll..." Asia looks away. "Can I wait with you?"

"No, Asia." Mica shoulders his duffle.

The hall light spills in when Mica opens it. He looks just like an angel when walks out. Asia takes a breath. Everything they said at dinner comes back to him. Mica wants the shell of him, Asia remembers.

That afternoon he calls Marcus and lays it all out for him.

"I don't have anything for you right now. And I don't know if anything will come."

"Mica already called," Marcus says. "He wasn't lying to you, Asia. He doesn't work for me anymore. Not since about a week after the funeral. Besides, I already knew about the song. I thought about leaving it out, because it was so painful, and I knew it would hurt you. But I knew Trace meant it for you."

There is a pause. Asia picks up the tape from the coffee table and stares at it. Marcus knew. They all knew. "I don't think I can..."

"Take a week. If you can't come up with the songs, okay. If all you do is use this time to get Trace out of you and figure out how to beg Mica to come back, it'll still be time well spent."

Asia collapses back onto the rumpled bed, inhales the scent of Mica from the pillows, and closes his eyes. Marcus goes on about how talented Asia is and how if he could just open that part of himself up.... He reminds Asia of the self-help guy he sees on TV late at night, between movies. "Do you need to talk to somebody about your depression?"

No, Asia thinks. I just need them all to stop talking about it. "One week," he agrees. "Then you can go on to find the next Trace for yourself."

"Asia." Marcus's voice is pained.

Asia knows he's being harsh, but he's got nothing left to spare Marcus's feelings. He mutters a goodbye and clicks the phone off.

Asia lies there long enough that the bedroom creeps from dim to full dark. He feels himself falling farther and farther away until sleep comes.

Finally Trace welcomes Asia into the blackness of his arms. Asia fits himself against the sharp angles of Trace's body, knowing that this is where he belongs. *I love you*, he tells Trace, accepting his cold kiss. *I need you to stay with me.*

But he doesn't. As tight as Asia holds him, morning comes. Sun finds its way into the room in slivers, splitting the dark away from Asia. He wakes numb.

Asia sits on the side of the bed, holding the cassette again. Asia turns it over in his hands, touches the tape where it feeds through. Slides his finger under and pulls, just to see how it feels. There's no divine intervention to stop him. He's not struck with lightning or anything. It doesn't matter, he realizes now. Whatever Trace's intentions were, they don't matter anymore. Asia pulls more of the tape up, then winds it back in. *You should have told me*, he thinks, and yanks out yard after yard of it.

He clenches his fist around the scraps, hard, feeling tears press at the corners of his eyes. He takes it all out onto the balcony and lets it go over the railing. Asia watches as it unfurls in the wind, the sun lighting the blackness of it up to silver as it spreads out over the city like cigarette smoke. He sucks in a deep breath and closes his eyes. There's no difference. He's done nothing to mend the ache, just pushed it deeper in.

Then late in the afternoon, the painting from Trace's memorial shows up at his door, attended by three guys and a tool kit.

"It's a gift from Para Bellum," one of them tells Asia when he questions them. "We can go ahead and hang it for you, if you want."

Asia stares at the huge canvas shrouded in butcher's paper. His act of defiance is obliterated now. He wants to tell them to take it away, burn it even, but instead he mumbles, "I'm not sure where it'll fit."

"It's eight by three and a half," the guy offers. He steps in and looks around the living room. "Y'got, what? Twelve-foot ceiling? How 'bout right there?"

He motions to a blank space of wall just to the left of the door.

"Okay." Asia sinks into a chair to watch them work. They free Trace from his wrapping and everything else in the room becomes unfocused for Asia.

When they finish, Asia opens his wallet to fish out a fifty for each. Then he's alone again.

24

Asia knows his week is slipping by, but it's only him and Trace now and everything seems frozen. When he sleeps, or passes out, dreams and memories smear into the same thing.

The rain that summer made all of Ann Arbor smell clean, like dirt and worms. The concrete step that Asia and Trace sat on was still damp enough to give Asia a chilled ass through his jeans, although it was eighty degrees even in the shade of the sloping porch roof.

"You just got me fired, Trace." Asia shook his head, knowing he should be pissed. "Now what are we gonna do for rent? We can't go back to livin' in my parents' basement."

"No shit." Trace wasn't looking at him, but Asia saw the curve of a smile. Trace was chipping the pastel blue polish off his nails. "It doesn't matter. You wanna work at Kmart your whole life? We're gonna get a gig and then you don't gotta worry about money."

"You don't know that," Asia protested, not because he thought he would win the argument, but because Trace expected it.

"I do know." Trace turned to meet his eyes. He grinned. "I know everything. Because I'm God and what I say happens."

Asia looked away. He didn't answer, because as much as he wanted to believe everything Trace said, he knew it wouldn't do any good in three weeks when they got evicted. Still, when Trace was so close to him, he couldn't concentrate on that. He found himself leaning in, letting their arms almost brush, before he pulled himself back. He stared at the chunks of nail polish Trace had flicked onto the sidewalk at his feet. As Asia watched, an army of ants converged on them, bickering over them, picking them up, carrying them off. Trace continued talking, not even noticing. He had no idea that he was the god in their world, casting pieces of sky down to them.

Asia wakes up, tears on his face, with the slim recollection of Trace as God. In my small world, he thinks. He wanders out to the living room window, but he's not looking at the city below him. In the reflection of the glass, Trace's standing behind him, in his own separate reality. Asia ruins the reflection by smoothing his hand across Trace's face. Then he lets his hand fall. Trace's eyes are on him. He remembers every time in their lives he'd felt them.

Asia turns and faces the painting, life-sized, still staring at him from the wall. He wonders how many people have that same gaze on their album covers.

Suddenly, the cavernous apartment that Asia usually feels lost in is too small. There isn't a corner of it far enough away from Trace's eyes.

He calls for a car and goes to put some clothes on.

It's darker in some parts of LA than others, but Asia isn't paying attention. It's not late by his standards. Just after midnight. And when he tells the driver to let him off in their old neighborhood in Glendale, the guy looks concerned. "Mr. Heyes, it's the middle of nowhere."

"I'll be okay. You don't have to wait," Asia assures, only slightly amused. He takes off toward their old building.

He doesn't know why he needed to come here. He begins to realize he's stranded now, but it doesn't worry him. He looks up over the roof of the building to where the neon cross of Queen of Angels Cemetery burns through the murky lights of the night. That's where I need to be. Asia smiles tightly. Queen of Angels is only a couple miles away and he thinks about walking up there, so he can touch the crunchy sod that covers the grave, but doesn't get the chance to think beyond that.

"Hey, asshole, gimme your wallet."

Asia turns, mystified at first. There are three of them, all big, standing on the sidewalk with him now, and he never heard anything. They wear hooded sweatshirts and their faces are hidden in the shadows. He reaches to his back pocket to obey, trying to remember if there is any cash in there. Then the one in front pulls a gun.

Asia's not scared. He looks right at it and wonders if the one Albrecht Christian used was bigger or smaller. He says, "It's okay, I'll give you my money."

"That's right, you will," the one with the gun agrees, stepping closer to him. Asia turns over the wallet. Take it, he thinks, wondering if later, they'll recognize his name on the ID, or just throw it away. As the guy's fist closes on it, his gun hand moves. Asia closes his eyes, expecting a bullet.

Pain lights up the inside of his skull. His head snaps to the side hard and he hears a crack in his neck as he hits the pavement. He chokes out a cry as the toe of a boot catches him in the ribs, once, twice. Then the dark takes him.

But it doesn't take him away. He feels the sidewalk beneath him, the pain in the half of his face that's on fire. The cold seeps in through his clothes.

"Asia."

He's dreaming. He must be.

"Asia, answer me."

"I don't want you," he tries to say, but it only comes out inside his head.

Trace is bending over him in the dark; Asia can feel his breath against the curve of his ear. It's a dream. "Trace."

"You have to get up." Trace maps the pain in Asia's jaw with his fingertips.

"You don't love me," Asia insists, clinging to the dark. He resists Trace's hands on his skin.

"How can you say that?"

"I would have done anything for you, Trace." Asia does open his eyes now. He struggles up to a sitting position, then to his feet. "I was ready to give you anything. How could you have not known that?"

Trace hooks one cold hand to the back of Asia's neck. The feel of his lips on Asia's, the taste of him, makes all of Asia's denials ridiculous. He opens his mouth, tries to feed Trace the warmth left in his body. What good is it to Asia now? He feels the city spin away from them and he lets it go. The ground beneath him softens, chills. The tang of smog in the air is replaced with something sweeter, damper. Asia can smell the coppery spice of the river, hear it slipping by. He opens his eyes to a warmer dark than the nights of LA. Home, he thinks, his breath catching so hard in his chest it hurts. Is he dead? Did he bleed out from a gunshot wound on the street in Glendale? He feels no regret, only relief.

They are standing next to each other on the muddy bank of the Huron River. "I knew, Asia," Trace says. "It scared me."

"Why?" Asia feels a wave of anger at being thrown away.

"Because look what I did to Albrecht and I didn't care about him like I love you." Trace smiles, reaching to train Asia's hair back behind an ear. "I wanted you and if I let myself take a little bit, it wouldn't ever be enough."

Asia wants to argue, but Trace kisses him again. Asia clings to Trace's sharp form. He tries to lose himself, dissolve into Trace.

When Trace lets him go, Asia opens his eyes. He feels the distant pang of

Mica's absence, but loses it when he glimpses the half-bright moon through shadowy tree branches overhead.

Asia knows this isn't a dream. He can smell the leather of Trace's jacket, feel the cool air around them.

Trace fishes his cigarettes and lighter from a jacket pocket. The brief flame illuminates his face. "But now you hurt yourself."

"No." Lies always come easy when Trace is with him. Asia rubs at his chest.

Trace pulls Asia's hand away, replaces it with his own. "I don't want it to be like this. You're starting to love somebody else now. All I can do is watch." He takes a drag off his cigarette, fingers abandoning Asia.

The water ripples like black glass. Trace stands again and crushes the cigarette under the toe of his boot. "It's cold to be dead, Asia. Even when I touch you, I don't feel anything. I can only remember feeling. Everything about me is an echo. I can't even really love you now."

Asia doesn't believe him. He climbs to his feet and grabs Trace by the shoulders. Asia kisses him, holding the memory of that first time tight, trying to wrap it around them. Trace puts a hand to the back of Asia's neck, fingers tangling his hair. Asia opens his mouth, needing the taste of who they were.

But Trace tastes of arid dirt. As he steps back, Asia licks his lips. "I don't care about anything else. I wanna be with you, Trace."

The ground shifts under them. The light of the moon amps up, burns away the soft veins of tree branches overhead. Asia gulps in one last breath of damp air before the night unstitches around them. He closes his eyes and kisses Trace again, refusing to be thrust away alone again.

"Look at me, Asia."

He obeys and they're standing in that damned bedroom again, surrounded by unrelenting white light.

Trace turns his back on Asia and walks to the wall of windows. "This is what being dead is for me. This room." He wraps his arms around himself. "You keep pulling me back here, when you just need to let me go."

Asia sits on the edge of the bed, amidst the tangle of sheets. He takes a deep breath of what lingers from Trace's suicide. "No, it's you, Trace. Like this was my decision." He laughs. "Like any of it ever was. I only ever wanted what you wanted."

"No, Asia," Trace says softly. "You were always the one I loved. But you never let me get close to you."

The naked brokenness of it takes Asia by surprise. Something shifts inside him again.

He has to look away from Trace's frozen eyes. "I wanted..." Wanting Trace had been like standing at the edge of a cliff. Asia had always known the fall would kill him. "I tried."

Trace comes to sit with Asia. His desolation cuts across Asia like Michigan winter. The impression of Trace's bones show under his flesh, like they're wearing through.

"I thought it would stop, after I did it." Trace's smile is hollow. "But you won't let it."

"Trace, I'm not doing this." But Asia hears the truth pounding between them. "I don't know how to stop it. Where would you go?"

"I can't stay here. Not in this nothingness." Trace drifts back to the windows.

This isn't some version of heaven or hell, Asia realizes. Not even purgatory. It's Trace's prison that Asia built for him.

"Okay, Trace." The words sound brittle on the sour air. They are all he can manage. He joins Trace in front of the glass. Asia blinks against the sunlight that streams over them.

He wants to kiss Trace again, but doesn't. Instead he puts his hand to the window. "It never mattered what you did. It didn't matter who you were fucking. It wouldn't have mattered if you killed me. I have always loved you. I still do."

Out of the corner of Asia's eye, he sees the curve of Trace's smile.

Asia pushes harder on the glass. If this is his world, he can make it do what he wants. The window implodes into mist, like he's broken a seal. It becomes an open door. He moves back. "Go."

Trace steps out into the unrelenting morning.

"Trace," Asia chokes out. The window solidifies again before he can follow. All he can do now is watch Trace walk away from him, into the blue morning sky of his death. He gets smaller and smaller, until Asia loses him in the sun.

The hospital is bright. Asia doesn't open his eyes at first, so the fluorescent lighting turns the insides of his lids pink. When he moves, his ribs ache, but numbly. He can feel no bandages, so they must not be seriously damaged. The pain in his jaw is sharper. When he feels it with his fingers, there are stitches. He takes a couple of lungfuls of disinfectant-laden air and knows. He didn't die. And Trace...

Mica is asleep in the chair by the bed. Asia smiles before he can stop himself, seeing the sky blue polish on his nails. Mica looks exhausted. Asia is so happy to see him. "Hey," he says, softly.

"Asia." Mica starts awake and gets up to step to the bed. He touches Asia's hand.

"Yeah." Asia smiles again, stiffly this time, feeling the stitches in his jaw pull. "Thanks for... I've been missing you."

"You're always saying that," Mica says. "You're lucky the ambulance guy that brought you in just bought *Ash*. He recognized you from the back cover. It still took Marcus almost a day to find out you were here. You didn't have ID on you or anything."

"I got mugged," Asia says. "Right in my old neighborhood."

"What were you doin' there?"

"I don't know." Asia closes his eyes for a second. Mica deserves the truth. "No. I was looking for Trace."

There's a space of a few seconds where Asia feels himself drift. He casts around within himself for something, anything of Trace that might still be there.

"Asia." Mica's voice raises, just a fraction. His hand tightens. "Asia, stay with me this time."

"I—" Asia rubs at his chest with his free hand, right over the hollow space. He tries for a smile. "I want to. I really—"

Mica cuts him off. "I understand if you can't love me. I know you tried. But Trace's dead. And you could have been killed, too. I mean, for almost twenty-four hours, I had no idea what happened to you."

"Mica, he left me." Asia says it softly. He doesn't understand what he feels with the words. Regret? Probably, but also a longing for Mica that isn't tainted with sadness. "Trace is gone. I let him go."

"He's—Trace is gone?" Mica echoes. "Are you okay?"

Asia laughs again and it sounds a little more like he means it this time. "You're probably tired of asking me that, aren't you?"

"No, Asia. I just want you to be."

Asia shifts so he can circle an arm around Mica to pull him closer for a kiss. So different, but he stops there. "I'm not okay," he says. "But I'm better."

25

Asia stays in the hospital another two days. The doctors treat him for dehydration. Somebody comes to talk to him about his diet. Asia is a little bemused at the fuss. In the old days, this would have been a trip to the ER that would have ended with an ice pack and aspirins.

When he's released, Mica drives him home. When they get through the door, Mica pauses in front of the painting. "Christ, look at him."

"Yeah," Asia agrees, but looks away. "It came while you were gone."

"Are you sure this isn't too much?" Mica asks. "I mean, you're still recovering."

Asia smiles. He shakes his head. "I know it's probably not the first thing you want to see every morning, but I can't just put him in storage someplace."

Mica frowns, but doesn't argue. Asia is glad, almost as glad as he was to see Mica's bag in the back of the cab along with his. Relieved that Mica is coming back to him, Asia catches him by the sleeve and pulls him close. "Hey, welcome home."

Mica takes a breath, "You, too." He turns Asia's head to kiss his injured jaw gently.

Asia is speechless, for a split second, at his beauty. When the kiss is done, he gazes into Mica's dark eyes, wanting to love him, wanting to say the words. Asia knows there's nothing holding him back now, but him. Asia melts against Mica, thinking, I've been so stupid to fight this.

Mica checks the answering machine and Asia smiles at the string of messages from Marcus, each sounding just a fraction more worried than the last. "Guess I'll call him before I order dinner, huh?" Mica says.

"I'll do it," Asia volunteers. He wants to convince Mica he can take care of himself, whether it's true or not. He reaches for the phone.

"I'm not going to push you," Marcus tells him, on the phone.

"Learned my damn lesson there."

"It's okay." Asia smiles, finding it easier to reassure Marcus. "I'm doing okay."

After Marcus hangs up, Asia goes to unpack his stuff in the bedroom. He moves slow, surprised to find himself still sore and tired in a way he wasn't lying in a hospital bed. It takes him forever to put his toothbrush away. His reflection gazes back at him, pale and drawn. He looks like he's aged years, not months since Trace died. Christ.

"Hey, I ordered a pizza, okay?" Mica appears in the doorway. "It's gonna be an hour or so. You wanna lay down?"

Asia shakes his head. "I wanna Diet Coke. And I want you to tell me what you've been doing lately."

"Well, there's Coke in the fridge." Mica raises an eyebrow. "And lately I've been hanging out at the hospital, with you."

"Yeah, this isn't exactly as romantic or exciting a life as you were hoping for, I bet." Asia feels heat on his face.

"Yeah, well, romance I don't need, and I could actually do with a lot less excitement, if that's okay with you," Mica tells him as they head into the kitchen.

Asia gets his bottle of Diet and leans against the kitchen counter. He tightens his grip on the glass, the hard chill of it grounding him. He closes his eyes and feels himself slip.

"You're going to fall asleep standing there, if you don't at least sit down," Mica tells him. "C'mon."

They end up in the living room, their backs to the portrait. Asia still feels its eyes, but he concentrates on Mica. Asia sets his drink on the table in front of them and leans his head on Mica's shoulder. He closes his eyes against the soft curve of Mica's neck and lets out a sigh.

It's another week before Asia begins to think of songs. Letting go empties Asia of Trace's music, too. For the first time in Asia's life, he's without it. Gradually, music of his own begins to take hold. When the songs come, they come fast. He writes them down, line after line on a legal pad. Each one comes out like razor wire, like an infection that he's carried for too long. They have to come up or kill him. He retrieves the twelve-string from the stand in the corner and begins to work out the chords. He works through the night, through the next night. He feels Mica's watchful eye, but Asia can't stop.

When he's done, he has twelve songs, all about the post-Trace world he lives in now. He calls Marcus. "I need a band," he tells him.

"Okay. Weird's workin' with Lionel on something, but Tommi—"

"No." Asia swallows and takes a breath. "No, Marcus. We—I can't do this to him. I can't drag him into this. Either of them. I need some other band and time in the studio with them."

Marcus agrees, just like Asia knew he would.

It's easier recording with strangers. With no history between them, Asia can sing about the post-Trace world. He lets Marcus decide what to do with it. Asia's sure nobody will want an album of him, but Marcus tells him he's wrong.

And he is. *After* sells as well as *No Outlet* and *Ash* did, so now Asia has three gold records.

It's Marcus's idea to start where Black Light's tour ended. Asia thinks he'll protest, but when it comes down to it, he says nothing. He lets them take him back home, finds himself at Joe Louis. It's been two years since Black Light played and Asia finds nothing of Trace here now. He sits on the riser in front of the drums, kicking the heels of his Keds into the plywood. The arena looms fifteen thousand empty seats large, stretching on until it takes up his whole vision. In his brain, he hears something like his own voice say, "I'm in hell."

"'S'a matter?" one of the roadies pauses to ask. "You wan' another soundcheck?"

No, he wants to run away, Asia thinks, but shakes his head. "It's fine."

He jumps down and wanders back to the green room. His stomach tightens at the sight of the massive amount of food and drinks spread out for the band. He throws himself onto a vinyl couch in the corner and tries not to want a drink. Or anything else he can't have.

Marcus sits down next to him. "This is pretty tough on you, isn't it?"

Asia only shrugs. "It's not supposed to be like this."

"No shit, baby. And I'm sorry as hell about it, but what do you do?" Marcus squeezes his shoulder. "This album is so good."

"Don't." Asia sits up, rubbing his face.

"It amazes me. Some people never write anything as good. And you... You come up with this the first time."

"Yeah." Asia rises to grab a fifth of Black Velvet. He unscrews the cap and takes a healthy belt. It burns and slams the breath from his lungs. He smiles. "All it took was Trace killin' himself. It was really fuckin' easy."

"I didn't mean it like that."

The smell of the whiskey makes Asia think of Trace, cold and stiff. "I hate it. I hate these songs. They hurt."

"I know." Marcus rises to catch him in a bear hug. "But Asia, you gotta let it out. You gotta get through it."

Asia pushes him away and goes back to the sofa. "I'm okay to sing, Marcus. Don't worry."

Nobody else bothers him. The band eats and drinks, milling around with girlfriends, boyfriends. After a month and a half in the studio with them, Asia barely knows their names. He can't care about them, can't let them be his band. He doesn't want a band. Press and groupies come and go. Asia lies there with his bottle, listening to Marcus deflect them all away from him.

Before curtain he hauls himself to the john to puke himself sober. There's nobody there to hold his hair this time and he doesn't care. Asia knows he needs to do this alone. He's glad Mica agreed to stay at the hotel until the show was over.

When Asia's done, the floor is so cold and inviting that all he wants to do is lie there all night, but he isn't stupid enough to think they'll let him.

The place smells sour now and so does he. He rinses his mouth and rummages around for clean clothes.

Jeans and a black tee shirt that bears the name of the album. Compared to the rest of the band, all leather and silver studs, Asia looks like a roadie.

In the wings, Marcus huffs the breath out of him with one last hug. Asia clings to him for a split second, but Marcus releases him and he follows the others onstage.

Asia is barely in his body but the rest of the band sweeps him along. The glare of the spot hits him and the crowd explodes on contact. Too much to hear: Asia feels it from the soles of his feet up. When he reaches for the mic, he can't tell if it's him shaking or them. It's like being trapped in a hail of voices.

He hears the opening chords of "After" over the collective gasp of the crowd. Asia's heart bangs against his rib cage in the next half-second. He tightens his hand around the mic and leans into it, closes his eyes.

He sings and it is like his voice has split into thousands of voices. He opens his eyes and sees a sea of faces, wet with tears in the dark, their mouths moving with his mouth. They share every syllable. They share his breath. The weight lifts.

In the wings, he finds Mica waiting for him. Asia passes off Trace's guitar to a roadie and sweeps Mica up into his arms. He kisses the other man hard, savoring the tiny gasp as their lips meet.

"Asia," Mica protests. "There are all these people."

Asia laughs, the words he's always wanted to say rising to the surface now, soft and easy. Asia kisses him again. "I love you."

THE END

ABOUT THE AUTHOR

Martha J. Allard is a writer of contemporary and dark fantasy. Her short fiction has appeared in magazines like *Talebones* and *Not One of Us*. Her story "Dust" won an honorable mention in *The Year's Best Science Fiction*, 19th edition, edited by Gardner Dozois. Her story "Phase" was nominated for a British Science Fiction Award. They are both collected in the chapbook *Dust and Other Stories*. *Black Light* is her first novel.

You can find her on her blog at marthajallard.blogspot.com.

ACKNOWLEDGMENTS

I owe thanks to so many people for this book. To Loren, for teaching me how to write a book, as we wrote the very first draft together, and for still teaching me. To Brian, who came up with exactly the perfect name for Albrecht's record label. To 'Chelle, for living with me during the worst bout of writer's block I ever had. And to Paul for being Marcus. And to Kelly for making me stop crying. Also to the Flint Area Writers, for their patience—which stretched decades: Nancy and Chris especially. To Melodie, for her hard, hard work in making the sentences say what I meant them to say. To Kacey, for pulling me through the last long haul, with as few carbs as possible. Seriously, thank you.

www.ingramcontent.com/pod-product-compliance
Lightning Source LLC
Chambersburg PA
CBHW070332260626
47160CB00003B/1026